KU-202-170

CODE NAME

WOLF

GIL HOGG

Copyright © 2013 Gil Hogg

The moral right of the author has been asserted.

Apart from any fair dealing for the purposes of research or private study,
or criticism or review, as permitted under the Copyright, Designs and Patents
Act 1988, this publication may only be reproduced, stored or transmitted, in
any form or by any means, with the prior permission in writing of the
publishers, or in the case of reprographic reproduction in accordance with
the terms of licences issued by the Copyright Licensing Agency. Enquiries
concerning reproduction outside those terms should be sent to the publishers.

Matador
9 Priory Business Park
Kibworth Beauchamp
Leicestershire LE8 0RX, UK
Tel: (+44) 116 279 2299
Fax: (+44) 116 279 2277
Email: books@troubador.co.uk
Web: www.troubador.co.uk/matador

ISBN 978 1783060 436

British Library Cataloguing in Publication Data.
A catalogue record for this book is available from the British Library.

Typeset in 12pt Bembo by Troubador Publishing Ltd, Leicester, UK

Matador is an imprint of Troubador Publishing Ltd

Printed and bound in the UK by TJ International, Padstow, Cornwall

BY THE SAME AUTHOR

FICTION
A Smell of Fraud
The Predators
Caring for Cathy
Blue Lantern
Present Tense
The Cruel Peak

NON-FICTION
Teaching Yourself Tranquillity
The Happy Humanist

1

My application to join the Secret Intelligence Service was tongue-in-cheek in the first place. I was making a living selling second-hand cars in Oxford at the time and in no desperate need of another job, but the opportunity arose by chance and I thought it would be interesting to test my skills against this avowed world of deceit. At the time, I was more interested in getting *into* MI6 than having a career as a spy; being accepted struck me as being a test of brass neck, like talking your way into the Oval Office, or the Cabinet Room at Downing Street. I was twenty-five years old then and an ex-Special Services officer.

I had always had a yen for the army and I had attempted to enter the Royal Military College at Sandhurst when I was eighteen. It was perhaps an exceptional ambition for a lad from Grantley Comprehensive School, rated one of the worst in the country. I had departed from that institution at the request of the head. Under the label *Disruptive behaviour*, a long list of misdemeanors too trivial to mention had been assembled against me. I had to go or be expelled.

I was quite keen to get an education, but at Grantley my talents were not recognised. Therefore I had taken charge of my own education at the local public library some time earlier – pleasant afternoons spent in a quiet seat when I was supposed to be in class. As I was said to be a 'disturbed youth' an arrangement was made between the school and the local authority for me to sit my A-level examinations. I passed all my subjects with top grades, and with my mother's help was able to scrounge the necessary references for Sandhurst.

Unfortunately, this early endeavour to fulfill my romantic vision and become an army officer came to a sudden halt; and as a consequence, I received a piece of advice which I have borne in mind ever since. The advice was delivered by Lieutenant-Colonel James Austen, the invigilator in a written examination at Sandhurst, designed to see what my class of would-be subalterns had absorbed the previous day from lectures on small arms. Colonel Austen halted over my hunched shoulders during the test, and with a curt "Excuse me," drew back the sleeve of my shirt to reveal the list of crucial facts and figures penned on the inner side of my pale white forearm just above the wrist.

Colonel Austen took me to his office. He smiled with charm. He had bright blue eyes, a sunburned face and wavy silver hair. He also had three fingers frostbitten from his left hand. He was a renowned mountaineer. In a tailored barathea uniform with service ribbons, he was a model of the man I hoped to become in later life.

"Barmby," he said (Roger Barmby was my name then) "I like you. You have charisma, a rare quality, and I don't mind your accent. You'd probably make a fine officer. You've done outstandingly well in the aptitude stuff, but I'm going to have to dismiss you. Rules, you know? Always remember this: we all cheat, but do it with elan, with dash. Above all, Barmby, don't get caught!"

The failure of my Sandhurst initiative at that time took me back to the Barmby boarding house on Cassel Street, Oxford. My mother, Gladys, was the proprietress. As her only child I had a small room of my own at the top of the narrow, five-storey town-house. I loafed about making a little money, as much as I needed without sponging on my mother, buying and selling second-hand motorcycles. I was fascinated by smart motorcycles and fast cars, and buying and selling for profit came naturally. Although I didn't think anything of it then, I was a talented salesman. Perhaps this gift was in my genes. I didn't know anything about my forbears at that time, except for Gladys, shrewd but uneducated.

Shortly after the Sandhurst episode, my mother was suddenly and unnecessarily killed. She was returning home at night after visiting a friend, when she was hit on the footpath by a fast-moving and silent bicycle, without a light. She died in hospital a few days later. Her death left me sadly without family. The large sum in damages, extracted from the myopic academic who was trying to improve his cardiovascular performance in the dark, was no compensation for Gladys's fund of cryptic common sense and affection.

I inherited the boarding house, and amongst the title documents I discovered to my surprise, a copy of a deed of settlement, in which the money to buy the boarding house was advanced by Sir Charles Conway of The Beeches, Grantley. The deed was dated in the year of my birth. In return, Gladys promised to keep confidential *Any matter whatsoever pertaining to her relationship with the Conway family.*

My mother had told me that she used to work as a servant in the kitchen at The Beeches before she bought the boarding house, and that my middle name, Roger *Conway* Barmby, was given out of her respect for the family. Naturally I was curious about my father, and there was an earlier time when I had questioned Gladys as closely as a son can respectfully question his mother. Her replies never went beyond 'Your father was a good friend.' When I asked her where she got the money to buy the house, she said, 'I inherited it from a good friend, that's all.' Her attitude was that Roger Conway Barmby had a lot to be thankful for, and ought to mind his own business. Gladys could be unyieldingly firm, and I knew then that I was never going to get any more information from her. I gave up trying.

I created a lot of fantasies about my father, but the reality I believed then was that he was probably a passing tradesman. My arrival would have been a deeply embarrassing matter to my mother, which in decency I finally thought I ought not probe. As to the inheritance, people do occasionally leave money to friends.

Now that Gladys was gone, and I had seen the deed of settlement, I was staggered by the notion that Sir Charles Conway could be my father. I was satisfied that there was no other inference I could draw from the clandestine document.

The Conway family were Oxford grandees. Sir Charles, in his day, had been Lord Lieutenant of the County. I visited the public library and read some of the papers on local history to add to my sketchy knowledge. Sir Charles had died in debt. The Beeches estate was sold, and the National Trust acquired the Elizabethan manor and a few acres around it. One of Charles's three children, all sons, had died in a safari accident in Kenya. The eldest, who had inherited the title, suffered from Huntington's Chorea, and was in a home for the disabled. Only the younger son, James, had survived fit. Little but the name Elliston Conway and a family history as maritime traders going back to the eighteenth century, remained. But Elliston Conway was a *name*, particularly in Oxfordshire, and I was tortured and enthralled by the idea that it could rightfully be mine – Roger Conway Barmby, or Roger Elliston Conway?

Not surprisingly, no father's name had been entered on my birth certificate and I hadn't even begun to toy with the complications of getting a DNA test. I decided to visit The

4

Beeches, which I had often driven past on the South Oxford High Road, always remembering, and not with any distaste, that Gladys had worked happily in that grand pile as a kitchen-hand. She always spoke well of the house and the family on the rare occasions when they were mentioned.

The mansion was open to the public on two afternoons a week to enable the hoi polloi to glimpse the treasures acquired on their behalf. I went through the stone gateway and walked up the drive to the front doors, past the rose garden, the lake and the fountains. As I neared the entrance, I passed through the neatly clipped miniature box hedges arranged like a maze, with curious apprehension. Imagine if this place was, in a sense, mine!

I paid for entry at the ticket box and ascended the marble steps, entering the dank-smelling Great Hall, a vast shadowy space hung with family portraits. A white marble staircase, with a tongue of red carpet rose before me and divided in two, swirling up to left and right. Shafts of light speared though the stained glass windows, casting puddles of colour on the mahogany panelling. I stood on the polished tiles inside the doorway, looking upward, while my eyes accustomed themselves to the life-size portrait in oils which dominated the hall from the landing where the stairs divided.

Roger Conway Barmby's quest was over. There, in the robes of a baronet, looking calmly over the heads of the curious tourists, was the face of a man who was unmistakably my father. I stared up at what could have been taken for a portrait of me in fancy dress; I stared until I was unsteady on my feet.

I hardly saw the finery of the rest of the mansion which I toured quickly, transfixed by the long, square-jawed face, the wide forehead, the grey eyes slightly downward slanting to the outward edges of the eyebrows, the sharp, straight nose, the pallor of fine skin, and even the hank of barley-coloured hair over his brow that was the young Sir Charles Conway, and was also me. I left the Beeches with elation, only tinctured slightly by a sense of the richness of the life that had passed me by; but I'm an optimist. I only look back with a kind of theoretical interest. I haven't time for what might have been.

I was much more concerned with what could be. Without any plan in mind other than to confirm my parentage, I continued my researches. I found that just seven days before my birth, Lady Lucy Conway, Charles's wife, had a son who was christened Roger James Elliston Conway, known as James. I wondered how painful this parallel pregnancy would have been for Gladys, who must have known of it.

James, I discovered, had attended Rugby School, completed a Politics, Philosophy, and Economics degree at Oriel College Oxford, married his undergraduate sweetheart, and departed to farm a thousand acres in North Wales. Already, he was a member of the National Farmer's Union, the parish council, and a supporter of local charities in Llangollen. The newspaper clippings made much of him, but to me he was distinguished only by his lineage; a dull figure whose sole ambition seemed to be to breed cattle, sheep and children.

I reflected that I was entitled to the name Conway. I became determined to take the legal steps necessary to make the change. I dropped the unbeautiful name, Barmby. It had occurred to me that people would confuse me with James, and if they did so, that might be to my advantage. Perhaps I increased the likelyhood of confusion by adding 'Elliston'. I became, by deed poll, Roger Elliston Conway. Now I had the name, and a lineage which I could, if pressed, properly defend.

The practicalities of becoming Roger Elliston Conway were small. As Roger Barmby I had no close circle of school friends, only a few casual acquaintances, and I scarcely ever saw any of Gladys's old friends. Gladys herself never had any relations that I knew of, so there was no embarrassing metamorphosis from Barmby to Elliston Conway.

My half-brother James had moved, virtually as of right, through Rugby and Oxford. James had obtained an upper second at Oriel College. An Oxford University degree would have been of great use to me; more than to a farmer in North Wales. In any event, I calculated that the real value in being Roger Conway – I intended to be careful to call myself that – of the Elliston Conway family, was not in noising it across every bar-room I entered, but in the quiet, unseen advantages of being discreetly known to have a pedigree. This would assure that certain doors would open for me – those of exclusive clubs, bankers, employers and society hostesses. I had already found, from my modest operations as a second-hand car salesman, that understanding the English propensity for snobbery was a necessary prerequisite for getting on in life.

2

The next episode in my career was, unwittingly, to provide a further qualification for the secret services. I had sold the boarding-house and bought an apartment in River Fields, an expensive new development on the Cherwell. My burry butcher's-boy drawl had yielded to nine months of elocution. According to a certain class of English person, including the elocution teacher, I now spoke, impossibly, *without an accent*.

As Roger Elliston Conway I appeared to be a well-educated, well-off bachelor. But I had no career. I whirled around the town in a Ferrari or a Lotus, and made a prosperous living from buying wrecks, getting their odometers rewound, and having them rebuilt and polished for sale. Although I never soiled my own hands with the technical functions of this trade, I took the financial risk and my skill was in negotiating the sale; it was an ignoble following for the son of a baronet.

Despite the Sandhurst fiasco, I was heavily influenced by books and films of Britain's nineteenth-century campaigns abroad, and still yearned to realise my idealised view of the life of an army officer. I therefore decided to apply for a short term commission in the army. I took some satisfaction in presenting myself as a young man from Rugby and Oxford, with a good degree, seeking to enlarge his experience before settling to a more routine career in the City. I thought, *what can the army do if it finds me out?* Only kick me out again.

With my paper qualifications, I was a veritable prize for the forces. Without difficulty I had obtained copies of James's university record and birth certificate, to which only modest alterations were required. My interlocutors fawned over me. I had no conscience in this, knowing that poor Roger Barmby, with his four A-levels, and his squashed vowels, although unacceptable as officer material, was every bit as good a man.

I was accepted by the army with alacrity, applied for special forces, and completed my officer training without a hitch, and with enjoyment. I liked the comradeship – something new to an only child – and the balance of physical and intellectual life. As one would expect of a person with my attainments, I was in the upper quartile of my class.

It was here that my boyish dreams began to be dissipated by cold reality. I had been attracted to the daring deeds of the Special Air Service – as portrayed in films and thrillers – and had never given much thought to the serious consequences of placing my body in jeopardy. When I took time to consider, and to talk to veteran officers who had endured the Iraq War and Afghanistan, I became conscious that the risk of being killed or maimed was grave. I began to wonder if this albeit short-term career I had chosen, this taster of adventure, was really wise.

The training regimes of the SAS were bone-cracking; hurling myself down cliffs, crawling through swamps and jumping out of aircraft. Later, I feared, real bullets, real mines and real shrapnel would add a different dimension of unkindness to flesh and bone. During the course of my training, I gradually, but keenly, began to appreciate the obvious: that the human body is a fragile thing in a life of conflict and that I had but one of them. With this realisation preying on my mind and active service in Afghanistan or Iraq looming up, I tried to make my specialty intelligence work. As adroitly as I could, I selected every option, every course, every task which led toward indoor work at HQ, and away from physically active operations in the field.

I was posted to Afghanistan with the 102nd Regiment, SAS, and remained firmly glued to a desk. I had taken the trouble to research the tribal system of the country, and beside the almost total ignorance of my fellow intelligence officers, could present myself credibly as an expert. The work was interesting, the mess life convivial, but alarming horror stories of experiences in the field seeped in. The sight of body bags and soldiers wrapped in blood-stained bandages was sickening. My appetite for the far frontiers of empire was now satisfied by looking over the wall of the barracks, and seeing the dust swirling down the road toward the low line of golden mountains.

After a year in Kabul, I was shocked to be told by the CO of the regiment that my very industry and excellence as a desk-bound analyst had qualified me for a place leading a team behind enemy lines. My particular understanding of the chaotic tribalism of the Afghans, trivial to a scholar, but impressive at briefings in Kabul, had earned me this assignment. Of course there was no logic in the assignment, but my limited experience had shown me that logic and common sense were not necessary attributes of military decisions.

"Sir," I protested quietly, "there are a number of field officers much more able than me."

"You're too modest, Roger."

"I'm just a computer geek."

"It's precisely your knowledge we need in the mountains, and you're as fit as any officer in the 102nd."

In the mountains. The words were heart-stopping. "But, sir…"

"Everything you say confirms the correctness of my choice," the CO said, putting his arm around my shoulder in a fatherly way.

The mission, codenamed Moonlight, was a joint product of US and British intelligence; armchair thinking, credible at face value, but (to me) impracticable in the bitter mountains. The team would gather intelligence in no-man's land, transmitting the deployments of the enemy to base. I was said to be essential because it was believed that I could identify, in the turmoil, who were enemies and who might be or become, allies. Personally, I doubted that on the stony, snow-flecked slopes, I would be able to tell one bunch of tribesmen from another.

It had not been difficult to make the confused and ever-changing pattern of loyalties of the warlords into a coherent design across a table at headquarters, but on a snow-blocked mountain pass, under enemy fire? I was reluctant to prick the bubble of my reputation, but I went a long way toward it in presenting my reservations. I approached my CO again.

"I must say that I have my doubts whether I can really add any value to the operation, sir. Identification of tribes and warlords' militias on the ground, by sight alone, in difficult weather, is going to be almost impossible."

"Good, Roger, good," the CO said. "I appreciate your caution. Very necessary. You are our best man here. If anybody can pull this off, you can."

My superiors had ordained that Moonlight would shine, and so be it.

I had kept myself physically fit, and looked the part of a field officer. I lectured my small squad of six with a confidence I did not feel. I lectured them until the scepticism that had at first filmed their eyes was dissolved into shining enthusiasm. The men were not fools, but they could not have realised that they were in the hands of a novice – indeed, a terrified novice. After a week, the team was as ready as it could be, packed inside the noisy fuselage of a Westland helicopter.

Disaster beset the mission from the outset. The chopper was to set us down at dusk, high in the northern mountains. The pilots could not find the drop zone. The blades of the chopper touched a cliff wall in a sudden gust of wind, and the machine crashed from low altitude. We all survived the fall and were more or less conscious, but stunned.

As I gathered my wits and struggled out of the burning hull, enemy firing began. Our noisy approach had given Taliban riflemen time to embed themselves behind the rocks which were scattered over the moraine of the valley floor. Suddenly, we were in a maelstrom of confusion, each one of the squad struggling to escape the fire and avoid bullets. The flames illuminated us like targets in a shooting gallery, while our attackers were invisibly tucked behind boulders.

I wormed my way out through the smoke and rubble, and hid in a pile of rocks nearby, unharmed. We couldn't have struck back. And I heard nothing from my team. I waited for dawn alone.

All I could see in the morning light was the burned-out shell of the Westland and scattered bodies. When I was satisfied that the area was clear, I crawled over and found two of my men and the two pilots dead, their bodies ignominiously stripped of equipment and useful clothes. I concluded the others had died too, in their hiding places, or perhaps been taken prisoner.

I retired to a cave. I had a small survival pack and a satellite transmitter. I reported the disaster, but leavened it with information on enemy deployments, identifying tribes, numbers and directions of movement; these were largely imaginary. It made the deaths seem less pointless and I hoped it made me sound valuable and worth saving.

I had a GPS device including a map. I started for the nearest place of safety, the US lines, probably a hundred miles away by the time I had found a way across the trackless mountains. Moonlight was over as far as I was concerned, and I judged that it was too risky to dally to find the pick-up zone, and then hide out until help came in four days' time.

I moved mostly at dusk or in the moonlight, and in the early morning, nearly starving after a week, and fed occasionally by friendly herdsmen. I saw no friend or enemy, herdsmen apart, but my satellite transmitter worked for that week, and I sent more imaginative bulletins. I hoped that I would attract enough interest in the enemy deployments to warrant an aerial surveillance in the vicinity and perhaps lead to my rescue as part of the exercise. My ploy failed. Although daring deeds in rescuing comrades are written about, I knew the unwritten rule was that the British and US forces wouldn't risk a chopper and pilots for me alone.

It took another six days to reach the US lines, by which time I could scarcely crawl. I was feverish and my guts had contracted into an agonising knot. I was scrubbed clean and put in a field hospital. Oh, the feeling of those clean sheets and the taste of sweet food!

Operation Moonlight would have been overtaken in a barrage of new missions and forgotten, but I allowed the US intelligence officers to debrief me. After all, they were entitled to know the story of this frozen, dust-covered, starving wraith who had crawled into their lines.

I had nothing much to say at first. There really was nothing to say other than the fact that I had been clawing my way across the mountains for nearly two weeks. But when it became apparent that the officers who gathered at my bedside with their tape recorders and notebooks were hungry to hear *something, anything,* I (myself an IO) understood their plight and obliged. They were bored with the routine of the base. I therefore told a story of the heroism of my men, fighting to the death, completely outnumbered, instead of the truth that they were shot like dogs in the dark. In contrast to my lonely and miserable starvation scramble across rivers and mountain passes, I spoke of watching enemy deployments during the day, and moving to new observation posts at night. I filled the US intelligence officers' notepads and tapes with a whole demography of war in the mountains. And I spoke to US war correspondents.

Operation Moonlight was exhumed from the grave. In the media game of point-scoring against terrorists, it was a success. The British and US commanders of the exercise basked in brief news media limelight, and I was an anonymous hero.

When I was released from hospital and delivered to the 102nd at Kabul, I expected a hero's welcome. I imagined the whole of the officers' mess gathering round me, rapt at my story. I found however that I was not popular. It was unforgivable that I had allowed myself to be debriefed by the US forces without calling in the British IOs, *and* I had breached the Official Secrets Act in speaking to US war correspondents.

"You've broken every rule in the book, Conway," (I was Roger no more) "including coming back from the dead," my CO said grimly. "You could be court-martialled for blabbing to the US press. But we're not going to do anything with you."

"I'm sorry you feel like that, sir. After all, you've had a very successful mission."

The CO glared at me balefully, knowing what a pointless shambles Moonlight really was, despite the favourable propaganda. And knowing, too, how impossible it was to make anything sensible out of the mass of intelligence on the movements and loyalties of the warlords, and their tribes, which my trek had spawned.

Shortly after this I was flown back to Britain and given a desk job while my commission expired. It was a happy goodbye on both sides when I got into a taxi outside the main gate at Aldershot Barracks. I had a record carrying an official commendation for leadership, bravery and endurance on active service. I also received what amounted to an apology from the Colonel of the Regiment, who always liked me and disagreed with my CO, saying that if there had been a witness to my account I would have been decorated.

Captain Roger Elliston Conway, ex-SAS, aged twenty-five, was back in the job market.

3

I had no thought of joining the intelligence services at this time. I returned to Oxford thinking that I might seek work in the City of London with an investment bank, but I wanted to take time to consider. To occupy myself I began to deal in second-hand cars again. The kind of person who buys a low-mileage Porsche or Aston Martin is one who likes a badge of style, even if he can't quite afford it. One of my customers (I called them clients) had collected another badge of a certain kind of provincial style: membership of the Leander, a pretentious but shabby club in Oxford. He suggested I join. I did and I was readily accepted.

The Leander was frequented by local businessmen, solicitors, and the odd don. It was a place for drinking rather than tasting, for eating rather than dining, for gambling and for pornographic videos, described as films, shown in the library. The food, the cod and chips apart, was unattractive, but the club could be a useful place for me.

I found that my clients were impressed by the confident ambience of the Leander, the marble veneer columns, the blotchy gilt mirrors, and the five-foot high oil portraits of petty merchants of yesteryear; they were apparently not deterred by the condescending and sometimes rude waiters, the stained carpets, the scratched silver plate, or the pervasive stale smell of past roast joints.

I studied the membership list soon after joining and set out to cultivate any members who might be of use to me.

One such was Marius Jacobs, a dissipated English literature don from University College. Marius was a curious mix. We met late one night in the upstairs bar, a grotty little cave where the rank smell of old beef could penetrate as light never did. We were both a little drunk. There was some good-hearted confusion over our drinks orders, and we introduced ourselves and began to talk.

"Oh, yes, Roger Elliston Conway," Marius said. "I remember seeing your name posted on the membership application list."

Marius, I was to find, had a precise memory for facts like that. It was enough. My name spoke for me. I think that after our meeting, Marius, who was ugly, liked being seen with me. I wear expensive and quietly stylish clothes, and I look noticeable in them. I suppose I could have been a model, if I had been interested.

In subsequent days we drank together on occasions, and I asked Marius about life at the college. I was genuinely interested. I had the slight ulterior motive that knowledge of a scene which I would never know personally might be of use to me. My regret at having missed an experience which might plausibly have been mine was faint. As I've said, I accept the way the cards fall although I play hard to get them to fall my way. Marius of course believed he was chatting with a graduate of Oriel. I have no respect for the truth (except in this memoir).

One day we were in the bar and Marius was disdainfully reviewing the prospects of his students. He said that some fools amongst them might even find their way into the secret services. Then he cocked his long head, looking out of the corners of his glistening eyes at me, and said in a jocular way, "You wouldn't be interested in joining, would you, Roger?"

My response was as flippant as the question, and we passed on to other subjects.

I was however taken by Marius's suggestion, whether it was serious or not. Selling second-hand cars was profitable, and becoming *something in the City,* which I had promised myself for the future, would be even more profitable, but nothing could detract from the glamour of a James Bondish career as a spy, and an operative against evil forces. Yes, there would be risks, but it was, I imagined, like fighting for one's country in a Savile Row suit.

A week later I was in the bar of the club with Marius, and when were on the second double-brandy, I reminded him of his earlier remark and said I wouldn't mind being considered for MI6. "Are you the recruiting sergeant, Marius?"

I put it very lightly. I couldn't be absolutely serious; he would think something was wrong.

He was very vain. He puffed up. "Well, I've shepherded a number of promising fellows through the portals. Poor devils."

"Perhaps I'm a promising fellow."

Marius looked at me in a knowing way, as though I had failed to resist an indecent suggestion. He made a palaver of writing particulars on a damp paper napkin. "Of course I remember all these things about you. Let me see. Roger Something-or-other Elliston Conway. Oriel. PPE. Upper second. Right? Rugby, I think. Oh, yes, the Conway family. They'll like you. They like dynasties. And the army. Captain, SAS. My dear chap, you're perfect!"

Two weeks elapsed, and Marius caught my elbow in the reading room in a friendly way, waggled his eyebrows and said I would soon hear something.

A week later I was returning to the apartment in Cherwell Drive. I came up the road fast in a Mercedes 300SL convertible, a slinky silver job, refurbished after a smash. The drive lined, with old plane trees which the developer had been required to spare, was usually bare of people, but I noticed a man in tweeds moving around uncertainly on the side opposite the apartment block and looking up at it. He didn't look like a burglar on reconnaissance; more like an inspector of some kind. Perhaps a bailiff. I had an uneasy start, combing through a list of people in my mind who might be chasing me. I pulled into the carport and cut the engine. Without apparently noticing the snooper, I locked the car and went upstairs.

I had several people pursuing me for sums of money which I disputed, but decided I was feeling unnecessarily guilty, and after letting myself into the apartment, went boldly to the front window and looked down. The man had gone.

I forgot about the incident until I went downstairs in the morning at eight, and found the man in tweeds was there, a few yards from the car. His clothes were crumpled and his complexion purplish. He looked testy. I felt a stab of unreasoning apprehension.

"Captain Conway?" The voice was thick and commanding.

"Who are you?" I asked, putting on an easy smile. "I think I saw you loitering around here last night."

The man was mean and unsmiling. "We need to talk somewhere." He moved his jaw upward to indicate the apartment, his tone more an order than a request.

"No we don't," I said gently. I looked at my watch, sprang the locks on the car and opened the door. I had a drive of fifty miles before me and an appointment with a prospective buyer.

The man stepped close to me, smelling of detergent soap and tobacco. "You've expressed interest in joining friends of mine in London," he said in a low voice.

Now, to my relief, I understood. I frowned, although I felt like smiling. "Have I? You seem to know a lot about my affairs."

"We sometimes look over prospects in advance, Captain Conway."

So this was MI6 in action. I had a sudden mental picture of myself in fifteen years' time – this man was over forty – checking on potential recruits in cold suburban streets at breakfast-time. I put my leg inside the door of the car. "Look, I have a business meeting."

"What exactly do you do, Captain Conway?" the man asked, his small eyes flicking over the lines of the Mercedes and my suit, a tailored gray woollen worsted, which unlike his own, draped without a crease.

"I don't discuss my business with somebody whose name I don't even know."

"Smith, I should have mentioned," he said tersely.

I bridled, unseen, at his arrogance, and for a moment didn't care if I scuppered the MI6 opportunity. "Sorry, Mr Smith, but you'll have to identify yourself a lot more fully before we can talk privately." I slid behind the wheel and fired the engine.

Smith moved close, blocking my attempt to close the door. "All right Captain Conway, no more messing around." He pulled a plastic card from the fob pocket of his waistcoat showing his photograph, and stating that he was a special adviser to the Home Office Department of Security. The name on the card was Edward Norrington.

I took my time with the card and returned it with a scowl. "It's Norrington now, is it? You know, Mr Norrington, I can get a card like that made up in about an hour."

I pushed him out of the way gently, closed the door of the car and drove off, glimpsing his indignant expression in the rearview mirror. I asked myself whether MI6 was testing my common sense, and then banished the idea of joining them.

Two days later I received a vague and brief note from Norrington's department making no reference to Marius Jacob, or the fatuous approach of Norrington; they simply asked me to call their number for an interview appointment. And so in this odd manner, my career in secret intelligence began.

Over a period of more than six months I was tested and seen by a variety of leisurely and enigmatic people – sometimes there were two or three of them, men and women, ex-soldiers or soldiers in plain clothes and as many civilians. The tests and meetings took place at offices in Whitehall and Victoria. Some of their questions were half-serious and many quite oblique. When I asked about *their* positions, they were uncommunicative. Efforts on my part to pin down what I would be required to do as an intelligence officer, apart from taking numerous courses on everything from Urdu to cryptography, were received blankly. It was my first practical experience of the barrier of inequality of information, which is a fact of everyday life in intelligence work. I was only entitled to know if I needed to know, and a mere would-be recruit was seen as having few needs.

There was plenty to say on my side in these many interviews. I rambled through my illustrious family. As Marius had said, the officials liked dynasties, and I gave them a good measure of Charles the gambler, and even Charles's father, the shipping magnate. I had school and university well researched and digested and my story off pat. I gilded the lily a little on my work, but told no untruth in explaining that I was a self-employed businessman, trading in machinery. Amongst these bureaucrats, a self-employed person was a wonder of self-reliance. On the sporting side, I confined myself to the second XV at school, and the actual county championship achievements on the track of James Conway.

My academic curriculum vitae was supported by a reference from a retired tutor at Oriel whom I knew slightly. The tutor was senile and confused me with my half-brother. I supplemented that with a reference from Marius Jacob, who had a destructive liking for being misleading. He knew no more of me than he had learned during our drinking sessions, but wrote of me glowingly as a friend, and a man of integrity with an acute brain. The two latter attributes may have been true, but Marius could hardly have known.

In all this, my military record was the clincher. I guessed that MI6 would have access to my file, so I had rounded it off with a letter from General Sir Humphrey Fraser, Colonel of the 102nd, rather than my sour CO in Kabul. Sir Humphrey kindly repeated what he had told me in the officers' mess; that I might well have been decorated for Operation Moonlight.

As the interviews drifted on, seemingly without end, I became confident that I would pass, but felt indifferent. I submitted to batteries of tests of intelligence and personality and leadership potential, always knowing what MI6 wanted to establish, and reacting appropriately. I have no doubt that I emerged as the strong, calm, reliable leader they were seeking. I found my questioners stodgy, snobbishly hidebound, and gullible. My anticipation of joining a service full of exciting projects, carried forward by dynamic and interesting people, had faded. But despite these dreary preliminaries, there *was* a cachet about being a secret agent. I was still determined to give it a chance. There was plenty of time in the future to think of that job in the City of London or New York, probably in an investment fund, and all the money it would make for me. Goldman Sachs and JP Morgan could wait.

4

My early months in MI6 are better forgotten, eighteen of them in a seemingly endless series of courses and conferences, everything from pistol practice to electronic surveillance. I didn't even have a desk, but was one of a rabble of trainees stabled in a common room at a dilapidated town house in Wimpole Street. In the short intervals between courses, we sat on tattered couches, with bare boards under our feet, drank coffee and mused privately on our suspicions about each other. Naturally, I set out to be pleasant and agreeable to everybody, including the crabby old woman who made the coffee.

The pay, I found, was pitiful but I had a useful sum in the bank – my inheritance from Gladys, the damages I won for her untimely demise, and the profits from my car dealing which were largely free of taxes in the manner in which I managed them. I added a couple of tailor-made suits to an already adequate wardrobe, and sauced them with a few shirts and silk ties from Gieves & Hawkes. My dress wasn't appreciated at the Mill (as the Wimpole Street base was called). My colleagues, when they were not wearing jeans, trainers and anoraks and looking as though they were going to a football match, affected sack-like off-the-peg suits, check flannel shirts and spurious club ties, like the crumpled Norrington.

I let my Oxford apartment and rented furnished rooms in a mews house off Welbeck Street, spacious, comfortable and quiet. I had to garage my Porsche 911; it was quite useless in London, but I kept it, thinking I might be invited to the occasional dinner in the home counties, and I could arrive in passable style. I enhanced my goodwill with my fellow trainees with two modest champagne parties over this period, and even by lending the Porsche on occasions. My colleagues regarded me as an upper crusty military type, but a 'decent chap' and good company – I was particular about being good company.

I was beginning to get bored and restive, thinking that even the world of used cars had more excitement in it than the intelligence service, when I received my first appointment. I was posted to US Liaison. It was considered to be a valuable appointment, and in my view, no less than I deserved. The appointment also usefully raised my stakes with my peers.

I flew to New York in high anticipation. The flight itself caused a slight problem. Determined to begin my new career with a flourish, I upgraded my mean economy airline ticket. I thought, why stop at business class on such a momentous occasion? I flew first class. At Heathrow when I boarded, I settled myself in the soft and roomy seat, attended by a dutiful hostess with a tray of delicate appetisers and a glass of champagne. I looked up to see a man in the cabin doorway. He was studying me. He looked irritable. Rather than a famous actor or politician, it was Cyril Hornby, with his sallow, egg-shaped head and tiny spectacles, clutching a worn, civil service-issue briefcase. Hornby, the head of my section in the US, whom I had met briefly in London, did not speak but tore himself from the cabin doorway and disappeared into the belly of the plane with the crowd.

At thirty-five thousand feet, I reflected upon this unpropitious sign with an ice-cold vodka, and a portion of lobster.

I did not see Hornby at Kennedy airport, having disembarked long before him. I presented myself, after an expensive cab ride, at the Rockefeller Plaza suite of my department. I was allowed to cool in the waiting area with my suitcases, for half an hour, with occasional refreshment kindnesses from the receptionist. Hornby himself did not materialise, but a smiling, flame-haired Cornishman named Yarham eventually appeared. He showed me my desk, in a glass-partitioned open-plan office and stood back while I admired its minimalist lines and cramped position.

"Not much, sir, is it? But I expect you'll be out a good deal."

"I hope so," I said, concealing my disappointment with a tight smile.

"Well, let me show you the apartment," Yarham said, with a knowing look that gave me a stab of concern.

Yarham took me in a cab, with my luggage, to a one-bedroom Greenwich Village apartment at the top of an old building, high-ceilinged and badly in need of decoration. The furnishings were mean and the place had the odour of the last occupant, a nauseating wet-dog smell.

Yarham looked at me, cocked his head on one side and said, "Not very salubrious, Captain Conway?"

"Or very clean."

"But it's a very good address, sir."

Later, Hornby received me coldly and made no reference to the flight. He lay back in his chair, looked out of the window, fourteen floors above Fifth Avenue, and fingering his ear, began to lecture. What emerged from his drone was that my lowly function would be to receive *published* reports from US departments of state, and to analyse and comment upon them. To me, US Liaison had implied hobnobbing with CIA field officers and cryptographers from the National Security Agency, hearing all the latest plots and plans of the most diverse intelligence services in the world. When I asked Hornby why the analysis I was supposed to supply couldn't be done from London, he regarded me pityingly.

"Oh, dear, you are virginal. Yes, it's perfectly possible to do this in London, and a lot cheaper, but always remember, Captain Conway, you have to find out as much as possible about what our American friends are doing."

"You don't think they tell us?"

"Not the truth, my dear Conway."

"But we have a special relationship."

"So does a grandfather with the granddaughter he is seducing," Hornby said wanly.

Hornby later introduced me to a number, but not all of the rest of the department. I thought that it was implicit in each meeting that I should speak to that person about work only when I had to; their work was something I wasn't entitled to know about, and shouldn't ask. It seemed that my colleagues would be wraiths who passed me in the corridor.

I was in New York. I was a spy. A spy with a growing pile of reports on his desk about new proposals for the postal service, the national cost of gas and oil production, the projected demands on the public transportation system over a ten-year term, the effect of legislative reforms on the insurance industry, and many other such absorbing subjects. At a glance, I could see very little intelligence potential in any of them. And I couldn't understand how, buried in these reports, I would even get time to have afternoon tea with my American contacts in the many departments that produced the reports, let alone spy on them.

It was at this point that Herbert Yarham came into my

consciousness in a serious manner. He had been appointed as my assistant. In the absurd lottery of departmental life Yarham was assigned to me, although there would be times when I would feel that I was assigned to him. He appeared at first as the man who would help with my files; he was a clerk, an administrator (although a trained intelligence agent). I had hoped for a Miss Moneypenny and I got Yarham. He was about five years older than me, and as tall, but bony and ungainly, with a hugely prominent chin, a thick stand of red-gold hair, and shining light blue eyes.

My first impression of Yarham as a worker was that he was dangerously enthusiastic, but I soon found that his knowledge of the form-filling, box-ticking and icon-clicking empire of intelligence was encyclopaedic. I also began to detect a particular subtlety and originality in his work which appealed to me. He knew the system, and took particular delight in outwitting it. He was drawn to puzzles and problems with nerdish pleasure. He was happy to sort out the paper – and computer-work messes I was beginning to create. With Yarham's help, I would gradually gain the reputation of producing comprehensive and well-written reports containing valuable insights.

Yarham's ability to concentrate on a small issue and gain enjoyment from it was refreshing, intent as I was on scaling the heights of the secret universe and pulling off great coups on the way. His ambitions at work seemed to be readily achieved each day, while mine were always short of fulfilment.

I found I could delegate most of my analytical work to Yarham. I would read the executive summary at the front of a report on, say, copper production and we would confer briefly. "Shall we say this? Or that?" I would ask. He would reply, "I would put it this way." A matter of a few minutes, a few notes on a scrap of paper, and he would retire to his modest corner to complete the task. Most of our work disappeared without trace into the sink of bureaucracy, but occasionally, Yarham's acidic analysis earned me some congratulations.

Apart from a few hours spent with Yarham each week, I was free. I had met a girl who was a courier for MI6, Laurie Hayes, and she began to stay with me when she was in New York. My Oxford and London girlfriends sent me affectionate cards and threatened to visit, but I always replied that I would be out of town at the time.

At first, with the flush of a new boy, I arranged to meet some of the researchers and civil servants who were involved in the reports Yarham was analysing; they were happy to elaborate their thinking to this British civil servant, and to have a winey lunch, stumbling over the list of questions which Yarham had invented. Since the authors of the reports were scattered across the US, there was an opportunity to travel out of New York and see the country. Sometimes Yarham accompanied me.

We recognised quickly that as a real means of intelligence-gathering, the visits were a nonsense and began to apply what we called the *Travel Test*. Yarham marked all incoming reports with the address of the authors and kept a list. If there was a place either or both of us wanted to visit for a few days (say San Francisco, Grand Canyon, Yellowstone Park), Yarham could be relied upon to find a report which would pass the Travel Test by relating to that location. We would then fix meetings with the authors of the report, concoct a slate of questions, and make the visit, allowing generous time for sightseeing. With Yarham's manipulation of the travel and expense account arrangements, we had regular and comfortable short breaks. And we did not neglect to include in our (really Yarham's) analysis of the reports, a snippet of information obtained from the authors which was not in the text of the report.

For a few months, these diversions, my girlfriend, the bars of New York, and some potentially useful connections at the Oxbridge & Ivy Club held my attention, but I was rapidly becoming disillusioned. The prospect of being a transatlantic version of the dyspeptic Norrington began to trouble me.

Then Nick Stavros called me at the office.

5

I met Nick Stavros at the Algonquin Hotel for lunch; we ordered Manhattans straight up and contemplated each other. Nick, from Wapping, looked strained. He was short and broad-bodied, olive-skinned, with black curly hair, and usually an infectious lover of life like his Greek forebears. One of the more able and amenable of my intake of recruits, he had secured a prized appointment in Washington.

Nick leaned back, sipped his drink and said, "You look as though you're enjoying the life, Roger."

I saw no reason to hide. "Well, I'm not enjoying the job, Nick. No. Don't be fooled by my cheery disposition. New York's the greatest, but you know, after a while you get choked on the parties, the bars, the movies, the galleries, the concerts – if you don't have a job. I analyse reports about the funding of interstate highways, and fascinating subjects like that. I'm thinking of getting out. Give me something real – real intelligence work I mean – to do here, and I'm the happiest man in the world."

"Uh-huh, could be useful, what you're doing," Nick said seriously.

I could see he was comparing his own pitch. "Then they can get somebody else to do it. What about you? What are you up to?"

I thought Nick had been appointed to liaise with the Central Intelligence Agency, but he explained it wasn't quite that. He was with C3, which I had never heard of. He said they kept in touch with certain overseas trade associations, and then his voice trailed away as he realised the evident nonsense of this spiel.

"Sounds like my job," I said.

If one rule had been hammered into the new recruits at every opportunity since we joined MI6, it was that we should shut up about our work to everybody, including colleagues unless it was a team effort. Nick was obviously trying to follow the rule. I felt no such constraint, because my small task at USL could be done by any member of the public, US or foreign. I insisted to Nick that my work was quite boring and almost useless.

I didn't mention my sense that things weren't right with Nick either, and our talk drifted to the pleasures of New York and Washington. Assisted by the lobster blinis and the bottle of Chardonnay we had ordered, I was beginning to appreciate the opulence of the shining walnut panelling and the frescoes, and trying to imagine the Dorothy Parker days, when Nick, encouraged perhaps by my frankness, startled me with a question.

"Do you know anything about *The Disciples*, Roger?"

At first I thought I hadn't been paying enough attention, and we had lurched into a spiritual discussion. Nick leaned over frowning at my confusion. "I mean the so-called club of Ivy League and Oxbridge operatives."

"Never heard of it. What do they do?"

"It's only rumours of course," Nick said weakly.

"What we live on. What do they do? Of course I can imagine all the professors and rocket scientists getting together and thinking they're a lot smarter than anybody else."

"Yes, maybe that's all it is, a sort of mutual arrogance club," Nick said thoughtfully.

"How about the name, *The Disciples?* Sounds… pretentious."

"That's what the rumours call them. I don't know if that's what they call themselves."

"So you think they do exist?"

Nick didn't answer directly. "I suppose the name suggests the game in a sneering kind of way. Disciples of what they would call Reason, disciples of Knowledge… or maybe disciples of nothing very much except their own collective ego."

"Guys who believe they know best how to run the planet?"

"Yes."

I was interested. "What are the Disciples reputed to actually *do*?"

"I don't know. I guess they have a brand of patriotism that's entirely their own."

"It's come up?"

"Yes, in a way."

"Tell me about it."

"I better not. I may be getting it out of proportion. Tell you what, come to Washington in a couple of weeks; things might be clearer by then, and we'll talk some more. I trust you, Roger, and I wouldn't like this conversation to get out."

I thought that Nick felt he'd imparted a special confidence, but actually he'd hardly said anything; it was no use trying to budge him to tell more. We closed the lunch with cognac and coffee, and reflections about the success or failure of some of our peers. I left him in Times Square slightly tipsy. Nick's words about trusting me remained in my mind, and seemed to suggest the importance he placed on the Disciples. I resolved to ask Yarham to find a report which passed the Washington travel test, fix the necessary meeting and book me a flight.

A week later, when Yarham and I were getting positioned at my desk for one of our lightning surveys of the latest crop of reports, Yarham said, "I was very sorry to hear about the death of your friend Mr Stavros, sir, and I've taken the liberty of cancelling the Washington visit."

I was shocked. "What *happened?* It's the first I've heard."

"Heart attack. The memo I saw said a British Embassy official died of a sudden heart attack."

Nick Stavros was my age and he had been passed into the service with the required high level of fitness. "Where did it happen? Do you know any more?"

"Nothing, sir. His file will eventually wend its way through our office when they've had a post mortem and signed it off. Would you like to see it?"

"I would, Yarham. Have you ever heard of the Disciples?"

He didn't hesitate for a second or misunderstand what I was talking about. He broke into one of his sunrise grins. "Certainly, sir."

"Tell me."

"It's a conspiracy theory: that the Anglo-American secret services are masterminded by a group of top Oxbridge-Ivy League dons."

"Do you believe it?"

"Like all conspiracy theories there's no proof one way or the other – only jokes around the coffee machine at morning break when there's a fuck-up."

As a result of the news about Nick, I declared a moratorium on work for that morning and slipped out for a drink at Giovanni's, and a quiet hour at the Museum of Modern Art.

Two weeks later, in a booth in O'Connell's Pub on West 52nd Street, Yarham produced, with a flourish, a printout from Nick Stavros's bulky personal file.

"Where do you get this stuff from, Yarham?"

"It's magic," he laughed.

I raised my Guinness in a tribute to his ingenuity, and began to flick through the documents. I expected the department had the same sort of dossier on me, a detailed biography and numerous reports, larded with barbed and niggling comments. But Nick was obviously well regarded, and marked for a distinguished career. One of the last documents on the file was an internal medical report by a psychiatrist saying that Nick was disturbed and needed a rest before returning to active duty. The file closed with a death certificate. "Do you see this, Yarham? It says he died of a heroin overdose."

"In diplomatic speak that translates as a heart attack."

"I don't believe he was a user. I didn't know him that well, but I had the impression of a deep down careful and controlled agent."

I decided to reinstate the Washington visit and see Sally Greengloss, Nick's girlfriend whom I'd met on a previous occasion in Washington. The suddenness of Nick's departure and the strangeness of his end, bugged me, and I had the time to be curious. I called Sally, a publisher's editor, whose number Yarham had located, offered condolences and suggested lunch when I was in town. We met on the terrace of the Colony Café overlooking the Potomac in Georgetown. It was a sunny day, and the soft-shell crab with spinach was delicious. I had a charming companion and I liked the role of solicitous friend.

When we began to talk of Nick, Sally sounded resigned. "It's hard to accept, but always on the cards for all of us I suppose."

She was far less perturbed than I expected. "He wasn't in any trouble was he?"

"What do you mean, Roger?"

I decided to share my wild imagination. "He wasn't murdered, was he?"

"What a rash and... crazy... thing to ask. I don't know anything about his work. *He's just died of a heart attack.* At one moment Nick was enjoying life, happy and healthy as an athlete, and the next he was dead. Sometimes this happens, young people just keel over."

"But Nick's death certificate recorded the cause of death as an overdose of heroin."

She gave a little cry which drew a few curious glances from nearby diners, and said that was impossible. "How do you know?" she asked.

"A friend of his told me. Another drinking buddy." I could hardly admit that I had ratted through Nick's personal file.

"I thought Nick didn't have any friends over here. Who was it?"

It was a hard, abrupt question and I instantly invented a name. "A guy called Freddie Coombs."

She stared at me; her engaging eyes had turned to beads. I couldn't work out why she was interrogating me so coldly. Perhaps she thought I was putting Nick down. Then she relaxed and mellowed.

"Nick was a fun guy who could push sensations to the limit."

"Have you seen him using?"

"Maybe a line of coke occasionally. Nick didn't come home from work one night. I was worried sick, but I knew he was in intelligence work which made unusual demands. The next day, about noon, I had a call from the Embassy saying Nick was in the mortuary, dead of a heart attack in the street."

"In the street?"

"Perhaps they got it wrong, or were trying to be kind," she reflected. "Did Nick ever say anything to you when he was in New York, about anything troubling him?"

I answered as a trained seal leaps. "No nothing healthwise. And he was very close about his work. I don't even know what his job was. We were drinking buddies in London during recruitment, but not much more."

She kept looking at me, and eventually seemed satisfied. I thought she seemed unsurprised about the drugs. I wasn't going to tell her what Nick had said about the Disciples, because it was a work observation that would be meaningless to her.

Later, I asked mutual acquaintances in Washington and New York a few guarded questions about Nick's death when I returned. As far as I could ascertain they were stunned or saddened, depending on how close to Nick they were, but nobody was perturbed about the bona fides of the event. However, Nick's idea about the Disciples, real or imagined, and his sense of concern about them, was the kind of thought that stays in the mind.

6

I had determined by now to seek a transfer to another department, or leave the service. And the prospect of Nick Stavros's job appealed to me, although I knew little about it specifically, save that it *had* to be more responsible than mine. The implicit message that Nick was carrying an onerous burden had come across by osmosis at the Algonquin. And it was inconceivable to me that any work could be less interesting than mine. I gathered also, from morning coffee chatter at the office (pay and promotion were subjects which were not verboten) that one or two of my more senior fellows at USL were also interested, which suggested that it was prestigious; the post would clearly be an enhancement of my present paltry role.

Although I found New York a delightful place to idle away my time, society within USL seemed to be non-existent. It was not that I hankered after the exciting company of my colleagues, but I reckoned that I could not advance myself with due speed unless I was able to meet and impress them outside the office. Nothing could be expected of Hornby, but otherwise my attempts to penetrate the work heirarchy socially ended with me paying for expensive lunches without any return invitations, let alone the opportunity to dine in the home of one of my seniors. Washington, on the contrary, where Nick had been based, a city of politicians, embassies and lobbyists, and presumably spies, was I fancied a place given to the art of entertaining.

I calculated that Hornby would view my proposed move with a certain ambivalence. He would be delighted to dispose of someone he detested, but competent operatives like me were all too few.

When I told Yarham that I might apply for Nick's post, to my surprise, he frowned and shook his head in disagreement. Later, as we eased ourselves into the shadows of one of O'Connell's booths, he dilated.

"That's a sure way not to get the appointment, Captain. Why don't you have a chat with Hornby and tell him that you've heard the vacancy will be coming up but it would be inconvenient for you to move to Washington?"

"That will get it?"

"You'll stand a better chance. Applications aren't a lot of use. The bosses do what they want, which is most often what you don't want."

"I should tell Hornby that I like New York so much, I wouldn't like to be disturbed?"

Yarham caressed his chin. "It would certainly increase his pleasure in releasing you, Captain. There's a certain perversity about appointments in the service, in which Hornby, like other managers, will conspire. You're likely to be posted to the place you don't want to go. If this had to be justified, it's a test of toughness and we're always being tested."

I was dwelling on this peculiarity when Yarham brushed the subject aside, saying, "I have a more interesting approach for you to consider, Captain. The result of my latest trawl through the OPB files."

I knew that Yarham did a regular and surreptitious survey of *Other People's Business,* in which he, as it were, looked through everybody's in and out trays. So much of the department's work was done electronically, that he was able to accomplish this with relative ease from his computer station. Yarham was an expert hacker. As an intelligence officer, he considered every intranet a target, and like a dedicated crossword-puzzler, sudoku fiend and computer geek, could not rest easy until he had conquered it. The OPB trawl was a practice that we both found very useful. When I questioned Yarham about the propriety and the risk involved he was very relaxed.

"Don't worry, sir, everybody does it to the extent of their know-how. We're all spies, and we spy on each other!"

Now, in the malodorous confidentiality of O'Connell's pub's booth, Yarham revealed a matter which would have life-changing effects for both of us. His eyes shone happily. "There's a top secret assignment coming up that looks important," he said. "It's a Washington posting. An email from Human Resources has gone round. Nominated candidates to go to London for selection. And there's around half a dozen of them – an indicator of importance."

"Me, nominated, Yarham?" I said, suddenly excited.

"No sir, not you. There's only one from the New York office – Leyton. He's more senior."

"So I'm out?"

Yarham raised his eyebrows and dropped his jaw open. His eyes were wide. "Not if the memo had been addressed to you."

"You mean?... Oh, come on, man, if you put me in the circulation by some jiggery-pokery, the mistake's going to be discovered in London and I'll be kicked out!"

"Perhaps not, sir. It's no shame to receive a misdirected email. London will have a guest list of a half dozen or so on the day. Nobody is going to be checking the candidates against the computer. Corporate fog will be fairly thick. And one very important point: Human Resources is a department which doesn't make mistakes, so your presence on the list, and at the selection, can't be a mistake."

I admired the sheer balls of the idea, and had nothing to lose. "If I'm there, I'm virtually certain of consideration at least, aren't I?"

"Quite so," Yarham said, nodding with wise amusement.

We finished another pint of Guinness, each considering the prospect and I agreed that Yarham should proceed to cast his spell over the computer.

I received no direct communication about the Washington post, but Hornby called me into his office several days later, and fixed me with a malevolent stare. "I see you've been summoned to London, Mr Conway." He had decided to drop the courtesy title of Captain. He pulled various contortions of his pallid face which indicated that this was a situation he didn't like, didn't understand, and indicative of a blunder. "How do you account for it?"

"I presume my merit has been recognised and my good record can't be overlooked."

"If over-confidence is what they're looking for, you could be appointed head of MI6, Mr Conway. Well, I daresay Mr Yarham can manage your desk until you get back."

"What if I don't come back?"

"It would be bad luck to conjure with that pleasant possibility, Mr Conway."

Hornby had a jaundiced view of me which I had to endure, having assisted in its creation. I certainly didn't mention how joyful the prospect of not returning to USL would be to me. Instead, I prepared for London with gusto.

When I arrived at Heathrow, I called the MI6 contact number to be told that there was a reception for the invitees that evening at the Mill in Wimpole Street. I paused at my department-selected hotel, the Holiday Inn in Welbeck Street, to shower and change into a suit and clean shirt. It was after eight o'clock when I pressed the bell on the front door at Wimpole Street. I was admitted by a secretary wearing an apron, and doubling as a waitress. Caterers with their own staff could never be let loose on an occasion like this.

Instead of being held in the threadbare common room on the ground floor, the function was upstairs. Here it was almost as shabby, but of pretentious proportions, with high ceilings, dusty architraves and drab velvet curtains. The party was well advanced, and liquor-fuelled, judging by the volume of the conversation.

When I entered, I noticed immediately that the occupants of the room were exclusively male apart from the waitress. They all looked older than me and were presumably senior to me – like Leyton, my New York colleague, who was in his mid-forties. Seniority was, I was beginning to learn, a product of the effluxion of time rather than merit. I was going to be in marked contrast to the other contenders, and I hoped that this would not raise questions about my presence.

I accepted a glass of watery yellow fizz masquerading as Champagne and eyed the crowd, all strangers apart from Leyton, who was standing to one side, alone. I greeted him warmly, but his social skills allowed no change in his glassy expression other than a sclerotic jerk of the head. I gave him a smile, wished him luck, and stepped toward the centre of the room. The uncertainty of such social moments is stimulating. Who will you meet, or will the gathering all hunch their shoulders, turn away and ignore you?

Out of the huddle of talkers in front of me came a small, thin, bent man, with oiled black hair which drooped down on one side of his forehead. His eyes were crossed and unnaturally bright. He flung himself on me grasping and pumping my hand.

"Roger Conway. Roger Charles James Elliston Whatever,

Whatever, Conway," he said in a loud voice that attracted attention. "I might have known you'd be here."

"Delighted to see you, Marius," I replied, clasping him around the shoulders like an old friend, surprised that my investment in cognacs at the Leander bar had paid off so well.

I quietened Marius, who was high, and drew him to the side of the room. I didn't want to attract too much attention, but clearly Marius regarded himself as my mentor and after we had exchanged a few trivial words on the high life in New York, insisted on making introductions. "Follow me, Roger!" he exclaimed, towing me across the room.

The first introduction was to Childers Amory, a name I knew by repute, the supposedly brilliant number two in MI6. In the flesh, Amory was about fifty, rotund, bald, swaddled in a dull blue suit. He had a hairy nose with large open pores on it, and hairy ears. He was seated at the end of the room furthest from the door, on a ragged chaise longue which looked as though it had been cleared out of an abandoned country house. The chaise longue was facing the cold fireplace; Amory thus had his back to the gathering, and a more or less private space where he could talk to a chosen few and drink whisky.

Marius left us, bowing like a courtier after the meeting, which included a quick mention of my background. Marius justified in a few seconds all the careful work I had done on Barmby. "Childers, this is Roger Conway, Rugby, Oriel and the SAS," he said.

A whole curriculum vitae and a sterling silver guarantee of quality, in three words! I imagined how Barmby would have fared in similar circumstances, in the unlikely event of getting such an introduction: "Childers, this is Roger Barmby, Grantley Comprehensive." In short, Roger Nobody. As things were, I was a person of consequence who had the entire attention of the esteemed Childers Amory.

He looked up at me, I thought with some pleasure, because I did look good; dressed in a tailored suit, handsome, youthfully promising and so immeasurably different from the other stale contenders. Childers Amory patted the couch warmly, inviting me to sit beside him. I *engaged* with him; I am very good at this. After all, I used to sell second-hand Porsches and I had swallowed *How to win Friends and Influence People* as though it was holy writ.

Amory spoke of MI6 in vague terms – the actual phrases he used to glorify the service were immaterial, but he went on for what seemed a very long time, ignoring the rest of the gathering. After a while he placed his hand on my knee, a gesture which was hidden from others in the room. In this conversation, I was like a master chef with a delicate sauce, stirring in the odd word very occasionally to make a piquant brew. As he talked, Amory moved his hand gently up my thigh as far as practicable and finally turned his pocked nose and watery eyes toward me. He pressed my hard thigh muscle.

"You're a very fit man… Why don't you come round to my flat tonight for a nightcap with one or two of the others, at ten or so, when we've finished here, Roger?"

"I'd like that very much, sir," I said, and tucked away the card Amory pressed covertly into my palm.

Marius Jacob approached us shepherding a tall, steel-haired man in a fine blue hounds-tooth suit whom he introduced as Sir Carl Bolding. "Roger was at Oriel, I think at about the time you were giving those rather controversial lectures about democracy, Carl," he said.

I panicked. This was the kind of confrontation I had feared.

Bolding, whom I had only heard of in my researches into the Politics Faculty at Oxford, but knew almost nothing about, looked hard at me. I guessed he had consumed a lot less liquor than Marius or Amory. Then, to my relief, a slight smile broke out. "Yes, I do remember you, I think. A better athlete than a philosopher, weren't you?"

We all laughed and I agreed. It was remarkable that Bolding remembered somebody as undistinguished as James Conway and confirmation that I had the family likeness. I was on edge that Bolding would ask me a simple question the answer to which, given my background, I *must* know, like who was my Politics tutor. I sweated. It was a yawning gap in my otherwise meticulous preparations. But the killer question never came. I parried Bolding's further enquiries about my undergraduate life, being slightly facetious and modest. I escaped from Bolding as soon as I could.

Marius trundled me round the room and introduced me to several more academics and departmental 'names' whom I guessed were serving on the interview panels the next day. By and large their eyes widened at seeing somebody other than a bespectacled fortyish bank clerk, or a bulky and graying ex-military man and this was enough for me. I was modestly amusing. I had been noticed. In their deliberations it wouldn't be, "Conway? Now which one was he?"

I judged that by this time I had met everybody of consequence. I declined Marius's invitation to rendezvous at a local bar and left the party quietly.

It was a cold but clear night, and I walked several blocks checking my watch before heading toward Grafton Way, the address of Childers Amory's apartment. Here, I knew, I would be on tricky ground. I had to rely on the hope that even a man as powerful as Amory would not expect to get his heart's desire in one night. And Amory might, in the intervening time, have gained some perception that his overture had been little more than the inopportune expression of a drunken urge. But having accepted his invitation, I had little choice but to take whatever risk was involved. Not to arrive at Grafton Way would be bad form; it would be remembered, and I was looking for a positive push in the selection process. As I walked, I also remembered a little of what I had read about Bolding. He was a controversial critic of the open society and an elitist.

Amory's rooms were on the third floor of an old mansion block. The lights were on. I was cold and it was ten-thirty. I rang and went up. He opened the door, whisky in hand, wearing only socks on his feet, his trousers supported by wide red braces. His shirt was open on his plump, gray haired throat. "Come in, my boy, I've just been reading about you."

I followed Amory into a small, hot, pink-walled and pink-carpeted lounge like a throat, where a computer screen shone on a side table. I was apparently the first guest to arrive.

"Your file wasn't with the rest of the batch. Can't think why. Had to call it up. I liked what I read, Roger." He clasped my arm affectionately and sought my eyes, but propriety required him to break off and serve me a drink.

As Amory swayed over the drinks cabinet, slopping out a whisky and water, I guessed that while the liquor had undermined his coordination, his mind was still functioning adequately. "You could be the man we're looking for, Roger, that balance of intellect and physical hardness, coupled with breeding. I'm an egalitarian myself, but I know the surest way is to choose men who come from a long line of traditional service, men with ingrained, inborn values. Pedigree counts, eh?"

"I hope to get the appointment, sir," I said, taking the glass from his hand, and choosing a separate armchair, rather than the couch. My responses could be, at most, echoes to the great man's aria.

"You don't even know what the task is," Amory said, standing over me for a moment.

I was looking upward into his wide, black nostrils. The power of knowledge, of so much secret knowledge, had produced a surge of adrenalin in him.

"I joined the service for exciting assignments, sir."

Amory lurched back to the couch, dropping on it heavily. "Exciting? Yes, you're that sort of man. And dangerous? Yes, you can handle that too. You could be the man, Roger."

"I certainly hope so."

"And loyal. Utterly loyal to me, to Bolding, to our service?"

"I'm certainly that," I said in a very low key, while Amory nodded affirmatively.

"You met Professor Kauffer tonight, and Dr Reich?"

I remembered being introduced to the two Americans, and had wondered why they were present at an internal MI6 proceeding.

"We work closely with them, Roger. You'll be working with them – if you're appointed. What's important here is the cultural affinity, the intellectual affinity between us. It's a bond. We must protect it, and work together to save our society against…" Here, Amory faded away, his sight unfocused. He waved a liver-spotted hand feebly. "Against marauders with weapons of mass destruction, and liberals who don't believe a threat until it's become a reality."

Amory threw the rest of his drink down his throat, stood up, and lunged across the space between us to sit on the arm of my chair. He let the tips of his fingers stray over my thighs. He giggled. "I like you a lot, Roger. I'm not sure I want to send you away to the US. I could use a man like you in my office here in London…"

I scented my ploy turning sour. "I'm very keen to get this job, sir. It means a lot to me, and…" I paused, sickened by my own grovelling. I was beginning to suspect that I was the lone guest.

"And I could see you in Washington, couldn't I?" Amory mused.

He was interrupted by a loud and extended buzzing on the entry phone, which he reeled away to deal with. A few moments later Marius, waving a bottle of vodka, Bolding and one of the US professors, Kauffer, stumbled in, wanting to party. I stayed for a few minutes, but refused another drink, and announced my imminent departure. It was a prudent move. I was the only candidate present at that point – if any had been invited.

"I want to be fresh for the morning," I said, which was taken as a riotous joke, as none of the others seemed to intend to stop drinking.

At ten the next morning I attended the Victoria Street office. There was a hiatus caused by the absence of my name from the candidates' list. I assumed a hurt and incredulous silence, and the lacuna was remedied in ten minutes without comment. As Yarham had predicted, it was not a mistake, merely a computer glitch.

I embarked on a day of meeting interview panels. The style was similar to my interminable entry interviews in being vague and imprecise, and only differed from them in being good-humoured. I sparkle in these circumstances. It was often difficult to tell what the oblique questions were driving at, but where they were designed to test my political affiliations, I ensured I toed the Amory-Bolding line, heaping on the clichés, hinting that liberalism could be dangerous in leaving one unprepared, and democracy was a delicate flower that had to be protected by being pragmatic.

I was frequently invited to talk about myself and I

burnished my faultless credentials carefully in front of the various panels.

At lunchtime I decided to take a walk along Victoria Street for some fresh air, and I met Marius Jacob as I was leaving the building. He took my arm and led me into a nearby pub. He hadn't appeared on any panel that I had seen, but was obviously working in some capacity behind the scenes.

He was in good humour and anxious to impress me with just how much he was privy to the inner workings of the event. "Amory thinks you're the man. What did you do last night, tickle his willy?" he asked with a suspicious laugh.

I denied this dismissively. "I suppose he makes a lunge for all the young men."

"But you are the Adonis of the moment. And what's more, the youth versus age argument apart, you're as good as any and better than most candidates. It's hit or miss anyway," he said derisively. "Interviews are misleading and paper qualifications don't always mean much. They know that. They *like* you, Roger. You're beautiful. I'd say you've got it."

Marius, raging with thirst after last night, sank the best part of a pint of lager in one pull, unabashed by his own indiscreet comments. I had a lime soda.

"What actually is the mission here, Marius?" I asked, matching his indiscretion. One of the absurdities of the service was that we were not allowed to know this with any precision at all. *Working with the US intelligence services in a variety of fields* was as specific as it got. But I banked on Marius's anarchic tendency to tell all.

"Ah, ha, the task!" he chanted, pleased with the question. He wiped the froth from around his mouth and absently smeared it over his shiny black hair. He assumed a mock-serious voice. "You know we're under threat don't you? The future of the civilised western world, i.e. our kind of people, depends on the Anglo-American intelligence services, de-da, de-da, de-da. In sum, Roger, it depends on Amory and Bolding and Professor Fartface from Harvard et al."

"I see. But the job I'm applying for, Marius. What's it all about?"

He looked me straight in the eyes. "Suicide bomber."

"No, seriously."

"I am serious. You may have to remove the US President, kill him if you have to."

I knew that once Marius was embarked on one of his fantasies he would not easily return to reality. "Oh, yeah? Why?"

"He's a dangerous liberal, pandering to opposition forces, allowing dissension to fester. *Under the scab of peace, the pus of threatening foreign armaments is swelling.* Ha, ha, ha! Let's have another!"

"Not me. So Amory, Bolding and Professor Fartface are taking political decisions now?"

"Political and military. And you could be our man at the party."

I looked at my watch. "I better get back. I sure hope I get the job. It sounds interesting."

I went back to an afternoon of interviews, heartened by Marius's assessment of my chances, but discounting his tomfoolery about the assignment. I thought the ultimate irony would be that Marius was a double agent, working for an intelligence service outside the Anglo-American alliance, and hell-bent on creating as much chaos as he could.

In the light of the drunken bonhomie with which officialdom had greeted the candidates last night, I expected that the day would finish with a party for the chosen man, but I was wrong. The panels seemed to expire rather than conclude. I left the Victoria Street offices at the bidding of a man I'd never seen before, who put his head around the door of the empty room in which I had been sitting alone for an hour, and told me snappily that I could go. I left without seeing either panel members or fellow contenders, and went back to my hotel thinking that my ignominious dismissal indicated that I was not the man. My return flight to New York left at ten in the morning.

I found a message waiting for me at the hotel which was an MI6 contact. I called the number and was directed to report to the Mill. It was a moderately good omen. When I arrived at the Wimpole Street house it was quiet, seemingly almost empty. An absence of other candidates, I concluded. A secretary directed me to the party room upstairs. There, in the gathering gloom, on the rickety chaise longue, was Sir Carl Bolding, a file open before him on a coffee table. I immediately felt exposed and unsafe. The room still smelt vaguely of stale spirits and tobacco, and emerged, in the half-light, in its full seediness.

"Come, in, sit down, Conway," Bolding said mildly. "We think you have the qualities we require, and we've decided to appoint you."

He didn't offer any congratulations. He simply stared at me. He was wearing a grey check suit that matched his eyes. In a way, he reminded me of Colonel Austen who kicked me out of the Sandhurst entry. Bolding was the same admirable kind of man. He and I, at least, dressed with panache and shone in this lacklustre environment.

"Thank you, sir," I said, deciding to keep my appreciation as muted as his. "Is there anything more you can tell me?"

"Not specifically. Dr Reich, whom you met last night,

will be your principal contact. You can and must trust him, Conway. In the last resort, he is the only person you can trust."

"But the department…"

Bolding let his head droop to one side, his eyes still intent. "You will work within the framework of MI6, GCHQ, the National Security Agency and the CIA. You will be as compliant as is appropriate, but Dr Reich is the *only* person you can trust. Do you understand the importance of what I say?"

"I do, sir."

This was the real universe of the spy that I had dreamed of inhabiting. It wasn't all boring paper analysis; it was a world of shadowy creatures who could not be trusted, whose loyalties were in doubt.

"You will be formally attached to the Special Collection Service. You know it, I expect?"

"Yes, of course." I had heard of the SCS with awe. I didn't show the elation that I felt. The SCS was a covert joint CIA/NSA organisation that specialised in bugging, burglary and bribery in order to penetrate foreign communications systems. It appeared to me that in one jump I had realised my ambitions. I was going right to the top of the spy ladder.

"It will be an indefinite secondment."

"In Washington DC?"

Bolding was still boring into me, trying to discern the impact of his news, and I believe a little impressed that I could be so impassive. "You'll be in the Washington section, usually called C3, the lead section for the whole agency."

That startled me. It was the late Nick Stavros's department. Obviously I wouldn't be doing the same job; mine was clearly much more senior if Bolding and Amory had to be involved in the selection. C3 was the department where the Disciples had apparently materialised to Nick, but my enthusiasm for the appointment at this moment overwhelmed any speculation about whether the influence of Bolding and the two US professors was actually evidence that the Disciples existed.

"We're looking for an experienced assistant from MI6 to support you, somebody handy on the technical side of IT preferably, or possibly with cryptographic skills."

"I can name a person, sir. Herbert Yarham in US Liaison, New York. A genius with the computer and a man with whom I can work."

"That was quick." Bolding's flinty eyes drilled into me again and there was a silence. "A genius, eh? They're always trouble."

"I mean his skills are exceptional…"

"A friend?"

I saw this one coming. I wouldn't be allowed a friend. "No. Just a colleague." Certainly Yarham was a friend and a confidant. What MI6 most feared was a confidant.

"You realise you'll have to work entirely as a solitary, except for Reich. Your assistant's knowledge of the task to be limited to the minimum necessary in your judgement?"

"Absolutely."

Bolding seemed to accept; he noted Yarham's name, and conceded that this might be another problem solved.

"I don't have to tell you how massive and uncoordinated our joint intelligence services are on both sides of the Atlantic, Conway. But there are a small group of us who are linked together by a common bond of intellect, who can see the way forward. We have decided that you have the qualities to join us, and help us."

"Thank you, sir, for your confidence which I shall

honour." I wondered then whether I *had* just been recruited by the Disciples. I was glowing. It wasn't until the silence had lengthened, and Bolding's stare had become frigid, that I realised the meeting was over.

7

I flew back to New York to clear my desk, and in two days, Yarham's appointment as my assistant was confirmed, something of a miracle of expedition for MI6. Yarham had initiated my promotion, and I had returned the compliment.

We were an ill-assorted pair on any visual inspection. Yarham's baggy, blue, chalk-striped woollen suits, his dusty black shoes and his tightly knotted ties of no particular colour or design, denoted no more than a cursory interest in his appearance. His manner was gauche and he was imperturbably, almost stupidly, good-humoured. We were nevertheless complementary. His skills, I had found, did not end with files and computer work. He fell easily into the role of batman, sergeant-major and aide-de-camp under my leadership and I will concede, at times, adviser. I thought I had made a wise choice.

Yarham was more than happy with the promotion – "Always hoped you might tow me along, Captain" – and he set about moving his young wife, upon whom he doted, to Washington.

My departure from USL was not the subject of congratulations. Leyton and his cronies could hardly conceal their envy. Even Hornby, who made one or two tart remarks about the pleasure of soon having a successor to me, was awed and to a degree affronted by my rapid ascent. But I thought he would be restrained in his personal report on me, not wanting to show that he was entirely blind to talent.

I concentrated on celebrating with Laurie – who, as a courier, would see more of me in Washington – and my bar-room friends at the Oxbridge & Ivy. Excited, but with a considerable hangover from a party at the 21 Club, I boarded a plane at Kennedy Airport bound for Washington. I was going right to the heart of the secret intelligence services as I had hoped and planned.

When I arrived at the Sheraton in Washington I called my new official boss, Gerry Clark, head of C3. Dr Reich, whom Bolding had mentioned, was not named anywhere in my joining instructions. Clark's reception was warm. "Come over and meet the guys, Roger."

The agency's offices were in a nineteenth century townhouse in Georgetown with flaky maroon paint on the outside, set back in a small, untidy garden. The image from the outside was dilapidated, suburban, when I had expected that we would be behind razor wire and security barriers in the heart of Crypto City. Inside, the premises were a contrast, modern glass and chrome.

Clark, Lieutenant-Colonel Clark of the US Army, to be precise, a fat man with a shorn head and rimless glasses, came to meet me. He extended a plump hand of welcome, ushering me into his office, which was tastefully furnished with grey leather couches and chairs, antique vases, and two abstract pastel prints to complete the spare style. Not a sign of the military, and Clark wore a civilian suit. He saw that I admired the room.

"We look after ourselves, Roger, even in these foreign outposts," he said, pleased.

Clark explained that the offices were an out-station, and that all their intelligence material was kept in Crypto City. He promised to take me there soon. "Getting in and out of the City is a big deal security-wise, and since we move about

Washington at different times of the day and night, and need somewhere to chill out, it's convenient to have this place."

We went to the top floor where he showed me the spacious room that was to accommodate Yarham and me. On the floor were three different computer screens and three telephones. "We'll talk about the hardware later. We can redecorate according to your taste, but the most important thing, Roger, is where you're going to rest."

Clark insisted on driving me three blocks to the apartment the agency had taken for me. While we were driving I mentioned that I had known Nick Stavros.

Clark said, "We take the odd specially selected rookie from MI6 for training purposes. Nick didn't fit in too well."

"What was the problem?"

"Inexperience."

I was going to respond that that was what rookies would inevitably suffer from at C3, but instead I contemplated my own inexperience. "Was that anything to do with his death?"

"I think the file's closed on Nick Stavros." Gerry Clark's doughy features showed no expression. He was preoccupied manoeuvering the car.

"Sorry, I shouldn't have asked."

"Right. You shouldn't."

It struck me that Clark had made an unintentional slip. He could have said Nick's death was because of a one in a million physical infirmity. He could have denied outright that Nick's death had anything to do with C3, but he didn't... But my attention was now captured by the new apartment in Glover Park, which was at the top of a four-storey apartment house, and overlooked an old, now disused cemetery, quiet, high-ceilinged and light. Cemetery or not, the area was spaciously green with many trees and the occasional fine mansion; a stark contrast to my Greenwich Village pad.

"Reminds me of something, the cemetery," I said.

Clark had no sense of humour and ignored me. "We'll deck this out for you. You know, whatever you want within reason."

"Regs, huh?" I guessed there was a thick book of regulations about the accommodation of personnel, as there was in MI6.

"We don't bother too much with that stuff here."

So far, for me in MI6, everything had been by the book, from the width of my desk to my economy class plane fares. I began to anticipate not only a fascinating assignment, but an enjoyable one, particularly when Clark rounded out my tour of inspection with an invitation to dinner at his apartment. What a contrast to my frigid colleagues in London and New York!

The Clark apartment was tucked away in a leafy lane near the campus of the Georgetown University, overlooking the Potomac. Carol Clark, Gerry's wife, with her green eyes and below-the-shoulder fair hair, greeted me. She had an enveloping physical presence and immediately interested me. Inside, the apartment was airy and chic – definitely showing the hand of a skilled decorator with a generous budget. A glance at the dinner table through the glass doors of the dining room indicated that there would be a few guests.

Gerry Clark bustled into the lounge and introduced me to a man who had been hovering over the bookcase. "Otto, this is Roger Conway, our new recruit from England, Otto Reich. Otto has a visiting professorship at Georgetown. He's a Harvard man."

I recognised the smoothly groomed Dr Reich instantly as the tousled and slightly drunk party player at Wimpole Street, and more important, according to Carl Bolding, *the man I could trust in the last resort*. Reich offered a hand and a

57

weak smile, but made no move to recognise me. And of course, I followed his cue. We were apparently strangers. It was the first crumb of cloak and dagger.

Harold and Felicity Kershaw arrived. Clark explained that I would be working with Harold. I instinctively disliked him. He had a long body, a beaten-up face, a thin layer of grey hair, small eyes, and large hands. He also proved to be boring and graceless. I guessed he was an agent who had spent a lot of time in foreign fields. His tiny, pleasant wife seemed to defer to him fearfully, and he had the misfortune to look cruel.

Carol Clark had a French cook, Mme Ducane, who served golden melon with prawns, Roquefort salad and filet mignon, with Cotes-du-Rhone, followed by strawberries with a Muscat de Beaume. At the table we discussed much except our common profession. In the shuffling between courses and afterwards, I had the opportunity to speak to Carol alone on the terrace.

"I'm looking forward to the Washington posting," I said, I suppose hinting that my mind wasn't *entirely* on the work I would be doing.

She searched the river, the breeze ruffling her hair and seemed depressed. She said, "Washington's a great town, but that's one of the problems for me. Gerry likes to stick to the firm when it comes to entertaining. Official dinners. Instead of having fun. We live quietly. I spend my time picking the kids up from school and ferrying them around to various clubs and games, under the hairdryer, on the massage table, or flexing my credit card in the boutiques."

As we went inside, she said, "Are you married, Roger?"

"No. I have a girlfriend who visits DC every few weeks."

Gerry Clark overheard us. "Why don't you help Roger get his place in shape, Carol? Take him shopping."

Carol agreed, and by the time we were on the third cognac, the arrangement was sealed.

My only contact with Dr Reich, table-talk apart, was a few words as we bumped into each other going to the bathroom. "When you leave tonight, don't go by cab. Walk down the road, and pick up a cab later," he said quietly.

When the time came to depart, I refused a ride with the Kershaws, let them get away, and then followed Reich into the tree lined street. He said he was staying nearby and we walked together silently for a hundred yards. We were now alone and out of sight of the Clark apartment.

"This is a number where you can reach me from a public phone by leaving a voice message," Reich said, passing a slip of paper. "Memorise it and destroy the paper. The number is probably not secure. All you can do is give me the degree of urgency on a code between one and ten, and I'll get back to you. For the moment, we'll have one meeting place which I will use when needed – the steps of the John Adams Building on this campus. Your code name is Wolf."

"Wolf?" I said, wonderingly, pleased at the connotations of the name. *The Assyrian came down like a wolf on the fold... his cohorts gleaming in purple and gold...* I thought that was how it went.

"The most you should have to do, Conway, is to say 'Five' on the tape, or whatever the urgency is. I hope you don't have to call me, ever. Most times, I'll be in touch with you. The code name is for any other situation when you may need to identify yourself. When I want you, I'll get through in a variety of ways depending on the circumstances, but if you receive a message with a nine in it, meet me in twenty-four hours at the Adams Building. Have you got that?"

"Certainly. Can you tell me anything about the... mission, sir?"

"This is where I'm staying, Conway. Goodnight." Dr Reich slipped between the shrubs on a lawn, and disappeared behind a hedgerow fronting a large, detached house.

Later, I treated myself to another cognac from the minibar in my room at the Sheraton, and lay in bed thinking about the evening. Carol Clark added a certain frisson to the proceedings. Kershaw seemed almost threatening. Gerry Clark was a nonentity. Reich had set up a framework of contact without ever referring to the mission. In fact no clear task had ever been defined for me by Bolding, Reich or Clark. The core of the job was a black hole. And I naturally dismissed the mischievous ravings of Marius Jacob about suicide bombers. But, I had my controller, the mysterious Professor Reich, and my code name. *Roger James Elliston Conway, Rugby* and *Oxford, ex-SAS, codenamed Wolf.*

"Ahhwoooo… " I howled out loud, as I settled down to a dreamless sleep.

8

I found the workplace at Georgetown congenial, having come from a functional glass-partitioned cage in New York, and a dark corner on a spotty couch in London. The thickly beige-carpeted room was lit by two tall, sunny windows with long, muted floral drapes. The three computer screens and three telephones at the side added a serious touch to the comfortably padded chairs around a long honey oak table. When I entered on the first morning, Yarham was waving a wand over the walls like a medicine man. He raised his finger to his lips for silence.

While I pondered whether this suspicion of our American cousins was justified, Yarham toured the surfaces of the room with his bug detector. Eventually, he waved to me. He pointed to the elaborate chrome central light fitting, and to one of the computers with a huge grin. The bugs were in there.

My expansive feelings subsided. For the benefit of our listeners, I confined myself to a short eulogy on the excellence of our welcome, the quality of the office arrangements made for us, and what a friendly and personable man Gerry Clark was, and took Yarham for a walk around the library lawn off Wisconsin Avenue.

"What do you make of it?"

"They want to make sure you're loyal, sir."

"We can't really remove the devices, or raise issues about them, can we?"

"Not without inviting them to bug us in some other way. Look on the bright side. We can communicate with them via the bugs."

"Who is *them,* Yarham?"

Yarham turned to me, rolling his blue eyes. "Colonel Clark?"

"I guess so." I was thinking that my apartment needed sweeping. Giving a more or less public performance from my bedroom, should Carol Clark happen to press her charms on me, was something to be avoided.

I knew from MI6 briefings that the euphemistically named Special Collection Service had a history going back to 1978. What the service collected was foreign cryptographic codes, ciphers and communication information. What was special about the service was that its methods were not restricted to surveillance, but included human intelligence, *humint* in the jargon of the spy world, gathered by unlawful means, often breaking and entering. The SCS operated worldwide, and Gerry Clark was head of the US operations. Although one would never have guessed it from his bearing or dress, Clark was having a distinguished military career, and had arrived at C3 from the Defense Intelligence Agency. Underneath the bacon was an acute mind.

Clark drove with Yarham and me to the SCS quarters at Beltsville in Maryland and showed us the *live* room where the electronic environment of target buildings is recreated to test surveillance equipment. But, as he explained darkly, "The wheel has turned. Interception of signals in air or space is being made more difficult each day by advancing technology. You'd think it would get easier as technology advances, but no, because the means to intercept signals advances at the same or a greater rate."

"So we have to go back to the guy in the fedora and grubby raincoat," I said.

"Yeah. You'll be looking for information *at rest* in databases or hard copy files. It takes the intervention of a human being to capture it. There's a lot of work out there for us, Roger."

I had the feeling that Clark was forewarning me of the kind of clandestine operation in which I would be involved.

My briefings in London had prepared me, up to a point, for the immensity of the operations of the National Security Agency, the biggest and most penetrating listening system in the world, but I could not have truly comprehended Crypto City until the day Clark, Yarham and I drove further north up Interstate 95 in Maryland to visit it.

We first had to progress through shields of razor wire, past bomb-sniffing dogs, past barriers, personal checkpoints and signs with dire warnings, before emerging in the surveillance city. Clark waved at the forest of tall buildings. "There's over thirty thousand specially cleared civilians, military and contractors here. The NSA have another twenty-five thousand in listening posts spread around the world. That's not counting your GCHQ. "

"I expect you can't fart here without it being recorded," Yarham said.

"You're darn right," Clark said, but he was on another wavelength, engrossed.

His eyes glinted behind his spectacles. The vastness of Crypto City still impressed him, like a kid meeting Santa Claus in a store. He was showing the place off and he loved it. "You're one big palooka when you get near the top of this heap of shit," he said.

Clark himself wasn't all that far from the top, highly placed enough to feel big, and that might have been what he meant.

He parked the car and took us to a building pretentiously fronted with white marble and red granite, which might have been an insurance company or a bank. We were entering through the Visitor Control Centre, the lobby dominated by a huge embossed version of the NSA seal on the wall, an eagle clutching the key of knowledge. While we were waiting for a clearance to enter (there were three separate barriers to penetrate, including one which operated on retina recognition and another on fingerprints) Clark remarked that there were seven hundred police in the local force, a SWAT team and a special operations unit of paramilitaries. "They call them *The Men in Black*. Bin Laden's pals aren't going to make it here. Feel safe, guys."

Yarham and I were given special clearance through the barriers on an advance authorisation arranged by Clark. We pinned on our PV, privileged visitor badges and entered the throng of blue badges of the indoctrinated. We were in a reflective glass and copper-wrapped building sixty-eight stories high, shielded from all sounds and signals. Clark gave us guidance in a low monotone, every step of the way. We traversed long halls, passed many closed office doors with numbers and letters on them, but no comprehensible names or signs. The walls had a variety of notices all counselling the same behaviour: don't talk.

Clark led us into a suite of small rooms with tan-coloured walls, each with a computer on the desk, bristling with cables and wires and a battery of monitor screens. He faced us with mirthless enjoyment, like a torturer, which is what he might have been at some stage in his espionage career.

"Polygraph. Compulsory for NSA employees at your level and includes secondees like you guys. You'll be in this room, Roger, Herbie in the next. The operator has your personal file."

The very word polygraph, or lie detector, makes intelligence people uneasy because we are all liars. However my fears of the great machine, much relied on by the Americans, had been put at ease by MI6, which gave an excellent course in how to beat the lie detector. MI6 thought it possible that the polygraph could be part of an interrogation by an unfriendly power, and we should therefore be prepared to defeat it.

When you are hooked up in the electric chair, a computer plots the anxiety around sensitive questions, and displays the level of anxiety on a graph; it takes its measurements from the skin, the blood pressure, the capillaries, the veins, the heart rate, the breath – everything that can change with anxiety.

I was packed into a padded seat, with electrodes attached to my fingers, straps around my chest and upper arm, like a candidate for execution. Now the examiner, a middle-aged woman wearing dark glasses (I think because she wanted to shield any emotions she might show), began to question me, and watch the reactions created by my answers on the various monitors. First, the routine about my name, address… and then more specific questions to test honesty, and political reliability. The MI6 theory, basically, was to lie back and think of England, to be as little involved as possible. I knew it worked, because I had already had practice tests and passed them all. My own life was such a rich tapestry of lies that there was no point in getting agitated about any particular one of them, starting with my name.

After the test, Yarham was confident; outwitting technical gadgets was his game, and Clark, without mention of the results, guided us to a more exclusive suite on the thirtieth floor, where we were again checked and identified. While we were waiting, Clark took a brief call. He gave us a humourless grin as he put the receiver down. "You know, we have a computerised assessment on the poly which only takes a few moments. You guys are both NSRs." He didn't elaborate, but I knew that meant *No significant response*.

We were shown into a small, luxuriously cushioned lecture theatre. Clark sat with us in the soft reclining seats, facing a stage with its curtain imprinted with the seal of the eagle and the key. Several other people came in and took seats at the back. Clark had not told me what to expect. After a minute, the doors closed automatically, the lights in the theatre dimmed, and the stirring sounds of the Marine's Hymn rose to fill the auditorium. I was at the core of the most super-secret place on the planet, shielded by miles of security barriers, police and military, about to become privy to secrets upon which the survival of our way of life depended.

When the spotlight flicked on, a woman had materialised behind the lectern. She seemed to be about forty five, but it was hard to tell under the lights. She was tall, shapely and wore a black costume, a white blouse, and a ruffle at her throat. Her black hair was swept up imperiously. Her face was pale and her lipstick violently red. She exuded authority.

"Good afternoon. Let me introduce myself to those of you who haven't met me. Rachel Fernandez, director of the SCS." She seemed to pause for applause, but there was only respectful silence. "I want to show you a highly classified film which details some of our operations and I will take questions afterwards."

The film which followed, with a Beethhoven music track and a voice over by the director herself, trumpeted the surveillance skills of the SCS, and emphasised the vastness and sophistication of the methods of collecting secret data, all kinds of antennae and receivers ingeniously hidden in a myriad of places. The film stressed the dangerous role of agents in collecting data from these sources. I had no questions after the showing, but others had, and I listened to the crisp responses of Ms Fernandez, more for their metallic certainty than the exact content. And then, when Fernandez pointed out the security and quantitative problems of converting online material to hard copy, Yarham stirred beside me.

"Is it true, Madam Director, that enough redundant hard copy intelligence reports are recycled every day to meet the entire daily needs of the nation for pizza containers?" he asked.

A silence fell, and so did the director's face. Then her lips managed a suggestion of a smile. "There's a lotta pulping going on, sure."

Afterwards, Clark shepherded us into an office as big as a hotel lobby to meet the director herself in person. The room was empty and shaded. The director's wide desk was on a raised platform. Backed by the US flag and the agency's seal, the high-backed director's chair might have been that of the Chief Justice.

Yarham leaned over and whispered to me as we settled ourselves. "Nice to be going backstage to meet the star of the show."

"Now you're in danger of getting ten years in a federal prison," I said.

Clark's spongy brow wrinkled at the impertinence. "The room is miked," he mouthed quietly, pointing a discreet finger skyward.

After a minute or two, when a quiet as thick as the carpet had settled, Rachel Fernandez sailed in through a side door, without glancing at us until she had taken her seat in the high chair. She leaned forward, clasping her hands on the bench, and smiled patronisingly. She was a very long way away and above us.

"It's all right, Gerry," she said, I'm used to the British sense of humour. Welcome, Roger. We're honoured to have such a distinguished operative join us. You're going to be a valuable asset."

Yarham got no more notice than if he was a stenographer. He was an appendage of mine. At the risk of contempt of court, I thanked Ms Fernandez. I noted without comment that I was only an 'asset'.

"Roger, there are aspects of our work which were not shown in the film... It would be an ideal world if we could collect everything we needed to know about our enemies by pulling it out of the air. And as you now know, we can gather an immense harvest of intelligence merely by sitting quietly in front of a machine. But we can't get everything we need that way. We *have* to resort to less aesthetically pleasing methods. In the interests of protecting our way of life we sometimes have to break other countries' laws, and even our own. Yes, our own laws too, regrettably, but hopefully seldom. These events are minor infringements measured against the importance of the integrity the United States and its allies. It's great and important work that we do, guarding our nation and its friends, and you have been chosen to play an important part. We rely on you!... Thank you."

The director bowed her head for a second and then rose from her chair, looking to a distant point on the wall behind us. Clark jumped to his feet and stood like a soldier on parade, and I followed, with the tardy Yarham well behind. Ms Fernadez turned away, her face as smooth and set as a figure on a ceramic vase. She strode from the room, leaving only a faint whiff of perfume.

Clark stepped in front of me, a short man whose belly kept him at a respectful distance. He looked up into my face, searching. "Impressive, huh?"

"Exceptionally," I said feelingly, taking care to avoid Yarham's face.

9

In his office in Georgetown, Gerry Clark, Lieutenant-Colonel Gerald Clark, United States Army, head of C3, with uncanny timing, unfolded a proposal involving the less aesthetically pleasing methods of operation that Director Fernandez had referred to at our introductory meeting. Gently massaging his stomach, and looking upwards, he explained that I had been chosen to play a leading part in Operation Screwdriver, which was under way. The next phase was in Washington. Some phases would be outside the United States. I would learn about Screwdriver on a need-to-know basis, as it progressed. Yarham and I would be working with his man Kershaw, who would brief us.

"This is a very important assignment, Roger. In fact I can't think of any operation more critical to the US nation than Screwdriver. And we're using you, a British operative, when we might use a more seasoned agent, because I'm told you have the complete confidence of *the powers that be*," Clark said, pointing the stubby forefingers of both hands at the ceiling and turning down the corners of his mouth.

Somehow an electric spark had come down from above – I assumed from Bolding and Reich and Amory – that Clark didn't like or understand and I hoped it wouldn't develop in his case, into what I called the Hornby Syndrome after my previous boss: grudging acceptance of a too-brilliant employee, and frustration at his progress. Clearly, Clark was uneasy, showing a lack of confidence in me, and hinting that he would not have appointed me. I promised modestly to do my best.

"Best isn't good enough," sneered Clark. "You have to succeed at *any* cost."

"Tell me a little about the job," I asked, realising it was something dirty and difficult.

"Harold will fill you in," Clark said with a gleam that confirmed my thoughts… and, yes, fears.

Had I over-reached myself? Wouldn't I be better at Goldman Sachs?

Later Harold Kershaw came up to the office I shared with Yarham to brief us. I say 'office' but it was rather a place to hang our raincoats and have a cup of coffee. As a consequence of the bugging we did our serious thinking out of doors. It was the first time that Harold had visited in our occupancy, and he looked around with feigned approval at the drapes and furniture, an outdoors man himself who despised comfort. He was empty-handed. His muscles bulged under his thin suit. I noticed his eyes were almost white, with a faint tint of blue, like a wolf, although a good deal smaller than a wolf's. The thought of this animal reminded me of my sterling codename, *Wolf*. I was the wolf, not Kershaw! With a codename like that, one couldn't help but take on some of the qualities of the beast.

Kershaw had broken teeth, a broken nose and a long, mean horsey face. His toughness gave off a certain unnerving attraction. He slouched down at our worktable which was paperless and shining, a barbarian in a lounge suit, and began without frills.

"Let me give you some of the detail. We're going to do an entry on this building in DC…"

"Shit!" Yarham said.

"Scare you, buddy?"

"No, but it's illegal, isn't it?" Yarham said.

Kershaw bared his teeth in a semblance of a grin. "Depends. You wanna get counsel's opinion?"

I kicked Yarham under the table. "No. Get on with it."

"We have a contact who will facilitate entry."

"You mean send us a written invitation?" Yarham said, his head with its long jaw tilted to one side.

"Yeah. As good as. Day after tomorrow I will be paying the contact off and getting precise entry info. Then we three will hit the building. Well, I will do the driving and getaway, and you two will do the entry. Inside, you will pick up papers relating to a secret operation, and hand them to me. Mission accomplished. Questions?"

"Whose building is it?" I asked.

Kershaw gave a dry cackle, and savoured the answer before he gave it. "Central Intelligence Agency."

"We are going to rob the CIA?" I said, concealing the surprise I felt. I had expected to hear the name of a foreign power, which I suppose would have made the plan slightly more palatable.

"Storm Fort Langley?" Yarham added.

"Right, the CIA, wrong, Langley. Langley is in Virginia, you dope. The building we'll hit is an outstation…"

"You mean the building *I'll* hit with Yarham while you're waiting outside?"

His mouth broke open like a bad plum. "Yeah," he said with unashamed amusement at this distinction. "You're the British action-man, aren't you?"

I ignored the remark and stared back into the ruthless white eyes and the cracked face.

Kershaw went on, "It's a luxury suite for the big brass in Pennsylvania Avenue, where they formulate plans and see people too shy or too busy to visit Langley."

"Couldn't we just write and ask for the file?" Yarham asked.

Kershaw gave Yarham an evil look.

"Are we at war with the CIA?" I asked.

"Yeah. Some of them plan secret operations for their own purposes that they don't tell us about. They've got their own political agenda."

"Can't we be told what that is?"

"Not by me. As far as I'm concerned, you two guys are bagmen."

With a hacking laugh, Kershaw got up, pushed his fists deep into his trouser pockets and shambled out of the room.

I took Yarham for one of our secure discussion walks in Wisconsin Avenue and raised the question whether I should speak to Professor Reich. I had doubts. I could raise them with Reich.

"You mean tell him that the burglary suggestion is getting out of hand? I wouldn't, sir. You told me Clark indicated that somebody above him had wanted you in on Screwdriver. It was probably Reich himself."

I could see this. "And after all, C3 does this kind of work overseas. But the National Security Agency raiding the CIA?"

"The CIA does what the President wants, and not everybody wants what the President wants."

"I suppose the CIA can get out of hand," I said.

"Maybe we're out of hand, sir. But it's better than if we were asked to do the British Embassy," Yarham said cheerfully.

The next day, Felicity Kershaw rang me and said that Harold had suffered a nasty accident. He'd fallen on the squash court that morning and broken his ankle. "He won't be in to the office until the doctor tells him it's all right to move around. The ankle is in plaster, and he'll need crutches. But he wants to see you urgently. He says he can't talk on the phone."

Yarham drove me in one of the Agency's cars out to Harold Kershaw's home at Wakefield Park, Virginia. I didn't quite know what to expect. I couldn't place Kershaw in a domestic environment. His natural setting seemed to be a bar or a nightclub, or at least a city apartment. Instead, I found a rambling mock-Tudor mansion set in at least an acre of fantastical gardens, with ponds, fountains and fake statuary, from Snow White to the Venus de Milo. And inside the house, amongst the schlock furniture with which the home was crammed, every sign of warm family life. The Kershaws had a big if not cosy nest, children, ample money, and very little taste.

Felicity Kershaw showed me to Harold, who was reclining on a sofa in a solarium with a view of the gardens. She served drinks and was swiftly banished. At first I thought Kershaw was in pain, and then I concluded that he was lined with anxiety about the break-in.

"You'll have to do the rendezvous with our contact, Roger," he said in a friendly tone. "Otherwise the bag job will be fucked up for a week or more and we need the product urgently."

"Sure. No problem. Tell me what you want me to do." I thought getting a direct briefing from the contact was better than cryptic orders at second hand from Kershaw.

"First, tomorrow, at the office, you draw the money from Aretha. I'll speak to her."

Aretha was the woman who handled all matters financial in C3, from expense accounts to personal tax and pay.

"One hundred thousand bucks. It's all requisitioned. You sign for it. I'll speak to her. Take it to your office and split it. OK? Fifty thousand you stick in the drawer of your desk. The other fifty, you hand over at the RV, when the contact has briefed you to your satisfaction. How and where you get inside the building, where to go when you're in. All the detail about security devices and patrols. All about the creeps that are still hanging out in their offices in the building. Make sure this guy tells you how you can navigate every inch of your way to get your hands on the product, and every inch of the way back. Wring him dry. That's what he's being paid for. To tell you how much dust there is on the window ledges. Savvy?"

"I'll question him. Everything depends on it."

"OK. Now, the contact is expecting fifty. He knows he has to give the utmost detail for the heist."

"What do I do with the stuff in my desk?"

"Hang on to it until I get in to the office. Tell nobody. Savvy?"

This sounded interesting, but not relevant to today's meeting.

Kershaw began to explain the details of the pay rendezvous. "The guy you will meet is an insider, very long service, senior, and he is the same guy who will let you into the building when we make the hit."

"When I make the hit."

"And tell you where to find the product. Simple. Hey? All you have to do is to grab the product, get outside and I will be waiting to chauffeur you to safety. I'll be able to drive no problem by then. It's my left ankle," Kershaw said, pointing to the plaster cast on his leg.

"It can't be as simple as it sounds," I said to Yarham on the drive back to Georgetown.

"I daresay not, sir. Kershaw seems to have assigned the interesting part, inside the building, to us, and kept the dull part for himself. Very generous of him."

"Interesting... but shitty," I reflected.

This was apparently the world-shaking kind of operation for which I had been recruited and promoted rapidly, heartily endorsed by the egg-heads who ran the intelligence services. The fate of the Anglo-American world might be in issue, but it was burglary, no more and no less. Yarham must have been thinking along the same lines.

"Probably a dozen lags in Wandsworth prison who could do this better," he said.

"What's the worst scenario?" I asked. "It's a CIA station, there'll be armed security roaming the building and if they light up... "

Yarham contemplated disaster with good cheer. "Two British Embassy officials, that's what they'd probably call us, killed in a car accident. Something like that, I should say. They have a way of ignoring the bullet holes."

That night, as instructed by Kershaw, I drove alone to a diner off the I 270 at Rockville at ten pm, carrying a small knapsack containing the money. I was wearing a red Dodgers baseball cap. The booths of the diner were dark and the place nearly empty. I wouldn't offend anybody by keeping my hat on. Again, as instructed, I seated myself as far from   the windows as possible, in the blue cloud around the fat fryer. Although I had eaten, not ordering wasn't an option according to the waitress.

"We get a lotta bums in here, lookin' for a place to zonk out," she said.

I ordered a Bud and a hamburger without the fries, and idled with a copy of *USA Today* which a previous patron had abandoned on the table. In the international news there was comment about the July 11th bomb attacks in Mumbai when over two hundred people were killed, and a headline reporting that Scotland Yard had thwarted a major terrorist plot to destroy British and US commercial airliners crossing the Atlantic. I couldn't help wondering whether what I was doing had some connection. I was right at the centre of Anglo-US intelligence and soon their plans, I thought, would have to be made clear to me. I was on a high about it.

At half past ten, when I was thinking the informer had let me down, a man of about fifty slid into the seat opposite. He had a thatch of silver hair crammed under a cap the same as mine. He looked as though he'd changed out of a city suit, into a sweater and slacks, designer gear. His throat was white. From behind thick horn-rimmed spectacles, he eyed me tensely. Then his eyes moved to the bag on the seat beside me. He began to rise, signalling that we should go. I dropped a twenty on the table and followed his ageing, out-of-shape figure. He walked with a limp. He looked like a well-paid, well-off civil servant, intelligent and perceptive. I had been expecting a security guard. What did he want the money for? A medical operation for his wife? A gambling debt? Maybe he just wanted more money the way we all do. I would never understand what had made him do this. Perhaps even some wacky idea about patriotism.

Outside, he led me behind the diner, on an ill-lit path toward the lavatories, moving into deep shadow under the trees.

"I've got to frisk you," he said, apologetically.

He ran his hands over me, looking for a wire and a weapon. "You'll have to show me inside the bag, too."

I held it open. He flashed a pencil torch on the contents. I could make out his slight smile in anticipation of receiving the compact parcels of dollars, but he carried out the search awkwardly, almost embarrassed. He wasn't an agent. He was a paper pusher. "I don't need to count it," he said, looking for reassurance from me, but I gave him none.

"OK. We talk here." He moved deeper under the branches of the old tree. I could hardly see him. He had a quiet, cultured voice. "You're going to pick up a *Very Restricted Knowledge* file, one of three hard-copy files that are regularly updated to contain the same material in each. There are no computer records on the project. The VRKs are either in personal custody, or in the security lockup, totally inaccessible. That's the rule. You go in at 10.30 pm on the night at the Jermyn Place entrance, right? It will be open and clear of security. I will make sure the closed circuit television cameras are off for twenty minutes. You'll be dressed in a dark suit, dark necktie, white shirt, black shoes. You have to look as though you belong. You'll have this tag on your lapel. Put any name on it. You need another? You'll have an assistant?"

I pushed the cards he held out into my pocket.

"You go to Level 4, Room 4002 by the stairs on the left of the foyer. There is little security about at this hour. It's their first break of the evening. If you meet a guard, you may have to bluff, but there's a ninety-nine percent chance he'll say 'howdy,' and go right on by. He will only know a few faces. Inside 4002 will be Gino Carmelli, deputy operations director on the project. He works every Thursday night until around eleven, eleven-thirty. This is absolutely regular. There will be some other workers in the building, not many, but nobody on his team. This is regular. The other workers will be in their rooms. They won't be socialising in the corridors. Carmelli will have the VRK file on his desk. You have to take it, silence him…"

"Take it by force?"

"You seem surprised."

"Not really," I said, sounding as careless as I could. "I just want to be sure."

"The only way. Take the file and get out. If you find his office door is locked when you arrive outside, use this." He proffered a key. "It's a caretaker's key, like in a hotel. There are no locks on the office doors that won't respond to this key."

"Why would he lock himself in, inside your secure building?"

"I'm covering every eventuality," the informer said flatly.

"Unless he's doing something funny in there."

"As I said, I'm covering everything."

"How will I know the VRK file?"

"It's marked. An orange cover, and it's likely the only one Carmelli's working on. When he goes home, he pushes the file into the late entry slot in the safe. You either take it from him while he's in his room, or you don't get it."

"One thing I want," I said. "Here's a mobile phone number and a phone. Anything goes wrong on the night before we get there, call this number and leave a message, 'Happy birthday'.

"It can be traced."

"My mobile will be in the river the next morning. You dispose of yours. Look, if this cracks up, it mightn't be good for you."

Even in the poor light I could see the tension in his features. He knew that a likely consequence of failure would be to crucify him. My mind was calculating the extreme risks in the plan, and trying to find alternatives, when a torch beam lit us both from ten yards away.

"Police! Stand still! Get your arms up! Don't move or you'll get a bullet."

I heard the informer groan quietly. Swaying toward us behind the blinding light, I could vaguely make out a uniformed deputy sheriff in a broad-brimmed stetson.

"What are you guys doing there under the trees in the dark outside this lavatory, huh?" he said, waving his Colt 38.

"Nothing, sheriff," I said. "We're just finishing off a business discussion."

"Oh, yeah? In the dark? I think somethin' homosexshool outside the lavatories."

He had advanced to within six feet, pushing away the branches of the maple, and he pointedly flashed the beam of the torch over each of our pelvic areas, but found no disturbing signs.

"Look sheriff, we were talking business. We're about to go home, but we wanted to cut out a guy with us, so we came over here," I replied, and the informer chimed his agreement.

"Don't give me that bullshit. I got to y' before y' got y' dicks out, didden I?"

I made another quiet denial and I could feel the resolve of the informer weakening. He was all but quaking in fear.

"I oughta take you guys in for immoral behaviour in a public place, and I damn well will if I see your asses anywhere around here agin. Now git!"

As we came out from under the maple tree on to the path, the deputy noticed the knapsack I had handed to the informer.

"Whoa, you two. Whaddya got there in that bag?"

"As I said, sheriff, we were talking business."

"I wanna see the business, sir, outside a lavatory in the dark."

The informer turned and held the bag open. The deputy flashed his torch over the contents, then put his hand in, picked up a couple of the packs, and dropped them back.

"Shee-it! Empty that bag on the ground, sir."

The informer poured the packets of hundred dollar bills on to the path.

"Jeez. That is one helluva lot a' green."

"This is our property, sheriff, part of a legitimate business deal," I said. I was very calm, but I could see this deputy cocking up Operation Screwdriver.

"Yeah, maybe and maybe not. Where's the coke?"

"This isn't drug money," I protested.

"We'll sort it out at the station. I'm takin' you two guys in on suspicion of immoral behaviour and drug dealin'."

Operation Screwdriver was coming unscrewed. It occurred to me that the deputy might change his mind for ten grand – just one of the packets. I tried to get the beat of the man. It could make things worse if I tried to bribe him and he refused. He was in his thirties, but going to seed. His gut hung over his belt. He had a childish look about his features, and dark, thick eyebrows which met between his eyes. He struck me as a kid who had memorised police manuals. I decided against offering a bribe.

We were handcuffed and bundled into the back of his cruiser. In Rockville, it was the sheriff who questioned us. We both gave our names and occupations. We both had cover names and jobs which would stand an enquiry. My name was Robert Courtley. I was an insurance assessor. The sheriff knew he had a couple of smart, educated men to deal with, and a strange situation which he could not understand, and was loth to let go.

"Sheriff, please," I pleaded. "There isn't the slightest evidence of any wrongdoing. I am not a homosexual, and neither is Mr Appleyard."

"Doing a legitimate deal you say, a fifty thousand dollar deal, outside a public toilet, in the dark, Mr Courtley? We gotta run you through the computers."

At last he agreed to let me make a call to my lawyer.

In fact I called Yarham, who was enjoying the conjugal

delights of his small apartment. I explained what had happened and he listened raptly.

"Herbert, I am being held on suspicion of immoral behaviour and drug dealing." I guess I sounded plaintive.

Yarham made a noise as though he was choking and said, "Oh, I'd say about nine out of ten for this one, Captain. Drug dealing and rumpy-tumpty! Very hard to beat. Nice one, sir. Very nice!"

"Herbert, please..."

10

Yarham, through Gerry Clark, engineered a call from the state attorney general's office to the sheriff's department which secured our release in three hours, but I had to face the withering contempt of Clark the next day. "You were supposed to meet the contact, not to fuck him!" he spat.

It was fortunately two days before Harold Kershaw could hop into the office on crutches, by which time the joke was stale, but my face was still red and I vowed to be ruthless on the break-in.

The night for the hit was close. At Kershaw's request, I opened my desk drawer and displayed for him the neat packets of residual dollar bills. He gave me the leering grin which dislocated his face and jaw, selected two five-thousand dollar packets, and pushed them across the table toward me. The remainder he scooped out of the draw and dropped in a plastic bag. He hopped out of the room without a word.

Yarham and I had another Wisconsin Avenue session to discuss.

"Skimming, I think it's called," Yarham said.

"Why let us in on it?"

"He didn't have an alternative. The hit had been set up and he'd requisitioned the funds."

"I suppose if Screwdriver is as important as Clark says it is, then it's running to a strict timetable, broken ankles or broken necks."

"And fingers in the honeypot on all appropriate occasions, Captain."

"I wonder if Kershaw's engaging in a departmental practice, to which we would have been introduced sooner or later anyway."

"Lovely, I'll pay off my mortgage more quickly," Yarham said.

"Kershaw was pretty cool. No explanation. What shall we do with the ten grand?"

"At the moment the money's hot and dangerous, Captain."

"You mean they could be trying us out?"

"Sure. Safest would be to let it cool, in the office, in the packets with Kershaw's prints on them."

"Yes… good point, Yarham. It might give us an edge, if ever we need one, with friend Harold."

At the office, Yarham placed the packets carefully in a file, with a note detailing their origin and checked them into the safe registry under the codename 'Grease'.

Carol Clark was as good as her word about the apartment. She came round alone and had a look on a Saturday afternoon. She was wearing a thin cotton sweater, a tight pair of designer jeans and soft white leather moccasins. Her blonde hair had been dressed to frame her face in curls. She looked a very appetising woman.

I was more interested in her than the decorating suggestions she was making, and I was quite comfortable at the Sheraton. In Britain I wouldn't be able to stay in a decent hotel, let alone be free of a get-out date. I wasn't anxious to complete the decoration process which Laurie had already offered to help me with and I could foresee a possible conflict here. But Carol took me out shopping in Georgetown, and we marched through a selection of small and exclusive shops.

She consulted me casually, but determinedly purchased mats, linen, towels, vases, lamps, prints, materials for curtains, even a dining room suite, with frightening speed. She wielded a credit card, explaining it was a departmental cost and simpler that way. Then, in a daze, I was in Bloomingdale's examining a king-sized pneumatic bed. We sat on it together. Her shoulder was pressing against mine. She turned to me and I could smell her peppermint breath.

"I think it'll be just fine, don't you?" she said.

I nodded agreement, knowing we had sat there a moment too long to be selecting a bed solely for me.

Two days later, on a sunny afternoon, we were in the apartment drinking vodka tonic with ice and examining the purchases which had now been delivered. When it came to the bed we both tried the mattress, laughing, bouncing around.

"Do you think you might want to sleep here, rather than the hotel, before you complete the furnishing?" she asked seriously.

"I might," I said, although I had no such intention.

"We could hook a piece of material over the window until you get the curtains up. That would give you enough privacy."

"Let's do that," I said, and tacked a new terracotta coloured sheet over the panes.

When my temporary bedroom had been prepared it was early afternoon and perfectly natural for us to come together in the mellow light of the room. Carol sighed as she came into my arms, and I held my finger to my lips – it seemed to be a common gesture in my business. I pointed at the light fitting and shrugged. Yarham hadn't been called in yet to do a sweep, but I had to be cautious. Carol immediately understood what I meant as the well-trained wife of an intelligence agent. She had no difficulty believing that I might be under surveillance.

I slipped away from her for a moment, turned on the ensuite bath, and left the bathroom door open. Carol was very hungry and passionate, and our muffled business was not inhibited by the bugs; if anything, the excitement of the surrepticious encounter was heightened. I thought of Gerry, as pale as a donut, and wondered what he would make of the hush and gurgle of sounds, if he was listening.

The time had come. At the Georgetown office, Yarham and I prepared for the raid on the CIA's luxury conference and planning centre at Jermyn Place and Pennsylvania Avenue. We had bought cheap grey suits, white shirts, dark ties, and black moccasins with grippy soles. We changed into these featureless clothes. We each had an outsize woman's black silk stocking, in case we needed to mask ourselves and a pair of latex gloves which we would don before entry. Although I had never remotely expected that my first real operation would have as its target the CIA, this was the kind of exploit I had joined the service for. It was certainly, in anticipation at least, proving to be as exhilarating as a Porsche at speed. Yarham was his usual nonchalant and cheerful self as we made ready.

Kershaw was waiting for us in the car, and on the way to Jermyn Place, he asked, "You guys carrying?"

When I said no, Kershaw reached a gloved hand into the dashboard compartment and pulled out two snub-nosed Smith & Wesson 38s. "Go on, put your gloves on and take them. They're untraceables. Scare value, in case you need it."

The chambers were loaded. In spite of my familiarity with weapons, I didn't have the US preoccupation with small-arms as a means of security, but we both tucked the guns into our belts.

There was little traffic about as we coasted down Pennsylvania Avenue. Jermyn Place was a small loop of street around a grassed square of buildings, deserted at this hour. Kershaw pulled the car in and checked his watch. We had about one minute to go.

"I'll be here or nearby when you come out, guys, rely on it." Kershaw's mouth opened up over his teeth in a sharkish grin.

It was no use thinking about the task. Just do it! I slid out of the car, followed by Yarham, sprinted across the grass, up the steps of the CIA building and confronted the darkened lobby. I had a pang of concern that the door would be locked, but it yielded, and we were inside. Nobody was about. We ran up three flights of stairs, seeing only a couple of people at a distance along the hallways. So simple. In a few moments, we were outside Room 4002 and the passage was empty. I tried the handle gently. It was locked.

Yarham, to whom I had entrusted the key, was ready, and he unlocked the door quietly. The room seemed shaded – not an office with somebody at work. I sidled in; it was a secretary's office. There was a vertical yellow shaft of light on the other side of the room – the slightly open adjoining doorway to Gino Carmelli's office. I moved closer across the carpet, able to look into a sliver of the room, across the surface of a desk, littered with papers.

Yarham and I studied each other's faces in the half-light as we listened. The series of sounds which emerged brought a dawning of enlightenment to each of us, the reason that Gino Carmelli locked his office. The unmistakable rhythmic squeak of a couch, the chesty, male intake and exhalation of breath at regular intervals, and the lighter feminine descant, always keeping time.

I whispered to Yarham, "I'll deal with Carmelli. You get the papers, and we'll leave our masks off."

I threw the door wide, and there, sunk on the leather couch, smothering the lady with his flab, was our man. He still had his shirt on, but fortunately not his trousers – he was in no position to pursue us. And by the look of the garments festooned on the chairs, the woman was in like undress.

I raised my voice, and put on my thickest US accent. "OK, Carmelli, FBI agents Docherty and Packard. You're under arrest for breach of security!" I pointed the 38 at Carmelli's unpleasantly hairy ass, while Yarham swept the documents from the desktop into a black briefcase.

Carmelli hunched round toward me with a groan of bewilderment, trying to get off the woman on the cramped couch. I could only see her head. She was a Latino girl, her dark hair fluffed up around her face which was very red from her exertions and Carmelli's deadweight.

"Now listen…" Carmelli growled in a tone which combined anger with incomprehension. He could see the gun.

"No, you listen, Carmelli! Don't move, either of you. I'm giving you a break to get decent in privacy. Then we'll be talking turkey about your offences. I'm taking these papers into custody. We'll be waiting outside this door. You have sixty seconds!"

Carmelli's mouth was frothing like an epileptic's as he and the girl struggled to get up. Yarham and I stepped out of the room, closed the door and bolted.

The hallway unfortunately was not deserted when we came out of Room 4002. At the far end, a flat-capped guard in khaki was ambling toward us. Our path lay in the other direction, and the stairs were within two hundred feet. We turned our backs on the guard, and moved as naturally as we could toward the stairs. There may have been something in the tension of our postures which disturbed the guard, and he called, "Excuse me, sir!"

"Ignore him," I hissed.

As soon as we reached the empty stairs and were out of sight of the man, we flew down the three flights, but before we reached street level, the guard was leaning over the balcony, calling "Sir! Sir! Stop!"

He must have called an alert, because there was another guard in the middle of the lobby, drawing his gun. Even in my panic I registered that their security was quite good.

I smiled at the guard, a real piano key job as I crossed the lobby, swaying in a relaxed way and keeping my gloved hands out of sight. "What's the problem, officer?"

I could see he was confused, and not immediately hostile to me. Alerts in the dark of the night didn't happen often, and he looked as though he was still waking up from a doze in front of the television. He didn't raise his hand – which now contained a gun. When I was close enough to him, still mouthing amicably, I hit him with my fist, a swift clip across the jaw, just the way I'd been taught by MI6 to get maximum effect. The guard hit the floor and his gun clattered on the marble.

I had a second's unease that the doors might be locked, but the one we had entered was still open. I could hear an alarm sounding, the clatter of feet, and muffled calls coming toward us. We were both outside in seconds, and running across the lawn in front of Jermyn Place toward the car. There was a burst of automatic rifle fire which shattered but didn't penetrate the glass of the entrance. When we reached the car it was dark and dead. I tore open the front passenger door and shouted at the bent figure of Kershaw, "Move your butt, shitface!"

Kershaw jumped to attention and started the engine. "Jesus! You guys were quick."

A hail of automatic fire from the front steps of the building hit the car as we snarled out of Jermyn Place.

"I guess they'll pursue," I said.

"They surely will. With their own cars and the cops. You got the product?" Kershaw said.

I looked around at Yarham who was searching the road through the rear window. He held up the black wallet. "Sure, we've got it."

Kershaw's face broke up with pleasure as he powered the car down Pennsylvania and squealed into Seventh Street. "Like lightning, huh?"

"Every cop in DC will be after us if you go much faster," I said.

"You whack anybody in there?" Kershaw said, slowing.

"No. I clipped a guard on the jaw."

"Neat. Clean. Carmelli? You hypnotised him?"

"Not a mark on his mind or body."

"Clever!" Kershaw sniffed, slewing the car dangerously. "We'll have to hear all about it. Look, I gotta plan. I can't move fast, see. If we stay in the car, and they run us down, it's all over, all your good work. Here's what we do. I bale out around Massachusetts Av with the product. You guys take the car on, have a ball, then bale out yourselves. Savvy?"

I looked around at Yarham, who was stiff-faced and I believe I saw a slight negative movement of the head. "OK, Harold. You choose the place," I said.

"Right. Anything back there?" Kershaw asked.

"Not at the moment that I can see," Yarham said.

"There will be." Kershaw turned on to K Street and followed a line of traffic to Franklin Park. There were pedestrians moving around between the restaurants and hotels on the other side of the road. "This looks like it. Don't you guys stay with this jalopy too long." He pulled to the kerb. "Now gimme the product," he said, turning to the back seat and reaching for his crutches.

The sirens were screaming, but there was no pursuer in sight yet. I jumped out of the car with Yarham, as Kershaw was struggling to get out.

"Where'n hell you goin'?" Kershaw yelled.

"Sorry, Harold. Change of plan. The product has to come first. Too risky to leave it with a man trying to escape from the cops on crutches. I'll take care of it. You look after the car, or go have a cup of coffee."

Kershaw's angry face had the eyes, jaw and mouth out of line. "You motherfuckers! You can't leave me here!"

"You've got your sticks *and* the car," I said, as I slipped behind the hedge on the sidewalk, followed by Yarham.

We crossed into a car park and paused in a garden, behind bushes near the entrance to the Hilton & Towers Hotel. I could hear the increasing wail of sirens.

"Do you think Kershaw will make it?" Yarham asked.

"The important thing is that we make it, Yarham. Think of the product."

Kershaw's indecent haste to get hold of the file we had risked our lives for left me with little sympathy. We strolled into the hotel lobby and went downstairs to the lavatories. I washed my face, combed my hair and we dropped the guns, gloves, black stockings and CIA passes in the trashcan. I tucked the papers into my shirt.

"I'm thinking of a beer," I said.

"I have a fair thirst, sir," Yarham said.

11

I settled with Yarham in a quiet corner of the Hilton's Lincoln
Bar, surrounded by empty couches and ordered Budweisers.
A few distant patrons were gathered around the bar and at
tables. We were in no danger of being overheard. As soon as
the waiter had set the glasses, bottles and a bowl of peanuts
on the low table and returned to the bar, I withdrew the file
from my shirt, straightened the few pages it contained, and
placed it beside the bottles on the table.

"Colonel Clark will no doubt be waiting anxiously to
view the treasure trove," Yarham said.

"Certainly, but don't you think a good intelligence officer
ought to read and understand the papers he risks his life for?"

"We're not mere postmen," Yarham echoed, craning his
neck toward the papers.

The sound of numerous sirens seeming distant but actually
close, entered the room.

"Kershaw's a survivor. He'll outrun the cops, dump the
car and hobble into the night," I said.

"He wasn't exactly pleased when you told him to use his
sticks."

"I fear we've made an enemy, Yarham. He might complain
to Clark, but how can he make it stick? We did the sensible
thing."

"He's the sort who get even rather than angry."

"We'll take care. He so wanted to go pegging back to C3
with the file!"

"And the credit," Yarham said.

All things considered, I was pleased with our evening's work; it was my first active service operation. Yarham had provided cool support. I appreciated too that I had earned a measure of respect from him for my ingenuity under fire.

"By the way, sir, am I FBI Agent Docherty or Packard?"

I smiled, but with the papers under my fingers, I was preoccupied. This was the kind of moment I had joined the security services to experience, a glimpse of the secrets that shape our times. I had a heady feeling that was more than the beer. "You realise, don't you, Yarham, that this is probably one of the most important pieces of secret intelligence in the world right now? God knows what the CIA are planning, but it must be something vital."

"I do realise, Captain. God knows what it is, and soon, you."

"Us, Yarham, us," I said, unable to keep my attention off the documents.

"Do you think we left a… signature tonight?" Yarham asked cautiously.

It was worth thinking about. I reluctantly turned to this possibility. "I don't think the CIA will know it was C3. Carmelli and one guard got a good look at both of us. But we're new, unknown faces. We have to hope that our informer sabotaged the closed circuit film. What else will the CIA have?"

"The car."

"It's a cut-and-shunt job out of a junkyard with no prints. It doesn't exist," I said.

"And I suppose Carmelli can't tell the *true story*," Yarham grinned.

"He certainly can't say, '*I was in my room, boffing my secretary, when suddenly…*' I speculated. "No, he'll probably come up with bullshit about toiling alone in the night, and being slugged by masked intruders."

"Then with customary paranoia they'll suspect everybody, Captain… Al-Qaeda and the Mossad, the FBI and MI6."

"No shortage of suspects," I agreed, sipping the beer and skimming the papers, handing them on to Yarham as I finished them.

I absorbed an obliquely written and somewhat shuffled story. When I had finished my quick study, I dropped the last page on the pile absently. I had a peculiar feeling. I waited for Yarham.

"What do you make of it, sir?" he asked, caressing his chin.

"No, what do you make of it, Yarham?"

"Well, it's not a CIA plan, is it? It's what the CIA are doing about a terrorist plan."

"Yes, and they don't seem to be doing much… dickering about… "

"History repeating itself, sir."

He was referring to the Cuban missile crisis in 1962, which I had read about, said to have been the most potentially dangerous moment in human history. What Yarham and I had just learned from the Very Restricted Knowledge file was that there was an operation by terrorists, nearing completion, to build secret missile launch sites in Cuba. The US coastline would be seconds away after firing, and Washington under two hours. It was anticipated that the low-flying rockets would be invulnerable to fighter attack, but if intercepted by defence missiles, would detonate their nuclear and germ warheads. It was 1962 all over again, with the terrifying technology of the new millenium.

Thinking about it, I said, "Whatever the CIA are doing, and this one file isn't the full story, it's not *exactly* a repeat of history. You remember how Kennedy dealt with the crisis?"

"You're testing me, sir. He gave an ultimatum, threatening an all-out attack on the Soviet Union unless the missiles were withdrawn. And Krushchev blinked. Dear old Mother Russia had too much to lose."

"Precisely, Yarham. Al Qaeda, in contrast, have nothing to lose. A threat to the bazaars of Baghdad, a few Saudi palaces and Dubai hotels means nothing to them. They'd welcome total immolation."

"Could include Mecca."

"It wouldn't matter. This is a crusade by Saladin against Richard the Lionheart," I said.

I pondered over the political sensitivity of the operation. The CIA had apparently discovered the plot without the aid of the NSA surveillance network – presumably from humint, flesh and blood spies in Cuba. The NSA had probably received sufficient intercepts of CIA business to understand that something questionable was happening, and their fellow agency wasn't telling them. Hence Operation Screwdriver.

"I suppose they've always been fighting each other, the NSA and the CIA," Yarham said.

"Never mind about the enemy when you can fight a friend," I said.

"Think of the lives in issue," he replied, long-faced.

"Never mind the lives, Yarham. Lives are just lives. Think of the *reputations* at stake. The President, his advisers, a generation of top Pentagon brass, not to mention the NSA and CIA bureaucrats, and the legions at GCHQ and in MI6. Their lives won't be in danger. They have their bomb shelters. But their reputations are not going to survive very long in a radioactive cloud."

"Reputations have a remarkable way of surviving, Captain,

despite the muck. I can't see our part in this tournament of masters."

"They might give us some brown shoe polish for our cheeks and send us off to a Havana beach."

"What do you suppose C3 is trying to do, apart from give the CIA a kick in the rear?"

"Ah, that's the question. The only thing I can think of, is that C3, or perhaps it's really the Disciples, want to zap Cuba, and maybe Dubai and Mecca too. This could be the excuse. A preemptive strike. They want to get tough. They want to discredit the President. And with General Madison alongside him as Secretary of State, they view him as a softie flopping on another softie."

"I'm sure jihadis draw the line at Dubai, Captain. They probably enjoy staying in the hotels. I won't say no to another beer."

I delivered Yarham in a cab to his apartment and waiting wife, and went on to the C3 bolt-hole in Georgetown where lights were still burning. Clark was waiting, coldly, *with Kershaw*, whose face buckled with ill-will.

"We thought you had hit trouble," Clark said.

"Not at all. I lay low for a while."

Clark licked his lips and paused. "You left Harold tonight," he said reproachfully.

I gave Kershaw an ingenuous smile. "I took the steps necessary to ensure the mission succeeded. It was Harold's decision to come with us in a disabled physical condition. I very much appreciate his dedication, but he was being too hard on himself."

"Harold was in charge, and this was your first operation with us," Clark said.

He sounded like a scolding schoolmaster. As a soldier he

probably wanted to impose a military model of authority. I had stepped out of line big time. But in this game he knew that we made up the rules pragmatically as we went along.

"Harold drove the car," I replied quietly. "There are ten fit people who could have done that. If it hadn't been my first operation (I let you call the shots) I would have objected to having a driver who could only move on crutches!"

Clark was deflating, and I now rested the captured file with its gaudy cover and large VRK lettering on the desk before him. His eyes became fixed on the file and my peccadilloes perhaps diminished in his mind.

"You've read it?" he asked suspiciously.

"In a public lavatory, in case somebody got it away from me later."

"Well you know everything, don't you?" Kershaw said, threateningly.

While Clark took notes, I explained the heist, including the FBI impersonation, and Carmelli's amour. Having, I thought, won the opening exchange with Clark, I was flattering about Kershaw's advice, his driving, and his determination to protect the file – which mellowed his scowl a little.

Clark congratulated me mildly, picked up the file, and shukked it affectionately. "A nice piece of humint. I'm always telling the sigint buffs, no matter how sophisticated they get, humint is crucial."

"What's the next step in Operation Screwdriver, Gerry?" Kershaw asked.

"We have to digest this first," he said, dismissing Kershaw and me, and no doubt relishing the opportunity to devour the file alone. Kershaw had to limp away in ignorance.

"Would you like to know what was in the file, Harold?" I taunted as we progressed down the corridor.

"I can wait for the official version, rather than get a load of horse manure from you."

As we left the building, I said to Kershaw, "I assume you lost the car, Harold, or are you keeping it for the maid to use when she goes to the supermarket?"

"I made out, after you dumped me," he said, grimly.

I offered him a ride to the parking garage, indicating my understanding of the difficulty on crutches.

"When I want you acting as my medical orderly, I'll let you know, smartass!"

I arrived at my apartment that night at two-thirty am. It was in full living order as a result of Carol Clark's ministrations, and Yarham had swept the walls, floors and all the furniture and fittings and found no bugs. There was a note pinned on the door. *You didn't leave me a key. I'm at number 12. Laurie.*

I felt encouraged by Laurie's determination to see me that night, in fact I felt a surge of pleasure. I was still high on the adrenalin of the raid. I didn't want to sleep. Laurie could easily have stayed at a hotel and waited until tomorrow. I had little compunction in knocking at the door of Number 12, which was on my floor, and in a short time, after the justified grumbles of my neighbour, a woman federal court employee, Laurie and her suitcase were in my apartment. I was full of anticipation, foreseeing a superb end to a successful evening.

Although Laurie was affectionate, once the door had been closed, and she had assured herself that I hadn't been out on the town, she had a womanly curiosity about the apartment which she didn't stifle. She was surprised. She broke away from my embrace and walked through the rooms flicking on the lights, putting her long legs down gingerly in this changed territory, rubbernecking.

She took in quickly the special touches that neither Roger Conway nor the NSA Regulations for the Housing of Overseas Personnel could have provided: the skilful use of the couches and carpets in pale greys, against the delicate reds, browns and greens in the drapes; the way a lamp with a big shade cast a soft moonlight on the shining mahogany dining table; the quiet abstract Klee prints on the walls; the dashes of colour from a few cleverly placed vases.

She finally turned slowly on her heel in the middle of the lounge to complete the panorama. "A decorator's hand or a woman's!" she pronounced.

I saw no reason to conceal anything, indeed I knew that the truth would be prised out of me to my discredit. "Gerry Clark's wife helped me."

"*She* helped *you*. Come on, Roger!"

"OK. She did it."

"What's she like?" The change of tack was as icy as it was sudden.

Laurie had scented that somebody else was trespassing on her territory, and regrettably I wasn't in a position to say that Carol Clark was a portly sixty-year-old grandmother. Not only that, the unspoken question was, why hadn't I waited to furnish the apartment with Laurie? It was what Laurie wanted and expected.

"She was very friendly, welcoming one of her husband's staff," I said blandly.

"I'm sure. How old is she? What does she *look* like, Roger?"

I pretended to make an assessment I'd never made before. "Oh, you know, late thirties, half-starved, straggly hair."

"Liar."

"Darling, it's wonderful to know you care."

"Uh-huh. A bored blonde."

I didn't admit that she was right on but feigned indifference. "And who paid?"

Laurie knew all about allowances for state employees. "Yes, that's an interesting point. C3 paid." This was safer ground for me.

"I don't understand... this place is... quite luxurious."

"I guess they feel it's a dangerous job, and their operatives need looking after. You ought to see Gerry Clark's apartment."

"How do you know what it's like?"

In my innocent wish to be truthful, I was making it more difficult for myself. "I went there to dinner. Hundreds of thousands of dollars in antiques, I would say."

Laurie nodded grudgingly, now no doubt thinking of Mrs Clark the hostess. I didn't tell Laurie about the skimming practice which might well be contributing to the furnishings. I persuaded her to join me in a Scotch on the rocks, and we chatted about other things, but she mounted the bed that night like a suspicious lioness sniffing her lair. After all, she knew Mrs Clark had probably chosen the bed itself, but Laurie had a sense of delicacy which would not let her enquire into such awkward details. For my taste, our lovemaking that night was a little perfunctory as a result of this conversation, but it spiced what had been, all in all, a very exciting and memorable day.

12

I had never managed to find out anything about Nick
Stavros's role at C3 beyond my early conversation with Gerry
Clark, when he seemed to imply that Nick had died on active
service, and I had mostly put Nick out of my mind. I would
have liked to know how Nick had stumbled across the
Disciples, in his minor role, but in a way, that question too
had been overtaken by my own personal involvement with
Amory and Bolding.

The rather sultry Sally Greengloss had also remained no
more than a number in my mobile phone with the advent of
Carol Clark, and of course, Laurie. I was therefore surprised
to receive a message from Sally via the British Embassy. She
had no other way of contacting me. *Hope things are going well
for you. Give me a ring, and come round for a drink.*

I called Sally, and two days later, on a Friday evening, went
to her apartment at Du Pont Circle. She had been very casual
about the invitation, but what was suggested on the telephone
as an end-of-the-week drink and a hot-dog, perhaps with a
few of her friends, happened as an elaborate and private
dinner of caviar and champagne in her apartment.

I had expected that, caviar or not, we would talk about
Nick, but Sally put the subject respectfully aside and I had to
accede. We chatted about our personal adventures, laughed a
lot, got mildly drunk, and I accepted Sally's invitation to sleep
on the couch in the sitting room.

It must have been about three am when I awoke, my

bladder bursting. I extricated myself from the room quietly, padded to the lavatory and shut the door. Before me on the wall as I urinated was a large mirrored medicine cabinet, which I opened. I have found you can sometimes get a fresh insight into a person, if you look at the pills and potions that they take. I absently picked up one or two bottles and examined them – holistic pills, vitamin supplements, herbal extracts, alongside aspirin and cough mixture; nothing unusual. And then I saw that there was a sliding panel behind the bottles, not exactly secret, but unobtrusive. I slid the panel open. Contraceptive pills and tampons. I removed a plastic packet I found; it contained about a dozen disposable hypodermic syringes. There were two other vials of powder, unlabelled. Just at that point I heard Sally stir. I quickly replaced the articles, flushed the toilet and went back to bed.

"Are you all right, Roger?" Sally asked, appearing in the doorway.

"Sure."

"I never asked you, but how are you getting on at C3?" she said, sleepily. "Does it make you wake in the night, sweating?"

"How did you know I was at C3?"

"You implied you were where Nick was."

I was sure I hadn't. "You could have rung me, then, instead of sending a note."

"No. I don't have any idea where C3 is sited. Nick never gave me a number. Are you liking it, Roger?"

I was surprised that Nick, who had been a stickler for following the rules, told her that he was in C3. Here we were, having this strange conversation in the middle of the night.

"Absolutely fascinating… I mean it beats having the Jaguar franchise for Oxford."

"Dangerous?"

"Would Nick have answered that?"

Sally gave a little groan of desperation, and went back to her bed. I lay awake for a while, wondering if the powder in at least one of the phials was heroin, and if it was, how this fitted with Nick's death.

Yarham had worked industriously on the C3 intranet, and the more complicated net that served the Special Collection Service at Crypto City and the NSA. The result was that our personal *Other People's Business* facility was in comprehensive running order. I had access to staff, administrative and financial matters, personal diaries and emails, and a certain amount of encrypted material coded *Umbra* (high level signals intelligence), *Gamma* (espionage information), and *Zarf* (electronic intelligence from satellites). The *VRK* files were of course inaccessible hard copy.

Yarham and I had a session about his OPB discoveries once a week as we circled the library or promenaded down Wisconsin Avenue, and gained a useful if patchy picture of what C3 was doing. In particular, we were able to watch the impact on C3 of our successful raid on the CIA. In the understated communications between departments within C3 and the NSA, there was a nuance of shock. The terrorist threat to mainland USA was real more than imagined, and potentially dwarfed 9/11 in effect. I got a justifiably high official commendation from a number of officers (never directly communicated to me) and there was a certain triumphalism in Clark's reports of a victory over an uncooperative rival agency. References in emails and memos to the next stage of Operation Screwdriver did not give even an oblique suggestion of what it might be.

"Roger, we're having another little dinner at my apartment on Saturday night, and now that you've settled in and completed your first assignment, I'd like you to come along," Gerry Clark said, beaming at me from the doorway of his office as he named the next day but one. "Short notice, I know."

The confections of Carol Clark's French cook were certainly to my taste, and the Mona Lisa smile I could anticipate receiving across the dinner table from Carol. But I wondered whether this was a more serious occasion. To test Gerry, I said, "I'd love to come but I've got a date at Ford's Theatre."

Gerry's chubby affability faded. "I like to make business as pleasurable as possible, Roger."

"Fine. No problem. I'll be there."

When Clark had gone, Yarham bunched up his fist with his middle finger sticking out and screwed the table. I nodded agreement. What could it be but the next stage of Screwdriver?

I had not seen Carol Clark for ten days, and on the day of Gerry's invitation she appeared in the office doorway – she knew better than to call me on the agency's phones or our mobiles. It was one of the privileges of being the boss's woman that she could wander unchecked through the secure corridors, completely in breach of the security regulations. As soon as I saw her, I put my fingers to my lips and pointed to the light.

"Hullo, Carol," I said formally. "I was just going to go out to the drug-store."

"I'm on my way too," she said, and we both left the building together. When we were strolling under the birch trees along the sidewalk, she added, "We haven't seen each other lately, really since I finished at your apartment."

Her tone was peevish. But the problem of bringing my dalliance with Carol to a mutually agreeable close occurred to me only remotely at this stage.

"I've been busy. You know, the job. And I'm committed to seeing Laurie when she's in town."

Carol sighed. "Oh, yes, Laurie. Roger, come to the dinner at five or five-thirty instead of seven pm. Gerry's going to be out himself until seven pm. I know him. He's like clockwork. He's playing poker with his cronies after work. The kid's are at my mother's. The cook will be the only other person there."

It was, for a few seconds, a groin-warming invitation, but quickly supplanted by caution. I was anxious about Carol's ire if I rejected her. I therefore accepted her suggestion with pretended alacrity, intending to be late, and use the time to question her about the guest list.

I presented myself at the Clark residence a little after six pm bearing flowers and a bottle of good Californian cabernet sauvignon. Mme Ducane opened the door and I noticed her remarkable face and figure again. She had very thick black hair, nearly shoulder-length with a slight crimp. She was of medium height with a full figure and mustard-coloured skin, perhaps of Algerian origin. Her eyes were bronze and lustrous as they settled on me. She accepted the gifts graciously, and walked before me into the lounge. She was wearing a thin, tight, short black dress in the warm apartment. As I walked in her wake, I could smell a hot female smell that was not from a perfume bottle. She looked over her shoulder and said casually, "Madame is in the room at the end of the hall," waving her arm gently toward the door. I hesitated at this casual gesture.

"Go on," she smiled, her purple lips parting over a neat row of contrastingly white teeth.

As I walked hesitantly down the hall I tried to clear my mind from the tawny cook, to favour the pink and white Carol. At the open bedroom door I paused, seeing a bed, smooth and empty, with the top sheet drawn back neatly to admit a body – or bodies. Only one meaning could be attached to being received in the bedroom.

Carol jumped out from behind the door with a yell which startled me and wrapped her arms around me. She was wearing a satin gown, and I was enveloped by her superficial softness with a scented, gym-firmed muscularity beneath. After this clinch, Carol began to undress me methodically, slipping my jacket off, undoing my tie. I wriggled around, showing good humour, but slowing the process. She hadn't yet spoken a word, unless her gasps counted.

"Now, wait a minute, Carol."

She then beckoned me to the bed, as I reached, automatically, to close the open door on my embarrassment.

"Don't shut the door, Roger, Marie might want to consult me about the table settings," she sniggered.

"This is very… dangerous," I protested, startled again by the implications.

Carol began wrestling me to the bed, her gown open, revealing those last few woman's undergarments which are the salad garnish of love. The problem of being drawn deeper into an emotional mire, hers not mine, was on my mind, not to mention privacy, and the possible, indeed impending arrival of Marie, and by ill-chance, even Gerry.

"What do you think, Roger?"

I saw Carol's attention was beyond me, and I turned to find Marie standing near the bed.

"Well, Monsieur?" Marie said, swaying her hips

I glanced uncertainly at Carol, and saw only amusement. I wasn't sure what was being promised.

Marie began to undress quickly in front of us, revealing a body astonishingly in contrast to that of her mistress in its swarthy voluptuousness. I watched this spectacle while Carol clung to me. And when Marie had stepped out of her last garment, a thong, she gave a whoop like a cowboy at a rodeo, and threw herself on top of Carol and me, and we rolled on the bed in a tangle. I was beginning to give serious thought to removing myself from this tangle of limbs and breasts, when I heard a voice echo down the hall.

"Carol, honey!"

Gerry Clark's tones were not particularly honeyed. He must have had a losing afternoon. He sounded scratchy.

"Goddam! Once in a thousand years, he's early!" Carol whispered.

In one fluid movement, Marie was out of the bed. She swept the pile of her clothes on the carpet into a corner, and slid into a long silk wrap. She went out the door, closing it behind her, while Carol crept to the door and locked it. I could hear Marie addressing Gerry. What was she saying? Perhaps that she was going to have a shower before dinner, and that Madame was dressing. But that wouldn't make any allowance for me!

I was gathering my scattered garments when Gerry came to the door and tried to open it. Carol grinned at me, kissed my cheek, and tried to undo my belt. She pointed to the bed. I was now in a confused state of shock and excitement, and whether my judgment was right or not, felt that despite all this ecstatic promise, the assignation could not in any measure be consummated. I was limp.

Gerry returned to the door. "Why have you got the door locked?" he whined. "It's my fucking bedroom too."

"You don't do all that much fucking in it," Carol said, calmly.

Gerry's image of her from outside the door was probably that she was sitting engrossed before the mirror of her dressing table, frowning while applying her eye shadow. "Yeah, well you can't fuck an iceberg," he said.

"I'm an iceberg? Really?" Carol tittered sarcastically, widening her eyes at me, and I caught the echo of years of stinging bedroom talk.

This two-way exchange had cooled Carol's ardour. Her mind was clattering with domestic conflict. "Listen Gerry, be sensible for once. We're having guests soon. I want to get dressed quietly without having Marie come in and ask me questions. I'll be out in a moment."

Carol managed this offhand response while her whole body was shuddering with anger and frustration. Gerry Clark gave an ill-tempered growl and moved away, and I finished putting on my clothes.

Carol's whispered directions to me seemed complicated and risky – exit through the sliding doors of the bedroom to the patio, descend the fire escape, drop into a neighbour's garden, mind the dog, go out of the neighbour's gate into the road, take a walk, and return to the apartment in five or ten minutes.

In a sweat I forgot to ask what kind of dog it was, and stumbled out on to the patio to negotiate the obstacle course. It was my good fortune that this detour was without event. I walked up the road thinking I would prefer not to return, but duty had to be done. I was going to attend a business meeting. Then I remembered the flowers and wine which I had brought and handed to Marie who had probably put them down somewhere in full view. Had Gerry noticed them? I was agonised. If only I could have disappeared completely.

Gerry met me at the front door of his residence at a few minutes before seven pm. "Ah, Roger first to arrive," Gerry said. "You look rather dishevelled. What's the problem?"

"It's a bit breezy out there," I said, following Gerry into the lounge. I saw the flowers and wine had been placed on the sideboard. Carol had not yet appeared.

"Whose is this?" Gerry Clark asked, picking up the wine and looking at the vintage. The room was so meticulously neat and understated in ornamentation that the gift was quite noticeable and demanded attention.

Rarely at a loss for a word, I was now fumbling for an explanation, or weighing whether I should profess ignorance, when a calm voice behind me said, "Monsieur Conway left the gifts before he went for a walk."

"Yes. Such a bracing evening. I was early, and I left the things with Marie."

Marie looked quite dull-eyed and lumpy in her apron, as she removed the flowers and the wine, and Clark thanked me. I reflected for a second as a man, and possibly a future victim, on the almost impenetrable deceptions of cuckoldry.

The events of the evening had moved so swiftly, I had not had time to find out from Carol in advance who the guests would be. This dinner was work, and could hardly be other than Operation Screwdriver, so the guest list was significant. Gerry fixed me a martini which I toyed with until the second guest arrived: Professor Reich, who again seemed to reach into his memory to place me. Then, to my surprise, Rachel Fernandez, the head of SCS, appeared. She had no personal intimacy. She was as commanding close up as she was on her dais. There were two more places yet to be filled. I thought one of them might be Kershaw, but instead, the pair who arrived together were Bolding and Amory. Bolding, elegantly suited in a fawn woollen check, was withdrawn and smiled only as a politeness. Amory's eyes sparkled when he saw me, and he rubbed his palm over my shoulder affectionately. Here, I concluded, were some of the top Disciples: Reich,

Fernandez, Bolding and Amory. I placed Clark as no more than a trusted stooge.

Despite Marie's tasteful efforts with the pate and orange duck, the dinner and the conversation were overshadowed by what was to come. Gerry was perhaps in awe of his guests, and Carol only made a faint attempt to play the hostess. She was very quiet, with a secretly enigmatic glance which she rested upon me occasionally. When the coffee and cognac were served, Carol left the table, asking to be excused in a way which suggested that she wouldn't return. Marie departed, closing the double doors to the lounge with finality, and the remaining six diners were left in silence at the table.

It was Professor Reich who spoke first and without preamble. "The first task is to find the precise location of the missile site. It's apparent from the CIA material that they don't know."

"GCHQ have no information on this, not one intercept," Amory said. "What about the NSA?"

"Nothing," Rachel Fernandez said. "It's very unusual. The equipment has been assembled under a blanket of silence."

"Aerial surveillance?" Bolding asked.

"Nothing," Fernandez said.

Bolding said, "Understandable if you compare the events of 1962. That was a big government-to-government operation. A lot of the traffic was in clear by the Cubans, and the build-up of vessels heading for Cuba was obvious. The U2s were overflying and getting pictures. This operation, in contrast, is completely covert, a lot smaller and more deadly. There's no need for perceptible shipping movements. All the on-site work can be performed underground. If you plan carefully, you don't need a lot of signals. And the Cubans don't appear to be politically involved, perhaps not even as willing hosts."

"So we need humint," Gerry said with a small grin.

"We do," Reich said, stiffly. "Do MI6 have any agents in Cuba who could help?"

Bolding deferred to Amory. "None of our sources is really in a position in Havana where we can expect useful information."

"Same with ours," Rachel Fernandez said. "We need a new team, pronto."

"That supports my point," Bolding said. "If you remember, the 1962 crisis involved major construction work, engineering, telemetry, not to mention money and politics. Information from many government departments in Cuba and the Soviet Union seeped out at all levels. Now, not only is the present operation on a relatively small scale, but my assessment is that the Cuban government isn't officially involved, and doesn't know anything about it. Our agents in Cuba aren't getting any information because there literally isn't any."

A pause, and their eyes swung toward me: Reich, Bolding and Fernandez, crystalline and abstract as though I was a specimen under x-ray, and Amory, warm and shimmering.

"This is where you come in, Roger," Reich said.

13

This was my moment. I was the answer to the jihadists' most damaging threat to the western world. I was like a modern Hannibal or Alexander. True, I had no vast army, but the effect of my mission couldn't be measured in elephants or warriors. It wasn't hard to see what the Disciples would want me to do.

"You want me to go to Cuba, locate and destroy the terrorists and their site?" I asked.

"Well not quite, but you're our chosen man," Amory said with a giggle.

"We want you to locate the site, period, Roger. Then report to us," Reich said in his clipped way.

I was disappointed at this more limited role; from Hannibal to Good Soldier Schweik in moments. But I gestured sagely, and said, "I'm honoured to have the assignment. Could I ask some questions?"

Reich made a giveaway gesture with his hands. "Anything."

"How long do we have before the missile site is ready?"

"We don't know. Really no time at all. It *could* be months, but probably weeks." Reich looked at the others for assent.

"Do I take any further action when I locate the site?"

"Other than to let us know the position, no," Reich said.

"What will happen when we know the location?"

Reich had assumed a sort of chairmanship. "Perhaps it's not good for you to know too much… but the missiles will obviously have to be destroyed."

"How?"

"I don't think we can talk about that," Reich said. "I appreciate your curiosity, but it's not in your interests to know. If you fell into the hands of the terrorists... "

"Trust us, Roger, to deal wisely and well with the intelligence you bring us," Amory said pontifically.

"What will the CIA be doing that is likely to affect me?"

Reich smiled wryly. "Trying to find out the same information, I would guess. But we'll be watching them, and we'll let you know anything useful."

"What will the CIA do if they find out the location?"

Bolding gave a groan. "Write a thesis about it, and then set up a committee to consider it, I should think. You don't need to worry about that. We'll watch them carefully and keep you informed."

"It's possible I could come into conflict with the CIA. After all, we're both looking for the same thing."

"Avoid them if possible, otherwise... treat them as you would any other unfriendly unit," Fernandez said.

I looked around at a ring of waxen faces, and had no need to question what one does with an unfriendly unit.

"The security of both our nations is in issue, Roger," Amory said.

"It's no time for half measures," Reich said. "Make sure nobody gets in your way."

I came away from the dinner with instructions that I would leave for Cuba, with Yarham, as soon as our false identities and papers had been processed, but with the vacant feeling, which every operative presumably experiences, that he is a pawn in a game he cannot begin to understand.

It had been my intention to make an excuse and decline a ride in Amory's cab, but now I decided that Amory was my one avenue of further information. I rode with him and

Bolding, asking not to be dropped at my apartment, and saying I intended to walk back from the city for the exercise. Bolding alighted at the Marriott, and when we arrived at the Hilton I accepted Amory's invitation to go up to his suite for a nightcap.

Amory had supplied himself with a generous range of duty-free Chivas Regal and cognac, making resort to the room-bar unnecessary. I fetched ice from the machine, and then dodged into a single armchair with my drink, and looked restive.

"What's the matter, Roger?"

"I'm very happy about the task, sir, but…"

"Childers."

"Childers. I feel a bit short on briefing."

Amory shrugged, and took a large gulp of whisky. "I understand, my boy… "

I interrupted, "The cause, what we're trying to achieve… of course I know that this threat has to be eliminated, but the larger implications if we were to unleash our missiles against Cuba, and the part the CIA is playing… "

"The CIA is dithering. So is the President. He's a ditherer by nature. He's so eminently political by nature that he's forever counting on the one hand this, and on the other hand, that. Result – inaction. And he's aided in this by Secretary of State Madison. General Madison is a dove. He seems to be a pacifist in an army uniform, and precisely because he wears the uniform, he is so plausible to the American people. *We* have to take the decisive action."

"We?"

Amory's face puckered pleasurably. "We. Our little band of Anglo-American brothers, Roger."

"The Disciples?"

Amory gulped again, emptying his glass and lay back contemplatively. "I believe that's what we're called."

I filled Amory's glass again very generously, watering my own, while Amory was supine with his weighty thoughts.

"But how can you command the resources, Childers?"

"Because, in the end, Roger, we command everything. With superior intellect, and all-knowledge, one only has to have one's fingertips on the levers of power."

It was undoubtedly the whisky, but I had a sudden picture of GCHQ and Crypto City embracing the globe with tentacles like an enormous octopus, poised to squirt its venom.

"The Cuban Crisis II will bring down the President, and discredit Madison," Amory pronounced confidently.

"You'll precipitate a strike on Cuba, Childers, if the President hesitates?"

"Certainly. And he will hesitate. And I will give you a further little piece of advice about your mission, because I like you, Roger, you mean a lot to me... You don't have to be too precise about the site location. I don't want you to take undue risks."

Amory was searching me now, his features crimped wickedly around his porous nose, watching for his meaning to dawn.

"You'll strike so hard that everything will be destroyed?"

"Everything in a wide area, my boy, so keep safe." His voice dropped from pronouncing political certainties to an affectionate burble.

Childers Amory raised himself from his chair and staggered toward me, collapsing at my feet, and shoving his body between my legs, his great bald head with its black-haired ears resting on my crotch. Fortunately, he spilled the remnants of liquor in his glass over my trousers, and I was able to spring up without giving offence, and go to the bathroom for a towel.

Had Childers Amory been a woman of my choice, this small event, the wetting, might have been used as an excuse to remove my trousers. As it was, in the bathroom, I mopped my brow rather than my trousers, and tried to work out an exit strategy.

I hadn't found out precisely how the Disciples would engineer their strike and whether it would be nuclear, but that would have to wait for a further opportunity. I returned to the lounge area of the suite, turning in my mind whether to plead a headache or pressure of work, and found that the liquor and jet lag had done their work. Childers Amory, the Disciple on whom the world depended for its security, was asleep on the carpet, his head lolling back, his mouth wide open and gurgling. I let myself quietly out of the room.

14

The arrangements for my departure from Washington were made rapidly, and I had an issue with Clark on only one point. He wanted me to take Kershaw, to work strictly under my orders. I refused, and insisted on Yarham. I told Clark I was prepared to go back to Reich if necessary and force the issue. Clark backed down.

Yarham, whose jaw hung open with pleasure at the prospect, and I made our few preparations. We needed no baggage because we would be changing our identities in Mexico City. For me, it was a matter of saying goodbye to Laurie – who understood the demands of the service, and happened to be staying for a few days – and asking the neighbour to feed my cat when Laurie departed.

Yarham and I were met at Mexico City airport by the expected man in a yellow Brazilian football shirt. He drove us to a safe house in the middle-class residential Petatlan district, run by Hector Rojas, a silver-haired Spaniard. Rojas said our papers would be ready the next morning, and we would be on an afternoon flight to Havana. I would become an English import-export dealer specialising in cars and light machinery, which suited me very well. As Daniel Garcia, I would be domiciled in Mexico, and travelling on a Mexican passport. Yarham, who had tolerable Spanish, would assume mixed parentage as Senor Roberto Rivero-Doyle, my partner.

Rojas lectured us on the implications of our new business,

and particularly the trade in stolen and second-hand cars. It occurred to me that if all else failed, this was a business I could manage with profit.

My new wardrobe of clothes was excruciatingly dull, and consisted principally of two used, tan coloured-suits in polyester, ugly brown leather brogues, and a varnished straw hat. The object, Hector Rojas said, was to look like a small businessman, sound and ordinary. The dark green and brown ties I was given underlined the effect. In keeping with this object we would be staying at an old but comfortable two- or three-star hotel. We would have a safe house to bolt to in an emergency. We would be met by an MI6 operative who knew Cuba.

"Your man in Havana," Rojas joked. "The MI6 agent will know nothing of your mission, just as, I remind you, I know nothing. MI6 will assist you in every way they can."

"That's a sort of kiss of death, Captain," Yarham said.

"I don't have any information about your communications to base or vice-versa," Hector Rojas said.

I showed Rojas our satellite phone disguised as a laptop computer.

Finally, he gave us a contact in Cuban intelligence. "Well, the contact may not be in the intelligence services, but has access. I don't know, I just get the instructions." He took me through a coded question about the yellow rose of Texas which I was to use when and if we used the Cuban contact.

The briefing over, Yarham and I donned our new clothes, had a good laugh at ourselves in the mirror, and I reluctantly abandoned a well-cut dark blue Saint Laurent jacket and a pair of Gucci loafers. That evening, Yarham and I spent an hour working out at a local gym – something we had begun in New York and continued regularly at least two days a week.

Then, in a leisurely way, in a torpor assisted by our exercise, the altitude and the tequila, we visited a number of local bars and clubs.

When, in one of the clubs, I asked Yarham whether the likelihood of a nuclear war overshadowed his work and worried him, he said, "I can't do much about it, can I, sir? Might as well enjoy the rum and Coke."

"Or to put it another way, Yarham, you and I alone, are doing everything that mankind can do about it. I doubt if James Bond ever had a task like this. Doesn't it… get the blood going?"

"Not as much as that girl," Yarham said, looking at the gyrating legs and flying breasts of the tinsel-covered dancer who was performing the samba on the dance floor.

I liked Yarham's refusal to acknowledge our intimidating task. For myself, there were moments when I realised that I was achieving, or had achieved, my ambition to penetrate to the very secret heart of the intelligence world. But there were other moments when I remembered, with slight yearning, the ease and freedom from care of being a car-dealer in Oxford. I remembered making a particularly profitable sale or an astute buy, and having champagne and a gourmet dinner with a girlfriend to celebrate; it had all been very uncomplicated.

On arrival in Havana we took a cab to the Hotel Comodoro in a Vedado back street. I was rather pleased with my room; it was old-fashioned, built perhaps in the 1920s and scarcely repaired since, but with a lavish approach to space. The high ceilings were dominated by fans; the windows were tall. The sitting room had a balcony covered in red bougainvillea, overlooking a busy street and market used by people rather than vehicles. The bed was a wrought iron monster. The ornate red drapes and mats were faded and plaster peeled from the walls.

We had time to sample a pina colada (what else?) on the balcony, before finding the Herradura Bar near the flea market on Calle 3, to meet our MI6 contact. I had already decided that our first step would be to visit the sites of the Cold War missile emplacements, the positions of which I had memorised from aerial photographs before I left Washington, but there were certain *supplies* I needed to obtain first.

I saw a man with a small dog in the rear recess of the dark bar. I identified myself as 'Wolf' which made me feel strong and invulnerable on the rare occasions I had to use the code. The MI6 officer was 'Neville.'

Neville was affable. "Please take a seat. I'll get you a drink. We can talk freely here."

Yarham and I ordered beer, and our host a whisky and water.

"I get sick of the sweet shit they drink here," he said.

When we had the drinks and were seated, Neville surveyed us through his spectacles, and gave a good-humoured nod of acceptance. "I'll give you an address you can use in an emergency. If you're on the run. Beyond that, what can I do for you two gentlemen, Mr Doyle and Mr Garcia?"

Neville was an Englishman in his late forties, balding, with silver hair and the coppered complexion of long exposure to a bright sky. He was too much at home in his cotton trousers and floral shirt to look like a tourist; rather the slightly uncomfortable expatriate. He was curious about our mission, but departmental constraints didn't permit him to ask. I wasn't going to satisfy his curiosity.

"Two 9 mm automatic pistols and ammunition, two flick knives, two pairs of knuckles, and two pairs of cuffs," I said.

Neville frowned and was more curious. "Really? Serious business, eh? I'm not sure I can do the knuckle-dusters immediately. I'll try."

The dog, a yappy dachshund tethered to a chair, peed on Yarham's shoe. Neville took no notice.

"Watch you don't get caught with the guns. Anything else?"

"Nothing," I said, and we finished our drinks talking in impersonal terms about the Cuban economy. We arranged to meet at the same time the next day to receive the weapons.

As we were getting up to leave, Neville said, "Would it help to know the CIA deployment in Havana?"

I already knew as much about the CIA in Cuba as the NSA could find out, but I wondered whether Neville had more. "Sure."

"They have two US agents in the city, headed by a guy named Savage. I'll give you an address and number. And they have a second line of Cuban agents of varying degrees of expertise and reliability."

"Thanks. Are you in touch with them?"

"Sure, I can tell them…"

"Don't tell *anybody* anything!" I cut in.

Neville was hurt by my vehemence. "I think I know enough not to do anything without your prior approval. I was just trying to be constructive."

When we left Neville still looked miffed.

I said, "We might want to get in touch with the CIA."

"Ask the CIA to help us, you mean? We may both be part of the one mighty civil service, but actually talking to each other, that's something else," Yarham smiled.

I forgot Neville and embarked on my next move of the day. Before leaving Washington I had plotted the GPS positioning of the projected missile sites of the early 1960s. Yarham and I took a cab along the Autopista La Habana-Mariel, to a location in Mariel where, with the assistance of his map-reading, we left the cab in a run-down area of failed factories and rotting sheds. Nothing vaguely resembling an old missile site was in view.

An old missile site was admittedly an arbitrary starting point, but I thought it might yield a few clues to what the terrorists were doing. What kind of site would be used, and where would it be positioned? Was there any possibility that the terrorists would seek to use an old site? My thinking on all this was unclear, save that having a look seemed to be a prudent step; it also postponed the vital question – what next? I had no answer to this at the moment.

The temperature was around eighty degrees. Grass sprouted through the broken tarmac. People were living under shelters, lean-tos of cardboard resting on the fences; they were living in doorways. Two strolling businessmen from Mexico in their tan suits stuck out like a dog's balls. We walked along the road looking as though we had come to buy it. Sullen eyes watched us from behind crumbling walls and piles of garbage. A crocodile of ragged children with dancing smiles began to follow us, laughing and occasionally daring to jump in front of us holding out their hands for a dollar.

"This is no good, Yarham," I said, feeling like the Pied Piper.

"There it is, sir," Yarham said, indicating a lot heaped with rubble and stinking trash, which did not quite disguise the heavy concrete foundations and the tangled steel rods which protruded from beneath the mess.

"You're right. Maybe it's completely blocked."

I was beginning to see that my idea of having a look at the old sites wasn't likely to be very productive.

"Might as well give it the once-over now we're here," Yarham said, patting a young girl of six or seven on the head. "I can't give you a dollar, love. If I do we'll be mobbed." He made his way off the road, and on to the lot.

Yarham found a hole covered with a plastic tent, which he removed; dark, smelly steps leading downwards were revealed. He looked at me questioningly. The children ringed us, chattering.

"What we're here for," I said. "You first."

"Not at all, sir."Yarham said, standing aside from the fetid black hole, and making way for me.

"From our briefing there are three sites," I said, starting to descend.

"That could mean miles of tunnels, Captain," Yarham said mournfully.

"Don't you think it's a good idea to go through the tunnels that haven't been sealed to see if there are any signs of the activity of our friends?"

"Wouldn't they find fresh sites?"

Yarham was beginning to erode the common sense of my move. "Probably, but we ought to check," I insisted.

"Why, sir?"

Yarham was always asking why, and in defence, I came up with a stray possibility which had been floating around in my head. "Suppose the nuclear warheads that were delivered, or said by the Soviets never to have been delivered, in 1962 are in fact here, in store, waiting for a new age rocket to carry them?"

"It's an interesting idea, Captain, but wouldn't the CIA, who have been nosing around for the last forty-plus years, have found them?"

"You'd think so, but as we know,Yarham, with intelligence agencies, anything is possible. The CIA would probably need a hundred years."

Yarham looked at me sadly as I conjured up a whole new mythology around missing warheads which might not exist. I went slowly, and with some embarrassment, out of the blinding light into the darkness, feeling for the cigarette lighter I carried as a useful tool. I never have smoked. The air was foul.

"Smells of shit."

"Very convenient lavatory for the locals, Captain."

I had just about decided to leave, and declare that we should return with torches to save face, when I noticed a faint light shining on the rough cement walls. We kept going and passed a candle guttering in a jar; there was now also a strong smell of incense and weed.

"Somebody's here. Having a party," Yarham muttered.

I asked myself whether we were heading for the terrorists' secret assembly room, or whether we were getting our mission messily mixed up with an intrusion into the living space of the community. My cheap shoes had softened in the sludge and were letting in liquid of a composition too revolting to think about.

Around a bend in the passage, we came upon an altar with candles, and before it, a coffin, open. We both stood still, transfixed with alarm. There appeared to be a corpse, lying in state, inside the coffin. There could have been other people there, watching from the darkness.

I was thrown back against the wall in fright as a piercing shriek filled the space – a noise which swiftly turned into a hysterical laugh. A figure jumped in front of me, naked from the waist up, and gleaming, a large-breasted female figure wearing a crown of feathers, and sparkling bangles on her wrists. The whites of her eyes glowed.

"Ayee! Senors!" she yelled in Spanish, "You have come into the house of spirits!"

While we were paralysed with uncertainty rather than fear, the woman anointed her forehead with blood from a dead chicken on the altar, and screamed, and as she did so, the corpse raised itself from the coffin – an emaciated man, naked, with iridescent skeletal white lines daubed down his chest, arms and legs.

"A judicious retreat, Captain, I implore you…"

Yarham and I scrambled up the steps, stumbling, splashing through the stinking mud, shouting apologies to the occupants.

15

"What then is the plan, Captain?" Yarham asked cheerfully, as we sat in the luxurious lounge of the Excelsior Hotel on Paseo de Marti in Centro, rather than the run-down Comodoro. We sipped fresh rum and Cokes, looking past the mass of purple blooms in vases around us, toward the traffic of coolly dressed, moneyed people who crossed the lobby.

"The plan, the plan, the plan?" I said.

I had no plan. My feet were wet, and I fancied I could smell them. Since our undignified retreat from the *santeria* ceremony in the bunker, I had been trying to think of one, or at least a different starting point. By tacit consent the idea of exploring the 1960s sites for signs of terrorist activity was abandoned for the moment.

"We need to find out whether our Cuban intelligence contact can tell us anything," Yarham said.

"And pick up the tools."

I noticed that a paunchy man with a thick neck, wrapped in a loose suit, had paused on the shining floor of the lobby and half-turned toward us, frowning, concentrating his gaze. I met his glance; there was mutual uncertainty. Recognition happens in milliseconds, but it seemed to take a long time for me to trace in my memory the precise lines of the pug nose and the thick lips... It was the man on the couch, Carmelli! I had seen his face for only a fraction of a second but it was unforgettable.

Carmelli looked away from me, bustled on his way, and swiftly disappeared into an elevator.

"Carmelli come to retrieve the CIA's honour, and his own!" I said.

"I fear we may have made a stupendous blunder in showing ourselves here, sir," Yarham said.

"He must be staying here, Yarham."

"They don't stint themselves, these servants of the people."

The Excelsior was one of about three locations patronised by rich foreigners. I was tired of playing the small businessman – that was why we had treated ourselves to a drink at the Excelsior, but now that I came to think of it, the Excelsior was the natural place to find the lavishly salaried, expense account-supported top men of the CIA.

"We better get our asses out of here, or Carmelli will be chasing us with a 45," I said.

We retired hastily from this cathedral of polished marble and white-jacketed waiters, to the dog-eared Comodoro. We washed our feet, and installed ourselves in my room. The risk of being seen from the balcony meant that we had to sit indoors and listen to the wheezing air conditioner. With clean socks and replenished cocktails, we considered our fate.

I turned over our few options – see the Cuban contact; try Neville for information about CIA movements at the risk of revealing our mission; and finally, home in on the CIA more closely, perhaps even tail Carmelli.

Yarham, tactfully, did not mention a further examination of the 1960s sites. The warmth, the rum, and the relaxed ambience of Havana took the edge of urgency off our conversation. I had made no decision, when there was a light knock at the door.

Yarham opened the door, and it was kicked back in his face, knocking him flat on his back. Two men were in the room, big, gymnasium-trained Americans in linen suits, ties, with lumpy, sunburned faces and short hair. Both had snub-nosed revolvers in their hands.

Carmelli had moved swiftly. The CIA had sprung into life, while we had forgotten our training and every spy film we had ever seen. In opening the door, we had acted like a couple of tourists inviting a heist.

"You move, you get iced," one of the men said, waving his weapon.

"I donna understand," I said, reverting to car-dealer Garcia.

"You will, punk, you will."

The CIA pair came round with their backs to the balcony windows, and held their guns on us. Between us was the empty couch on which Yarham and I had been sitting facing the windows. We were all in the ante-chamber of the suite, which contained only the couch, armchairs and a low table. Multi-coloured tiles, strewn with a few old rugs, covered the floor.

"We're goin' to have a little talk with you guys," the speaker continued calmly as they took up their positions.

I could see now that the man who had only frowned hatefully, and not spoken, did not have a conventional pistol in his hand. He was holding a dart gun. They were going to tranquilise us, and remove us to a place with more scope for interrogation. That would be life-threatening. Although these were two young men with college education and law degrees who no doubt faithfully remembered their mothers' birthdays, they were also brutal goombahs in the Kershaw mode, who would kill without conscience. I was sure Yarham would have assessed the situation as I had, and understood the need for instant action.

Although I was unarmed, I had been taught a technique to deal with this kind of event which the melancholy MI6 instructors called *The Gas Chamber Alternative*. When you are destined for the gas chamber, you will surely die if you don't act. The essence of the technique is action, a whirlwind of physical action which confuses the planned approach of an antagonist. I had never employed the technique before, and at the time I had learned it, thought it rather puerile, desperate and dangerous. But now I could see, graphically, that it was better than nothing. Action, but what action?

When my eyes met Yarham's I moved my head slightly to indicate the windows, and thought Yarham signalled readiness, his chin hanging down below his open mouth, oddly relaxed. The talking man signalled me to come closer.

"I wanna get to know you better."

He was lining me up for a shot by his accomplice with the dart.

Between the man and me was the heavy, upholstered couch, sitting on small brass wheels, easily mobile on the tiles. I stepped forward to comply, but then dived behind the couch, twisting and heaving it forward with my shoulders toward the gunman. There was a wild shot, and I felt the heavy furniture collide with the man and smash him against the closed windows, shattering them.

Yarham took advantage of the momentary distraction of the other man, and charged him like a lineback, carrying both of them through another pane of the glass doors to sprawl on the balcony.

When Yarham and I sprang back from our work, we had two dazed CIA agents on their backs, and a pistol spinning on the tiles. I scooped it up.

"Let's go," I said, grabbing the satellite phone, and while our assailants were struggling to their feet, we were out the door and down the stairs.

"Not the front," I cautioned, thinking that there might be reinforcements there, and that our attackers would be in immediate radio contact with their team.

We made our way out through the kitchens, and melted into the crowds on Calle D heading toward the Malencon.

16

After I had bought antiseptic cream and plasters from a pharmacy, I retired with Yarham to a shadowy bar, replaced the drinks which seemed fated to be interrupted, and dealt with the cuts on Yarham's scalp and hands.

"What's next, Captain?" Yarham asked with his foolish grin.

It would not be possible to return to the hotel rooms. "I'll send some cash in the post or the hotel will report us to the police, or maybe I can get the MI6 man to compensate for the damage."

We were wearing shirts and trousers, and our suit jackets were no loss. Each of us had money and a passport in a body belt. I had the satellite phone, and the pistol I had picked up from our attackers. Nothing of any value, to the CIA or anybody else, had been left behind. The false memoranda and invoices which were meant to bolster our identity as Mexican domiciled car dealers were in my belt, although that identity was almost useless now. We could check into another hotel, but I assumed the CIA would set up a fairly comprehensive surveillance on hotels; they would have plenty of scavenging dogs, hired for a few pesos, to sniff the streets.

"I think we pick up our tools and go for the safe house, work from there," I said.

"Do you think the CIA will haul in the police to find us? It would be easy enough for one of the CIA men to complain, say, of a theft. We're missing. Hotel room damaged."

"Perhaps, to make life more difficult for us, but my instinct is that they'll keep clear of the police." In an hour we had changed from respectable businessmen into fugitives. "We'll need to be cautious on the streets anyway."

"I've always fancied having a beard like Fidel," Yarham said.

It wasn't such a bad idea. "We'll ask Mr MI6 if he can provide wigs."

We hung out in a grotty bar, fortified with warm, greasy empanadas and rum, until the time for the meeting was near, and then slunk through the back streets to the assignation at the Herradura bar. Our man was waiting in shorts and open-toed sandals, slumped back easily on a bar stool, a white t-shirt stuck out over his bulging belly. He had no luggage that I could see. He looked at us with curious humour, and noticed Yarham's plastered head and fingers.

"Started work, eh?"

"Have you got the stuff?" I asked.

"Yes, but we have to pick it up elsewhere."

"We need disguises. Maybe wigs, a moustache, something to darken our skin, dark glasses."

"Fancy dress, eh? OK. Cops after you?"

"Could be. You need to discreetly fix up our bill at the Comodoro Hotel and compensate for the damage to my room, or they will be."

"It's not that easy," Neville frowned.

I knew he was considering the administrative bother – the requisition for funds, the reports, the explanations. "Don't wait until you've discussed it with London, will you?"

Neville hardened. "What happened?"

I explained the damage, but not the cause.

"How did it happen?"

"You think of an explanation, and peddle it to the hotel manager."

"I have to make a report," Neville said, sourly.

"You know the *need to know* routine."

Neville accepted this reluctantly. "The police aren't all that sharp. But there are a lot of informers around."

"I want to use the safe house."

The hard look turned to the annoyed. More admin work. "You're all done, then? Waiting to leave?"

"No."

"If you operate from the safe house it won't be safe for very long."

"Too bad. Right now we need somewhere."

This gave Neville a problem. Disturbed in his cosy and probably tranquil post, he could feel himself inching toward trouble.

"Why not set up another safe house immediately?" I asked, thinking we might have to bolt again.

"I'll handle my department."

"We might need it. I'm serious. Don't let me have to ask, and find you can't deliver."

"I said I'll handle my department."

The meeting finished coldly. Neville's visitors were a bloody nuisance. He gave directions to the safe house, and agreed to meet in fifteen minutes, in a nearby electrical goods shop, where the weapons would be handed over.

"The shop is only a few minutes away. Wait here, give me five minutes, and then follow," he said.

When Neville had gone, I moved to the front of the bar, from the dark recess we were inhabiting, and looked up and down the street through the strip of dirty window that was not plastered with advertising. It was a lucky move, made out of caution rather than foresight. Some of the patrons eyed me curiously, but I wasn't worried about them. Through the window I saw one of the CIA college boys who had raided the hotel, the trank operator, crossing toward the bar. They were apparently searching aggressively.

"Let's move," I said to Yarham.

I went out back toward the lavatory, kicked open the back door, waded through a heap of rags, old newspapers and empty liquor cartons, to enter the next-door premises. It was a cookhouse, with the door open. I walked through a haze of barbeque smoke, followed by Yarham, toward the restaurant at the front. Nobody seemed to take notice of us. We slipped out the front door, and heads down, dodged down alleys toward our rendezvous. At one point we had to pause to make sure we were going the right way and Yarham held my arm.

"Some questions arising out of that, Captain," he said, blocking me from moving.

"Like, how did Trank know we were there? Maybe he was just searching routinely," I said.

"How many bars are there in central Havana? Big coincidence turning up at the Herradura. And if he followed us, why wait until after our meeting?" Yarham's head was inclined quizzically.

"He was tipped off?"

"By our MI6 colleague, perhaps, Captain?"

"That's uncharitable, Yarham. Maybe Neville has unintentionally let his CIA friends know he has pals coming to town, and they're following *him*, to get a line on us," I reasoned.

"Despite what you said about telling nobody?"

"Perhaps he let it slip before that, before we even arrived, said he had a couple of guys coming in from the States."

"He did look taken aback when you told him to keep quiet. But we're keeping our meeting with him?"

"We have to take the chance, Yarham. We need the weapons, and we need the disguise material."

"You have a gun, and a disguise won't be much use if Neville can't be trusted, Captain."

Yarham was right, but I blustered on. "True, but it's my gut feeling we ought to do this."

As soon as we appeared in the cramped, narrow shop, lined with dusty radios and record players, each bearing garish signs blaring their cheapness, a black Cuban greeted us and led us to the back room. Neville was there, looking nervous, sweating too much for a long-time resident. He held a backpack in his hand.

"It's all in here. Not the stuff you asked for this morning or the cuffs. I'll deliver that to your place as soon as I can. If you want to get back to me at any time, go to the bar, buy a drink, and leave afterwards. I'll be there twenty-four hours later."

"That's a bit like sending smoke signals," Yarham said.

"Make it two hours," I said.

"No. It's the best I can do," Neville said, seeming pleased at the delay. "I have to rely on a man to come to me, and I live quite a way from here."

"Does your man have to go on horseback?" Yarham asked.

"Look, Neville. These are prehistoric communications you've set up. We may need assistance quickly."

"Sorry. I don't know anything about your mission. It's the best I can do."

I made a mental note to deal with Neville later, in my report. "Good old MI6," I said, taking the pack and testing its weight. It was solid. I thought of questioning Neville about the CIA pursuers, and decided it would give away more than it revealed. I shrugged my shoulders in desperation. "We're out of here."

Yarham felt the pack uncertainly as I hefted it. "Could I see if I have a right-handed gun, sir?"

I hadn't thought to check the contents. I dropped the pack on the floor and looked inside. Neville closed the door. The two cheap flickknives worked well enough. Then I pulled out a 9 mm Colt semi-automatic. I slid out the empty magazine clip and racked the mechanism. The gun was new, in fine working order. Yarham tested the other.

Yarham plunged his hand into the pack and retrieved two boxes of shells. With one of his daffy grins he held out the boxes so I could see the labels; they were .38 shells. "Tricky loading with these, Captain."

I looked at Neville.

"Shit!" Neville started miserably, "They gave me the wrong ones. Give me those, and I'll get some more to you tonight."

We made our way cautiously west across the city to the Buena Vista area in the Playa district, where the house was. We took most of the day, dallying in bars, travelling on buses, and waiting in a lonely spot in a nearby park until dark. Yarham told me his life story, and I entertained him with tales of my adventures at public school and Oxford. But then our talk turned to more serious matters, because I was conscious that the safe house was likely to be bugged, and we couldn't take the chance of doing any of our planning there.

"Do you have any doubts about our mission, sir?"

"Of course I do, Yarham. Any sensible person would. If it's true the CIA and C3 are fighting each other, and it seems to be, who can tell what the outcome of this nuclear threat will be?"

"I was thinking along a different line, Captain. Why have we been sent here? I mean, *two people*, when they could have sent ten or fifty, or alerted the Cuban government, and made the whole thing into a huge search and destroy mission?"

"I can think of a lot of reasons. Politics. We can't expect intelligence agencies to do the sensible or even the obvious thing. Neither the Disciples nor the CIA really know how urgent the threat is, and they seem to be assuming they have sufficient time. I guess that with all our sophisticated surveillance machinery there's a reluctance to believe that such a threat could be brought to fruition without it being known long in advance. Second, the Disciples want to get one over the CIA. They don't want a CIA triumph here; that would reflect credit on the President. They also want to dislodge the President. So they want the problem to escalate to a crisis, as in 1962, to show the President and the CIA are inept. Then they will take a last-minute victory by forcing the bombing of Cuba, engineered by their own presidential candidate, McDonald, and right-wingers amongst the Joint Chiefs of Staff. We will presumably have found and passed the necessary information to them to enable them to pinpoint the strike."

"Humble information-gatherers."

"Humble, but not minor, Yarham. Yes, we're confirming the map references so they can zero in the bombs. And they know we probably have more chance of finding out something useful than if they sent an army of lead-footed agents in."

We agreed that this was more or less the rationale of what we were doing, and although Yarham mumbled something about not being entirely convinced that we were working in a just cause, I pointed out that the ultimate safety of people on the US mainland was in issue, and I suggested that we should leave the politics to those who seemed to know so much. Yarham assented, and we decided to move on in good faith.

The safe house was in a middle-class district of modest detached houses of two or three storeys, walled and heavily barred against burglars. As we – alone – moved along the street, the dogs behind the walls stirred and barked excitedly. There was no sign of life in the house, no light from the windows. Yarham rang the entry-phone, and when I was beginning to think we must have the wrong address, the speaker came to life with a mumbled answer.

"This is Wolf," I said. Eventually the gate was opened and we were led inside by a brown boy of about eighteen, wearing only a pair of shorts. Pedro, the man I had been told was in charge, was waiting, smoking a cigar, coughing and dropping the ash down his T-shirt on to his paunch.

"So senors. I show you your rooms. Very, how you say, very leetle? Not much. OK for a short stay. I bring you food and drink."

The house was, as Pedro said, plain. It was just about devoid of furniture. Pedro lived in a caretaker's apartment in the basement. The reception and dining rooms were empty, bare boards with fade marks on the wallpaper where pictures had hung. Another room contained a kitchen table and half a dozen plastic chairs. The bedrooms had only single beds with bare mattresses and a small dresser. All the floors and walls were bare.

"Lavish," Yarham said.

I didn't like the place either, but we made the best of it. Pedro brought chilli beans and rice with enchiladas and salad to the kitchen table. We had a couple of bottles of wine, and played checkers provided by Pedro until the early hours. We did not talk about the job until we retired to the bathroom, and sat on the edge of the bath with the taps full on.

I said I had little doubt that MI6, under the leadership of Amory, was fully supportive of me. Neville was either a bored operative who had gone to sleep in a comfortable post, or he was working with the CIA on his own initiative.

"Hasn't got anything much right, has he, sir? No usable guns, only a couple of flickknives."

The problem with intelligence work," I said, "is that you began to question the bona fides of everybody around you. Maybe we're a bit paranoid about Neville. Let's assume, for the moment, that he's an idiot, a Brit who's gone native, screwed himself up on whisky and sun and cheap jiniteras."

"A bold assumption, Captain, if I may say so."

I began to wonder how long it would be before Carmelli ran us down. After I had switched out the bare overhead bulb in my bedroom that night, I spent time at the window, looking out on to the ill-lit street, listening to the occasional dog, starting at shadows, wondering if Yarham was right about Neville, and realising that we had not even started our urgent mission.

17

In the morning, I went with Yarham to a cheap men's outfitter recommended by Pedro and we purchased more relaxed clothes, slacks, loafers, T-shirts and light jackets, sunglasses and baseball caps. I consigned the remnants of my Mexican car-dealer outfit to the garbage with pleasure. Then I called the number I had been given for our Cuban contact, mentioned the number of my call box to the answerphone at the other end, and waited. An hour later there was a ring. A woman's voice.

"Wolf calling."

With very little hesitation, she answered, "Go to the fountain in the Heroes of the Revolution Park. Carry a bunch of flowers. In two hours."

I purchased a small bunch of flowers at the gate of the park, and sat nursing it on the edge of the fountain at the appointed time. I sent Yarham off to circle the area and see if he could spot anybody who might be interested in me.

It was an exquisite day, warm but not blistering, with a clear, duck-egg blue sky. A few people were resting or strolling near the fountain which sent a cooling mist into the air. The colours of the grass and flowers and trees seemed unnaturally bright. Three children tried to sell me a candy bar in a crumpled wrapper, which I purchased after we had all laughed a lot. Then a dirty and garishly dressed beggar approached me. He held out his tin and I put a few pesos in. He looked at this, frowned and rattled it in my face for more.

I eventually gave him more, and he wandered off, spitting discontent through the stumps of his teeth.

A girl had taken a seat on the wall a few feet away while I had been occupied. She turned in my direction. She was pale and quite pretty.

I smiled and put my hand on my chest. "Wolf."

"Wolf?" she said quietly, inclining her head. "Those are pretty flowers you have, what are they called?

I held up the red blossoms of hibiscus. "The yellow roses of Texas," I said.

"Follow me," she said.

I walked a few yards behind her. She was wearing a thin knee-length dress which was smart and expensive. She had a tooled leather handbag over her shoulder, and the way she stuck her chest out suggested complete confidence. She left the path after a hundred yards, and began to walk up the slight slope into the trees, tiptoeing so that the thin heels of her white slingback shoes didn't sink into the turf. I caught up with her in the seclusion of the wood. When she turned to me, I could see she wasn't as young as I had imagined. She was a tall, well proportioned woman in her late twenties.

I presented the flowers to her with a slight bow, and she took them gracefully.

"How can I help? And will you please take your cap and dark glasses off so I can see you?"

This was more my idea of what my role *ought* to be, assignations with beautiful spies in a garden. I did as she had requested, and I fancied she was pleased with the result. She studied me for a few moments and then nodded her head. "You're very fair, aren't you?"

"And you, senora, are both dark-haired, and very fair."

This puzzled her, but she said nothing. She waited on me. "I want to know about the terrorist missiles," I said.

She hesitated, thought for a moment, and then gave a small smile. "It's expensive."

"How much?"

"Half a million dollars in cash."

She had named the price as though it was absolute.

"I don't have that much on me."

"But you can get it – the richest nation in the world."

"How do I know the information will be good?"

"You don't. You have to take the risk."

"It seems very risky."

"Not if the security of your country is at stake."

She had a point. "OK, I'll get it. Shall we go and have a drink?"

"No. You must wait here until I've gone. Get in touch when you have the money."

"Wait. What kind of information can you give me? The position of the sites, the state of readiness. Where supplies are deployed. How many warheads there are in the country. Where they're located. How many people are involved. Who they are. Where they live. These are the things I need to know."

"Sure. I'll get everything I can."

"How long after I call you?"

"A few hours maybe. I know it's urgent."

"OK. What shall I call you?" I asked, but I didn't think she'd offer a name.

"Dolores," she said, and as she brushed past me I could smell her faint perfume in contrast to the rank smell of the vegetation around us. I noticed that her left hand was loaded with a wedding band and two sparkling diamond rings.

I waited for a couple of minutes as she had asked, and when I came out of the trees she had gone. But Yarham would have watched our contact, and I had instructed him to follow her. I waited for Yarham in the park, fending off beggars, children, and jiniteros and occasionally discussing with various vendors the varieties of dope, booze and people that were for sale. I also composed, in my head, my satphone message to C3 calling for the money. Half a million dollars was nothing when I thought of the crisis, and C3 would readily see it that way. Yarham returned in about an hour and a half, quite pleased with himself.

"I followed her in a cab. I told the cab driver she was my wife and she was screwing around. He wouldn't let her out of sight. You'd have thought she was *his* wife. She went to a very plush condo in the Flores area. Seventeenth floor."

"Can we find out who owns or leases the seventeenth floor?"

"I already have. There are three big apartments, three names."

"A Dolores amongst them?" I didn't for a moment think she would have given me her real name, but one asks the obvious.

"Carlos and Dolores Martinez."

"Well done, Yarham. I wonder what Dolores does. She sounds bossy, like some kind of manager, an accountant perhaps."

"One of them has a law firm, Herrera & Martinez. It's on the name-plate."

As there would be a delay in getting the money, we agreed that Yarham would follow Dolores for the next few days and find out as much about her as he could. I would visit the ex-missile sites and see if there were any signs of activity, or any other clues that might lead me to the terrorists; which actually meant I would idle about on bus journeys or stay in the house and read a book.

Yarham, with his fiery hair hidden beneath a baseball cap, dark glasses and a dense black walrus moustache, had some further success in tracking Dolores Martinez. She might have been a lawyer or perhaps a clerk in her husband's office. Yarham found out where her office was, where she went for lunch when she was alone, where she shopped at lunchtime, and he followed her on an afternoon visit to another apartment in the Siboney district. After sharing a bottle of aguardiente with the concierge, he learned that these visits were regular, one afternoon a week. The apartment was occupied by Alfredo Arias, a senior figure in government – Yarham concluded this from the fact that Senor Arias was driven to his work at the ministry each day by a chauffeur.

"Is she a lover, a messenger, what?" I asked Yarham.

"Senor Arias is always at home when she calls. The concierge reckons he's an expert with women, and if he's ever seen a lady going to meet her lover, she is the one."

I felt a pang of envy of the bureaucrat Arias. Dolores was an interesting creature. I requested information about Arias on the satphone – my messages were encrypted and sent in a microsecond burst, almost undetectable, except perhaps by the latest Russian equipment. The answer, similarly dispatched, confirmed Arias's high governmental rank, and said he was regarded as a possibly friendly independent.

I was becoming bored with my fruitless journeys to find old missile sites. And a little tired of Yarham's tongue-in-cheek questions about my success. I decided upon a slightly different tactic. I waited in the lobby of Dolores's building until she came out for lunch. The first day, she had a meeting with a woman. The second day she was alone and I followed her, determined to speak. She went into a fish bar – not a place I would have chosen to dine in myself. I slipped into the seat next to her. The customers sat on high stools randomly next to each other, and the fishy delicacies were visible beneath the glass counter. The odour was very strong, the décor rough and the prices cheap, but the place seemed clean and efficient.

I removed my cap and shades. "Hullo Dolores."

She looked at me, crestfallen. "You've been following me."

"No, I wouldn't do that. I had business in the building, and when I came out of the elevator I saw you. I admit I followed you in here, but I do want my lunch. By the way, my name is Dan Garcia."

I could see that her better judgment was telling her that the chances of a casual meeting were remote, and that she should leave immediately, but she turned, eyed me slowly, sighed, and said, "All right. Let's lunch."

I ordered glasses of cold white wine and we picked at the quite tasty plates of raw white fish and prawns in vinegar, while she told me of her education in the USA and Spain, and her husband's busy corporate law practice, her husband, and her childless marriage.

The best way to sell a second-hand Porsche to an older man or woman is to ask about their children. I was selling myself rather than a Porsche on this occasion, but the same principle applied. People delight in titillating their own egos by talking about themselves, and they see their children as reflections of themselves which they like to dilate upon, either to commend or complain about. Dolores had no children but she did have a story of a neat, orderly, middle-class life.

I couldn't understand why she was involved in spying, but that wasn't a question to table. For my part, because one has to trade intimacies, I admitted I was English, American by adoption, an exporter and importer of cars based in Mexico City, doing a one-off task out of loyalty to my country. We parted warmly after three quarters of an hour, and I knew I had penetrated her skin. Perhaps we had told each other a pack of lies about ourselves, but there was a warmth there, a connection.

Four days following the request to Washington for funds, I arrived at the safe house after another frustrating day of touring a site. When Pedro admitted me he said, "Your friend is here." I was mystified for a moment. Then I walked into our spartan dining room to find Yarham, and sitting across the table from him, on which there was a small suitcase, the bulky figure of Kershaw, his face cracked in one of his mirthless grins. I tried not to show my disappointment.

"I broughtcha the lolly. The whole three-quarters of a million."

I had thought it prudent to apply the Kershaw technique, and request a sum to cover 'additional expenses'. "Good. That was a quick delivery. But surely you didn't bring that through customs?"

"I picked it up in town from the Bank of Chile by special arrangement."

"I could have done that."

"Gerry didn't want you to be troubled. He wants me to work with you."

"I don't have a job for you," I said, silently cursing Gerry Clark, who had managed to get his way. Clark didn't trust me, but I couldn't expect that he would, spook to spook.

"Then I'll find one for myself," Kershaw snorted.

But, despite my annoyance, it occurred to me that Kershaw was like a Rottweiler who could be used against Carmelli and his goons if necessary. I retreated, told him our problems about being followed in a whisper. Kershaw relished the idea of tangling with Carmelli. Then I pointed to the ceiling which dried up the flow of talk.

Dolores and I met to discuss the exchange of money and

information at a small and unfashionable restaurant in La Habana Vieja. We had a secluded table. My guess was that the designer-label Dolores did not mess with the dirty business of exchanging information, that she was really a middleman for somebody else, perhaps even Alfredo Arias.

When we were settled over iced Campari sodas, she said, "You bring the money, and I arrange for you to meet the man."

"Who is he?"

"An important person in government."

"Why is he doing this?"

"For the same reason you are. Patriotism."

"Patriotism at a price?"

"He must fund the political movement which will save Cuba."

"Is it Arias?"

She looked shocked. "It's a man. What do you know about Arias?"

I gave an unconcerned gesture. "The people who asked me to do this are carrying on intelligence work all the time. Senor Arias is a respected figure."

"Bring the money. The meeting place will be a hotel room. Tomorrow. I will not be there. The man will be. You have to trust us."

We had hardly touched our salads. Dolores looked bright-eyed, excited. "Have some more wine," I insisted, pouring from the bottle of white wine I had ordered.

We finished the bottle, talking idly, but not focusing too much on precisely what we were saying. We were in a cocoon together, apart from the other diners. I was conscious of the sensual proximity of our bodies, and it was more intoxicating than wine. Cuba is a place for love-making, relaxed, warm, and fleshy.

"Why don't we continue this at my hotel?"

She gave a small sign of assent. There was no doubt about her attraction to me. How much of her feeling was counterfeit, spurred by lurking suspicion, and perhaps fear that I wasn't what I seemed, I didn't know or even care at that point. I had no hotel, but I soon remedied this when our cab arrived at the Hotel Santa Isabel in Plaza de Armas. It was stupid to head for such an opulent venue, but my thoughts were pelvicly inclined at that moment, and nothing but the best surroundings would suffice.

I pushed my Mexican passport, containing a credit card and a hundred-dollar bill, across to the reception clerk, and was rapidly allocated a superior room.

The clerk leaned across the desk toward me. "For you, senor, it's no problem. But your Cuban friend..."

We both looked across the lobby to where Dolores was sitting, straight-backed and proud, on the edge of a chair, flicking the pages of a magazine, oblivious. Did she really look like one of the jiniteros? I took another hundred-dollar note, slipped it into my passport, and handed it to the clerk. "She's a Spanish lawyer."

The clerk extracted and palmed the note expertly, moved his head, giving me the accolade for imagination. "As you say, Senor Garcia." He slid the entry-card across the desk.

As soon as we crossed the threshold of the room, Dolores said, "This is lovely!" She unceremoniously dropped her bag on the carpet, kicked off her shoes, and walked to the window. She drew back the curtains to reveal the trees of the Plaza sleeping heavily in the heat. I stood close behind her, my botanical interests weakening. She turned, and wrapped her arms around me, fragrant and soft.

18

The room had a fine view of the tops of the lime trees, the basking buildings, and the deceptively gentle blue sky touching the distant sea. Dolores had pale skin which, with her ebony hair and eyes, suggested a cream veneer over mahogany blackness. She insisted she was a creole of pure Spanish descent, prized for her whiteness. It didn't matter a cent to me one way or another, but her admiration of the whiteness of my body was touching and useful, although she had seen very little of it.

I suspected Dolores wasn't a trained espionage agent but a go-between, acting perhaps out of patriotism or political loyalties or love. She could be objective and businesslike, but that was the façade of the lawyer which could possibly be pried away to reveal the yearning, sexually passionate woman underneath. She seemed to have little idea of the personal risk she was running. I liked her, and I was inclined to despise those who were using her.

Dolores disappeared for a moment to use the bathroom, and I plotted how to lure her from the floor to the bed, feeling that in a strange way, now that we were alone, she seemed more distant. On her return, Dolores opened the wardrobe doors and found an empty space. "You don't stay here at all?"

"No. I took the room for us, this afternoon. Because you are very beautiful."

She sat on the end of the bed and pulled a small chrome-plated semi-automatic pistol out of her handbag. "And I came here to find out more about you – but I liked you." She pointed the pistol at me.

"Is that a cigarette lighter?"

"I don't smoke."

"Let's go over the money exchange arrangements." I was hopeful that she would put the gun away if she was at ease. And we might even use the bed.

"You come alone. You bring the money, you get the information. It's as simple as that," she said flatly.

Dolores might have been a woman whose tender feelings for a man could melt the trip-wires of her judgment, but I couldn't budge her. "It's a big risk," I protested. "The information might be poor, or I might be robbed or suckered in a con game."

"Sure it's a big risk. Yours. Now let's go." She stood up and walked to the door, still holding the gun.

We parted from the Santa Isabel with a meeting fixed for twelve noon the next day at a hotel out of town to be named.

At the safe house, Kershaw was restive with inaction, and inquisitive. Gerry Clark had never told him what was in the VRK file. All he knew was that our break-in at Pennsylvania Avenue had touched off another skirmish in the war with the CIA. I had no intention of telling him what Yarham and I were doing. I told him I had reservations about our MI6 contact, Neville, and that he had to keep watch in the house for the moment to protect us from the CIA goons.

That night I walked with Yarham in the park and we were able to talk.

"Don't you think it's all gone very smoothly with our Cuban contact, sir?"

"You mean too smoothly? We meet. She's beautiful. She leads us to the precise information we want. We pay. We catch a flight for Mexico City. Yes, it's a dream too easy, isn't it?"

"There might be a need to be prepared for action tomorrow when we hand over the money."

Yarham was right. It seemed to me to be preposterous to walk into a stranger's hotel room with half a million dollars in cash and hope you were going to get good value. Because it was sure that we weren't going to walk *out* of there with the money if we were disappointed with the information. But we had to find a way to act on the proposal. I thought of sending somebody; that meant going to the meeting without the money as a testing operation. Yarham? I couldn't ask him to do something I was hesitant to do myself. Well, I could, but I wasn't going to on this occasion.

"I'll send Kershaw. He can look after himself."

"I can tail him, and provide back-up if necessary," Yarham offered.

And so it was agreed. We returned to the house and brought Kershaw out into the street for a briefing. I told him it was a trial operation for a handover of the money and receipt of information. He was to assure himself as far as he could that the contact was genuine, to specify that we would choose the next meeting place and obtain a contact number. I explained that Yarham wouldn't be far away. It sounded simple.

Kershaw's small, white-cold eyes glinted in the dark as he absorbed the task. "What will you be doing?" he asked.

"I'll be in bed at the safe house, sipping my rum and Coke and reading a book. Do you want this job, or do you want out?"

"I can do it," he said offhandedly. "I need to know what the info you're payin' for is about."

"No you don't, and it's better for you if you don't," I said, perpetuating ignorance once again with use of one of my masters' hallowed phrases.

Kershaw was dispatched to an address in Santa Maria del Mar, a tourist hotel, received that morning from our contact number, with Yarham not far behind. Kershaw must have been observed carrying an empty suitcase for effect, and identified as a stranger, because when he arrived at room 412 of the Hotel Hermosa, it was locked and unoccupied. We were back where we began.

I arranged another meeting with Dolores Martinez. She was chilly, but agreed to meet at a room at the Santa Isabel. Dolores' capacity for passion did not overcome her petulance, and she remained as stand-offish as before. We had an inquest into the failure of our mission. Dolores opened with an icy indictment.

"You let me down," she said, turning her back on me, as though I was her lover.

"My friends wouldn't let me do it, Dolores. They said, *Send somebody to make better arrangements.* So I did, and it didn't work. OK. Let us try to do better."

"I got a lot of heat because you didn't show."

"I'm sorry about that, but at least we meet again..."

"This could go on all year!" she said impatiently.

"I don't mind. It would be a pleasure," I said.

"You're supposed to be on your country's business. Can't you be serious?"

"In return for the information I told you about, yes."

"Where, then?"

I had given thought to this – and to the possibility that Dolores would offer to do the deal. It seemed to me that one place was as vulnerable as another, and I had decided to sacrifice the safe house. I wanted to get Dolores on to unknown ground where I had support. Yarham, Kershaw and I could leave the house immediately after the handover. I told Dolores I would give her the address of a house when she was ready to come.

"Why not here? Then we can make love," she said, brushing her hand down my thigh in a gesture which seemed theatrical. She had to reach across the coffee table where we sat opposite each other.

"No."

I wasn't going to take the chance that she would send somebody into the hotel to whack me and collect the money. Her gesture was not loving, and half a million dollars was at stake.

Dolores was firm about the Santa Isabel, saying she couldn't go alone to a strange place, but I was equally adamant.

"You know you can trust me, Dolores. I care for you. If you bring the information, you go away with the money. This can't hurt you or your friends."

"You could take the secret information from me and send me away without the money," she protested. "Just like we could take your money and give you nothing. As I said when we met, the risk has to be yours."

"I represent the US government, Dolores. We wouldn't send you away without the money. We don't do business that way."

"Oh yes?"

I wasn't going to defend the morality of the US government in the face of her cynical stare. "Look, a compromise. We'll meet in a restaurant, do it in two instalments. I'll tell you what I need to know at our first meeting for two hundred and fifty thousand. If that goes OK, we set up another meet in the same or a different restaurant, for the rest of the info and the balance of payment."

"No way!" she said, firmly. "It has to be the whole amount… but a restaurant is OK."

Despite a little discomposure, Dolores was still thinking clearly. The concession to meet in a restaurant went some way toward restoring my belief in the genuineness of the deal. Perhaps Dolores's friends really were patriots working for a better Cuba, rather than conmen trying to fiddle the US government.

"Let's do that, Dolores. The total sum in a restaurant. But I name the restaurant."

"OK," she said, still distant.

That night, in the park, I explained the plan to Yarham, and we took a long cab ride to inspect a number of restaurants. Later, we discussed the different layouts, from Las Ruinas on Parque Lenin, to La Torre on the top floor of the Edificio Focsa, a hundred and twenty five metres above the city. The high restaurant had the advantage that if thieves snatched the money, they wouldn't be able to exit easily. Finally, however, we chose Los Dos Apostoles, a spacious, quiet, middle-class establishment in Vedado on Calle 16, approached through a short pedestrian shopping mall.

Yarham left a message at our contact number in the morning, and made a reservation at Los Dos Apostoles.

Having debated the merits of chaining the case to my wrist, I loaded the cool half-million in hundred-dollar note packets into a backpack, and slung it over my shoulder. I was wearing a plain white T-shirt with a thin, cream linen jacket which concealed the bulge of the Colt in my waistband. I arrived in a cab at the entrance to the shopping mall at one pm, the appointed time. Yarham would be in the crowd watching, but I couldn't see him.

I paid the driver generously with a ten dollar bill, and struggled out of the rusty old 1939 Ford cab on to the sidewalk, hitching the pack. I was tense, but I was eased by seeing Dolores Martinez about twenty feet away, watching in the reflection of the window of a jeweller's shop. She looked at her own diamante wristwatch, squared her shoulders and began to move down the mall ahead of me, toward the restaurant.

I had the feeling that this was going to go well. There was a press of people around me. Suddenly a man stepped forward, a nondescript mulatto in a suit with an open shirt, and a sincere look of concern. "Excuse me, senor," he said, pointing above my head. I was distracted for a second. I looked up to see if anything was going to fall on me. Then there were two men alongside me, containing me gently from either side. They could have been passers-by in a sudden crush. One said quietly, "You'll be OK, senor."

Too late I realised I was being held in a vice. I felt the tugging at my back. Another person was behind me, taking the weight of the pack. And then, as suddenly as the press of bodies had started, I was on my own, packless, with a fragment of the shoulder strap, which had been razored off, at my feet. I stopped while the crowd surged past. I spun around, saw Yarham's undisguised jaw. He veered off in pursuit of the men.

I had been mugged like a greenhorn tourist in front of a hundred people, hardly one of whom gave me a glance, but hurried on down the mall. I was torn between pursuit of the men, or Dolores Martinez. I couldn't have recognised any of the men. I felt very, very sick and angry. I blundered a few yards to the doors of Los Dos Apostoles, shoving people out of my way.

I pushed past the head waiter to survey the room. I scanned every chair and table. Just quiet people eating or preparing to eat, taking no interest in me. No Dolores. I walked into the woman's lavatory. No Dolores – only a bouncer outside wanting to know what I was doing. Yarham, breathing heavily, appeared beside me.

"The maitre d' says no woman like Martinez has come in here in the last few minutes. The thieves got the bag away on a motor scooter. No chance to get them. I didn't even realise you'd been boxed in by the thieves until they broke away. It all looked so innocent. After they cut off your pack, Captain, they passed it back along the mall to other members of their team like seasoned rugby players. They just melted away. I'm fairly sure the pack went with a pillion passenger on the motor scooter."

"How's that for an MI6 operation, Yarham?"

"Leave it out of your memoirs, sir."

19

I was not so concerned about losing half a million dollars of the US taxpayers' money as I was about my complete misjudgment of Dolores Martinez. Her portrayal of the soft, conscience-bitten intermediary had been consummate, when she was actually a brass-necked thief. I couldn't whine to Clark, Fernandez, Bolding & Co, *you gave me the name of a thief.* Dealing with crooks was part of my game. This one was on me. My cock had run away with my brains and our task was no further ahead.

I sat on the wall of the park with Yarham that night, and we shared a bottle of rum, laced with Coke. I was punishing myself. We had checked on the Martinez apartment and made enquiries at the legal office, only to learn that both Dolores and her husband had fled. The apartment was available for letting, and Carlos Martinez was taking a sabbatical from his practice in Acapulco.

It was impossible to keep the failure, and at least an outline of events, from Kershaw, who was ecstatic. He rocked with gales of hoarse laughter: "She made a cunt of both the big dicks!" Needless to say, I did not invite him to join Yarham and me on the wall of the park and share our bottle.

"I wouldn't worry too much about it, sir. We still have a quarter of a million petty cash."

"I'd like to... " I was going to say "wring Dolores's neck," but I had to admit she was an alluring woman, and her duplicity would have made her more interesting were the results not so personally embarrassing.

I took a grave line. "We're not getting anywhere, Yarham."

"True, Capain. Sadly true. I suppose we could check out the site positions you were given more carefully," Yarham said, I think flippantly. He had never supported my idea since the *santeria* ceremony.

"Poking around in shitty tunnels, abandoned long ago? No, Yarham, we have only one worthwhile contact left in this place. Do you know who that is?"

"Could it be our colleagues in the CIA?"

"Regrettably."

"Ah, yes. You mean we... what do we do?"

"We take the initiative with them, Yarham, find out what they know. Then at least we might make some progress."

"When you think of it, Captain, the CIA have had since the last crisis in 1962 to find out about the possibility of a missile strike, and all that diddle about lost warheads. I daresay they have found out *something*. But how can we actually lay our hands on it?"

"I'm not too optimistic, but it's our only chance. We target Carmelli tomorrow. Find out where he and his boys operate from, and..." my voice faded.

"And what, sir?"

"Mmmmm. We'll work that out when we've found them."

With these simple – crude – intentions, we retired to the house, dined on Pedro's tasty brand of chilli beans, rice and tomatoes, and finished off the rum with Kershaw, enduring his wisecracks about the mugging. I promised Kershaw an active role tomorrow, although, other than a raid on the Excelsior Hotel, I had formulated no clear plan. Fortunately, he was used to taking orders, even when he didn't like them, and it was only necessary to hush my lips to stop his questions. By eleven o'clock we three had settled a second bottle of rum. We were drunk, and ready for bed.

I slept dreamlessly until about two am by the illuminated digits of the bedroom clock. I woke up suddenly, with a headache from the rum, sensing somebody in the room. It wasn't a dream when the light went on. A man was at the end of the bed, levelling a gun at me. He had a pyramidal head, a small shaven dome, broadening out into a wide jaw which sank into his wider neck. His thin mouth, turned down at the corners, was like the trap of an excavator. It was Carmelli.

"Geddup Mr FBI Smartass."

Another, younger man, whom I recognised as the tranquiliser gunner at the Comodoro Hotel, swept into the room. He clipped me over the jaw with the butt of his automatic, pushed my head and shoulders down, and snapped a pair of handcuffs on my wrists from behind. The noises I could hear from adjoining rooms suggested the same thing had happened there. Yarham and Kershaw, handcuffed, were herded into my room.

Trank threw a pile of clothes at us, collected from the other two bedrooms. "Phooie! You guys smell like a distillery. Had a party, eh? You better dress each other best you can," he said with a cackle. "It could get cold – and hot where you're going."

"What happened to Pedro?" I asked.

"The gateman? He moved out. Went back to the farm," Trank said.

It was hardly possible to dress while handcuffed, and it was a bad sign that our captors didn't particularly care whether we were dressed or not. We pulled on trousers and wrapped shirts around our bare shoulders, helping each other, while Carmelli and his two men searched the premises. They found the only things I had to hide – the quarter million dollars and the satellite phone, which were in my bedroom wall, behind a loose board.

"We can always do with a bit of small change," Carmelli said, shaking the bag of money. It could have been a bag of bird droppings for all the pleasure he showed.

Then they gagged us, and manhandled us downstairs and out to the street, where we were pitched in the back of an old van like sides of meat, and our ankles were hobbled.

The journey in the back of the van took a half-hour and ended with the vehicle edging down a slope. I could hear the swish of the sea, and there was a humid, salty smell. We were covered with blankets, carried out of the van, and dumped one by one, in the cockpit of what smelled like a fishing boat. The boat's diesel engines were already thumping slowly.

I could feel Carmelli and his men settling themselves on board near to us. The craft seemed small. The engines revved, and the boat began to move. After a few slight swells as we left what must have been a harbour or a river mouth, the hull of the boat settled to cut smoothly through the waters of the Straits of Florida.

It wasn't hard to work out what was going to happen. Carmelli wouldn't be taking us on a voyage if all he wanted to do was to grill us. He could have done that at the house, or elsewhere on land. And he surely wasn't returning us to the US. We were going to be shark bait. It was another case for the *Gas Chamber Alternative*, except that we didn't have the immediate freedom required for that response. It was impossible, at the moment, to see how we could make any physical move.

When I thought it over, I questioned how Carmelli found our house. We were coming and going a lot, and as we always wore baseball caps, dark glasses and sometimes a moustache or wig, it was only remotely possible that we were followed to the house. It was also possible that Neville had wittingly or unwittingly turned us in. The timely withdrawal of Pedro seemed to confirm that Neville had something to do with it. But the important point, and what made me almost despair, was that we got drunk and went off guard. I had encouraged Kershaw to drink last evening, but on any other night he had the guard duty, and we would have had a reasonable chance of defending ourselves. I had made two abysmal mistakes in twenty-four hours, and I set about thinking how to get out of this one.

After about quarter of an hour at sea, the blankets and gags were removed and we sat up. The boat was indeed small, about twenty feet, with only a small wheelhouse. The lights of Havana were falling away fast, and we were heading into a womb of blackness, with only an occasional distant flash of lightning on the sea. After about another half an hour, Havana looked like a diamond and gold necklace on a black velvet cushion at Cartiers'.

Carmelli cut the engines. The boat rocked gently. The sea seemed untroubled. The faces of Kershaw and Yarham, lit dimly by the instrument lights, had hardened into painful lines as they waited their fate. Harkness and Burton (I had picked up their names as we travelled) sat together on the stern transom, both nursing Uzis.

Carmelli came out of the wheelhouse, bent down and kicked me in the ribs. "You're going to tell me all about your career, Mr FBI, and who the hell you are. You sure gave me some pain."

"And then?" I asked.

"Don't be too concerned about the programme, asshole. If you talk good, I might just crush your balls and let you take a late night swim with the skinny dippers at Playa Santa Maria del Mar." His guffaw sounded cruel and the other two joined in.

I knew this was coming, and I was prepared to talk for a thousand and one nights. I thought a measure of truth might help, might pull these animals, who were supposed to be on our side, around – if they believed me.

"You want to know what happened – I'll tell you. I'm an MI6 agent, Roger Conway…"

"That's the funny accent, is it?"

"I was asked to get hold of the VRK file by the NSA. They arranged entry to your offices through a contact in the CIA. The NSA were worried they didn't know what you guys were doing, and thought things might get out of hand."

"Bullshit!" Carmelli said, but I could see that inside his pyramid skull he was turning over the serious possibility that what I had said was the truth.

"Which government you working for, scumbag?" Harkness said, coming forward and kicking me in the spine.

I was ready to go into a heavy routine of pleading – we were in sister services, we served the same government, I was only following orders – all that, and beneath the deck grille, I had my hands on one of the bilge cocks. If all else failed, perhaps I'd send us all down. In some ways, the thought of surrendering to the warm water was less fearsome than being kicked into unconsciousness by these hoodlums.

At that moment, a searchlight flashed on from a hundred yards away. Another boat had drifted down on us unseen. Carmelli gunned the engine of our boat, and headed away at full throttle. A loud Spanish voice on a megaphone commanded us to stop. Burton fired a burst back at the searchlight, shattering it. Our boat had an astonishing turn of speed from its twin engines, and I now suspected it was more than a fishing craft.

I could see that Carmelli was confident of outrunning what might have been a pirate boat, but was more likely a Cuban patrol boat. If it was a patrol boat, and Carmelli was caught, he would be in difficulty explaining his three prisoners, and the quarter million dollars. I assumed he must have stashed the money on board for safe keeping – he wouldn't have left it in the van.

To the Cuban coastguards, the scene on our boat would look like a drug vendetta. And I wasn't sure if it was capable of being explained to the satisfaction of the Cuban government – mistakes and misunderstandings in foreign intelligence services – if Carmelli chose to stop the craft and we were all handed over to the police. What were we doing in Cuba anyway? We had entered unlawfully. Not even the intervention of our own governments could answer that satisfactorily. We would be outlaws in the eyes of the Cuban government, however patriotic our calling.

Carmelli's decision to run was therefore the right one, and in any event, once he had fled and returned fire, there was no going back.

The pursuers didn't give up, as Carmelli's cursing confirmed. The persistence of the chase meant that it was a Cuban government boat. Carmelli's two gunners loosed off more bursts in the direction of the patrol boat, and there was an answering flash of firing. Yarham, Kershaw and I sank down as slugs slammed into the woodwork of the hull and cabin. The pursuer had what sounded like a medium machine-gun firing bullets of around 15 mm, capable of smashing the wooden superstructure of our craft to chips.

Carmelli, seemingly a desk-bound slob, handled the boat with the verve of an experienced skipper. After a few minutes I spelled out of Carmelli's oaths that the Cuban boat was about as fast as ours, and it apparently had a radar system that kept it on our course. Feinting and weaving in the dark would not achieve much.

The Cubans began to open up more consistently with

the machine-gun. The deckhouse glass was shattered, and Carmelli wounded. He collapsed in the wheelhouse. Burton took over the helm, and changed course frantically, keeping his head as low as possible, but the patrol boat was always there in the darkness, a nemesis.

"Help Gino, will ya!" Burton yelled at Harkness.

Harkness crawled forward, and bent over Carmelli, groping around his throat for a pulse. "Jesus, Gino's *dead!*" He looked at his bloody hand and sounded surprised.

As Harkness was pulling himself upright, Burton jerked the wheel to the left in a violent attempt to shake off the Cuban boat, and Harkness, shocked for a moment by the discovery of his dead boss, was taken off balance as he moved aft. The hull lurched steeply, and it looked for a moment that it might take water and swamp. Harkness let out a choking cry, and toppled over the low transom into the water. His cries were lost in the roar of the engine, and the crack of the patrol boat's machine-gun.

Burton, engrossed in the pursuit, did not hear Harkness's cries. In a few moments he turned round from the wheel to look for his partner. "Where's Jed?" he screamed.

"He fell overboard," I shouted.

"Oh for fuck's sake, what are we doing?" Burton moaned in desperation, alone with his prisoners and a gunboat blasting his ass.

Burton was like a kamikaze at the controls of the power boat roaring into pitch darkness. He was howling to himself like an animal.

Below the open-planked deck which supported us, I had kept my hands on the bilge cock. Being taken by the Cubans had become emphatically the lesser of evils, even if it meant time in a Cuban jail. When there are only nasty options available, the least worst becomes desirable. My thoughts about having ruined my career disappeared. Through the gap between the decking and the hull I deliberately started to turn the ring screw, and felt a rush of cool water as the bilges began to fill. The craft pounded on, but soon began to lose its top speed, and respond more sluggishly.

The water rose to the level of the deck planking. Burton, crazed, noticed the difference in speed and handling of the craft too late. He left the throttles wide open, and stepped down toward us, seeing the deck awash.

"We're fucking well sinking!" he shouted.

I could have lashed out at Burton with my feet, and it was likely that I could have brought him down, and we three manacled men might have overcome him. Or he might have retaliated, and gone completely beserk. Instead, I shouted, "It's all over, man. Give up, unless you want to swim to Florida."

Burton turned back to the wheelhouse in desperation, shut off the throttles, and hunched over the controls, sobbing.

The boat heaved to, rocking in the swell, settling deeper. The patrol boat was out there, quiet. Another searchlight lit us. It took five minutes of questions and instructions over the loudspeaker before the Cubans felt it was safe to come alongside. Our craft now had only three or four inches of freeboard. The three of us inside were virtually afloat. I tried to persuade Burton to release us, in case we drowned, but he was too distraught to move. The Cubans eventually persuaded him to act.

"I don't have the key!" he shouted. "Harkness had it."

I explained to the Cuban lieutenant, with Yarham's help as interpreter, that Burton and the dead Carmelli had robbed us, and were going to drown us when we were intercepted. I didn't mention Harkness. Burton could only swear incoherently in response. The Cubans considered the position quietly. They probably didn't believe me, or care.

"We take you all into custody and investigate. Maybe you stay in jail for a long time. Maybe years," the lieutenant in charge smiled.

That much was true. Months, probably years, in a Cuban jail. Our mission aborted. My career in MI6 finished. I told the lieutenant that there was a bag of money behind the controls. He waded forward and found it. He opened the bag and saw the profusion of neat bundles of notes. Dawn was lighting the sky faintly. I watched the faces of the lieutenant and his wheelman. It was likely that they had never seen so much money before that they could actually touch.

"What is this, senor?" the lieutenant asked.

"My present to you for saving our lives. Two hundred and fifty thousand dollars. You take the money. Put us ashore at the nearest beach, and we will go away. We will vanish, vamoose, never to trouble you again. And please get these cuffs off."

The Cubans were impassive, but clearly wanted time to consider, and we were moved from the launch at gunpoint to a lockup cage on the rear deck of the gunboat. We watched the *Santa Maria* (only now could I see the noble name) go down with Carmelli's body. The fact that the Cubans didn't want to save the body seemed significant.

"Think they'll buy it, sir?"

"Wouldn't you? You're a coastguard. Maybe you have a secure job and a small salary, but it's risky work, and you have a family who need things, things you know you'll never ever be able to provide, and suddenly you stumble across a pot of gold that's yours for the taking. You see, Yarham, it's one thing or the other. If they hand us to the police, they have to hand over the money to the police too."

"Have to?" Kershaw said.

"If we were to tell the police that there's a big sum of

money missing, appropriated by the coastguard, the police would be unrelenting in their investigation and surveillance of the crew. These men know that. It's not worth the pain. On the contrary, if the coastguards let us go, they know *we're* not going to come back, or complain about loss of the money. They're in the clear with the money. As far as they're concerned we're running drugs. We're criminals. We'd only end up in custody if we tried to complain about the coastguards. No, it's money for them, freedom for us."

"Why are they taking so long then?" Kershaw asked.

"Counting the pile so they can believe their luck, and fondling a few notes to see if they're counterfeit. Reasoning out the sequence of events I just gave you."

Without any further words with us, the wheelman started the patrol launch for the Havana shore at full power. It wasn't clear to me where he was going for half an hour, until he cut the engine a hundred yards off the Boca de Cojimar. While the boat pitched, the crew put a small inflatable in the water, and a crewman climbed in and started the outboard. Yarham looked at me, his jaw sagged down in a grin.

The lieutenant spoke to us when the door of our cage was opened. "I'm going to take a chance with you and put you ashore. You'll end up in plenty trouble if you get in the hands of the coastguard or the police, so don't get caught." One of his men with a giant pair of cable-cutters clipped the chains on our cuffs.

"OK, thanks officer," I said.

We had a deal that was cheap at the price.

166

20

I stood on the quay at Boca de Cojimar. It was five in the morning. The low sun had turned the sea to molten brass, and it hushed on the sand. The houses along the front were shuttered and yellow in the early light. A pair of gulls swooped overhead; the quay with its lumpy flagstones was deserted. I was chilled, dressed only in a wet pair of trousers, with a shirt wrapped around my neck like a scarf. I squeezed the water out of the shirt and put it on. We were all stilled for a moment, stunned by our ordeal.

I whispered to Yarham, "We need to talk to Burton."

Burton had not fared well. He had regained some composure, but was still reeling from the death of his partners. He was probably wondering whether to try to break away, realising that we could not be friends. Yarham grabbed him, and then Kershaw helped to hold him. Burton was in no state to resist.

"We'll go back to the van," I said to Burton. "If you don't have a key, we'll wire it," I said. Hotwiring cars was something I had learned while still at the Barmby boarding house.

Yarham took Burton's wallet and extracted the money. "We can afford a cab," he said, waving a wad of notes.

"If you don't come quietly with us, we'll hurt you. Savvy?" Kershaw said to Burton.

We walked the streets in the direction of the Via Monumental, hoping to get a cab. The streets were filthy and uneven if you had bare feet. We passed refuse trucks, bums asleep in doorways, roadsweepers, sanitation workers pumping drains, but no taxis. We stopped at a stand where a grubby mestiza woman with a pocked face was serving sweet lukewarm liquid from a flask. Her customers were drunks who'd come-to after a sleep on the beach and tramps like us. She was also selling hard little cakes with what looked like dead flies embedded in them; these we declined. But the stewed, milky coffee, nauseating to the well-fed and rested, was like the finest wine to me. She waved a half-empty bottle of aguardente at us, and cackled through her broken teeth. We each took a shot in our coffee for a few more pesos.

As we walked, clustered around Burton, he showed a willingness to talk which was possibly a result of shock, and the fact that we four all followed the same profession more or less, shared a language more or less, and a culture more or less. He was the youngest of us – I guessed in his early twenties. He was chubby-faced, a baby, and I wondered whether he was a fully trained intelligence agent. He had certainly forgotten a basic lesson about keeping his mouth shut. Yarham started him going with classic questions about home and family, and then on to college and the Central Intelligence Agency. Talking about Mom, and the farm in Idaho, and law school and basketball, was a warm-up for the tough questions he would have to answer later.

Eventually we got a cab. I had to pay the driver in advance, we looked so disreputable. I asked Yarham to tell him we'd been to a party and gambled our shoes away. When we arrived at Boca de la Chorrera where the van was parked, it seemed to have been left unvandalised. Then a black youth of about twenty came along and held his hand out. He had looked after the van by arrangement with Carmelli, and I paid him off with Burton's money. My wiring skills were not needed because Yarham produced Burton's key. We climbed inside, Yarham in the driver's seat. Kershaw and I got in the back on the tray with Burton. But we weren't going anywhere.

Heat had already started to build in the cramped metallic interior, and I pushed my sweating face into Burton's. "The way this can end for you is that my friend here" – I indicated Kershaw – "takes you to Havana International Airport with a one-way ticket to Mexico City. That's the best scenario. All other scenarios are ugly. Clear?"

Burton nodded. I had reasoned that Burton could not be released in Cuba. He would go to the local CIA with dire results for us. The only solution was to ship him out of the country, or hold him incommunicado during our task. In the meantime, he seemed sufficiently disorientated to talk. He had already shown his incomprehension that two intelligence services reporting to the same government should be fighting each other, to the prejudice of their common objective. Yarham had got Burton to understand that our objectives were actually the same as his.

"What was Carmelli going to do with us? Who did he think we were?" I asked Burton.

"He didn't know who you were, just foreign agents trying to screw up our plans. Also I think he was angry about the Penn Avenue break-in, which resulted in his butt getting kicked."

"What I told Carmelli on the boat was true. I'm from MI6. We're here to get intelligence on the terrorists. Do you accept that?"

Burton hung his head. "Yeah. I don't see who else you could be."

"If you cooperate with us, you get to go home, OK? Will you do that?"

Burton nodded a guilty assent.

"Where did the tip-off about the house in Buena Vista come from? Was it street info, or from within?"

When he hesitated I knew it was an internal leak. He was a kid. "I don't understand why one outfit is selling out another, shit... I think we got it from MI6. The English guy."

I looked at Yarham. "Then we can't go back to the house," he said.

"Or to Neville. How much money do we have?" It was the grand total of Burton's wallet. "Two-sixty dollars. Enough for clothes and somewhere to stay while we get more money," Yarham said.

"Where's your HQ?" I asked Burton.

"At the hotel. The Excelsior. We have adjoining rooms with an anteroom. We work out of there."

"Plush," Yarham said, holding up a Ving card he'd taken from Burton.

"Good. We'll have a look, later. How many guys in your team?"

"Just the three – was three." Burton hesitated and smothered a sob. "We were on our own. Gino felt kinda personal about getting the goods back to Langley, didn't want a whole mob of local agents crowding in, takin' the applause. It was goin' to be a big deal for us three."

"Were you in touch with other field agents here?"

"Only if we needed equipment. They didn't know what we were doing."

"What equipment?"

"Guns, this van, the boat."

"OK, we'll get some clothes, have breakfast, and visit your hotel. Maybe we can take a shower there."

Yarham left us in the van to buy underwear, shirts, trousers and moccasins for the three of us. He returned in an hour.

We dressed awkwardly beside the van. When we were passably clothed, I committed the care of the van to the black youth, in case we needed it later, taking the satellite phone with me.

We found a small café on Calle 4 where we ordered Spanish omelettes, fried bread and coffee. After a silent meal – we were ravenous, we took a cab to the Excelsior, and went up to the CIA rooms which had *Do not disturb* signs on the doors.

We entered and our first move was to use the coffee machine to make fresh cups of hot, black Cuban coffee. I set Kershaw to watch Burton, while Yarham and I searched the rooms. "Ask him if he can point us in the right direction. It'll save time," I said to Kershaw.

We were very thorough. We took the rooms apart. We looked under the carpet, took out the wardrobes and bath panels, opened up the mattresses, got inside the TVs, and went over the curtains and pelmets. Burton provided useful advice, and claimed not to know about the other pieces we found that he hadn't mentioned. We finished by noon with a laptop PC, a bundle of notepaper, two notebooks, five thousand dollars in cash, several cassettes of tape, a cassette recorder, two revolvers and boxes of shells. The rooms looked as though they were ready for redecoration.

I dispatched Yarham to find a hotel somewhere where we could hole up for the next few days, study our find, and talk to Burton.

While Yarham was away I had a long, hot shower, using the perfumes and unguents that hotels provide for their guests which I usually ignore. Then, while Kershaw was taking his turn in the shower, I tried to get Burton to work the PC. Whether he was playing dumb, or genuinely ignorant, I couldn't decide. We made no progress.

Yarham returned in two hours, task accomplished, though apologetic at the result. I had to accept that in the shapeless jacket and trousers he had borrowed from the closet in the Excelsior, and without luggage, this flame-haired gringo was not well placed to check into an establishment of any quality. With customary cunning, however, Yarham had purchased a suitcase, which he had carried, empty, on his search. He returned with the suitcase, into which I placed our haul, and we departed.

On the way to our destination, the Club Atlantico at Playa Guanabo, in a cab, I stopped to purchase toilet gear. The Atlantico was not a peso hotel for Cubans, but a run-down beach hotel for tourists. It had long grass in front, a peeling sign, faded paint, a half-awning over the swimming pool which sagged, and the pool itself had a dusty scum on top. We had two large rooms with cracked walls, a terrace, a shower and a lavatory. The rooms were shady, even if the beds were short, narrow and hard. An insidious *agguanco* rumba beat came from nowhere and throbbed through the entire premises. Yarham looked crestfallen.

"Cheer up man. You did well. We should imbibe the Cuban culture at all levels," I said. "And talking about imbibing…"

"I asked the desk boy to bring four Cuba libres," Kershaw said.

I liked the idea of four rather than three. It made Burton seem like an ally.

I settled on one of the beds to consider our haul. Despite his calling, Gino Carmelli was an inveterate note-taker. That had been my thought the night I looked through the door from his secretary's room, and saw his desk covered with handwritten papers. He was a pre-PC man. And here was more proof, jottings, which I guessed would form part of a longer report. It was my good fortune.

I took about an hour and a half to get a dim picture of what was happening from the notes and the cassette player, and consulting with Yarham. He worked with Burton on the PC, and managed to locate a few files. Kershaw wasn't much help because he didn't know what we were looking for, and he wasn't very sharp, but I had decided there was no point now in keeping anything from him.

"The way I see it," I said, when Kershaw produced the second round of Cuba libres, "is that a man codenamed Gomez from Al Qaeda or some other jihadist group is here, masterminding operations. He has technical help from a scientist or engineer codenamed Hertz. They have two mobile platforms – built on thirty-ton trucks with hydraulic stabilisers, under cover. The rocket fuselages have been smuggled in, in short sections. There are only four rockets; they are kit-sets under assembly. The chemicals for fuel have been imported and stored. There are four warheads, which Carmelli estimates in the one hundred kiloton plus range. That is about six times more powerful than Hiroshima. Compared with the ICBMs of thirty years ago, this model is less than a quarter the size, has a longer range, and flies very low in the atmosphere. There is a foreign, Arab, technical team that can handle the assembly and firing without local help. The cover for their work is that they are a construction company building housing units. It that it, Burton?"

"Yeah. It's crazy."

"I think you've done good work," I said mildly, thinking what a brilliant intelligence coup it was, and how indebted I was to the late Gino Carmelli. "What has Carmelli done about this information?"

"Nothing. We were about finished when Gino saw you in the hotel. He was going to put a report together after we'd… "

"After you'd murdered us. I understand."

I had seen the initials *AA* in Carmelli's notes. I guessed his principal informant was Alfredo Arias, and Burton confirmed this. "Was a woman involved, Dolores Martinez?"

"As a go-between."

Burton also confirmed that they paid half a million dollars. It seemed that Dolores had decided that patriotism ended with talking to the CIA, and it was time for her to make some private profit from the NSA.

Yarham sniffed. "You can't blame her. And no price inflation either between deals which was reasonable."

"And the Al Qaeda team are staying at Campismo Mercados in Pinar del Rio Province? What is that, Burton?"

"Yeah. I've been out there. It's a motel or hotel. Isolated. They do riding and trekking from there when they're doing normal tourist business. Once it was the centre of a big private estate, Rancho Mercados, before the revolution. Al Qaeda have booked it out. There don't seem to be any other guests or vacancies."

"How many of them?"

"We estimate ten plus a couple of bosses, Gomez and Hertz."

"So how do we get to them, Burton?"

"I guess at the Campismo they wash and pray five times a day, but they do their whoring and drinking in Santa Cristobal town a couple of miles away. They spend, so the Cubans have beefed up a night club, brought in a new band, more girls, you know."

"You've been there?"

"Sure, just to observe."

"What did you see?"

"Guys drinking and dancing and picking up whores."

"And where do they go to work?"

174

"In an old run–down part of Mariel. There are lots of junk yards and contractor's yards there."

I got a map of Mariel and made Burton identify the site. "How do they get from Campismo Mercados to Mariel?"

"They have a hired bus. All together. Every day. There and back. Seven days a week."

I thought we had about everything we needed from Burton. I concluded that he didn't have the guile or the experience to mislead us badly. "OK, Burton. You've done your part. I guess all this will check out. You go to the airport when we receive the money for your fare from Uncle Sam."

"You have the money from the Excelsior stash."

"We might need that in the meantime. Don't doubt me, Burton. You'll be going."

I went into the other room alone and sat down with pencil and paper. I didn't think it necessary to verify Burton's account or Carmelli's findings: they sounded completely authentic. Burton's contribution would have been difficult to fabricate convincingly. I decided to take a chance. If there were errors or if Burton had misled us, I'd just have to send a correction later.

I jotted down notes for my report to C3. I was proud of it, the complete intelligence I had been instructed to gather. And all acquired from the CIA. Of course, I did not reveal that. I said, *My surveillance and enquiries have revealed...* Nor did I mention the unfriendly CIA activities, or their two casualties. I requested a further half-million dollars urgently for further important information. Clark would question this, but the quality and precision of my report and the importance of the mission would ensure a further prompt payment. My computer encrypted the message, and it was sent in a microsecond burst.

Afterwards, in the cool of the evening, I left Burton with Kershaw, and walked along the lightly peopled beach with Yarham. Red clouds were massing for the sunset. The sound of different South American and Caribbean rhythms from half a dozen radios intertwined: salsa, rumba, samba, reggae, cha-cha-cha. We found a small bar on the beach, and sat sipping pina coladas, watching tourists sun themselves. I needed an easy hour while the memories of the Carmelli nightmare subsided.

"That's it, is it, Captain? Tidy up and go home?" Yarham said, hopefully.

"Technically, yes... The Disciples will then play their game of political and military brinkmanship, and get their men into power."

"Does 'technically' mean the job is done, but we're not going home?"

"You want to see wifey, Yarham – and I don't blame you, but yes... I'm thinking about it."

"I'd rather not put in any overtime on this one, Captain."

"We could establish what the *timing* is on this crisis, Yarham. That's the one thing missing from my excellent report. Is it going to happen in a month, or in six months? It's important for the Disciples to know that. They'll want to know how much time they have for their political manoeuvres in Washington."

Yarham looked alarmed. "It is very important to find this out, but I can't see why we should nominate ourselves to do it."

"It would be quite a coup, and we're probably best placed to find out. Don't look so unhappy, man."

"I detected a certain inconsistency between the completion of our work and your request for further funds." Yarham spoke with funereal gravity.

"Well, I thought that if we were going to answer this timing question, we might need money."

"It's rather a generous sum, Captain," Yarham, said stroking his jaw.

At the same time, I was also thinking that it was comfortable to be awash with dollars. "If we're going to go on here, we've got to be solvent, Yarham."

"Certainly, sir, but I would prefer not to be sitting on the beach when the US strike," Yarham said cautiously. "Cuba will be flattened. Pity. I'm getting to like it here. Nice climate. Friendly people. The atmosphere is free and easy."

"Don't worry, Yarham. The Disciples have a lot of domestic machinations and back-stabbing to do before they get to the point of an actual strike against Cuba."

"That may be so, Captain, but look at it another way. Forget Washington. Suppose Gomez is ready to unleash *his* rockets *now*?"

"Good point, Yarham. Virtually instant retaliation by the US, you mean, and pffft! – we're all gone? Brings a certain tightening of the scrotum to our activities, doesn't it?"

"My scrotum is already as taut as a drum, Captain."

"Hence the importance of solving the timing question."

It was actually very difficult to focus on imminent disaster as I basked in the sultry air and watched the near-naked asses of the sunbathing girls, the children dipping in the vast, flat, ultramarine sea, and the small white hulls of distant yachts.

When we walked back to the hotel, I was still confident enough to think I might win further plaudits from my masters by solving the timing question. I was also thinking about dinner, and hoping the cuisine would bear no relation to our mouldy premises.

As I approached our rooms, I saw the door was open. I ran forward. I found Kershaw on the floor, half-conscious and bleeding from a head wound, a heavy glass ashtray bloodied by his side – and no sign of Burton.

"He's bolted," Yarham said. "We've saved the air fare."

21

Kershaw seemed to be concussed, and we called a doctor who prescribed rest, produced pills from his black bag, and charged a hefty fee. It was too risky to remain at the Club Atlantico, and we decamped that night to a small hotel up an alley in the Boca Ciega area. I decided that when we had more time, we would find a better place.

I reasoned that Burton, who was naively straightforward in his thinking, would go straight to the local CIA, and tell them everything. He would blame us for the deaths of Carmelli and Harkness, trump up a story. The likely result was that we would have some of the local resources of the CIA looking for us with extreme violence in mind. The only saving point in the debacle was that Burton had been left with the impression that for us, the job was over and we were going home. If we weren't found in a couple of days, maybe the CIA would relax their search.

I had, however, now finally decided that I would pursue Gomez and Hertz at least to establish the likely timing of their assault. When I announced this to the recovered Kershaw the morning after our move, his white eyes squinted. He knew the risks, but he was too much of a tough guy to back down. Yarham simply cracked a grin and swallowed, his adam's apple bobbing. For me, the tension was lessened, if not removed, by the fact that our intelligence suggested that the Gomez team still appeared to be working on their weaponry.

Within twenty-four hours I had a signal that the money was

available at the Bank of Chile, as promptly and unquestioningly as I had predicted. I stowed the greater part in a locked holdall, the security of which would, I knew, haunt me whenever I went anywhere without it. I gave a substantial wad each to Yarham and Kershaw, and took enough for myself to pay for taxis, a new and better hotel for a couple of weeks, and some new clothes – including the inevitable dark glasses and a collection of sun hats and baseball caps.

After fixing these domestic details, I hired a car and driver and with Yarham and Kershaw, drove to the town of San Cristobal. When we left the car, we arranged to meet outside the Church of Santa Antonio, in the Square of the Revolution at around eleven that night. Then – it was seven in the evening, we split up. Kershaw who was nearly back to normal, and Yarham, were both to keep me in view and assist if necessary.

I was dressed like a tourist – straw hat, garish silk shirt, which is what I pretended to be. I had a number of unsolicited offers from young men who wanted to be my personal guide, and I chose Jose, a mulatto youth of about twenty-five, with sufficient English, who looked clean and streetwise. I started our relationship with ten dollars, which was more than sufficient for the whole day and night, and let him know there was more to come.

My thought was that if the Al Qaeda team came to town and spent money, the locals should be able to identify them at least as benevolent strangers. I had to have a guide who was desperately keen to earn more bucks, and who would consequently talk, and talk.

Jose took me through a succession of churches, civic buildings, parks, gardens, cafes and restaurants. I encouraged his chatter, and he was quite instructive. I was beginning to feel I knew the town of San Cristobal which had few industries or attractions, and seemed to live as a junction of roads and railways. I steered the conversation toward Jose, his family, the people, how they lived, what was happening in the town.

What was happening for the majority, according to Jose, was what we would call poverty, but there was always that Cuban buoyancy, a catlike delight in the sun, a respect for Castro, and an understanding that free healthcare and education were valuable. As we sat by the fountain in the square, Jose mentioned the hotels, and I asked him to tell me about Campismo Mercados.

"They pretty broke. Instead they have foreigners there, working in Cuba. Like a hotel."

"Do the foreigners take Cuban jobs?"

"No. They have their own work. Maybe good for Cuba."

"Where?"

"Mariel. They come here to enjoy themselves."

"Where do they go?"

"To the Bar La Costa and the Sol Night Club. There are girls there. Nice girls. You want a girl? I can get you."

"No, but I'd like to try these places. Have a drink. OK? We go."

Jose set off enthusiastically. He was sure I wanted a girl and was being coy. The Bar La Costa was thick with cigar smoke. At one end of the bar, a beaded curtain swayed, catching the light, as patrons and girls passed through into the exciting darkness beyond. Music was being strummed and beaten, teased out into a rough rope of sound through an audio system by a trio of black Cubans on a small dais.

The tiny dance floor, testing ground for whether you liked your chosen girl enough to go through the curtain, was crammed with macho men clamping the firm, round asses of their partners as they moved, locked pelvis to pelvis. Other men stood around staring, like buyers at a cattle fair, or sat at tables drinking. Jose and I took seats at the back, where we could watch.

"Are some of these men the foreigners from the Campismo?"

"Some. Why you ask the Campismo all the time?"

I was being too obvious. And I was finding I couldn't tell a Cuban from a Saudi. "Let's go look at the nightclub."

"Eets early yet. Not much action. We wait. I get you a girl…"

He beckoned one of the girls with her elbows on the bar waiting for a partner. She came swaying toward me, big breasted in an almost transparent floral dress with a belly hole in it, and he whispered to her. I turned away from her inviting smile.

"We go, Jose," I said, and headed for the door, with Jose trailing behind, protesting the quality of the girls.

At the Sol Night Club I paid our dues, and found there were very few people there. The band hadn't started, the bartenders were still stacking the bar, and a woman was vacuum-cleaning a strip of carpet outside the toilets. Two coffee-skinned men, whom I thought were mulattos, were having an argument with a white-jacketed Cuban who looked like the manager. I sent Jose down to the bar to get me a daquiri and took a seat to watch the altercation.

A girl flounced up to the trio and said something. One of the men grabbed her by the wrist, and tried to drag her toward the door. A muscular, black, shaven-headed Cuban in a tuxedo intervened and broke the man's grip on the girl. He grabbed the man by the back of his shirt and the back of his trouser belt, and propelled him across the floor and out of the door. The expelled man's companion retired too, a few yards behind, still arguing with the manager and gesticulating.

When Jose returned with our drinks, I said, "What was that about?"

He shrugged wearily. "Fight over a girl. Who pays who. How much. The foreigners are always fighting over the women."

"Is he from the Campismo Mercados?"

"Sure. He thinks he's a big shot. He spends plenty, but always trouble with the women. You know Cuban women have spirit. They don't lie down like dead. They don't take orders. If they like, they fuck. If they don't like, they don't fuck."

I was more curious about the protester. He was about forty, heavy, with a thick moustache under a bulging nose. I would try to remember him. Although he'd got the worst of it, the man had carried himself as though he was used to getting his way. "Do you know anything about the man?"

"Why you so interested?" Jose said, slyly.

I feigned indifference. "I like to know about people. If you want to talk, talk. If you don't, it's OK." I finished my drink and made to rise.

Dollar signs were preeminent with Jose. "I tell you senor, I tell you. I work here sometimes. Make a little money behind the bar. He is a drunk. Makes trouble. But he is big boss. He wants that girl. He fucks her once, wants her every time. She doesn't like. She makes plenty without him. A star girl. Problem."

I received Jose's words in an offhand way, and wandered outside. Jose called after me that I would have to pay again later if I wanted to come back. I gave Jose another ten dollars, thanked him for his help, and said goodnight.

At the church, I met Yarham and Kershaw. Kershaw was drunk, feeding a depression from his lapse with Burton which we hadn't chided him about. Yarham hired a driver at an

182

exorbitant rate to take us to Havana. While Kershaw slept in the car, we guardedly discussed our plans. Yarham had identified a couple of men he thought were Middle-Eastern, but like my find, it was a case of *so what*? The next step was to see what we could unearth in Mariel – and the obvious way was to follow the work bus.

It seemed extraordinary to me that Gomez had created a little ghetto at Campismo Mercados, but in a way I understood it. They were here for months, in a foreign culture. They could keep each other company, and be more readily subject to control if they were living together. But there were serious risks in making your whole group an identifiable target. It was an inept mistake.

The next morning we hired a Suzuki Samurai jeep with a soft top from Transtur using the forged Cuban driver's licence Yarham had removed from Burton. Yarham bribed the clerk heavily to get to the front of the queue, and the clerk paid little attention to checking the document or the photo-identity. I carried out a reconnaissance on the road between the Campismo Mercados and Mariel, selecting a place where we could wait the next morning.

With the move to an old but reasonably quiet and spacious hotel in the Vedado area, the Hotel Yara, which had in addition a park for the jeep, I felt we were making progress again.

We were in position on the Via Luis Fernandez at four-thirty the next morning – it had occurred to me that Al Qaeda might work unusual hours, or perhaps prefer the cool of the morning. It was a sensible move, because an old twenty-seater bus, wood-framed, with peeled paint, huffed out between the skewed gateposts of Campismo Mercados in a cloud of smoke at five-thirty. Kershaw drove, following the bus on the empty road at a distance, and closed up after forty miles, when we were approaching the outskirts of Mariel.

When the bus seemed to have finally finished its snail-like journey around the oily pools of water, through the mud and potholes of the back-street wasteland, we were a block behind in the jeep. The sun was well up now, and lifting the rags of mist which hung over the low-lying ground like a noxious gas.

"Stick it off the road beside the tin fence and we'll get out and walk," I said, and Kershaw parked and disabled the vehicle, disconnecting wires under the bonnet.

The bus was pulling away by the time we came near to it, but several figures could be seen, walking in twos and threes in the same direction. There were a few other people around trudging to work even at this early hour and I didn't think we had been noticed. It wasn't necessary to split targets between us, as all the bus passengers seemed to be going to the same place, which coincided with Burton's information that as far as he knew, there was only one site.

Yarham and Kershaw dropped back, and I was about two hundred and fifty yards behind six men huddled in anoraks despite the rising temperature, the last of the passengers, who never looked around as they walked. We were crossing uneven waste ground which smelled like an infill site for garbage; beyond it was a yard, with a fifteen-foot galvanised wire fence. One of the men stopped to light a cigarette, and I pretended I was scavenging, kicking the earth, bending over to examine a stone, but they showed no curiosity about me – if they saw me. The men filed inside the gate of the yard when it was ponderously unlocked, and locked behind them by a guard. I turned away, and walked back to the jeep.

I was pleased with my observation, and it tallied with

what Burton had said. I'd have to get into the yard to find out precisely what stage the terrorists had reached in their work, and how to do this was occupying me, as I turned the corner of the tin fence where we had left the 4x4. I found the smart, royal blue Samurai, which a few minutes ago had been equipped with bulging, maxi-grip tyres, possibly the pride of the rental fleet, sitting on its axles in the mud, with an open hood and a broken windscreen.

Yarham's amusement was complete when he caught up a moment later. "Couldn't steal it, though, could they, Captain?"

I hired a car back to the hotel in Havana. Yarham and Kershaw now had reservations about my plan to squeeze another ounce of glory out of the mission, which they expressed in hints. They wanted us to prepare a plan of the area and return to Washington.

Yarham had exercised his skills and money on Havanautos to produce a similar Japanese vehicle, in case I decided that we should continue, and when he returned to the hotel with the new jeep, we conferred on the patio beside the pool, with assistance from a couple of strong rum and Cokes. Kershaw was in Vieja calming the no-doubt outraged manager of Transtur about the loss of his Samurai with a wedge of dollars.

"Is it really practicable for us to find out the state of readiness of the rockets and warheads, Captain? Nobody is going to tell us, and short of penetrating that wire… "

"It could be months before they're ready," I said calmly, although I doubted it.

"But as a result of your report, Washington already knows enough to become nervy. The US could turn Cuba into a piece of burnt toast, and we'll be two of the black specks."

"No. They'll wait until they hear more from me. While

we are in play and cool, Yarham, Washington will hold fire. I deliberately didn't tell C3 the locations we knew about from Burton at the Campismo and Mariel, to forestall any hasty desire to loose off."

"Burton implied the CIA thought Al Qaeda had a way to go yet. But he didn't know."

"*So we have to know,* Yarham. We can't risk panicking the Disciples. They're first-strike crazy. Are you happy to hang out for a while longer?"

"I wouldn't say happy, Captain... but it's a good cause, and if you say so."

Yarham's usually irrepressible sense of humour was frayed. I did not reveal to him, because he was understandably anxious about his skin, the full ambit of the plan I was forming – to do so would only have alarmed him unnecessarily.

I had at least tentatively decided that the objective I could strive for was not merely knowledge of when the rockets would be ready, but destruction of them, and their operators; *the mission as I had originally envisaged it* at my meeting with the Disciples at Gerry Clark's apartment. Complete destruction of the threat would be the great prize.

And there was another thought which made that prize even more tantalising. Assuming Burton had told all to the local CIA, I thought that *they* would not content themselves with a report to Langley. They had lost two agents and the report would be a virtual admission that they were second-class operators. Instead, they would rely on what Burton said, and would seek the same prize as us. Destruction of the missiles would be a contest between the CIA and C3.

I went to bed high on the idea that I could do the virtually impossible.

22

My first instinct was to try to enter the launch site at Mariel and see for myself what was happening. And then I decided it was too risky. The site would probably be guarded around the clock, so surreptitious entry would be unlikely. A break-in would involve conflict and alert Gomez. Instead, I ordered Kershaw to move to Mariel town, and start daily, and if necessary nightly, surveillance. He had to be there when the bus arrived. And he had to find out who and what, apart from the bus workers, went in and came out of the site. We might be able to infer, from the nature of the traffic, what the state of readiness was. It was an important independent assignment, and Kershaw accepted it without demur. I think he rightly felt excluded, and was glad to get away on a project of his own.

I had conceived a very ambitious plan, far beyond the immediate orders of my masters, but I considered I could argue that I was interpreting their likely intentions in a situation where time could be of the essence. And it was a plan which, if successful, would reflect no little honour upon me.

With Kershaw posted to Mariel I could concentrate on the Campismo, and San Cristobal town, with Yarham. The plan I had formulated in my head went broadly like this: assemble the necessary weapons; dispose of the ten or twelve Al Qaeda or most of them; then strike and destroy the Mariel factory. I pushed the problem of how to deal with the warheads, together with our means of escape, to the end of the list. I wasn't exactly in a position to ask for technical advice about neutralising atomic weapons.

I had no means of acquiring weapons from the Disciples. I had the money to pay for them, but no vendor. There were only two sources of supply that I could think of: the CIA and the Cuban government. Even the CIA might not have the grenades, explosives and mines cached in Cuba that I needed, and of course even if they did, they wouldn't sell them to me. That left the Cuban government, and the dubious Dr Arias.

Arias was playing politics with this dangerous development, and hoping to unseat the government. Fidel Castro had just handed over power temporarily to his brother, Raul. Arias had helped the CIA, and he might be prepared to help me – for a consideration. I told Yarham we must pursue Dr Arias for further information about the Cuban government's position. I concealed from him the fact that the approach would really be for arms.

He responded bleakly, reluctantly agreeing to help. "Dr Arias may get us in the missionary position, Captain, as before."

"We don't know whether Arias was behind the heist in the shopping mall. It may have been a little private enterprise by Dolores Martinez."

The question was how we were to approach this important security-conscious bureaucrat now that Dolores Martinez had disappeared. I was sure that with the codes and information the Disciples had given me, I could establish a trustworthy identity for myself which Arias would accept, but to do that I had to corner him somewhere in a calm frame of mind. I could convince him of the desirability of supporting our cause, if only I could create the opportunity.

"You're thinking we could go to his apartment, force our way in, cool him down, and then talk?" Yarham said impatiently.

"He's probably got a security guard on the premises. There could be shooting." I meant that we could get shot.

"We block his car in the morning, get the driver out at gunpoint, and you two have a nice chat," Yarham tried, more seriously this time.

"Possible, but creaky. Anything can happen on the road, like the unforeseen presence of cops, or a hidden security guard on a motorbike."

"I've got it, sir. Ring his office and make an appointment to call," Yarham joked.

I disregarded his cynicism as I thought for a moment. "By God, Yarham, you've got it!"

"If you go in, and you're rumbled, you'll never come out, sir."

"Money opens doors, Yarham. Surely we've learned that."

In parallel with my initiative to see Arias, I had to get a line of sight on Gomez and Hertz. It would be little use destroying the bus and its passengers (my intention) if their leaders were not on board, unless they could be otherwise ambushed at approximately the same time. Another visit to the Sol Night Club and possibly even surveillance of the camp was required. Yarham therefore drove me to San Cristobal in my tourist outfit, with little more in mind precisely than watching events at the Sol for an hour or so and trying to identify Gomez and Hertz. I decided it was prudent to employ Jose again, and arranged by phone to meet him outside the club. Yarham left the jeep in the custody of a boy, and shadowed me.

The Sol presented an entirely different picture at eleven at night. The lights were subdued, and although the jineteros were still trading, there were tourists, and numerous women who were obviously partnering the male with them for the evening, and had come for dinner, the floor show and a little dancing. I sat through a loud girlie cabaret act of legs and bosoms that looked as though they were rehearsing to understudy the chorus at the Tropicana; their sheer sexual exhuberance overcame the sloppy beat of the music, and the uncertain choreography.

"You want I get you a girl? Beautiful!" Jose asked after the show.

"I'll have a pina colada."

"You gay or something? I get you a boy. Very nice boy."

I declined. "A pina colada."

"Whatsa matter you don't fuck? You want me?" he smiled, raising his eyebrows engagingly.

"No, Jose. I like to talk. I have AIDS, SIDA you know? My dick is no good. We talk. I pay you. You tell me about all the great people here. Amuse me."

Jose looked at me with an uncertain kind of repulsion. "SIDA you got? OK," he said slowly, seeing the commission he had hoped to earn on sex disappear. "We talk."

It was at this point that my attention was jolted by a woman who had just stepped into the limelight on the dancefloor. I couldn't mistake Dolores Martinez's expensively coffeured black tresses with gold lights, and the slender stateliness of her tall body, so unlike the plump fat-fed jineteros. The man she was with was swarthy, rounded, an inch shorter than her, with thin black hair and a short black beard. He was about fifty; not a Cuban, but an Asian of some kind. He didn't hold her too close. He was showing her off. She was scintillating in gold. He was wearing a white office shirt, open at the neck and rolled to the forearms, and the dark trousers of a suit. He had a proud bearing.

"Who is the woman in the gold lame dress?" I asked Jose.

"I don't know her name. She's with the big man from the Mercados. She comes here sometimes with him. They watch the show. Why you always ask about Campesino Mercados?"

"I didn't. I asked about the woman. You mentioned the man. I told you I'm interested in people. Beautiful women. To talk about."

I was rapidly working out the connection between Dolores and Gomez – assuming this man was Gomez. She had already sold him out to the CIA, according to Burton. That must be true. She was their principal informant. And if she was still close to Gomez, she wasn't just a go-between and a thief, as I had thought. She was a spy, still on the job, working for the CIA. She couldn't have been working for the Cuban government, or they would have moved in to clean up the rats' nest of terrorists long before now. I admired her bravery, and her cheek with money which quite overshadowed our sleight of hand in C3. My much earlier sympathies for her returned. I didn't quite understand her loyalties, but I thought she was a very sophisticated operator. If Gomez found out what she'd done, he'd choke her without a qualm. I didn't begrudge her the half-million she had filched from us, sore as I felt about being duped. I wanted to talk to her again. I wanted to find out more about her... I wanted to make love to her.

I told Jose I felt ill and would have to go. I said it was the pills I had to take. As we were pushing through the crowd, a jinetero grabbed my arm. "Come dance with me, honee!" She engulfed me with her soft breasts, and drew me a couple of paces toward the dance floor while I tried to free myself, and remain pleasant at the same time. As I turned politely to go, I saw Dolores, staring at me blankly through a space that had suddenly appeared between all the moving bodies, like a rent in the clouds on a windy night. We were riveted together for a fraction of a second by mutual glances of surprise. What flashed between us in that moment, like a video in re-run, was our brief past together. I looked away, and followed Jose outside.

I paid Jose off, and waited in the dark for half an hour until Gomez and Dolores came out, with two other men. A driver with a black Toyota saloon was waiting for them. They drove away taking the road toward the Campesino, rather than Havana. I assumed that Gomez didn't want to hit the high spots, but couldn't resist going out for an hour or two – and Dolores would be persuasive.

When we climbed into the jeep, I asked Yarham to head for Mariel. "I want a report from Kershaw, and he can't come to us."

"Where does tonight's little venture get us, Captain?" Yarham asked, sounding exasperated.

"I made an important discovery tonight," I said, and I explained. I could see that I was going to have to confide completely in him, and I hoped he was up to it. "I want to work out a way of neutralising Gomez, and Hertz – if we can identify him."

"You mean killing, Captain?"

"It's a very good cause, Yarham. Think what they'll do if we leave them loose."

"What about the other engineers and technicians, ten of them?"

"Unfortunately, them too. Well, most of them. We don't have to be fussy about detail."

Yarham soothed his massive jaw ruminantly as he deftly handled the wheel of the jeep with one hand. "Exigencies of the service," he pronounced deliberately. "And considerably less than the population of Washington or New York."

"Very much smaller. Can do?"

"Certainly, Captain," he said unwillingly. "But what with? We've only got those two pea-shooters we pilfered from Carmelli."

"Arias."

"I'd already worked out that you hadn't told me the full story about Arias."

"Only trying to save your feelings, man."

Yarham gave a big grin. "I can take it, sir."

At Mariel we picked Kershaw up at his lodging, and shared a bottle of rum in the jeep, parked in a backstreet in the dark, while Kershaw reported. He was sure that there was only one site. He thought that with the exception of two or three locals, the Mercados crew were the only workers. There was twenty-four hour security on the site as I had expected, including dogs. Other than local market lorries delivering food and building supplies of wood and cement, he'd seen nothing significant in the way of traffic going or coming – except that he had sighted an eight-wheeler Demag with a superstructure that looked like a mobile crane entering the wire enclosure. He produced a blurry photo on his mobile.

"It could be a firing platform," Yarham said.

"Keep looking," I said, bestowing what was left of the bottle on Kershaw, as we prepared to pull away.

That night I asked Yarham to find out whether the black Toyota sedan was a regular part of the Gomez fleet, and if it was, where it took Gomez and when. Yarham went off with the jeep in the morning, while I purchased a new wardrobe for my encounter with Arias – a light grey suit which fitted passably well, a white shirt with a green silk tie, and a pair of brown brogues. It was smart without being expensive, about right I judged for a US secret agent.

I had fixed the appointment with Arias by the simple expedient of ringing his secretary and making a request, as Yarham had facetiously suggested. My name I gave to the secretary was Smith – so obviously false to a person looking for falsity. I explained to her that I was visiting from England, and had met some friends of Dr Arias there. I had to make Arias curious about this visitor without alarming him. There had been a delay on the telephone line, and I had expected a further interrogation, but to my surprise the appointment was fixed for eleven the next day.

One of Yarham's tasks, when he was finished tracking the black Toyota, was to drive via Mariel and get a report from Kershaw, but he came back that night without one.

"Kershaw wasn't in his room. The room had been turned over, sir."

"Just a rough search?"

"No, a ransacking. Furniture broken up, curtains torn down. Dog shit, or maybe human shit, on the mirrors."

"A message?"

"Only an implicit message of hate."

"Kershaw had nothing there that could worry us."

But I was concerned about him. There was nothing to do but wait until he made contact. I ruled out going to Mariel. Either Kershaw was able-bodied and would report later, or he was in such serious trouble that any effort by me would be ineffectual.

I had taken to dining quietly with Yarham in the hotel on recent evenings. It was a pity we had to keep our heads down, because there were a few Havana restaurants I would have liked to try. At our hotel the food was disappointing Caribbean-style fried vegetables and fish, only interesting if you didn't have to confront it night after night. I established that the cook – not a chef I'm afraid, appreciated being presented with a bottle of good rum, and was at his best away from the hotel menu. He could produce an acceptable version of orange duck or garlic chicken vesuvio on request. Afterwards, we would drink cognac and make our plans for the following day.

Yarham had followed the Toyota that morning. He found that it departed with two or so passengers including, Yarham thought, Gomez, for Mariel, at about ten in the morning, and was taken into the compound of the site.

"That gives us a serious problem," I said. "If we were to hit Gomez on the road, it would be at a time when his men were at the site, and we'd have to assume they'd hear of it somehow. The opportunity to catch all of them together in the bus might be lost."

"Equally, Captain, if we zapped the bus at six am, Gomez wouldn't follow his normal routine."

We mulled over different schemes which might throw a noose over the whole gang at once, but none seemed to have satisfactory timing and we left the nature of our attack unresolved.

I thought about Kershaw that night, and he didn't phone the hotel. In the morning, after breakfast, leafing through the hotel papers as a matter of routine, I found in the tabloid *Cuban Star* a story of a gruesome beating at Mariel. A photo of an unidentified, unconscious white man was included. His mutilated body, found on wasteland, was lying on its back, and despite the blurred quality of the photo print, and the swollen and bloody injuries the man had suffered, was recognisable as Kershaw: the short grey hair, big forehead and the long, irregular face, now more irregular than ever. I worked though the rudimentary newspaper report with Yarham's assistance. The assault was described as a drug duel, but the other duellist was unknown.

"We can't go near him, Yarham. We'll be identified and…"

"Or worse. Leaving Kershaw to the tender mercies of one of Fidel's hospitals is no bad thing, sir. Fidel is good at hospitals."

"We couldn't even send Kershaw a card without making it tough for him. We've lost thirty-three per cent of our force."

No doubt the Cuban police would be standing around Kershaw's bed. I drew a blind in my mind, closing off the man who had been.

"Oh, that's a crude measure of loss, Captain. I'd say Kershaw was fifteen percent."

"I was only trying to be generous to a troubled man."

23

"Just when we were beginning to work together," Yarham mused.

"Kershaw was all right... Somebody is sending us a message. The CIA or Al Qaeda?"

"An angry CIA?" Yarham decided.

I thought that was probably right. I couldn't see Kershaw being taken by the people he was watching. He was too fly, and they were too busy. But somebody who was also watching might have noticed him watching, or somebody who knew him may have seen him. I was thinking of Burton.

"I think we should assume the CIA are working on more or less the same lines as we are. So be aware when you're snooping around the Mariel or San Cristobel," I said.

I sent Yarham off for a repeat of yesterday, had a long bath, and dressed for my visit to the Ministry of the Interior. Other than putting in a short satellite report of Kershaw's hospitalisation, there was nothing further I could do for him or about him. My report said no more than *Injured in action*. I could get away without details at this delicate stage. Kershaw wouldn't talk, and he would remain a mystery body to the authorities, ultimately consigned to a prison. His timid wife would be bereft in the rambling pseudo-manor with its plaster Grecian gods.

I arrived at the Ministry in the Capitolio National at ten-forty-five am on a brilliant and hot morning. I had walked through the Parque de la Fraternidad on the way. Havana's morning lethargy had worn off, and there was a burst of energy from the bicycles and clanking cars, and more bounce and colour in the pedestrians.

The corridors of the Capitolio were wide and dark and long and cool, lined with half-shadowed portraits or painted with Rivera's murals of the struggles of Maceo and the workers. The floors were polished granite, the carved doors designed to admit giants.

I was shown through various barriers, past bureaucrats by whom my meeting was verified and my body searched. I was carrying proof of identity in the form of a forged British passport in the name of Smith, acquired at high cost from a local dealer. It was a poor effort, but good enough for this purpose. I progressed through the fortress, and came to an ante-room presided over by a uniformed officer, where I was invited to sit down. I remembered with an unpleasant tremor that if Dr Arias rejected my case, and had me arrested, I could, as Yarham had suggested, disappear into a deeper, darker hole within this battlement. I crushed the thought. A half a million dollars was surely an inescapable lure.

If offices are the index of importance in government, Alfredo Arias was very important indeed. When I was invited to enter – at precisely the appointed time – I had difficulty finding the man at first. My eyes were dazzled by the expanse of shaded glass along one wall, the richly sculpted moquette of the multicoloured carpet, and the oil paintings of more than life-size soldiers, some mounted on horses, in scarlet, blue and green uniforms, which hung on the walls. It was as though I had stumbled into a gallery or a museum.

I peered one way and then another. There was a movement behind a desk at the end of the room. The relatively small figure of a man on his feet in a brown linen suit, advancing toward me, a grey-eyed creole, with a skull of sleek, dark hair. Dr Arias had a bearing of Latin impatience, struggling, in competition with the splendour of his room, to narrow the focus down to himself. We cannoned together in a brief handshake.

"Meester Smeeth from England, please sit down and tell me about yourself," he said, sweeping me on to a couch at the side, and taking a seat beside me. He thrust his face forward to occupy my full vision. The fumes of his expensive after-shave were slightly intoxicating. There could be no pause to admire the room.

I came straight to the crux. "I thought it most diplomatic to use the name Smith, Dr Arias. My codename is Wolf. I'm an agent for MI6, working with the US on anti-terrorism. My name is Roger Conway." Arias's expression never changed as I gently delivered this surprise. "I was given a special code for you in Washington – *The yellow roses of Texas.*"

I knew that the code phrase had been originated in the utmost secrecy, and was probably only known to Arias and Dolores Martinez. Arias drilled me deeply with his glare, and then his expression softened.

"I've been expecting you."

I wasn't going to tell him about my financial adventures with Dolores, because he spoke as though this was my first contact, and I didn't want to get into side issues. "I want to ask for your help."

He nodded very faintly, as though help was something he didn't do. "What exactly?"

"A small quantity of arms."

"What for?"

"To deal with Gomez."

He frowned, confused. "You will deal with Gomez? What about your famous Central Intelligence Agency? They will deal with Gomez."

"My mission is separate."

"MI6? But you work together?"

I had to change course and give Dr Arias the answer he wanted. "Of course. We each do our separate part." It was clear he was confident that the CIA would remove the Gomez threat, and that was the deal he would have made when he sold Carmelli the information.

"But I don't understand what *you* do, Meester Conway."

"It's very simple, Dr Arias. Now that we have surveyed the task on the ground here in Cuba with our friends the CIA, we find we need further arms. We haven't the time to bring them in from the US or elsewhere. We look to you, our valued ally, to help us, for which we will gladly make a contribution to your fund for the future."

Dr Arias went through a long moment of stony consideration before he could see. "And with these extra arms you will deal with everything?"

"Everything. The terrorists and their works."

"Yes, how much contribution do you have in mind?"

I told him a quarter of a million dollars, and specified the grenades, automatic rifles, high-explosive and anti-tank mines I required. I handed him a slip of paper with a quantified list. "The actual cost of these items is relatively little, and so there will be a substantial contribution to your campaign funds."

"Certainly, but the risk of getting them to you is great," he smiled.

We parted with an agreement which I did not like, but had to accept, that the money would be handed over first, to a representative of his, at a bank in Vedado, and that the delivery of the arms would take place at a drive-in on the Pinar del Rio Autopista the day following the payment. But, all in all, I returned to the hotel with some satisfaction that I had not only made the deal, but confirmed definitely that the CIA were planning a strike against Gomez.

Yarham was slightly questioning when I explained the arrangement to him. "We are dealing with an important man in government," I protested. "Surely we can trust him on this? It's not a petty matter. Cuba's whole future is at stake."

Yarham continued to stare at me as though I was talking drivel. I pressed on: "I know politicians tell lies, but this is… " I struggled to find the appropriate words.

"The opportunity for a very big lie," Yarham said, slumping his head toward one shoulder as he habitually did when confronting the utmost idiocy.

"OK, maybe you're right. I'm a sucker. Hell, as a second-hand car dealer I ought to know very well if you don't get the money when you part with the car, and vice-versa, you don't get it all! But what alternative do we have?"

"There you have me, sir."

I was sitting at the hotel bar when Yarham returned that night, with an irrepressible grin suffusing his face. "Got some interesting news, Captain, and a present for you in the jeep."

"You know I like presents," I said.

I followed Yarham downstairs to the weedy lot surrounded by a broken stucco wall which served as the car park. Yarham opened the jeep and drew back a blanket which covered the rear deck. A human body, on its side, bound and gagged, lay there. The man's face was red and his eyes bulged with semi-suffocation.

"Burton! You've come back to us!" I said. "How good to see you."

"I found him skulking around in San Cristobel, followed him into a side street and… persuaded him to join us."

"How eloquent you must have been, Yarham. I hope you told him we're not doing airport transfers any more. Not even if he has a complementary flight on Air Mexico."

"Shall we take him for a ride, Captain?"

Burton bucked and groaned at this prospect. I closed the door on him. Yarham got behind the wheel, and we drove to a lonely area near Bauta on the Carretera Central where we could talk to Burton without interruption. Yarham sat him up in the back and removed the gag. Burton looked weak and vulnerable, and anxious about his fate. His anxiety had caused him to mess his trousers, and the stench was revolting. It also seemed to me to be a sign of extreme apprehension based on guilt.

"Burton, I don't want to spend much time with you," I said, "because you need a bath. I told you the only good scenario was the one where you caught the plane to Mexico City. You could be on your way home to your Mom now, in Idaho. You didn't listen. Pity…" I stared at him for a moment, watched the childish mouth falter. "Now tell me about Kershaw."

"I didn't do anything to him."

"But you saw him at Mariel and identified him to your CIA colleagues."

"I didn't know… I didn't expect…"

"You knew they'd kill him or nearly kill him, because you were going to kill us when we went for that little voyage on the *Santa Maria* with the late Gino Carmelli. That's how you guys work."

Burton didn't say anything. His lips trembled.

"I'll take that as an admission. We won't talk about Kershaw any more. Tell me about the CIA plans to hit Gomez."

"I don't know them!"

"Then you better start imagining them. You are the man who brought the local department of the CIA into this. Until then it was your well kept-secret with Carmelli. When you escaped from Kershaw, you contacted them, told them Carmelli's mission, and in pursuit of glory, they've taken it over. You are right at the heart of it, son."

"No!" he protested, his eyes wet.

"Well, Burton, I don't have any more to say to you." I turned to Yarham "How shall we dispose of him?"

"Here, in a ditch?" He snapped open the flicknife obtained from Neville, and Burton let out a sad little sound.

I considered. "Wait. I think Burton has to disappear."

"OK. Suppose he takes a swim a mile off the coast, Captain. We can hire a boat, deal with it tonight."

"Agreed. There's a certain poetic justice in the method. Gag him."

"No! I'll tell you all I know," Burton whined, predictably and sensibly because he would have realised we now had no alternative.

I sat in the jeep, prodding Burton with questions, until a tolerable picture of the CIA activities and plans, which weren't greatly different from ours, was created. The CIA had been funding dissident Cubans, and had accumulated a cache of arms over a period. They had, according to Burton, a core of two US special agents, as well as their wider network of local agents. It was going to be a two-pronged attack. First, a strike at the ranch, and second at the site, a military exercise to wipe out the terrorists and their work. The event, which was expected to make international waves – and would, was going to be used by Arias's party to help destabilise the government in the popular mind.

When the interrogation was over, I decided we should keep Burton on the floor of the jeep tonight, with Yarham and I taking turns to keep watch to see that he didn't get loose. I overruled Burton's request for a shower and fresh clothes. I would decide what to do with him tomorrow.

When Yarham and I were enjoying a cognac after a late dinner, all taken on the patio where we could see the 4x4, I said, "You wouldn't have used that knife, would you?"

"No sir, but I could get close to it. Would you have dumped him in the Florida Strait?"

"No, but I might have taken him out there to scare him further if it had been necessary. Remember that feeling we had on the Carmelli cruise, with the dark water swirling past a few inches away, and the thought of sharks below? I don't have any sympathy for him."

"What are we going to do with him, Captain? We need the vehicle."

"And he stinks so much, we can't cart him around with us." We came to no final conclusion and I went to bed.

My stretch as guard was from three am, and I spent the rest of the hot night in a deckchair on the patio, from where I could view the parking compound, watching and listening. During that time I considered various ways to deal with Burton. I had seen some killing in Afghanistan, but that was war. I wasn't squeamish about the need to eliminate Gomez & Co, and was prepared to do it because they were psychopathic would-be mass murderers.

While I disliked Burton for his part in Kershaw's capture, which might have been greater than he admitted, I somehow couldn't bring myself to execute him. And yet his continued life was a threat to the lives of both Yarham and myself. Nor could I order Yarham to do that which I wouldn't do myself. Oh yes, I could, but I wouldn't on this occasion. I therefore had to have a scheme which effectively got Burton out of the way for say a week – the time it would take us to wind up this affair.

One possibility was to hire a local pilot to fly Burton to Jamaica, or even Haiti. But there was always the possibility that Burton would return promptly. A more ambitious international flight would involve a delay in getting a good quality forged passport for him, and we didn't have that much time. I could hide him in an old mine shaft – there were plenty of disused workings, but that would put his life at risk if the water or food ran out, or put us at risk if he escaped. At last, when the sun was coming up, and my stomach was rumbling for breakfast, I had a better idea.

I had the hotel serve our breakfast of watermelon, yoghurt with honey, cereal and hot rolls, on the patio. All remained quiet in the car park, but we could not afford to take our eyes off the jeep.

"We deliver Burton to the police, Yarham."

"With a label to say CIA spy? Whatever made you think of that, sir?"

"Our voyage with Carmelli. Imagine if the coastguard had handed us over to the police. How long would it have taken to establish who we were? That we were not drug smugglers? And to justify what we were doing in Cuba? No passports, no other ID."

"Trying to justify the unjustifiable… a very long time."

"We'll buy some heroin on the street, dope Burton, fill his pockets with the drug – and, adopting your suggestion, tie a label on him. The Cuban police will have a party."

"As long as we don't have to bath him, Captain."

24

That morning I received the first instruction by satellite that I had received from my bosses at C3. Decrypted by my computer, it said *Return immediately*.

"Not much dubiety, Captain." Yarham had difficulty concealing his pleasure at this order.

"None. Perhaps they fear Gomez is going to fire his missiles, and they're going to strike first. They want us out of the firing line."

"Decent of them, I suppose," Yarham said.

"Do you think they care about us?" I asked.

"Actually, no, Captain. I don't think they give a damn."

"Then there must be another reason."

But Yarham wasn't following me. He was off in a dream of his own. He said, "You probably gave them enough in your report to get on to the site. And they'll have space photographs." He couldn't keep the lightness out of his voice.

But I wasn't quite satisfied with the order, and I went out to a newsagent on Calle M where I knew I could get a pirate copy of yesterday's *USA Today* or the *Washington Post*. I scanned the national and international news in both papers, and found that while there was considerable agitation about possible terrorist attacks, and a presidency under severe pressure to be more hawkish, there was nothing specific about declaring war. The focus was on the Middle East, not Latin America, and there was nothing about the Caribbean. I believed that any move the USA made would be likely to be signalled in some way in the press a few days before. Just as nature is said to abhor a vacuum, so humanity abhors secrecy; it is unnatural and virtually impossible to achieve.

When I returned to the hotel, I said to Yarham, "I think the Disciples are getting ready for a move on the home front, perhaps using the photographs of the site as evidence to embarrass the President. They don't want any more action here. They want a hot threat at home to terrify the voters into electing a president with balls. Their man."

"What about the local CIA boys here running wild?"

"The Disciples probably don't even know what the CIA's local lads are up to. And we haven't told them."

I was wondering whether I should report to C3 that if I didn't hit the terrorists, the CIA would. Then, as a matter of agency pride, they might let me try to get the blow in first.

"Shall I organise a boat to take us to Jamaica, then, Captain?" Yarham asked, sweeping the line of my thoughts aside, only too glad to conclude that our mission was over.

I considered it. The mission *was* over – and accomplished expertly. We could make a quiet escape without passports. From Kingston, Jamaica we could organise ID, and fly to Washington. Safe. Pats on the back. Back to Laurie, and the cat. But I couldn't help wondering whether, if we hung out longer here, there could be any kudos for me in taming the CIA, and eliminating the terrorists. And Dolores Martinez remained on my mind. I dreamed of her at night. I desired her. I was curious about her secret. Agent? Double agent? Crook? She haunted me.

"Shall I, Captain?"

"No… no boat, not yet. We know we have a week or two before Gomez lets go," I said.

"But we don't know when Washington will let loose," Yarham said, dropping his chin.

"If the US strike first, Yarham, they'll use conventional weapons, take out the site."

"That's a comfort, sir, if we happen to be on or near. Blown to bits, rather than fried to a crisp."

"It's true there are risks. But don't you think we have a duty to find out more about this dangerous situation?"

"If you say so, Captain."

I sent Yarham off to purchase the heroin and syringe for Burton, and when he returned, I counted out a quarter of a million dollars from our hoard, and carried it in a plastic bag to the Brazilian Bank of Commerce. Inside the august grey marble portals, a dark-suited man came from behind the counters, using my real name. I mean Roger Conway. He took me to a private interview room where he asked me to tip the contents of the bag on to the table. He examined one random note, and then counted the packets once only, like a man used to counting hundred-thousand dollar packets. Then he took an envelope out of his breast pocket, and slid it across the table. "I was given this to hand to you in exchange. I'm not aware of the contents, but I take it they are in order." He gave a faint smile.

I thanked him and looked at the envelope. "I presume… "

"That's fine, Mr Conway. You can leave it all with me," he said, standing up to conclude our meeting.

I hung on. I slit the envelope and read the typewritten slip with road directions on it. I gulped, but this was the way I had agreed. I felt the payment in a bank had an air of respectability about it, and that it would be beneath my dignity to rehearse the details of the planned hand-over of arms. I was sure the banker would have charmingly told me, if I tried, that he didn't know what I was talking about.

The following morning at four-thirty am I drove the jeep past the police station on Padre Varela, while Yarham, in the back seat, had the rear cover open. The streets were nearly deserted except for the odd sanitary worker or bum. There was a slow, sleepy atmosphere, stars fading in the sky, the populace struggling to their feet, which was why we had chosen this time.

Burton had been carefully doped that morning with a quantity of heroin which Yarham had discussed with the dealer. The dealer presumably did not want to kill his customers, and was keen to give advice about the size of a shot, because of his claim about the purity of the drug. I did however invite Yarham to run a series of punctures down Burton's forearm veins to complicate the issue of whether he was a regular user.

Burton was conscious now, eyes half-open, and in paradise, collapsed on the steel tray of the jeep. Yarham slid Burton's bound body, labelled *CIA spy*, out of the back, as I slowed the vehicle. Burton had a heavy fall on the flagstones at the foot of the station steps, but would have felt nothing. I accelerated away.

"The jeep still stinks. Clean up the floor when we get back, will you?" I said.

Our next move that day came in the afternoon – the rendezvous to collect the arms. We drove out on the Autopista an hour before three pm and patrolled up and down. There was an intermittent stream of traffic, old buses and ramshackle trucks, with the occasional twenty-ton semitrailer, snorting and roaring at its inferior companions. We pulled in to wait at the appointed place, a tree-lined rest bay twenty kilometres east of San Cristobal. It would be quite possible to transfer the load of arms without being seen by passing traffic. It was a good choice which seemed to corroborate the genuineness of the deal. We waited. I thought of Dolores, what she might be doing. In bed with Gomez? Or Arias?

"It's three-fifteen, sir."

The tone rather than content of Yarham's words gave me a few misgivings. Had I been suckered again?

Yarham persisted, to my annoyance. "Suppose Arias took the money and did nothing. What could we do? Write a letter of complaint to him? Instruct our solicitors to recover it?"

"If you don't shut up, man, I'll brain you. Arias thinks we're part of the CIA effort which he has already helped. He wants us to succeed. And he's had good money for his fund. Why shouldn't he produce the arms?"

Yarham sat at the wheel with a composure that suggested he was humouring me. He looked forward at the empty tree-lined track, slightly amused. I got out of the jeep and walked up and down until it began to rain. It was fine being a secret agent, and there were glamorous moments, but there were also long periods of waiting. It was five pm.

"We'll give it another hour. There's been a slip-up on their side. I'll get back to Arias if there's no delivery," I said tersely.

There was no delivery. I drove back to the hotel seething. I went into the bar and ordered a Scotch. I tossed it off, and ordered another. I reviewed my previous plans and their outcome. Could I have played it any differently? Then Yarham came swinging into my vision, eyebrows raised, his jaw hanging down. He slapped a *Cuban Star* newspaper on the bar in front of me.

"There's your answer, sir."

I knew enough Spanish to read the headline and straplines. *Arias Arrested. Senior Government Minister Detained for Sedition. Other Arrests...*

"Half a million down the plug-hole," he added.

"And the security police looking for us, I have no doubt."

"I'll organise the boat to Jamaica, Captain."

"Yarham, rid yourself of this childish wish to go home. You're a Boy Scout now."

"I'd like to see my wife."

I didn't blame the uxorious Yarham for wanting to see that little woman. I thought what a relief it would be to spend a night in the peaceful USA in the arms of Laurie, or in my fantasies, Marie, the cook, with her fuzzy armpits, but perhaps not Mrs Gerry Clark. "One more visit to the Sol Night-Club, so you can practise the samba, and amaze your wife."

It had been raining when we arrived at the car park behind the church in San Cristobal. The moon had appeared and the trees were glistening in the darkness. Yarham engaged a minder for the jeep, and we headed for the Sol. It was eleven-thirty when we took our seats in the half-dark fog of cigar smoke, as far from the dance floor as we could get. The main show was over, but there was the promise of another at one am.

We ordered Cuba libres, a salute to the expensive Dr Arias. Perhaps it was foolish to have come. I was bankrupt of ideas. What could one do, armed only with a couple of pistols and flicknives? I wanted to see Dolores once more – at a distance, and then perhaps we'd go. And I hoped, I suppose, in a distant part of my mind, that some opportunity would present itself to checkmate both the CIA and Gomez, or at least that I would pick up a scrap of information which could be massaged into a valuable intelligence coup.

On the third Cuba libre, Jose appeared, his hands in his pockets, slouching over his hollow chest. "I see you Meester. You have a friend, huh?"

"I don't need you tonight, Jose."

He laughed suspiciously. I invited him to have a drink, and he said he didn't mind, by which he meant he wanted one. He sat down. "You still watching the famous people, eh?"

"Just enjoying."

"You don't fuck. You watch," he said knowingly. "American who watches."

"I drink," I said lightly, but Jose was worrying me, because obviously I was worrying him. He knew I was a phony.

While we talked desultorily and watched the dancers with half our attention, I saw Gomez and Dolores standing in the midst of the tables. Then I lost sight of them in the crowd. When I tried to find them, searching the darker restaurant tables at the back, I couldn't see them. They seemed to have come in – and then gone. I felt apprehensive, and in any event, we weren't doing anything useful. I was simply indulging my imagination.

I took a five-dollar bill from the roll in my breast pocket, and pushed it across to Jose. "For your drink, when the waiter brings it."

"Don't go yet, senor. Stay and watch." His lips pulled back and exposed his teeth with a humour that exceeded the occasion.

I gestured to Yarham and we stood up and made our way toward the door. "Short, but not very sweet," he said.

Outside it was raining again, and I paused on the porch. I could see Gomez and Dolores standing to one side under umbrellas, with a few men around them. Dolores looked pale and strained but scintillatingly beautiful in the lamplight. The men wore white shirts and were unconcerned about the rain which soaked them. I looked away, stepped through a row of doormen, pimps and touts, and walked briskly across the courtyard, head down, with Yarham beside me.

I felt somebody grab my arms from behind, and pinion them, while somebody else slipped a cord around my neck and drew it tight. Nearly choked, I was propelled toward a waiting car, rammed into the back seat, and the door slammed and locked. Much the same had happened to Yarham. The driver, in the front seat, had an automatic in his hand. "Sit back, men, or I kill you."

The thick voice, the difference in tone and pronunciation struck me. He was from the Middle East, one of the Gomez gang. He was joined by another man in the front seat who took over the gun, but never spoke. He stared at me with black, malign eyes. The driver backed out of the courtyard of the club, and there were two other cars with headlights, waiting to move. We drove the few miles, which I recognised, to the Campismo Mercados. The other cars were following.

The car turned up the path to the gate and stopped outside a long, single-storey wing of the building. I was taken inside into a room that looked like a cheap motel bedroom, with two mean single beds. I was tied to a chair, wrists over the chair-back, ankles strapped to the front legs of the chair. After a few moments Yarham was brought in and tied in the same way. Then we were left alone. We never spoke. That was the discipline. Not even one of Yarham's awful flippancies. Somebody would be listening, and watching.

We were left for perhaps three hours, and I was drifting off into a nighmarish sleep, my head lolling uncontrollably, when the door opened. The man I had identified as Gomez came in. He was wearing a dark blue silk dressing gown with small white spots, quite tasteful. His fat neck showed. His muscular legs were bare. He wore sandals. He had evidently risen from bed; it was, I estimated, around three am. I thought of Dolores. Had she turned over and gone back to sleep? Had she even stirred? Gomez looked fresh, his beard neatly clipped, his scalp shining through his carefully combed black hair. He took a seat opposite us.

"Let me introduce myself. I am Rahman Malmuni, head of this project."

I had no doubt that he felt free to give us his name, or as much information as he liked, in the knowledge that we would never leave the room. The only reason he had to keep us alive was to learn who we were, and the schemes we had against him. And he would press us ruthlessly, and separately, knowing that keeping us together would be unfruitful; one person's strength encouraged another.

The theory, according to MI6, was that if you face certain death after interrogation the less said the better. A fairly obvious view, but the point was that unharmful specific answers always led to further questions, and the MI6 psychologists believed that a captive was more likely to be worn down, and unnerved, once he was tangled in a chain of specific answers. The tempting thing, however, was to try to spin your life out a little longer by apparently being helpful, and it was a tactic I had used myself with advantage.

"Come now, American spies… introduce yourselves."

Gomez waited attentively with a smirk. He might have been entertaining a lady friend at afternoon tea. Eventually, without any change of expression, he said, "Very well. I am going to choose one of you to have a chat with me, and to give a little more… accessibility, shall we say?… I shall have your lower body clothing removed."

He beamed at each of us in turn, unhurried. "What am I going to do then? What do you think?"

I thought, sickened – something to do with my cock and balls!

Gomez produced a gold cigar case and lighter from the pocket of his robe. He selected a cigar, sniffed it with concentrated pleasure, and took his time lighting it – removing the barrel from his mouth and examining the glowing tip. Satisfied with the evenness of the burn, he rested back in a cloud of smoke.

"A really good Havana here, in Cuba, is a delight. Mature, but with a freshness that is lost in packaging and transport overseas, don't you agree?" He raised his hand, pinching fingertip and thumb-tip together to signal the superb.

My mind had frozen, rejecting any further contemplation of what baring my *lower body* could entail. I fervently hoped that Yarham would be chosen for this operation.

"Now," Gomez began gently, leaning forward confidentially, "whichever of you it is, the spy with the red hair, or the spy with the golden hair: my colleague will bring a thin cord. He will tie a torniquet – you see I have a very good English vocabulary. I spent a year in Fulham in London. There is a language school there. And the girls! A tourniquet will be tied at the base of your cock, or if he, my colleague, pleases, at the base of your balls. I don't trouble myself with these details. So! Now you can guess what happens next." Gomez drew heavily on the cigar, his eyes half closed. He sniggered.

I was running with moisture, and so was Yarham, yet neither of us spoke.

Gomez laughed. "The red spy will have an excellent view of the gold spy, or vice versa. I can promise my friend's knife will be razor sharp. The removal of your cock, or balls, will take just a second. Food for the cat!" Gomez stood up, opened the door and shouted, "Hussein!"

Hussein was the one who had held the gun on me in the car. He was a very short, fat man, still in his clean white shirt and black trousers. He had a long kitchen knife in one hand and a coil of cord in the other. His expression was morose, a workman absorbed in the job he was about to perform.

"Which spy do you want, my friend?" Gomez asked him.

Unhesitatingly, Hussein pointed at me.

"Wait, I think I prefer the red. Do you have a view, Mr Red? Would you prefer to give the honour to Mr Gold?" We waited, a minute of terrifying silence for me. "OK, take the gold," Gomez laughed.

Hussein bent down to untie my belt. He began to pull at my trousers. He dropped them to the floor with my underpants. I felt his fingers on my shoulder as though I was being anaesthetised and my body was already partially numb. My head pounded with the dreadful anticipation.

"No, no, wait, Hussein. I think Mr Red. Yes, I insist, Mr Red." Gomez collapsed on his chair in a fit of coughing and chuckling, clapping his hands on his knees.

Hussein sighed, and moved expressionlessly to Yarham. He untied Yarham's belt, tore open his flies, and using the knife, hacked away his underpants. Yarham's cheeks were death-white. The great jaw clamped shut. His flaccid cock and balls hung over the edge of the seat.

"What is it to be, Hussein?" Gomez asked. "Wait. Does Mr Red have a view? Your cock or your balls? A difficult choice, eh? Perhaps Mr Gold has an opinion. What would you advise, Mr Gold? Cock or balls?"

Hussein picked up Yarham's dick and dropped it contemptuously.

"Very well, then. Proceed," Gomez said, taking that gesture as a decision.

Hussein cut a short length of cord, but I could neither watch nor suffer this ordeal any longer.

I tried to sound calm. "I'll tell you what you want to know, Mr Malmuni."

A sign of life flickered from Yarham.

"Of course you will. Ha, ha!" He signalled Hussein to leave the room. "No, leave your tools my brother. You might need them yet."

I had toiled in my thoughts since our arrest to find an acceptable story to tell. I could probably bank on Gomez knowing nothing specific about the C3 operation, or Carmelli's CIA fiasco. All Gomez would know, I guessed, was that to carry out his project, he had to evade the Cuban Secret Service, and might come under surveillance by CIA agents. I would have to take the chance that Dolores was not a double agent who had revealed everything. But it would only make Gomez lose patience if I claimed we were ordinary tourists doing the rounds of the nightclubs. No, I had to *give something*, or Yarham would lose his dick.

"We're nothing to do with the CIA, Mr Malmuni. We're British. And if you've lived in London, you'll know the English accents."

Gomez was thoughtful, and too good at poker to show surprise. "You are intelligence agents?"

"Yes. British."

Gomez nodded. "Working with the CIA?"

"No. We don't talk to them, but our bosses in England might."

Gomez was suspicious. "You come here, you liaise. You talk together. You share."

"No. Like two separate companies."

Gomez relaxed slightly. Whether he believed or not, he understood. "What are you doing, then?"

"We have had agents here for sixty years or more. Routine visit. We went to the nightclub to have a drink, watch the girls."

"You hang about for several days, watching, asking questions. You don't like girls."

"My colleague liked the club, the band, the floorshow, so we came here more than once. Wherever we go in Cuba we hire a local and ask questions. It's our job."

"You have AIDS?"

I could see why Gomez had preferred to emasculate Yarham. "I'm HIV positive. I take a lot of pills."

217

Yarham's stupified eyes enlarged. Gomez looked nauseated. "Your names and department?"

I gave him the names we had assumed in Mexico City, telling him that because of our Latin connections we worked in Latin America. I said we were astonished that we had been picked up and asked him why. Gomez preened himself, wriggled comfortably in his silk gown and lit another cigar. He looked as though he was preparing to talk about himself.

"I don't believe you. You tell a very fancy story. Don't tell me such lies!"

I was at my most plaintive. "We really are from British intelligence."

"You know what we're doing here don't you?"

"I haven't any idea. I never knew you *were* here until you kidnapped us."

"Two members of British intelligence arrive. They start asking a lot of questions about our processing plant."

I had talked us into a corner and there was nowhere to go. "That's what we do. We're always asking questions. Mostly we don't find out anything worth telling our boss about."

Gomez laughed at first. "I don't believe you. Yes, I will believe you are British agents. No, I won't believe you know nothing about us. What am I going to do with you?"

"Let us go and we'll go on our way… " It was a fatuous request. Jose had told all. I wasn't believable.

"You think somebody is building a rocket site here?" Gomez said jokingly.

"I doubt it. It didn't work in the sixties. It won't work now."

Gomez the leader was considering. "Technology has moved on since the sixties. The island is well placed. A rocket can fly lower and faster now, and deliver a bigger warhead.

Theoretically, Washington and New York could be destroyed. Flattened. In a few hours."

"It's possible technically," I said. "But if Kruschev couldn't do it from here, nobody could."

"September Eleventh was utterly impossible and unthinkable until it happened."

"But the US would retaliate against Havana, and probably Riyadh, Baghdad, even Mecca and Medina. Millions would die, including us, here!"

"Martyrdom!"

"How could you possibly develop such weaponry in the Middle East?" I asked, determined to keep him talking, although I knew the cause was lost.

This riled Malmuni. "Ah, you greedy westerners screwed the balls off Eastern Europe after it collapsed, and their scientists found a home in the Middle East... You have to give clever people something to eat, not tell them to take their doctorates and fuck off... "

He was interrupted by a piercing, intermittent alarm, the weird, strident shrieking of a beast in pain. His homily ceased. His confident expression froze. Yarham and I were forgotten. He stood up quickly and rushed out of the room.

25

Roped to the chair, powerless, the alarm drilled into my head painfully. I could hear shouting and boots thudding along the corridor outside the room. The knife and cord still lay on the bed. I made efforts to move my chair closer to the bed, although the hope of getting hold of the knife was slim.

"We'll never do it this way. Let's try to get back to back, and you might be able to have a go at my wrists," I said, and Yarham silently complied.

As we struggled, propelling our chairs with our toes and shifting our weight, there was an explosion from outside which shook the flimsy wooden building, then another and another. Plaster and dust fell from the ceiling.

"It's a raid!" I was filled with hope, and made a frenzied attempt to jerk my chair to back Yarham's.

Then the door opened, and Dolores Martinez came in, hugging a bundle wrapped in a towel which she dropped on the bed. She gave no greeting and hardly looked at us. She seemed unreal and she moved in a cloud of womanish sweat. She held her fingers to her lips. She had a knife in her hand, and quickly severed my bonds at the wrist, dropping the knife on my lap, my bare lap where my penis lay shrivelled and inert. At any other time this would have been a pinnacle of embarrassment. She moved like a sleepwalker. Her black hair with its gold streaks hung in disarray over her damp forehead. Her breasts swung loose under a thin T-shirt. She wore a pair of tracksuit trousers. The pink painted toenails of her bare feet looked incongruous. She fled from the room without a word.

I cut my ankles free, and paused, before I attended to Yarham, to flick the towel off the parcel Dolores had brought. It contained a Uzi submachine-gun and magazines, and a Colt Double Eagle 45 with a box of shells. When Yarham was free, and had dragged his trousers up from his ankles, he grabbed the Uzi without any direction from me. "Fucking bastards," he mumbled to himself.

"Go easy with that thing. You know it?" I said, as he clipped in a magazine and racked the gun fiercely. But he seemed to know what he was doing. He cradled the gun in one arm and picked up the knife. He had been crazed by his experience with Hussein.

I checked that the Colt was loaded, removed the safety catch, and pushed the box of shells into my pocket, as the door opened.

Hussein, carrying an automatic pistol, was framed in the doorway. Behind him issued the din of automatic rifle fire and exploding grenades. He stood still, his moon face impassive, but his eyes flickering, startled at what he saw. In that second, and before I could begin to react, Yarham dropped the Uzi, and hurled himself at Hussein, plunging the blade into his throat. I dragged them both inside and shut the door. Hussein collapsed on the floor spouting blood, jerking like a dying turkey, and Yarham was still at him with the knife.

I was splashed with blood, and Yarham's shirt and trousers were soaked. "Steady on, man, or the dry cleaning bill will be enormous."

Yarham had hardly spoken since the emasculation episode, and he had a wild look in his eye. I could understand it. He'd been scared near to the stopping of his heart. He wasn't listening to me. He made as if to go out of the door.

I grabbed his arm. "We're not going out there until we have an idea what's happening, and a plan. And you're going to follow my orders, understand?"

He nodded reluctantly. "If I'm going to die, it'll be with my boots on, firing this!"

"More importantly, with your trousers on," I said.

Heavy small-arms fire was going on within the building, and as far as I could tell, very little from outside. That seemed to me to suggest that the CIA had actually got a commando party into the building. It couldn't be the Cuban police or army, because they would have set up a siege and megaphones, and demanded a surrender. I stood still. I didn't intend to risk my skin by rushing into a firefight.

"We need to get better observation, Yarham." I drew up the blind cautiously, to disclose floodlit lawns, and beyond, a wood. "Not a sign of life, this side. Those lights are very powerful. The ranch would never have installed them. They're part of Gomez's defence system."

"I think the action has all been on the other side of the building," Yarham said. He was coming to.

We had to cross the hall and have a look out of the window of the opposite room. When I opened our door I could see that the opposite room, which was open, was deserted. We slipped across the empty hall into a bedroom lit by the outside floodlights. The beds were upsided and resting against the shattered widows as barricades, and there were three dead men on the floor, slumped over their weapons. I turned one over with my foot. He had been shot in the head. He was wearing the familiar white shirt, open at the neck, with rolled sleeves.

"They look like Gomez's people. Keep a count, Yarham. We have to notch up ten."

The gunfire was still going on more sporadically now at

the other end of the wing. I crept up to the open window and looked out. The area, lit only by lights from the motel and flames from adjoining buildings, presented a quite different picture. Cavernous holes had been blown in the road and the lawns. Lumps of earth and rocks were strewn across the gardens. It looked as though there had been a bombing raid. Bodies lay on the ground. I counted five.

"So what happened?" Yarham said. We were both astounded at the carnage.

"My guess is that the CIA planned a commando attack on the building, fine, but failed to anticipate that Gomez had set up booby trap defences, fearsome defences. I'd say the whole building is ringed with mines, even that peaceful side we saw. The CIA hit the minefield and to give them due credit, some kept on going, and are still at it!"

"Where do we come in, Captain? Or go out."

"I think we practise masterly inactivity until the shooting is over, then work our way down the hall, go through each room, mop up any opposition, make a body count, and retire to the missile site. Oh yes, and we'll get you some decent clothes. You look as though you've been working in an abattoir."

I thought that there was a strong likelihood that the CIA would have cut the telephone lines from the camp, not wanting any calls from staff to the police or the army, but I was aware that intervention would come soon. The Gomez team were occupying the Campismo Mercados as sole guests, but there were Cuban staff and management. A frightened Cuban servant had only to walk to San Cristobal, or use a mobile phone. The police or the army or both would arrive soon. Yarham and I therefore had to be out of this place quite quickly, and this gnawed at me for ten or fifteen minutes as we waited, listening to the gradually reducing gunfire.

"Come on, man, let's go. One room at a time. Shoot first. I'll guard the rear," I said.

"How do we know the difference between CIA and terrorists?"

"Unfortunately we don't. Equally, the CIA will think we're terrorists and shoot first, and the terrorists will think we're CIA and shoot first."

"So we kill everybody?"

"Can you think of a safer way?"

We agreed that the only exception was Dolores Martinez, and began to move down the hall, Yarham in the lead with the Uzi. The rooms on the left were generally empty and untouched, those on the right had seen action, with the furniture turned over, and smashed windows – and the occasional body. I could distinguish now between the CIA and Al Qaeda. The CIA were wearing khaki denims with camouflage patches. The terrorists still wore their black trousers and mostly white shirts. We moved methodically. I kicked each door open. Yarham entered first, his gun cradled at the ready, while I kept an eye on the hall.

The gunshots had ceased. We paused to listen. There was silence. A man came down the hall toward me, a blur in the poor light. I fired. The Colt had a whack like a cannon. The man dropped without a murmur, his throat pulped. He was in the dress of the terrorists. I stepped over him, the fumes from the Colt pricking my nostrils, and we went on, from room to room, counting the toll.

"These guys intended to fight to the death, and they have," I said.

At the end of the hall, where the most intensive hand-to-hand fighting had taken place, the woodwork and doors were splintered by high-velocity bullets which had penetrated the thin construction. With two more rooms to go, we stepped into one where two men were on their feet, bending over, examining a dead man. They spun around at the noise. The bigger man, in denim, with a black beret on his head, had his hand at his side holding a revolver. The smaller man, with a black mask over his head revealing only his eyes, had a submachine gun cradled in his arm which he was bringing to the ready.

I was standing behind Yarham's shoulder. I took in the red complexion and the neat ginger moustache of the big man. He probably had a family in Montana. Instantly, his light eyes searched us, two bloodied Caucasians, trying to place us, seeing fighters and concluding foes.

I wanted to say, "Wait, man. We can talk. We're on the same side," but words were useless. His companion's gun was nearly up. It was kill or be killed. Yarham sprayed them with slugs as though he was putting out a fire.

I did not pause, but continued the search. The lobby and office were deserted, the staff shack a few yards from the house was in blackness. We changed our shirts for white T-shirts we found in a drawer in one of the bedrooms, and went over the body count – nine Al Qaeda, no Gomez, and thankfully, no Dolores. It wasn't surprising that the pair had escaped while they had the opportunity. There were six dead CIA inside, including two Caucasians who might have been the leading US agents, and the rest Cubans. A quick search of the bodies inside the house revealed nothing, except that one of the Caucasian CIA men, whom we had counted as dead, had a shoulder wound. I shook him into consciousness.

"Listen, buddy, we'll get you out of here and fix your wound. We need a vehicle. You got a vehicle? You'll end your days in a Cuban army prison if we don't get you out. We don't have much time."

The CIA agent was in too much pain to resist, or to

trouble about precisely who I was. Any saviour would do. I was banking on the fact that the raiders had a line of vehicles nearby, and that their vehicle minders had probably fled. It seemed easiest to solve the transport problem this way, rather than try to hi-jack an Al Qaeda vehicle, assuming we could find one. I prodded the CIA agent into the lead, and we gingerly followed the tracks of others through the devastated part of the minefield. I looked across at the staff shack and saw a light.

"Swap guns, Yarham, and take our man to the gate. Wait for me there. I'll go across and have a look at the staff quarters, just to be sure. There's a light showing. I think the local staff will all have run like hell."

I moved out of the moonlight into the shadow of the staff building. The blinds were closed. I crept through the open doorway in darkness into a hallway. I heard a woman's voice speaking low, but edgy, full of emotion, and speaking in English – I assumed it was the common language of Dolores and Gomez. I stepped into the room, a seedy lounge leading to the bedrooms. Gomez had laid his revolver on a side table covered with greasy magazines. He was standing before Dolores, who was hunched on the edge of a chair, her arms wrapped around her breasts protectively.

I had the Uzi with my nervy finger on the trigger. "Don't make me kill you in front of the lady," I said, thinking at the same time that I was a damn fool not to gun him down without a word.

Gomez smiled thinly, but at ease, and I knew he would be as ready to lose his life as his comrades had been. If he had been alone, I'd have killed him without any preface. And if he moved, I intended to kill him, Dolores present or not. Dolores looked up at me blankly, gave an involuntary cry and lunged forward, whether out of relief or to shield Gomez, I didn't know. In the instant that she stepped in front of the barrel of the Uzi, Gomez fled out of the open door behind him, and along a back verandah. I followed, loosing off a burst as he jumped over the rail. He disappeared down the hill, into the dark foliage of the wood. Pursuit was out of the question.

I went back to Dolores. "Come on, we've got to get out of here."

I took her arm and pulled her along, down the path to the gate. She still had bare feet and moved with difficulty over the sharp stones. Yarham and our CIA prisoner were waiting. The CIA man led us down the main road for a hundred yards, a journey made in a silence, broken by his heaving breath and moans. In a lay-by, there were two jeeps and two sedan cars, but no guards. I decided that a battered Subaru sedan might be the least obtrusive. The keys were in the ignition, the tank was nearly full. In a few moments we were on the road to Mariel, with Yarham at the wheel, Dolores slumped in front beside him.

I attended to Wayne – as he identified himself – in the back of the car. I stanched the bleeding from the wound in his shoulder, and applied a tight bandage from one of the medical kits in the car. Yarham drew my attention to a train of lights a couple of miles away, approaching on the winding road, winking like glow worms. We were driving without lights, and I ordered Yarham to pull off the road, into a field. We waited in the hot darkness, the old car smelling of engine oil, grimy plastic seats, and a faint scent from Dolores. In a few minutes an army convoy of four armoured cars, an armoured personnel carrier full of troops with rifles, and a staff car came past us. As soon as they had disappeared, we got back on the road and made all speed for Mariel.

I had decided that Wayne could be of further use to us. He looked to me to be around thirty-five, and that almost certainly meant he was a fully trained agent, and a party to the CIA plan of attack. He wasn't badly hurt; the muscles and blood vessels in his upper arm were torn, and possibly the bone was chipped; although his wound could poison. He was in serious pain. He was shaken by his ordeal, and in a receptive state of mind.

"Wayne, I want to tell you who I am. I'm a British agent of MI6, working with US intelligence. I'm here to do the same thing you are – put these terrorists out of business. OK, the attack at the camp was costly, but we can still go on and destroy the site."

"Three of us?" he asked, seemingly untroubled by my thin explanation.

"Four, if you include Dolores. Sure, we can do it. Tell me how you were going to do it." Dolores was still hunched over and did not react to my inclusion of her.

Wayne didn't take very long to weigh up the pros and cons of revealing the plan. "I don't know whether I should be talking to you guys, but I guess I heard you were around… and OK we want the same thing… We reckoned on wiping out Al Qaeda at the ranch, making the destruction of the site a demolition job."

"Makes sense. What about the fissile material in the warheads? What were you going to do with that? Did Langley give you specific instructions on how to handle it?"

Wayne hesitated. "Tell you the truth, this is a kind of save-the-world mission, and we've never had instructions from Langley. Red Lomas, the chief, said we just go ahead and do it, and take the applause afterwards. We were going to drop the warheads down a thousand-foot nickel mine shaft and throw in a few grenades to block it off."

I didn't know any more than Wayne did about disposal of nuclear warheads, and it did not sound like a very satisfactory idea.

"Tell me about the actual demolition of the rockets and launchers."

"We were going to blow shit out of them. Drive in a couple of trucks loaded with HE. Detonate the explosives. There's a lot of chemicals on site for rocket fuel. Would have been a blaze you could see from Miami."

"We can still do that, Wayne. You have the trucks and explosive in place?"

"Yeah, but what does MI6 have?"

I gave a little laugh. "We don't have anything at the moment. We're only in the planning stage. You guys have beaten us to the punch. So we have no option but to try to finish off what you started."

"I understand... go ahead..." Wayne groaned, and closed his eyes.

"No problemo," Yarham echoed, coming further out of the cataleptic state that had gripped him since his dick was endangered.

I gave Wayne a needle full of morphine, and let him lapse into a stupor. I was feeling rather pleased, already framing a report in my mind about how I led an assault on the Al Qaeda terrorists against almost insuperable odds, wiping most of them out, and how I went on to demolish their site.

"Ambitious, don't you think, Captain?" Yarham said, startling me as though he knew my thoughts.

"Let's see how we go. If friend Wayne's associates have set it up, we need only light the fuse, so to speak."

Yarham grunted irritably. "If I was Gomez on the loose, and saw my plans being wrecked, and death didn't matter a damn, you know what I'd do?" He paused, and I switched my mind to Gomez, whom, in the flush of victory, I'd ignored. "I'd arm a warhead and get a rocket away without waiting for the fine detail of plotting its course, and if I could, I'd arm any other warheads and detonate them on site."

"Gomez doesn't have the capability to do that immediately, man!" I said loudly and confidently, although I had no confidence.

26

Yarham's suggestion about Gomez unsettled me. I argued with him whether Gomez would want to hurt an inoffensive country like Cuba, and whether Gomez would have the personal expertise to arm the warheads; whether technically the warheads could be exploded on the ground without a lot of work. But in any event there was no doubt that Gomez was a complete nihilist, and left free, a menace.

"If you're right, Gomez will run for the site. We'll find him there," I said. "Is that right, Dolores?"

I hadn't begun to think about how to deal with Dolores. She had joined us like a shadow. She stirred, and spoke expressionlessly. "I think so. He is a very determined man. And there's something I should tell you. Although the missile firing is not ready, one missile has been placed on readiness. This was done for this kind of emergency. Discovery by the Cuban authorities, you know. It will take maybe twenty-four hours to arm and load. Ayoub Sabri, whom you may know as Hertz, was killed at the ranch, but Malmuni can do it."

"We'll have to move our collective ass," Yarham said, cheered at the suggestion that we had twenty-four hours.

"Oh, and by the way, Dolores, thanks for what you did back there," I said, but she showed no sign of having heard me.

I had to travel to Mariel via the Hotel Yara in Havana, to retrieve the money and the satphone. It took a long time, and except for Yarham at the wheel, we were comatose by the time we reached Mariel. There, I prodded Wayne into consciousness, and he directed us to an old factory, in a rickety block of similar premises, guarded by an armed Cuban. The guard accepted us as part of Wayne's force when I half-carried Wayne through the doorway. I sat him down in the office cubicle inside the doors. I intended that we should take the place over for our operations, and I ordered Yarham to bring the car inside and close up. The factory had been cleared from its previous use, and on the broken concrete floor were two ten-ton trucks loaded with explosive.

"We were going to drive them through the gates," Wayne said.

"Can you handle one of these?" I asked Yarham.

"A kamikaze run, you mean?" he said, cocking an eyebrow.

"No," Wayne said, "we aimed to give the driver and his support crew time to get out, and detonate electrically."

He showed us the mechanisms. Apart from switching on the radio controls, the vehicles were wired and ready to go. The guard had the keys.

"What about the warheads?" These worried me.

"They're on the site. It is in fact the workings of an old nickel mine. We didn't expect serious opposition. Maybe a few Cuban guards. We aimed to drive in the trucks, settle the resistance if any. Dump the warheads down a shaft, follow them with a few grenades, then retire and blow the trucks."

There, with changes in the dramatis personnae, was my plan.

Wayne had been very helpful. He had lost a lot of blood – my first aid was not very effective – and apparently he was suffering. I promised, in return for his help, to get him to a doctor. I was doubtful about Dolores, whether she might act as a magnet for Gomez, who might by now realise that she had sold him out. I decided to leave Wayne, Dolores and the car in the factory with the guard, while Yarham and I made a reconnaissance of the site.

"I'll take Wayne to a doctor while you do that," Dolores said.

It made perfect sense. But, while Dolores had saved our lives, she was a spy and a deceiver, a woman of strange allegiances, a woman whose mind I simply could not plumb. I didn't trust her, fascinating as she could be on a relaxed occasion. And I didn't want to lose sight of her, in case somebody as obsessional as Gomez might be drawn back to her out of love or revenge – enabling me to deal with him, as I should have done at our earlier meeting.

"No. It's too dangerous. When I get back from the recce, in about an hour, we'll all go together. There's one other thing I'll ask you to do, Dolores. Find out how our man Kershaw is. I don't even know the name of the hospital."

Dolores agreed and I told her the story of Kershaw's misfortune. "Give me a phone and I'll see if I can trace him," she said.

In the first light of dawn, we walked the several blocks of filthy, uneven and deserted streets. Yarham had an old piece of canvas over his Uzi. I had the Colt in my belt. As we stumbled along, a couple of drunks getting back from a party, I began to consider how we would make our entry. Our chances of doing so surrepticiously were slight – there were dogs and guards. I was thinking of climbing the wire at the rear, when Yarham reminded me.

"Mines, Captain."

If Al Qaeda had booby-trapped their living quarters, the likelihood that they would have done the same at their workplace was strong. Therefore any entry other than the main gate was dangerous. When we were a few yards from the gate, we tucked ourselves away behind a rusty iron fence. I could get a view across the compound to the crumbling brick buildings within. There were signs of movement inside the wire. Dogs roamed the compound, barking occasionally. Through the cracks in the doors of the building, lights were shining.

"I think we do it all in one, like Wayne's pals. We bust in through the gate with the trucks," I said.

"Sounds easy, Captain," Yarham said ironically.

It was in fact very dangerous, and near suicidal if there was determined opposition, but I could think of no other way. I only wanted to recite the plan, to hold it up to the light in all its naivety.

"Suppose the grenades we throw down the mineshaft set off the warheads," Yarham said.

"I wish you wouldn't bother me with these theoretical difficulties, man."

We walked back to the CIA factory in silence. I left Yarham and the guard to keep the area under surveillance while I drove the Subaru, with Wayne and Dolores, to find a doctor.

"Your friend Kershaw," Dolores said, "I found out from the newspaper office. They remembered the story of the beaten up white man. They said he died."

I had expected this. "He was badly beaten. I'm sorry. He was doing a good job."

Nobody else said anything.

Dolores directed me to a relatively prosperous part of the town outside the main shopping and market area, with small but expensive detached houses. She accompanied Wayne into the doctor's surgery – which was not officially open, while I waited outside. I had given her enough money to calm the medico if his sleep was disturbed or if he was touchy about treating a gunshot wound.

I had bought Wayne a pair of trousers and a T-shirt at a market stall, and had struggled in the car to remove his denims and dress him, to avoid suspicion. After twenty minutes, during which I began to regret my generosity with my time, Dolores came out to the car. "The doctor says Wayne needs to go to hospital."

"We'll take him to hospital when I've finished the job, in a few hours. I might need him. Get the doctor to give a painkiller."

"It will knock him out and he won't be able to help."

"Not too much then. Is the doctor reliable? I mean will he keep his mouth shut?"

"He ought to. He's been paid enough."

I didn't want to get involved in admitting a patient with a gunshot wound to hospital. I might find myself in custody, answering questions. I didn't want Dolores involved either. At this point, although I didn't say so, I planned to dump Wayne at a hospital casualty department without explanation, when I was ready to leave Mariel. Dolores pleaded that we couldn't continue to drive Wayne around, and as a compromise I agreed to leave them both at a hotel while I went back to the factory. But we couldn't go to a hotel until I had bought Dolores shoes, a jacket and a comb. These small tasks took an interminable time. The market stalls were still setting up.

I at last obtained two adjoining rooms on the first floor of a small hotel, the Avila, in the downtown commercial district. Money assisted the reception staff to avoid looking too closely at our unkempt condition. We helped Wayne upstairs and put him to bed.

"I'll watch him, but if he gets too bad, I'm going to call a cab and take him to the hospital," Dolores said.

"You could get into trouble if you do that. I have to leave it to you."

"Good luck with… what you have to do."

I had to believe she would stay with Wayne and wait for me, unless Wayne's condition became too acute, because there was no other course for me. We went into the next room. She said she would lie down, but didn't feel tired. I put my arms around her and thanked her again for saving our lives.

"I don't even know your name, and it's not Wolf, is it?" She summoned up two small dimples in her cheeks which I had never noticed before, and I told her. "Rojairr, I like that," she said.

"And I don't know who you really are."

"Isn't it obvious?"

"Gomez's lover?"

"That's what you call business… But he is a man. A strong man."

When she said Gomez was a man, I took it that she was paying him a high compliment, a mix of sexual power and drive. "You were trying to get him to leave you at the camp, to get away?"

"Yes, my feelings… "

"It's hopeless dealing with him, Dolores. He's programmed to kill or be killed on this mission, didn't you realise this?"

"Yes, but… "

"And you were Arias's lover?"

She shrugged. "He too is an impressive man. He has no chance now. He wanted the best for Cuba."

"You really cared for him?"

"Yes."

"Two men at once?" I asked, thinking of my own paltry position between two such giants, and feeling slightly put down.

"Two *men* – why not?"

"Why did you do me out of the half-million?"

She laughed faintly. "Because the CIA plan was going

forward. I didn't want complications. Did you feel bad?"

"I did. What did you do with the money?"

She was wistful. "Some I kept. I like money. I need it. Some, most, I gave to Alfredo."

"Why were you working with the CIA?"

"Is there any other game in town?"

"Mine."

"I didn't know about you, Rojairr. You were very charming, and interesting. You had the password. And the money. But I wondered about you."

I still couldn't fathom whether she was a patriot or a moneygrubber, but even in her stained clothes, with dishevelled hair, and bruised-looking hollows under her sleepless eyes, she was a deep well into which I wanted to plunge. I closed my arms more tightly round her, and felt the wild surge within her own body, as though these memories of her lovers had excited her, or she wanted to bury the memories in the sweaty present, in that plain room, on the narrow bed, with the unconscious Wayne a few feet away.

I laid her down gently, and lay beside her, and she unfolded like a flower. We clung to each other until the last waves had subsided, and there was only the reality of partly undressed wet bodies, and the smell of human juices. It was so far from my ideal of the luxurious penthouse suite above a blue harbour, where I would bed the beautiful spy, but no less sweet for that... Only now I began to chastise myself for wasting precious time when I had urgent work to do.

"You're beautiful, Rojairr."

"But not serious, like Arias and Gomez?" I said, levering myself up off the bed, and going into the bathroom.

"You're fun. You take me away to... to a make-believe world," she called.

I returned to the bedroom, to the grim present of Arias

and Gomez. "So who do you really work for, Dolores. Yourself?"

"I thought it would be obvious to you. The United States."

"Tell me another."

"It's true. You don't have to believe me. It doesn't matter between us one way or the other."

I gave a silent groan at the nonsense of my calling. "You're kidding. You mean you're a US agent?"

"Sure. And citizen."

"Which department?"

"You wouldn't know, Roger, and it doesn't matter. It's in Washington. It's called C3."

27

I left the hotel grinding my teeth at Dolores's revelation. It was no use asking why I wasn't told that C3 had a fully trained Cuban operative in place. The answer was that nobody in C3 had thought I needed to know, or probably nobody knew that I didn't know. Maybe Dolores wasn't rated very highly alongside the machinations of the Disciples. It was no use thinking how much easier my task might have been had I known who Dolores Martinez really was, because it was too late.

Instead, I tried to concentrate on the demolition job. It was necessary to go through with it now, rather than wait for darkness. I had to assume Gomez was arming a missile, and there was always the possibility that the Cuban army would latch on to the site. I would have liked to finish Gomez, but I decided that Yarham and I would have to get out of Cuba immediately after the demolition, whether we got Gomez at the same time or not. We didn't have time to chase him further.

I drove the car down the rubbish-strewn lane approaching the CIA factory, dodging rusty oil drums and wooden crates. I turned in to the factory doorway and Yarham was waiting, an old straw hat pulled down on his head. He looked every bit like one of the dirty, unlucky people who roamed these streets. He approached the car before I climbed out.

"I've seen Gomez, riding around in his black Toyota. He was at the site for a while, and then out. Are you sure you weren't followed?"

It was a possibility I hadn't even considered. "I don't think so. There are so few cars, I think I'd have noticed. But get your Uzi, and we'll take a ride, see if we can pick him up."

We patrolled the streets around the site, looking for the Toyota. We made a wider sweep into the town. "I think it's right to do this, but we can't give it much more time," I said.

"There!" Yarham shouted. About three blocks ahead of us, idling in the sparse traffic, was a mud-splattered and dented black sedan. "I think that's him."

I thought we could pull alongside Gomez's car, force it off the road, and hit him, gangster fashion. I would have to wait until we were in a less populous area, but the desolate streets around the site would be ideal. I kept a couple of blocks behind. Gomez was heading back in the direction of the site. He was well in front for a few minutes, easily in sight, and then he disappeared. We drove a few blocks, peering into the distance, and around corners, but no Gomez.

"He must be going back to the site. This is the general direction," Yarham said.

I drove hard in that direction, but saw no sign of him, only empty pot-holed streets with abandoned rusting car bodies. "What would he have been doing in town?"

"He has to eat," Yarham said, reminding me that we hadn't eaten for hours.

I had a dismal thought – about Dolores and Wayne. "Gomez couldn't possibly have found the hotel, could he?"

"Do you want to check, sir?"

I thought it would be a cautious move. I drove back to the hotel fast, keeping my foot down on the wheezing engine, and using the gears until the car screamed. I pulled up outside, and raced through the lobby and upstairs. I could see from the landing that Wayne's door was ajar, and that gave me a jab of anxiety. Something had gone wrong. When I reached the door, I halted involuntarily. It was apprehension. I gently pushed the door wider. Inside, Wayne was prone on the floor. He lay in a red flag of stain, his face blue, eyes half open, his throat cut.

I had a sick feeling in my guts as I strode across the room, and thrust open the adjoining door.

Dolores had made a fight of it. The bed was tossed, and the sheets flecked with blood – but she was not there!

I clattered down the stairs and ran back to the car. "Wayne's been killed and Dolores abducted. This is zero hour," I said to Yarham as we drove back to the site. "We take the trucks, and go in now."

"Very good, Captain," Yarham said unenthusiastically. "What are you going to do about Dolores?"

"There's nothing I can do. Gomez has her. He could have killed her at the hotel, but didn't. What that means, I don't know. I think we have to… regard her as dead."

"Going after her at all shows he's not thinking straight. He should be getting the rocket away," Yarham said.

It was one of those practical observations which made me value Yarham. "She betrayed him. His feelings for her must be a strange concoction of passion and hate, enough to divert him. And he has time. Dolores said that there were chemical processes which were prolonged, fuelling I suppose."

I felt that luck had favoured us so far, Yarham and me, and couldn't be expected to last; I ought to shorten our programme. The driving in and detonation of the trucks would be sufficient. We would retire immediately. The warheads would have to take their chance in the blast. Then, at last, we would be on our way with all speed to the south coast to hire a boat for Jamaica. Dolores was heavily on my mind, but, as in the case of Kershaw, I couldn't help her now. I explained my abridged proposal.

"I think that's a better plan, sir," Yarham said, relieved. "Have you thought that Gomez only has one place to take Dolores?"

"The missile site? I know."

"It doesn't make any difference to the plan?"

"No. If we delay, we're in danger of not doing the job, and that could be fateful, one life against many lives."

At the factory it took a half an hour to get the tired engines of each of the trucks started and warmed up. We were nearly asphyxiated by the diesel smoke in the shed. I rehearsed Yarham on the procedure for the radio detonation – at least that equipment was new. I bestowed the radio control on Yarham with his technical skills.

When the two trucks were running throatily, we each mounted, and they roared in low gear, their arthritic chassis creaking, as we came out of the factory doors, into the lane. I had my automatic with me, and Yarham had the Uzi. Other than those two items, the only piece of valuable equipment was the satellite phone which was locked in the Subaru, with the holdall of cash under guard by our Cuban helper.

I gripped the wheel with clammy hands, and moved the slack gear-shift up as the vehicle gathered speed. This was the moment.

When we were crashing through the ruts three hundred yards from the gates, as agreed, we moved abreast on the road, and accelerated up to about twenty-five miles per hour. The gates were opposite an intersection, and if we could stay together, we could hit the gates directly without reducing speed. I kept looking across to make sure I was keeping up. I could see Yarham grinning and waving – a display of bravado which I encouraged with a thumbs up sign, as we bore down on the gates, the two vehicles grinding along wheel-to-wheel.

I put my arm up to shield my face as the bumper struck the wire gates, but the truck crunched through easily, tearing away the wire and pipe frame without even breaking the windshield. I let the vehicle go on across the compound at a lower speed, to splinter one of the shed doors that had been visible to us in our surveillance. Yarham's vehicle smashed through the other door seconds later.

Our plan, which seemed to have worked, was not to try to drive right inside the shed, where we might be vulnerable, but merely to shatter the entrance and retreat.

I leaped out of the cab. I could see one of the vehicular launching ramps, and a crane, with a rocket suspended in its claws to be loaded. There were no people about; even the dogs had been scared into retreat. Just inside the door was the black car. Gomez was here somewhere – and, presumably, Dolores.

Along one wall was a row of shining tanks with gauges, pipes, and what looked like condensers or coolers. An instrument panel glowed with lights; a bank of computer screens flickered. The air had a sickly sweet smell, and there was a sense of life and activity about the tanks. All this I absorbed in a flash.

I heard the chatter of Yarham's Uzi and a feeble return of fire. A voice boomed out of a loudspeaker. "Don't move, Mr Gold. I can see you. I have cameras everywhere. You can't see me. I have you covered. Drop the weapon. Your brave companion, Mr Red, has run away. You will die if you run." It was Gomez. "Move inside," he commanded.

I stood still, and a shower of automatic rifle fire pocked the cement floor at my feet.

"Move or die, Mr Gold."

I moved. I dropped the Colt and looked around as I went nearer to the platform. Gomez was at the controls above me, looking down. "I don't think your brave friend will do anything drastic while I have you and Mrs Martinez, and I need only a little time. You will have a front- row seat for this major attack on the US mainland."

One of Gomez's men marched me upstairs to the platform. The crane had swung the barrel of the rocket into place on the launcher. Apart from the man on the crane, and the one holding a submachine gun on me, I could see no others. And there couldn't be many more. Gomez confronted me on the platform. "Welcome to the performance, Mr Gold. A once-in-a-lifetime performance for you to see, ha ha! Come join the audience, I think you know Mrs Martinez."

He gestured to a rack, further along the platform, to which Dolores was tied, arms outstretched, ankles lashed, head slumped like a crucified sinner. She lifted her head as the worker behind me jolted me in the spine with the barrel of his gun. I remembered the blood on the sheets at the hotel. Her cheeks had been slashed with a knife, her t-shirt torn open and her breasts slashed. Her chest was a curtain of blood. She was expressionless and speechless, but her eyes contained cold chips of crystal.

"A woman's beauty is transitory, eh, Mr Gold?"

I was full of inexpressible rage against Gomez, but all I could do was murmur to her, "Don't give up."

I had to let Gomez's man lash me to the rack alongside Dolores, while Gomez returned to his technical work at the instrument panel. I kept as tense as I could, so that when I relaxed, the bonds might be slightly looser. I could see that the man wasn't used to this task and he did it poorly – but for the time being I was held tight.

While Gomez's attention was off me, I struggled unobtrusively, but feverishly, to free myself. I watched the crane man retreat. Another man appeared with various tubes and wires which he fitted to a panel near the base of the missile. Gomez had become absorbed in his controls and the progress of the work. But without looking up, he spared a moment to taunt us about the expected victims. "Not the fate of three thousand, Mr Gold, but the fate of three million," he said, and then returned to his instruments. I guessed he would come back to us to taste the moments before launch.

If, as seemed likely, Yarham had escaped, would he detonate the trucks and blow me to pieces as the best way to save possibly three million people? It was a simple sum, and Yarham would understand it. After all, it was the same reasoning we had applied to Dolores.

At that moment, a piercing intermittent alarm, like the one at the Campismo Mercados, sounded. There were shouts in a language I didn't understand, and the crane driver and the man who had tied me picked up submachine guns and scuttled into cover.

I assumed Yarham was trying something on. There was a rattle of gunshots. Gomez disappeared from the platform. Dolores had torn one wrist out of the bonds, and she quickly undid the other, and her ankles. She had no time to free me before Gomez, gun in hand, appeared at the head of the stairs. She screamed, and threw herself at him, an avenging fury. She caught him off balance, and together they tumbled down the stairs. The speed and savagery of her onslaught had momentarily overcome Gomez, and he was stunned in the fall. Dolores landed on top of him, at the foot of the stairs. She plunged her long-nailed fingers like daggers into his eyes, again and again. Hearing his cries, his men turned their guns on her, and riddled her body. Then they took cover and started to exchange shots. I concluded the fight was with Yarham, who was cautiously behind the black Toyota.

Out of panic, I had managed to tear my wrists out of my bonds by this time. I picked up Gomez's semi-automatic pistol which was lying on the deck. Gomez, below, was crawling around in sightless circles howling like dog, while his eyeballs dripped out of his face like broken eggs. Dolores, nearby, was a bloody heap. I slipped downstairs quickly. I kicked Gomez as I passed, but I didn't kill him – that would have been a kindness. I took a couple of shots at Gomez's defenders, and ran to join Yarham behind the car.

"Let's get out of here, double quick," I said.

We retired carefully, Yarham keeping up a steady return of fire. We began to get the impression that the terrorists, technicians rather than riflemen by choice, weren't minded to attack, and were glad to see us go. Nobody had guessed that the trucks were not merely battering rams, but bombs ready to explode. We dashed across the compound into the road. The dogs were cowed by the noise, and those which chose to attack were shot by Yarham. There was no pursuit.

At five hundred yards, I ordered Yarham to operate the radio control. I felt a sharp ground-shock like an earthquake, then another. And with a skull-crushing roar, an inferno exploded out of the site, sending a fireball up hundreds of feet into the air. As the rocket fuel ignited, the fireball pulsed further and faster with successive explosions. The sky was filled with a black-leafed orchid of gargantuan dimensions.

The heat and smoke of the blast soon engulfed us, and we had to jog with little visibility, choking, for the last half-mile to the CIA factory. The loyal guard was still there. We took him with us in the old Japanese sedan, and with Yarham driving, found our way out of the town. We let the Cuban out on the fringes of the town, with a roll of dollars, and pointed the nose of the car toward Marea del Portillo on the southern coast. As we moved south, a curtain of pitch darkness behind us blotted out the sun.

"Do you think the intense heat might... set off the nuclear warheads, sir?"

"Yarham, I'm thinking of a glass of red wine and a steak, but keep moving at a brisk pace, will you?"

28

I decided that it would be too risky, for a variety of reasons, to pause long enough on the island of Cuba to have a bath, shave, a few bottles of wine and a good meal, badly as I wanted these things. Instead we embarked dirty, smelly and hungry on the boat which Yarham chartered at Marea del Portillo, bound for Jamaica. It was a fast cabin cruiser, used for deep-sea marlin fishing, basic but effective, with a Cuban skipper and a boat boy.

The skipper asked no questions after the price was settled. When Yarham asked the skipper about food, he pulled out a bottle of good Caney rum, and pointed to the maize fritters wrapped in newsprint, on the bench in the galley, which I supposed he had bought at a local stall as a snack.

As we headed out of port I felt the rum warming my belly and I gnawed at the *fritura de maiz*. I jotted down the report I proposed to send by the satellite phone, which I had composed in my head as we jolted across Cuba in the car. "It's important to get a report back soonest, Yarham, because our masters have certainly got wind of events here – and they're likely to panic." The explosions at Mariel would have been detected and photographed.

"How will you explain the ahh… pause in compliance with the order to return, Captain?"

"Say I didn't get it."

"Then you better chuck the phone overboard when you've sent your report, because it's logged in there."

"Thanks, Yarham. I need you to keep me straight on these things."

"It'll be a difficult report, Captain, because it has been a not uneventful mission, and there are some interesting aspects to cover." Yarham tiptoed awkwardly over the words.

He had touched on a sensitivity that had been exercising my mind. "It's important that we both tell the same story, man. You know, just in case we get separated."

I was probably being over-cautious, because the likelihood was that Yarham would not be debriefed. Although he was in practice my assistant, he was officially an administration officer, and his grading meant that he didn't, in the view of the authorities, have the wit to form a view worthy of debriefing. The only reason he had been able to take part in a field operation was that I had the clout to insist upon it. At the same time, he was fully trained in field operations.

"I'd appreciate your guidance," Yarham said.

"It's occurred to you, I suppose, that there's nobody to contradict what we say?"

"Indeed, except Burton. It gives you a certain… freedom of interpretation, sir."

"Burton is a jailbird and a drug smuggler, and we haven't risked our lives to write a report that shows anything but the professional excellence of our work. Agreed?"

"Absolutely, Captain."

"Very good. Something like this, I thought." I handed him my scribbled note. *Al Quaeda were ready to release nuclear missiles targeted New York and Washington within hours therefore immediate response necessary. Led force supported by the CIA which destroyed all known Al Qaeda personnel and missile site. Heavy CIA casualties.*

"Very short and snappy, sir. How will you get over why you didn't call in aid from Washington?"

I squinted out at the sun-dappled sea, and thought about this. "Mmmmm. You mean taking too much on myself? C3 being peeved that they couldn't initiate a bit of precision aerial bombing surgery on the Cuban mainland? Well, try this. I pencilled: *Al Qaeda found to be on countdown to release nuclear missiles targeted New York and Washington. Immediate local response essential. Insufficient time to call air strike. Led force supported by CIA in attack. Destroyed all known Al Qaeda personnel, including missiles and site. Heavy casualties. Returning.* Now, how about that?"

"That's it, sir. Pretty impressive. You don't intend to say anything about Carmelli and the coastguards, or the fate of Burton?"

"Not at the moment. What's the point? It'll only start up a whole lot of internal enquiries. No, I think we should make a virtue out of CIA support."

I went over our venture in detail with Yarham as the fibreglass hull of the boat hammered across the rippling sea, and sent the report on the satphone. Then we sluiced away the maize grease with large drafts of rum, and both fell asleep in the cabin, exhausted.

I awoke from jagged dreams when we were skimming smoothly across the entrance to Montego Bay, toward a mooring. I thought it wise, however, to avoid the bay, and get our skipper to drop us at a more quiet spot along the coast, to avoid the coastguards and immigration police. A few miles on, we waded ashore at a green inlet with a few yards of deserted beach, and hired a local person to drive us in his car to the Montego Grand Hotel.

Since we were both grubby, in rags, and without any appreciable luggage, I had to embroider a story of the privations of big game fishing at sea, at the reception of the Montego, Grand Hotel, but the production of a large bundle of US banknotes, and a lavish tip, enabled us to get luxurious rooms, shower, and sleep overnight.

In the morning, we ventured into the boutiques to buy clothes. We spent a day eating and drinking and contemplating our good fortune. That evening I sent another message to C3 requesting new documentation to enable us to fly to the US from Jamaica. When the documentation arrived via the US Embassy, I crushed the satphone with my shoe and dropped it in a dumpster. In the two or three days this formality took, Yarham and I had a vacation by the sea. We still had about two hundred thousand dollars of our supply left, and I debated with Yarham what its fate ought to be.

"Suppose we each take a hundred thousand and leave the rest for Uncle Sam?" I suggested.

Yarham moved his jaw around, and said after a while, "I'm very grateful for the offer, and I don't want you to think I'm moralistic about this, but I'd prefer not to."

"Too much? Take a smaller slice."

"It's not that, sir. I can manage without any of it."

"Good for you, Yarham. I was just testing to see if the shield of truth, and the sword of honour, were in place."

Of course, I had been thinking that the Kershaw method ought to apply, but I marvelled, not at Yarham's probity, which every good batman ought to have, but at the fact that clearly the money wasn't important to him, even though we were sampling the delights of a five-thousand-dollar-a-day suite at the Grand. Yarham was the man who was happy with things as they were. I was the man who was yearning for an ever more brilliant future. Other than purchasing a greenhide Vuitton bag to contain the money – and the stylish clothes I had bought I made no decision about it.

We returned to Washington on a sunny afternoon, well rested, to be met by C3 agents and taken to the Georgetown office for a preliminary debriefing. Gerry Clark was there to greet me, unctuous and expectant. I had glanced at the newspapers on the flight, and apart from the usual rumblings in the Middle East, there was nothing to suggest that the US mainland had been in danger from terrorists. Cuba was not mentioned.

"We're all waiting to hear how you did this, Roger. It's quite a coup for C3. Yeah, it's turned out differently than we expected – but then field ops often do. We thought we'd be dealing with the threat from here."

"There was no time. I had to deal with it, as I'll explain."

In the presense of Clark and two senior C3 agents whom I knew only slightly, I spun my story of cooperation with the CIA in the person of Carmelli, Harkness and Burton; buying information and arms through Dolores and Arias; surveillance of the Campesino and the Mariel launching site; Kershaw's unfortunate discovery and death; a skirmish with Cuban coastguards on a reconnaissance in which Carmelli and Harkness were killed, and Burton taken prisoner; and my decision to attack at the Campesino, based on intelligence from Dolores that a launch of the missiles was imminent. I spoke of talks with the local CIA in which my leadership was accepted. I admitted that none of us had anticipated that the Campesino would be so heavily defended, but with Dolores Martinez, a wounded Wayne, and Yarham, I went on to destroy the opposition and the Mariel site.

It was a neat, sequential account, only at variance with the facts in immaterial respects. I calculated that criticism of Carmelli's thuggery, and the fiasco with the Cuban coastguards would do nobody, including myself, any good. The only problem could possibly be Burton, who I anticipated would probably serve a few years in a Cuban prison for drug dealing, if the Cuban legal machinery was allowed to come to rest without intervention by the US. And even if diplomatic pressure led to his release, there would be little he could contradict that would bring him credit. I would simply challenge his memory of events if necessary.

Clark & Co were astonished at what I had undeniably accomplished, and not in a mood to probe my story. And characteristically, the loss of Kershaw, Dolores and the CIA agents evoked no more than a casual mutter of regret from them.

Later, after I had filed a full written report, in view of the public silence about our exploits, I instructed Yarham to get busy on the OPB files and find out how my standing was in the agency. As I expected, it was accepted that I acted with speed of thought and valour, and avoided a national disaster and an international crisis. The Disciples seemed to be reconciled to not being able to play political brinkmanship with the presidential candidates on this occasion.

Much was made in departmental memos of the astonishing cooperation between C3 and the CIA, as though the concept of frankly sharing information with a fellow agency was novel, startling, and slightly risqué. Actually working together in the field was as unusual as intergalactic travel. And for two agencies to agree to be led operationally by a member of one of them was against the laws of nature. A new era of cooperation between agencies was heralded by the more far-seeing, and it was recommended that I should spearhead this, and be promoted to director level. A number of the big brass commented that I would make an ideal director of the CIA – certainly true. Only my lack of US citizenship stood in the way of this consideration.

I was conscious that Yarham, who had shared my adventures, was still plugging along as grade GSO2, an administrative grade which meant that in reporting terms he didn't exist. I recommended that he be promoted to a grade1 field agent. I am a grade AAA special agent and I was assured that subject to passing a few tests which I knew would not deter the wily Yarham, that would happen. Gerry Clark supported me wholeheartedy. He was getting a piggy-back ride to distinction on all of this, as the wise and discerning manager of agents. I couldn't begrudge him a benefit I would have taken myself.

The other avenue which I instructed Yarham to pursue was a list of the names of all C3 agents with British or US citizenship – I was mindful of the debacle with Dolores, and I was determined to know, on all subsequent missions, who my agents were. After much trouble, Yarham was able to produce a list containing names and grades, derived from the payroll computers. Dolores was there – for the moment – listed as a grade A special agent. I felt sad whenever I thought of Dolores.

A few days after I arrived from Jamaica I was summoned to the office of Rachel Fernandez. She sat on her high throne and looked down on me. She was very tense. She had my written report in her hand. After a few moments she stood up and descended to the floor level where I was, and sat in a chair next to me. I was in the aura of her heady perfume. She looked rigid, older, her skin as stiff as parchment.

"I've read your report, Roger, and you've done a superb job, but I want you to tell me in your own words about your mission."

I never drop my guard for a second with any members of the intelligence services, high or low. I gave her my now well-worn spiel, which was no doubt recorded on her office tapes as I spoke.

"Tell me more about your contacts with Dolores Martinez."

Ah, Senora Fernandez had a personal interest, but I remained deadpan. "She arranged the arms purchase, and gave the dispositions of the terrorists. I spoke to her only fleetingly on this."

"How did she know the dispositions?"

"I don't know. She had some kind of contact with the terrorists."

"Why was she at this rancho place when the CIA attacked?"

"Maybe she was with them."

"Where was she at... the end?"

"With our group. She died in hand-to-hand fighting at the missile site."

"Your group...?"

"Yarham and myself at this stage."

"How do you actually know that she died?"

"I saw her body."

"How do you know – in the heat of a gun-battle – that she was dead, actually... dead?"

I was expressionless before Rachel's imploring tones. "You don't want to know that. Believe me, if she had any sign of life, I would have taken her with me."

Rachel Fernandez was hurt and frustrated by this thin story, but the people in the secret services are, in the end, the victims of their own parsimony with information. She put her hand, holding a white handkerchief, to her forehead. "She's my niece, you see, and we were very close."

It was a touching display, and I could have told a tale of heroism but I didn't. Rachel Fernandez would have to accept the limitations of the service. If the details of Dolores' exploits were unravelled, questions would be asked about my performance of my duties. I moved on a different tack. "You mean she was a C3 agent? I didn't know that. It might have been helpful to know. As far as I was concerned, she was a friendly contact. She died bravely, that's all I can say."

"How *can* you say that? Do you really know?" Fernandez said fiercely, seizing on my generosity of spirit.

I maintained a sympathetically wooden expression. "Because all our group died bravely, fighting against madmen who were determined to die themselves. Dolores survived the Mercados raid with Jack Wayne, a wounded CIA agent. Wayne and Dolores made up the four of our party to attack the Mariel missile site. Dolores was helping Wayne to hospital when he was murdered, and she was taken hostage. In the final showdown, she freed herself and fought against the terrorists with Yarham and I, but she died."

After a long, withdrawn silence, Rachel Fernandez said, "Thank you, Roger, for telling me."

At home in my apartment, which Yarham had swept afresh and found to be bug-free, I had reclaimed the cat, disposed of the pile of bills, circulars and letters which nearly blocked me from opening the door, and read Laurie's loving letters. There was also a note from Sally Greengloss suggesting dinner, and one from Carol Clark, saying she knew I was back (breach of security by Gerry) and was looking forward to seeing me soon. She left a mobile number for me to call. The *soon* was underlined in a way that I felt was threatening rather than affectionate, but Carol was the doorway to Marie the cook, whose heavy, sculpted breasts and lidded eyes I couldn't get out of my mind.

As I had expected, Gerry Clark gave me a dinner invitation after a few days, which I assumed was an assignation with the group of Disciples who concerned themselves with me. In the meantime, minor stories had appeared in the newspapers about insurgency in Cuba, and a huge industrial blaze in Mariel, but the articles, which hinted at US involvement, were speculative, and my story remained under wraps.

I called Carol and we met in a coffee shop on M Street. She confirmed that Amory, Bolding and Reich would be at the dinner. I was looking forward to basking in their admiration. But instead of suggesting a threesome including Marie, as a preliminary to the official dinner, I opted for a separate date when Gerry was away. The risk of trying to combine the visit with a top-level conference was too much even for my iron nerve, and one must be in a position to linger over such pleasures. Carol's attitude when I joked about another threesome was to be slightly put off. "So you really liked Marie?" she pressed, as though I shouldn't really have noticed the vibrant woman who jumped into our bed with glee.

"I hardly had time to shake her hand, Carol. I thought your idea was a good one, and we ought to give it a chance."

"OK, I'll fix it," she said coolly.

I could see Carol wasn't a woman of catholic sensuality. She wanted to please *me*. I thought that she was becoming dangerously attached.

I was surprised to get a call from Sally Greengloss, insistent that we meet for dinner. I couldn't remember how she got my apartment phone number, which I'm cautious about handing out. I had disregarded her note, because I had always been disturbed by the Nick Stavros affair, and the grim threat of the Disciples as Nick saw them. There was no point in dwelling on it; Sally reminded me of Nick. However, I didn't feel all *that* strongly, and I responded to Sally's pressure in the way one often does when there is a warm and inviting voice at the other end of the telephone. We made a date.

I mentioned my concern about Nick Stavros to Yarham, and happened to add that I was having dinner with his ex-girfriend. A day or two later when we were perambulating around the park, Yarham said, "I assume you noticed from the list, sir, that Sally Greengloss is a C3 agent."

"This is getting to be a habit with my women. Is Laurie on the list?"

29

I was jolted by Yarham's revelation because it hit me like a splash of cold water that I had amateurishly failed to appreciate Sally Greengloss. "How the devil did you find out?" I asked irritably, knowing that in the matter of getting such details right, Yarham was supreme.

"The list. I happened to be looking through it and noticed her name. It's unusual. Could that mean she's on the job with you, sir?"

I took some time to consider. Sally knew Nick and I were in the same unit; she had assumed that, and I had admitted it. If she wanted to be friendly, why couldn't she reveal she was too? Unless, as Yarham suggested... "What job could she be doing on me, do you think?"

"Some kind of staff loyalty check?"

"I suppose that's feasible. I know C3 does it, all the agencies do. Finding out whether the business of the Disciples shakes me. A mid-term report. It would make sense."

As a result of these thoughts, my dinner at the Cirico's Restaurant with Sally was much less carefree than I would have wished, although I didn't show it. We drank champagne, and followed it with a Chardonnay to accompany the red snapper. The wine and food were delightful, the conversation not so, because I suspected a double edge to it. To Sally's questions about where I had been recently, I answered, "On holiday in Florida, lying on the beach."

"Well, you have a little tan, but surely you weren't alone?"

"No, Sally, I wasn't," and I gave her a wink – enough to stop this line of questions. I doubted that Sally would have been told officially about my mission. She might have got the buzz from C3, if she ever mixed with other agents, that I was the man of the hour. And she could have linked that with the increasing stream of still inconclusive newspaper reports of US involvement in Cuba. In any event, she changed direction.

"I've been thinking about Nick a lot recently. Do you ever think about him?" she asked in a melancholy voice.

"Well, no, to be honest. His death was very sad, but I didn't know him all that well."

"You know Nick talked to me before he died about the Disciples?"

She was homing in directly on what I had assumed was her real preoccupation. I gave her a blank look. "Sorry, you've lost me."

"You've never heard of the Disciples?"

"At Bible class when I was a kid. Did Nick get religious?"

"Don't the C3 guys talk about them in the bar?"

"C3 guys don't talk together much, and never about the job."

"Nick said the Disciples were a clique in the intelligence services on both sides of the Atlantic. He was worried about them."

She was watching me intently. "So what?" I asked.

"He told me he told you about the Disciples, and you were coming to Washington to talk it over with him."

"I don't know what Nick said to you. What he said to me was he had some worries about the job, and maybe if I came to Washington some time we could talk. Nothing specific. He was a cautious guy. He didn't even tell me what he was doing."

Sally didn't seem satisfied. She wanted to know if I'd ever heard any talk about a powerful clique in the intelligence services. I fudged the answer, saying there were all sorts of myths in every organisation about who held the power, and I let my attention drift rudely to the occupants of other tables, only half-listening to her. There was a certain stiffness between us at the end of the meal, and we didn't linger. Neither of us seemed to be able to move the conversation back into personal intimacies.

When the cab arrived at Du Pont Circle, I responded to Sally's weak suggestion that I should come up for a nightcap, by saying I had a pile of work to do tomorrow, and needed an early night. On the way home in the cab, alone, I concluded I had passed the steadfastness test with Ms Greengloss, if that is what it was intended to be.

However, the conversation with Sally Greengloss re-aroused my curiosity about Nick Stavros. I asked Yarham to find out all he could in his OPB browsings, and he approached me a few days later with his efforts.

"It's all a bit past its sell-by date now, Captain, and a lot of the files have gone into the shredder. But the story I've picked up from half a dozen sources, and spliced together, is that Stavros was involved in a black bag mission in Washington which went wrong. A member of the public was killed. There was a powerful intervention in the case before any charges were laid – somebody from the Disciples, I don't know – and our man responsible for the killing, none other than Kershaw, walked free. Stavros went to pieces. He didn't want to work for this kind of outfit. He might even have threatened to talk. There were internal enquiries and proceedings. He was declared unfit for work on medical grounds, suspended on full pay – and you know the rest."

"Do you think he could have been murdered, Yarham? I mean this *is* Washington, not Kabul."

"Do you remember what Rachel Fernandez said in her

induction address to us, sir? *We sometimes have to break our own laws.* I'd like to say Stavros couldn't possibly have been killed by our own people, but I can't."

"Sally Greengloss and her hypodermic," I said, remembering my fumblings in her medicine cabinet in the middle of the night. Actually, I could accept that Sally Greengloss might be a loyalty examiner for C3, but not that this lightweight slip of a woman could be a part-time executioner of wayward C3 agents.

An experience I hoped would be distinctly more pleasant was that of my afternoon with Carol Clark and Marie Ducane, which took place when Gerry flew to LA for a conference. We had the quiet and luxury of the Clark apartment (the children were staying overnight with friends) and plenty of time. I arrived for lunch with champagne and flowers, Marie tickled our palates with a salmon souffle, but Carol seemed to brood over the luncheon table, gulping the wine. We three had a shower together, and jumped into the king-size guest bed. The performance was fun, but not as much as it might have been if Carol had been more than woodenly cooperative. She managed, subtly, to dismiss Marie, the servant, soon afterwards, and the two of us remained in bed.

I was certain then that Carol was going to be a burden, and now that I had had the opportunity of sampling her charms on more than one occasion, I decided she was too demanding and dangerous. Also, she was too bony for my sexual taste, a skeleton of a woman compared with the pneumatic Marie. When it was time to say goodbye – I declined coffee and drinks – I went into the kitchen to say a word to Marie. I slipped a paper with my cellphone number on it into her apron pocket, and whispered, "Ring me, please.

I like you very much," and then I kissed her full lips and felt her hard nipples burning into my chest – until I noticed Carol, very pale, in the doorway, watching.

After this slightly unsatisfactory afternoon, I drove one of the company cars to Wakefield Park, Virginia for my appointment with Mrs Kershaw. I was the only human link for her with Harold's demise, and I thought it was the appropriate act for a commanding officer. I found the Kershaw mansion, its Tiger Balm Gardens immaculate, with all fountains and water features pumping industriously. Inside the house, in the hugger mugger of plastic furniture and antiques, Mrs Kershaw was in good spirits. She had already received a call from Gerry Clark, and a bland note of regret from the Department of Internal Affairs. I explained that Harold had died in an accident, an explosion, in Afghanistan, and there had been no suffering. Mrs Kershaw sought no details, and did not seem concerned about recovery of the body.

"We always knew Harold's work was dangerous," she said, "although he never used to talk about it. So it's not exactly a surprise, Captain Conway. He left us very well provided for, I think with this in mind."

My memories of the Kershaw method of personal provision were only too clear, and to a degree I had adopted them myself. After a glass of fruit juice, Mrs Kershaw showed me out. "Did you know Harold was gay, Mr Conway?" she asked pleasantly, as we dodged the palms and fronds in the jungle of plants which lined the hallway to the front door.

"I hadn't the slightest idea." My picture of Kershaw, his home and wife apart, was quite the reverse; a tough man, who would have been likely to go for tough women, and be hard on them.

"Yes, after the children, we drifted, you know. Harold had his friends, and I have mine. It was all perfectly amicable. We were very close. Like brother and sister."

As I threaded my way between the pools and the box hedges clipped into weird shapes, I reflected that I should suspend my judgment on everybody I knew, and expect surprises.

My other experience with the US widows of the attacks at the Campesino and Mariel was to attend a small memorial service at the Remembrance Chapel at Arlington Cemetery, at the invitation of the Secretary of State. Incredibly, this was not a public event but a sop to the widows, who were told that a public funeral would be held later when the events involving their spouses could be made public. The directors of the SCS, C3 and the deputy director of the CIA were present, and I was very much the centre of eyes as the sole survivor. Yarham, who had literally pulled the trigger on two of the dead, I excused, and I noticed that Mrs Kershaw was not present.

The event raised curious conflicting feelings in me. I sat at the front of the chapel, dazzled by the light on the stained glass, and soothed by the fountains of flowers arranged around the pulpit. I heard a rabbi and the ministers of two Christian denominations make sense of what I regarded as chaos, believing, as they had been told, that the events happened in Afghanistan.

I knew that only in films do goodies and baddies exclusively kill each other. In reality, as I had learned from Afghanistan and Cuba, men who bear arms are as much in danger of death from their *friends* as a result of accidents, personal quarrels, and service rivalries, as they are from the enemy.

For a while after the service, at the request of the clerics, I sat in the lounge and had afternoon tea with the widows, fine-looking, vigorous women, and some of their healthy, restive children. There were quiet questions, mostly to find out how well I knew their husbands. Other than Carmelli, Harkness and Wayne, the wounded agent who went with us from the Campesino to Mariel, I didn't even know the names of those who were killed, but I gave suitably warm and soulful replies. The widows, for the most part, wanted to be close, for a moment, to a survivor.

I thought that if the widows could see some integrity in the situation, and take some consolation, from what I alone knew was a virtually uncontrolled near-tragedy, I ought to support them. Here was the dilemma of the secret service. The women wanted to confirm that their husbands did not die in vain, but on an important mission for their country. The question they asked in different ways was, inevitably, *You've told us it was important, now please tell us why it was important?* With the deputy director of the CIA, Rachel Fernandez and Gerry Clark hovering near, I had to ask the widows to accept my sincere assurance that all I could say was that the occasion of the deaths was very important to the USA.

The bereaved women were impatient with the secretive attitude of the intelligence agencies which had employed their men, and I could see that they were wondering what could be so important about a raid in Afghanistan? Was something ignominious being covered up? Cuban Missile Crisis II was like a live cat trying to get out from under a blanket.

The dinner at Clark's was the big professional event on my return, not only because I would receive well-deserved adulation, but I would hear about the next step in Operation Screwdriver. And I fancied that there would be a further, yet more exacting, mission for me. The National Security Agency, the CIA and the Administration had done an effective job of keeping the Cuban crisis off the front pages of the newspapers. They were following a policy which Gerry Clark described to me as *Don't frighten the horses.* It occurred to me at the time that this might be a blunder, but the intelligence establishment is ossified in secrecy; suggesting it part with information is like asking a beggar to give up the coin in his fist. And the news stories had continued to appear, firmer each day and week, as the news media continued their unremitting search for answers. There were US and foreign journalists digging in Cuba, and the families of bereaved Americans asking questions.

I had not been in touch with Carol since the threesome, and I decided to behave like a normal guest on the occasion of the Disciples' dinner. No more covert eye signals; no more fingers caressing a thigh under the dining table; no more slyly pressing my groin against an ass on the terrace. The evening was plainly business, and I therefore presented myself without the usual gifts.

It was Marie who met me at the door, eyes lowered, her markedly curved body camouflaged in a black pleated dress, and topped with a frilled blue check apron. I made no attempt to be personal with her in that shared quiet moment as I stepped into the hall, and was still wondering whether she would ring me. I was received by the other guests with obvious interest and pleasure, Reich, Rachel Fernandez, Bolding and Amory. Gerry, outshone by his employee, was quiet. Amory of course clung to my hand, and placed his other on my arm, while he looked up into my eyes like a girl on her first date. Rachel Fernandez, possibly as a result of her confidence at our earlier meeting, was a little softer than her usual self. And there was a new man there, General Rudolf Schmiesser, whom I had heard of as the new nominee to be chairman of the Joint Chiefs of Staff.

Carol Clark did her formal duty as hostess, spending a few polite moments with each guest, except me. The talk was all social chit-chat: plays, books, concerts, personalities outside the intelligence services, the stock market. The flow continued wearily during the excellent Tuscan-style meal, served unobtrusively by Marie. I thought that people were asking themselves how long they had to keep this up, when there were more important things to discuss.

We moved rapidly through dessert and coffee. Marie placed a decanter of brandy, and one of port, on the table. Carol excused herself in the final way she had – and received a murmur of thanks for her efforts. Marie closed the double doors, and I was alone with my cell of the Disciples, and Gerry Clark.

Bolding held his brandy balloon up. "Wolf, well named, a toast to you on your successful mission."

All raised their glasses and drank to me, and I thanked them. By this time both C3 and the CIA had independently verified the carnage at the Campismo Mercados, and the fiery melt-down at the launching site. The CIA was embarrassed about its lost field agents, but quick to claim credit for their part. The NSA and C3 were preening themselves as leaders of the enterprise. The White House and the Senate Defense Committee were deeply impressed by my decisive action.

And there was no doubt about the horrible reality of the threat. The name Gomez had given me, in the unguarded moment when he intended I should die, Malmuni, was real, and had been traced to an Iran-trained rocket engineer who fitted the profile of the person who would be needed to build and command a site. Covert photographs had been obtained by the CIA of the Al Qaeda dead at the Campismo, and matched with known terrorists with technical training. In particular, a Saudi scientist, Ayoub Sabri, who had worked in Iraq, filled the likely specification for the scientific brains on the project. There was therefore independent evidence to substantiate my report, and no doubt about its veracity.

"What I'd like to know, Roger, is how you brought the CIA onside," Reich asked. "That was an incredible piece of conciliation and persuasion."

"When Carmelli and Harkness were killed, I said to the surviving agent, Burton, that we should talk to the local CIA, who Carmelli had wanted to keep out, and join forces. When I got intelligence of the countdown… "

"Who gave you that, Roger?" Rachel Fernandez asked.

"Dolores Martinez, my local contact."

"How did she know?" Fernandez pressed.

"She was in touch with Gomez. When I got this message, I met with the local CIA, explained that we had to act immediately, proposed a two-stage attack – one at the ranch, two at the site, and that's what we did."

"Why didn't they push you aside and do it themselves?" Schmiesser said, puzzled.

"Carmelli might have wanted to do it himself, but he was dead. We had to have a leader. It was a time for quick decisions. I supplied the arms and the plan, and I venture to say I was the only person capable of seeing the project through. Nobody was thinking departmental politics. They were thinking, *how do I save my country?*"

The Disciples all sat back as though they had suddenly remembered that a lot of agents in the field were actually motivated by patriotism, and might, in an extremity, be expected to put their country ahead of personal aggrandisement.

"It's a great achievement," Reich said. "You know, Roger, we didn't expect such a rapid development. OK, you coped splendidly, but we were looking to that little Cuban problem to, shall we say, deal with some of our problems at home. A Cuban missile crisis like the sixties, which we thought we would have, would have put the stoppers on the President's second term, and consigned his doveish advisers to the ashcan of history. Now the Cuban situation has gone away, and thank God for your efforts, but our problems haven't been solved. The President is squaring up for his second term, with General Madison at his shoulder preaching righteous mumbo jumbo."

Despite my complete understanding of the chronic paralysis of the communication nerve in the intelligence services, I asked the obvious question: "Why didn't you let the crisis hit the headlines?"

Reich opened his eyes, and swept a knowing glance past Amory, Bolding and Rachel. "Roger, you're a superb man of action, but this is a political judgement. The President and Madison would have looked like heroes, wouldn't they? Decisive action to save the country. The very action we all know they're not capable of. Oh no, we couldn't let them have that coup. We have to keep it completely under wraps."

I wondered whether I should express any dissent in a forum crowded with such enormous egos. The devil in me shook my head in quiet disagreement. "On the contrary, the situation could have looked like inability to protect the nation, only averted by quick thinking on the ground. *My thinking on the ground.*" It was a point I thought I could rub in without seeming too arrogant.

"Nobody is doubting the crucial nature of your intervention, Roger, but we are talking here about *news management in the USA*, not your undoubted courage and decisiveness in Cuba!" Reich replied, colouring.

"Of course you can spin the facts one way or another, but would a president who came within seconds of having his two principal cities annihilated by terrorist attack, ever be trusted again?" I said mildly.

A silence fell around the table as the large brains of my listeners pondered this alien line of thought. They were considering whether they might have missed a trick.

Reich came to first, twirling his wineglass by the stem. "An interesting and dangerous speculation, Roger. One can never be sure of micro-management of the news. Leave that aspect to us, and now we need to talk of other matters." He looked at his watch.

I could see that Amory, Bolding and Fernandez were not so dismissive. They were measuring the depths of their predisposition to keep events secret, and thinking that they might have been submerged in those depths.

Bolding tossed his silver mane. "We should get away now, Otto."

"Why don't you join us in the car, Roger, and we'll finish this off?" Amory said to me, baring his teeth in a leer.

We said our goodnights to Gerry Clark, and from the doorstep, I could see a long-wheelbase black Lincoln waiting below. Clearly, the intention was to exclude Gerry, at least at this point. And there was no driver for the Lincoln, either. He got out, into another car, handing the keys to Rachel Fernandez. We were able to sit comfortably in the Lincoln with the rear seating arranged conference-fashion in facing seats.

Rachel, behind the wheel, pulled slowly away, and obviously intended to cruise for as long as it took us to confer. I was about to hear the last stage of Screwdriver. I had wondered what it might be, knowing that as far as it involved me, it was likely to be hazardous. Whether it would also be unlawful – in the US – I couldn't be sure. I had therefore taken a risky precaution. In my pocket, no bigger than a silver dollar, was a highly sensitive digital recorder with a tiny chip, capable of storing hours of conversation. It was standard issue for senior agents in C3. If I was caught with the device I would never be trusted again, but I wasn't entirely sure I could accept the mission, and even if I did, I wanted an insurance policy.

General Schmiesser, who had contributed little during dinner, led the talk by common consent. He was hunched down on the seat, his neck retracted below the level of his wide shoulders, his skull resting in a hollow. He looked like a frog. His eyes did not blink but moved about, quivering. "The problem we have is Madison, Roger," he began with utter directness.

"General Madison?" George Madison was the Secretary of State for Defense.

"Yes. You know him by repute."

Madison had something which few at the top of the political tree possess, a blameless reputation. A lifelong civil servant, he had amassed no great wealth. Absence of attacks in the media confirmed that he had contented himself with one wife, and apparently lusted after no other women or men, except perhaps in his heart. He was respected for a high intellect which had placed him at the top in most of his military career since West Point. He was a devout Christian with a quiet charisma which projected his clear views of right and wrong. His dominating influence on a liberal president was well known, and obvious in practice. In a former age, he might have appeared as a Christian warrior or a crusader. In this age, his enemies branded him a Christian fundamentalist.

His alleged lack of sympathy for either the Arab cause, or Israel, evoked a deep unease in the capitalist heart of the USA.

"He's a dangerous man. A crypto-president. A threat to America. His creed is more important to him than common sense," Schmiesser said passionately. "Without him, this president will melt like a tub of lard in the oven."

"There's never been such a subversive influence in high office in America at a time when we have to defend ourselves against all comers," Reich said.

"Except maybe the Kennedys," Fernandez observed as she wheeled the car along smoothly.

Reich added, "And Madison's a maverick. You don't know what he's going to do in the name of justice. When a hoodlum robs your home and beats you up, and you land a couple of blows in retaliation, Madison is the guy who insists on the hood's right to sue you for damages."

There was an acceptance of this verdict in the car. I had the chilling feeling that we were steering toward treason and murder. "What do you want me to do?"

"Get rid of him," Schmiesser said. The others nodded agreement.

It was no use me complaining that this was murder, or against the law. I knew a few corpses more or less made no difference to the Disciples. If in their view it was necessary to commit what the statute book described as a crime, their views were a sufficient justification. They considered themselves guardians of a way of life. If the end was considered just, the means could be found, whether the target be high or low. I was the means.

I realised I might use the recording I was making to protect myself in an unusual extremity, but I could not wash my hands of my predicament by sending the recording of this conversation to the Attorney-General. I probably wouldn't live to see the result, which would be no more than the slightest unnoticeable tremor in the vast US establishment, where I suspected the fingers of the Disciples reached everywhere.

I therefore received the news without emotion. "How do you propose?"

"We'll set it up for you," Schmiesser said, with evident pleasure, assuming my acceptance.

No more was said. We cruised to our various hotels and apartments in silence. It was like the silence immediately after sexual intercourse, replete with pleasure and relief – for my companions. There was nothing to add to this conversation; it was unsurpassable. Vital matters had been dealt with in a rational and effective way, leaving a lightness, a sense of ease – but not with me.

30

I explained my new assignment to Yarham on our morning walk. This was a complete breach of security, but I had to trust somebody. His chin hung down, and he smiled at the passing girls as though I was describing an afternoon tea party.

"I know Madison is a pain in the hawk establishment's ass, but isn't this going a bit far, sir?"

"Just a bit, Yarham. Any thoughts?"

"Apart from getting the earliest possible bus to Tierra Del Fuego, it's difficult. If you refuse the assignment, you'll fall out of favour, so to speak."

"So to speak," I echoed grimly.

It was an impossible situation. I had clambered to the top of the intelligence pile, and I expected to spend some time in the sun. Instead of that, I was confronted with a task which was dangerous to the point of being suicidal. And I remembered Marius Jacob's prophetic words about being a kamikaze. If I declined, I would be regarded as a failure, and probably a failure who knew too much. I might receive the Nick Stavros treatment.

We strolled on for a while. I stopped to talk to a panhandler, gave him a dollar, and then went back to Yarham saying, "Do you think it's a situation where we could rely on the TIFU factor to work its way?" The TIFU, *Typical Intelligence Fuck-Up*, was as well-known and as ever present a phenomenon in our business, as in every disciplined service.

"You mean allow events to take their course, and rely on… ?"Yarham's eyes opened wide.

"Rely on the carefully laid plan to go awry."

"With a nudge or two,"Yarham added.

It was chancy, but I didn't doubt that Yarham could cleverly drop a bolt in the crankcase. I said, "Look, I want to come out of this with distinction, man. My credentials are excellent now, and I don't want shit all over them. We'll have to be very imaginative."

"I appreciate that, sir,"Yarham said, frowning and shaking his head negatively.

Otto Reich called me about a week later, and we met in a secluded corner of the Georgetown University campus. We sat in the shade under a tree. Reich had a handful of books which he placed between his legs. The book on top of the pile was Hobbes' *Leviathan*. Reich was certainly a major proponent in the war of all against all. In his jeans and tweed jacket, he looked the part of the greying, tousled professor with the student he was tutoring. But underneath his superficially laid-back manner was an icy and cunning machine.

"We've been giving the project a good deal of thought, Roger. And what we want, broadly, is an event which is an accident, or at least ambiguous in the public mind as possibly an accident. It might be thought of as an act of terrorism, if not an accident. Do you follow me?"

"You don't want a John Kennedy-style assassination."

"No. Too crude. And too shocking for the people. We have the means at our disposal and we have to be sophisticated."

"I'm glad to hear it, Dr Reich. I'm a good shot, but not a marksman. So what have you got in mind, gas, poison?"

Reich twisted his neck and looked at me, his cavernous eye-sockets very close, with misty eyes. His lips rose to reveal his brown teeth in a rictus. "Call me Otto. You like to have your little joke, don't you Roger? You're very cool. No, certainly not gas or poison. This is an accident, remember."

"There are chemicals that disappear."

"But leave awful suspicions. We don't want the national media on an everlasting crusade asking *Who and what killed Madison?* We want a national tragedy, a funeral, a memorial service, sweet and fading memories. And that is why we rule out any event at Madison's home. Violence in the home disturbs the nation, especially when it happens at this high level."

"No violence in the home. Quite."

"We could defeat the security of any home easily, but it wouldn't solve the problem. A car bomb is a possibility – that would be terrorism, not an accident, but it's neat…"

I intervened again in the learned professor's thoughts. "Extremely neat and quite conclusive, sir, but Madison's car will be screened every day, probably twice a day, immediately before his driver uses it. It means you'd have to bring other people in to subvert the screening, and they'd have direct knowledge. If you help to put a bomb in a man's car, there's not much doubt about your intentions, Otto."

Reich parted with the idea reluctantly. "The thing about a car bomb is that if you do it right, it's only the occupants who get hurt."

"That's a humanitarian thought, Otto."

Reich jerked his head around toward me fiercely. "I'm serious, Roger. We don't want to kill any innocent bystanders."

"I'll remember that. And since Madison works in the State Department, his work environment is practically invulnerable.

That leaves weekends when he's moving around the state with his family…"

"No, weekends with the family are sancrosanct, Roger, like inside the home."

"Of course, family values. Then, when Madison makes a public appearance."

"That's a possibility. There's a confidential visit of the big brass to a new missile site coming up, and a ceremony for war veterans which might include the President. These are real possibilities. We don't know which. We're working on it, and we'll let you know. But let me ask you, how do you feel about this project?"

I looked him straight in the eyes, unblinking. His eyes looked messy, like oysters on the half-shell. "If it's my duty, I'll do it."

He put his hand on my shoulder warmly. "Good man. I knew we could rely on you. It's an act of patriotism. The act of a brave man."

"There's only one thing that troubles me, Otto."

"Tell me, and I'll fix it."

"A close-out."

Reich looked at me blankly at first, and then his wet eyes ignited, and he began to savour the technique of killing the assassin after his work is done, often used by the Mafia, and in top political killings. The tactic was to cover the trail back to those who gave the order. He moved his cheeks to suggest good humour. "As a good agent, I expect you to think of everything, Roger. But no, there is no possibility of a close-out here. We trust you completely. You must trust us. You are one of a handful of the most valued agents we have. We honour you, Roger."

I came away from the meeting with Reich with very grave misgivings. Yarham's suggestion about a bus for South

America seemed a possibility. I fingered the tiny recorder in my pocket as I walked down the hill. It was no answer to the forces that were gathering around me.

I had a telephone call from Marie Ducane. I arranged to meet her for coffee in M Street in the afternoon, and then took her to my apartment. She proved, as I had thought, to be a strong-smelling woman of seething passion, and I had a few carefree hours with her. But I was all too soon back to my cogitative walk with Yarham. I recounted the conversation with Reich, which Yarham received with slight amusement. "What's funny?" I asked him.

"It bodes well for us, sir. A ceremonial event gives us a measure of control, and can be... derailed."

I didn't feel so confident. "Really? What about the close-out?"

"A ninety per cent certainty, wouldn't you think?"

"You believe they'd do that to me?" I was affronted for a second, the uniquely valuable and important *me?*

"You are, if you'll forgive me saying so, Captain, a small part of a grand design which nothing and nobody must prejudice. Eliminating you – us probably – afterwards would be a prudent move."

I had wanted to believe the earnest Professor Reich. *We honour you, Roger.* Did they mean to honour me posthumously? Their concern was the supremacy of *our kind* of world. The Disciples undoubtedly held the constitutions and laws of our two countries above and beyond all else, except where, in their view, the constitutions and laws had to be broken in order to preserve and strengthen them. My untutored mind detected something cock-eyed in this position. But the point was that Yarham was right, deflating at it was. A mere life, my life, was as nothing to them.

"Very well, then. We calculate that there will be a close-out," I said.

"The wisest thing, sir. And, I suggest, an advantage in some ways."

"I don't follow that at all!" I snapped.

"Suppose we were to find out details of the close-out plan. We would have a ready-made band of miscreants who could take the blame for… anything untoward which happened."

"We turn the close-out team, trying to kill us, into crazed subversives, terrorists responsible for… whatever happens?

"Simple, isn't it?" Yarham laughed, caressing his chin.

"Oh, an elegant solution as the academics say. But we're going to save Madison, not kill him."

"Quite, but somebody may get killed and it pays to have somebody to blame."

"Like love, easy to imagine, but not quite so easy to achieve in practice."

"We don't have any option, Captain."

"I could get a fast camel out of here, or have a nervous breakdown and ask to be shipped home."

"My advice about Tierra del Fuego was hasty, sir. Wouldn't the Disciples come after you on the next bus, with all the formidable tracking technology of this millennium?"

"What about losing my marbles?"

"Would you be entirely happy resting in bed, knowing who might be outside the door with a gun or a needle?"

We agonised about it, but I finally came round to Yarham's view that I was locked into a venture from which it would be difficult to extract my life, let alone any credit. This was where my ingenuity, skill and self-sacrificing service to Anglo-American intelligence had taken me.

31

In the days that followed, I determined that the only way to save myself was to attempt to think ahead of the moves of the Disciples. It was a near-impossible task, because they were largely invisible, and they had seeped into fissures in our society at which I could only guess. Naked on a street corner in effect, I was enclosed in the Reich-Bolding-Amory-Fernandez-Schmiesser cell. I would be placed in a set-piece action to carry out my task of killing Madison at a public ceremony, not knowing who my enemies were.

I could be shot down by any guard, soldier or guest. Yarham and I conferred endlessly as we walked the days away in the pale sunlight of autumn. I had instructed him to redouble his efforts on the OPB trawl, and extend it as far as possible with safety, to try to determine what our hidden enemies were doing.

"Nothing found at all, sir, so far, except that there's going to be a small reception for you on Capitol Hill, the Defense Committee, possibly the President, and the British Ambassador. Top secret. They want to hear at first hand how you saved America."

It didn't surprise me, and in a way, it was my due. Although I would always have to remain largely anonymous, the Cuban Crisis II as an incident itself was gradually beginning to emerge in the press, as journalists collected the facts. A sudden impetus had been given to disclosure by the Cuban government, which had made a complaint to the

United Nations about armed aggression by US Special Forces. The raid at Campismo Mercados and the holocaust at Mariel were now part of the public record, and it was only a matter of time before the US president would be forced to make a statement to the nation. Intense curiosity was building up, not least on Capitol Hill.

"Those who know a little can't believe how close disaster was," I said.

As Yarham foresaw, I received an invitation, and on the day, at the appointed hour of six o'clock in the evening, made my way through the security barriers at the Capitol, in the wake of Rachel Fernandez. We passed through shadowy corridors, where anterooms buzzed with other unknown earth-shaking events, to a small reception room. The room had plentiful green velvet cushioned chairs arranged casually, a thick green carpet, and a table loaded with pastries, cakes, and bottles of red and white wine. I was introduced to the British Foreign Secretary, as well as the British Ambassador, a variety of members of the general staff – including General Schmiesser, and the Secretary of State General Madison. The director of the CIA, and the head of the NSA, and of course, a selection of senators from the Defense Committee were also present. They all seemed to be hungry and thirsty. I ate and drank very little during the introductions and preliminary talk, although I did not feel overawed by these important people who really knew very little about my world, or indeed the world they were trying to govern.

The chairman of the Defense Committee called the room to order, and mumbled that the events that were about to be disclosed were top secret. Rachel Fernandez made a short speech in which she emphasised the key role of C3, and the proof, as a result of the Cuba episode, of the critical practical part our intelligence services played in the security of the nation. "Now," she said, "I want to introduce Captain Roger Conway of MI6, who works for C3 as part of our Anglo-US intelligence partnership, and who led our forces in the crisis."

The audience settled themselves in chairs, and I leaned back on a table, half-sitting, facing them. I had honed my story in a dozen debriefings since Cuba. In some respects it was certainly a travesty of the truth, but the leaders of a nation do not want to hear that one of their intelligence forces is squabbling with another, committing internecine burglary, assault and murder. My narrative revealed the joint discovery by the CIA and the NSA of grave terrorist subversion which had to be investigated on the ground, by *humint* immediately and which might have been a mere rumour. And then the further discovery, by me alone, that the urgency was more than we had ever thought, and the consequent need for immediate action to wipe out the threat. I took them through the bloody night at the camp, and the raid on the missile site, emphasising the courage of our men, with a degree of cool understatement. I'm a good storyteller, and every one of my listeners was rapt, some were pale, living the terror of those few hours. With their hunger for gory facts, the audience reminded me of the US debriefing team and the war correspondents in Afghanistan. I gorged them. At the end, they were silent, sated.

The chairman of the Defense Committee creaked to his feet, recovering himself, and giving his fulsome thanks. "Our people will only know in heaven what you have done for them, Captain Conway." Then there was warm round of applause, and I was surrounded by questioners.

One senator asked me about Agents Carmelli, Harkness and the luckless Burton, still languishing in a Cuban prison. "How did Burton get into the hands of the Cuban authorities as an alleged drug smuggler, Captain Conway?"

I had skipped over these details in my account. "I was working with Carmelli and his men, and we hired a boat to skirt the coast on a reconnaissance. The Cuban coastguard tried to board us, and Carmelli thought we could outrun them. The patrol boat had a machine gun which cut us up. The incident ended with Carmelli and Harkness dead, and Burton captured – presumably handed to the police later. I escaped with two men, diving overboard and swimming to shore in the dark."

"Misjudgment, huh? Carmelli's decision to run."

"No. Bad luck being caught by a patrol boat. We couldn't afford to be taken, or we'd all be in jail in Havana now, and New York and Washington wouldn't exist…"

"God forbid," somebody gasped.

General Schmiesser came up to me at the end, when I was about to leave with Rachel Fernandez, his face puckered into dozens of deep vertical lines, and his eyes quivering as though they were about to overflow. "You spoke very well, Roger. You did us credit. I don't know what we're going to do with you." I felt his huge, rough hand encircle mine.

In the middle of that night I dreamed that Schmiesser was crouching before me, as he had that night we rode in the black Lincoln, and the plan was hatched. He repeated his words of the afternoon. What I had interpreted at the time as a compliment, that I deserved a reward for my efforts that was so great as to be hardly quantifiable, had now become a malign reflection, almost a threat from this supremely powerful man. *I don't know what we're going to do with you.*

"You're having a bad dream, Roger," Laurie said, moving the warm palm of her hand across my chest.

"Just solving a problem, my love."

"Solved?"

"Yes."

"Then turn over and give me a cuddle."

It was true that my dream had given me an insight into how the last phase of Operation Screwdriver should be handled. I awoke with a sense of a burden lifted, had an American breakfast with hotcakes cooked by Laurie, while I mixed a couple of large Buck's Fizz.

I tried out my idea on Yarham when we left the office that morning, at coffee time, for our stroll.

"They don't trust me, man."

Yarham brushed a thoughtful hand across his flaming hair. "It would be wise to assume that, sir. It goes with the close-out."

The truth was, I had up to now had difficulty believing that the Disciples meant to kill me. I was brilliant and I was loyal – so far, at least. I hadn't really subscribed to Yarham's comic cynicism as far as it applied to me. The Disciples could kill anybody, but I was unique, and uniquely useful, honoured by the most powerful people in the US. Surely they couldn't eliminate me like a bug? This unduly optimistic trend of thought had been dissipated by the malevolent wrinkles of General Schmiesser, the alien touch of his hand, like a bunch of thistles, and those words, reinterpreted in my nightmare: *I don't know what we're going to do with you.*

"All right, then. We also make distrust of me a planning assumption. How does that play out?"

"Doesn't it mean that although you have the task of killing Madison, the Disciples will do it if you don't, and blame you?"

I supposed that was what it did mean. "If I succeed in killing Madison, well and good for them. They kill me, and blame me. If I don't succeed with Madison, they kill him, kill me and blame me. Either way, Madison dies, and I'm one dead terrorist. And possibly you too."

"Thank you for including me, sir. This approach is very helpful."

"*It is?*"

"You don't have to make any plans to kill Madison yourself – bombs, guns, etc. Think of the equipment and planning. It's going to save a lot of effort."

"I'm glad about saving effort, man. I wouldn't want to work too hard on this. It's not my way. So we just turn up at the ceremony, and dodge the bullets?"

"Perhaps. But if there's no shooting, merely an explosion, the whole event may go down as an accident. It'll be easier for us than Campismo Mercados or Mariel." Yarham affected a serious look, but there was a wild shine in his eyes.

I was nevertheless very unhappy. "But what about my reputation as a faultless operator, Yarham?"

I had a call from Otto Reich for a rendezvous on the Georgetown Campus, and we wandered together across the lawns for a time in a gusting wind, which swirled the falling leaves in arcs. Using my anorak as a ground sheet, we finally settled under the same plane tree that we had used before, although it was nearly bare now. How easy it was even for two senior spies to develop a bad habit about a meeting place. And I had the recorder in my pocket, another habit I was developing for these meetings. I had determined that if anything happened to me, the tapes should go to the *Washington Post*, but it was no consolation.

Reich had no books on this occasion, but it would not have surprised me to see a copy of *The Prince* protruding from the pocket of his tweed jacket.

"It'll be New Mexico. Fort Gaines, in late November, Roger."

"That's the trial of the new R40 missile?"

"Ah, you know of it. Demonstration is probably the word. Show the generals and a few select politicians what they've bought with their money."

"How many people?"

"Perhaps a hundred. It's ideal. A remote army base. Small audience. We control the news media. Unfortunate accident or terrorist incident. You'll be appointed to head security, so you'll have the opportunity to make whatever arrangements you want..."

"And take responsibility for the outcome."

"With your skills, the outcome need not concern you."

"That's very flattering. I'll need full details of every proposed step in the ceremony, and details of all those attending. I'll have to go to Fort Gaines, and have an engineer show me over the site."

"That can all be arranged."

"And, in addition, I want to be specifically appointed as Madison's chief of security. I want it to be understood by Madison and his staff that on site in New Mexico, my word about what Madison should do, or not do, from a safety point of view, is final."

"Certainly, and a very understandable proposal." Reich chortled deep in his chest, the first time I had seen him show any humour. "Especially since you are going to... ah... administer the *coup de grace*. I'll make sure Madison and his people are briefed on this. You're not sticking your neck out personally, are you, assuming so much responsibility for Madison? Afterwards there'll be a thicket of enquiries, and you'll be at the centre of them."

"It's good of you to be solicitous about me, but no, I need to control my man."

"You're the expert."

"I'm not an expert executioner, Otto."

Reich swung his cavernous eye-sockets around to regard me closely. "That quaint sense of humour of yours again, Roger."

"Will you be there?"

Reich gave me his bland look, the tolerant professor. "I'm afraid I don't get to go to the party. But Schmiesser, naturally, will be there, and Rachel. We'll all be rooting for you."

"I'm glad to hear that. Does Gerry Clark know?"

"Nobody knows except us and you. Clark will be ordered to facilitate your requirements."

"What did you think of the President's statement?"

Reich jerked around toward me again, pursing his lips, disturbed. "Crap. Yellow-bellied crap, like I'd expect from him."

The President had appeared on national television the previous evening, and admitted in low key that US Special Forces had undertaken a mission in Cuba for the purposes of self-defence. He said that our intelligence services had discovered that missiles were being prepared for firing into the US by terrorists. The US had to defend itself, and would continue to defend itself against such threats. Seven US personnel lost their lives for their country. The mission had been directed strictly against the aggressors, who were not Cubans, and no civilians had been involved.

The statement was the bare truth as far as it went.

"I thought he did rather well," I said, to bait Reich.

Reich had reddened. "As I've said to you before, Roger, you're off limits."

"But the President has quietly claimed Cuban Missile Crisis II as his. Don't you see that?"

"It doesn't matter what he's claimed, because you are

going to put an end to all that at Fort Gaines," Reich said angrily, getting up to go.

With the information from Reich, I was able to plan. I flew with Yarham in an army Gulfstream jet to Fort Gaines. It was a VIP plane for generals, and had a steward, and a bar which we sampled en route. On arrival, I met Colonel Stanley, the adjutant, who gave us a quick tour. As far as Stanley was concerned, I was General Madison's security adviser. I saw enough of the R40 silo and underground control room to appreciate that these were ideal confined spaces to have an explosion. Colonel Stanley gave me a plan of the underground.

"One grenade would do it," Yarham whispered.

Assuming the close-out team doubted my ability to perform, and were going to do my job for me, this was very likely where they would do it. The usual army ceremonial would be held on the tarmac above ground, where it was planned to erect a small covered grandstand and dais. This was too open to be a very favourable area for the would-be assassin.

"The problem, Captain, is to stop Madison going underground," Yarham said when we had an opportunity to talk alone on the tarmac, in the sun, under a white, windless sky.

"Not if he was accompanied by Schmiesser, the one person who can't be sacrificed. If Madison stays close to Schmiesser, the darling of the Disciples, and heir apparent to head the Chiefs of Staff, he ought to be safe."

By cocktail time, I had seen enough, and felt sufficiently relaxed to enjoy the quality of the Californian Cabernet Sauvignon which Colonel Stanley provided with the dinner hosted with one or two of his military colleagues at their club. We had an amusing evening swapping yarns, before Yarham and I, somewhat inebriated, were piled on to our aircraft. But I flew back from New Mexico with the germ of an idea.

What was before us now was to identify the close-out team, the killers who were being recruited to act against us. Yarham diligently searched the NSA intranets to which he had access, and although it was possible for him to observe the top secret official preparations for the Fort Gaines ceremony, it was impossible to discern beneath the guest lists and transport minutiae any clue about the identity of the close-out team.

I therefore adopted a different tactic. I pressed for a complete biography of every person, including Fort Gaines personnel, who would be anywhere near the ceremony – a stipulation I had made to Reich when we first spoke. When Gerry Clark questioned why I needed it – not knowing my real task, I told him Reich had already agreed. Clark knew I had been appointed as Madison's personal security chief for the ceremony and could hardly refuse, although he snorted at what he described as my bureaucratic approach. Eventually I received the information. Then I set Yarham to verify the bona fides of each person in detail. Many, of course, were patently in the clear, and he eventually narrowed the list down to three CIA agents, who were additional to the security detail provided by the 101st Artillery stationed at Fort Gaines. The rest of the guests were high officers of state, elected representatives, scientists, engineers under contract, and service personnel, all of whom had careers which Yarham had scrutinised from national records. These people were not sensibly open to question.

"Good work. There's a high probability it is one or more of these three," I said to Yarham.

"It could still be one of the big bugs, if one's going to think laterally."

"Which one?"

"Rachel, Gerry Clark, Schmiesser himself."

I dismissed this. "They get others to clean the latrines. They don't want the faintest smell on their fingers."

A check on the backgrounds of the three CIA men showed they were all seasoned field agents with experience in Colombia, Guatemala and Afghanistan. The leader was Scott Maxell, a heavy like the late Kershaw, and not to be trifled with.

"Right or wrong, they *look* like the men for the job. Killing is what they do," I said.

"Where do you suppose they get their orders, sir?"

"I'd like to know the answer to that myself. Not from the CIA Director. The CIA is the Disciples' enemy. That's where we started, Yarham, in Pennsylvania Avenue. But the Disciples have their way of subverting people. I wouldn't be surprised if they have some agents scattered through the CIA."

Yarham's jaw hung down lugubriously as he slowly agreed.

Our reasoning was all a bit creaky. "Maxell & Co as the close-out team will be our working hypothesis. We'll just have to see how it turns out in practice," I said.

"Oh, one final point, Captain. You realise that Sally Greengloss is on the list, the only C3 person apart from Clark."

"Yes. I don't know what to make of that, but I can't see the Disciples or whoever is managing the close-out giving the killing job to her. We could have maximum violence at Fort Gaines. She could have to kill Madison as well as me. No, the Disciples will field a heavy team."

"When a slight girl has a gun, it's the gun that kills, Captain."

32

I was well aware that although I had made suppositions about what might happen at Fort Gaines, the possibility was that events would turn out differently. It was an uncomfortable time, because I could not relax and declare the problem too confusing to worry about, when my life – not merely my career or reputation was in issue. However, I did manage to divert myself to a small degree, in Laurie's sometimes long absences, with the beautiful brown Marie, whose steamy desire kindled and rekindled my own.

I found out that she was twenty years old, and a violinist in a chamber music quartet. What attractive skills for a young woman! She had reached concert standard on the violin, was a delightful cook, and a sensual lover. I attended two of the quartet's concerts – and had interesting suppers with Marie afterwards. It was her ambition to join one of the city orchestras, and she was tutored by a virtuoso twice a week. Marie was charming, freshly earthy, and I liked her very much.

Unfortunately, Carol Clark discovered our liaison, or possibly assumed it, and began to make risky telephone calls to me demanding that we meet. I tried to reduce her obsession by seeing her for coffee occasionally. Cutting Carol off without a word wasn't an option. If I did, I knew there would be an emotional explosion, the consequences of which I couldn't foretell. It may have been that Gerry Clark would be outwardly complacent if he knew about us, but I calculated that under the milk pudding expression, he was a good hater – he was, after all, an expert in a ruthless business. And so I spent a couple of hours, on odd afternoons, trying to persuade this intense and I thought rather bored blonde housewife that I was too busy for a twosome or a threesome with her – she hadn't fired Marie, but certainly, Marie *was* an irreplaceable cook, a social asset, and Gerry's belly was a large part of him.

After the last of our fleeting meetings, Carol persuaded me to walk her to the parking building in the wintry half-dark, and then, when we reached her car and I was holding the door open for her – probably in sight of the video cameras – she hitched her skirt, pulled down her pants, and unzipped my trousers. I didn't have any sexual thoughts in my mind in the moments before this, but her actions, in the shadowed and cramped space between the vehicles had a volcanic effect on me. I pushed her on to the back seat, and I have to say, because it was unexpected, had a thoroughly exciting experience. But I vowed to stay in a crowd and out of the dark with her henceforth.

My interest in the sensual life began to diminish in the October days before the Fort Gaines ceremony. To persuade my superiors that I was proactively pursuing my role, I indented for a small quantity of a new type of high explosive grenade, plastic explosive, fuses and timers. These were locked in a steel trunk and under Yarham's care, flown out to Gaines and stowed in the R40 silo. I told Colonel Stanley that they were for counter-terrorist measures. I planned that we would carry at least one grenade each, but otherwise I did not actually intend to use the items.

I had photo-identification cards printed for everybody who would be present, including the 101st unit's perimeter guards. An army detail was appointed who would check the identification of all guests, and identify any irregularity to me, or the presence of any stranger. Colonel Stanley remarked that he had never known such tight security. I was as ready as I could be.

I flew out to New Mexico with Yarham two days before the event, and spent the time pacing the site, walking the underground tunnels, and worrying unnecessarily. On the tarmac above the silo, the stand and dais had been built, and festooned with red, white and blue ribbons. The ribbons fluttered in the wind. Dust and spindrift blew across the tarmac. Under the pale sky the place had an abandoned look, as though the ceremony, and the tragedy, were over. Hidden beneath my feet was the most far-reaching destructive weapon that man had yet produced.

On the first day, when I returned to the officers' mess in the afternoon, there were three men in starched white shirts with dark ties and short haircuts waiting to meet me. Colonel Stanley named them as Scott Maxell, Barney Coultas and Terry Sneller. I introduced Yarham and we all touched, rather than shook, hands. We settled down in chairs facing each other but the CIA boys were in no hurry to make conversation. They smirked. They obviously felt very much in control.

"So what are you guys doing here? The show isn't open yet, and there's nobody on the gate to take your money," I asked.

Maxell, older than the other pair, with a stained oak face and prominent grey eyebrows, shrugged. "Just dropped in to case the joint."

"That's diligent. Any points you want to make, I'll be glad to hear. I'm looking after security."

Colonel Stanley, slightly embarrassed at the obvious hostility, offered us all a drink.

"We've heard of you, Captain Conway," Coultas said. "What're you captain of, anyway, a cruise liner out of Havana?"

"Your guys I fought alongside in Cuba were the bravest of the brave," I replied gravely in the silence that followed Coultas's remark.

This got to Maxell. He held up his hand. "Right!" he said, signalling to the others to be more respectful. He asked me about Cuba, as I knew he would, and I played up the role of Carmelli and the CIA. We ended having a drink together, and talking about field experience, although I was an apprentice alongside Maxell. I was reflecting on whether this man had been detailed to kill me, when I got a call on my satphone.

"It's Otto," a strained voice said.

"Just a minute." I went outside the mess on to the parade ground. "Yes?"

"Return to Andrews Air Force Base immediately. We'll meet you there."

I looked at my watch. "I barely have time. And no plane."

"A plane is being organised for you now. Do it."

I left Yarham to keep an eye on Maxell & Co. A Learjet was warming up on the Fort runway. On the flight, I tried to work out what had gone wrong. Why was I required to be seen personally, when a coded message on the satphone would suffice? Reich had sounded very tense.

The only external factor I knew which might trouble the Disciples was the success of the President's recent national address. Although some media sources had criticised his statement on the Cuban crisis as being too little too late, by far the majority reaction, if the opinion polls were to be believed, was that it was a no-nonsense account of a piece of business well done. The President was getting good marks for avoiding posturing, avoiding scaremongering, and keeping

America safe. To a public terrorised by the thought of terror, modest competence was attractive. The President's poll ratings were as high as they had been at the start of his term, and his re-election was starting to look like a foregone conclusion.

Before we landed, the co-pilot said he would be refuelling, and the ship would be ready to take me back in half an hour. An officer met me as I descended to the tarmac, and escorted me to a room on the base. There were two worried people present, slumped at the plastic-covered conference table – Reich and Rachel. The blinds were drawn. They scarcely greeted me, waved me to a seat, and Reich began looking down at the table.

"We want you to call it off, Roger."

I appeared to be incredulous, and I *was* surprised at this late failure of nerve. I rocked back in the chair and exhaled heavily. "Seriously? Just nothing?"

"Yes. Go out there. Be the security boss. Make sure nothing happens, and above all, make sure Madison stays alive."

Since this was already my intention, I could have acquiesced with ease, but I wasn't going to let them off the hook so easily. I scowled and made it look like a difficulty. "But the preparations are already made, the events are in train…"

"What do you mean? For God's sake, you can stop what you've started, can't you man?" Reich said, purpling.

"I hope so," I said without confidence.

"You *hope* so, Roger! Jesus, tell us what you've done," Rachel said.

I shook my head in refusal. "It's better you don't know. If anything goes wrong…" I revelled in playing the *Need to Know* card against them. And in their bellies, they didn't want to know. Assassination was vile medicine. Too vile to talk about, let alone swallow.

"Roger, I want your undertaking you'll do everything necessary to stop this. Everything," Reich said. His usual throaty confidence had an imploring note.

"May I ask why the change of mind?" I asked, guessing readily enough, but wanting to be awkward.

Reich's instinct was to cut me off with one of his jibes about my maladroit political sense, but in this extremity he was beholden to me. "It's not the appropriate time, that's all."

"I can see that myself. The President will get back into office with or without Madison. Even if we kill Madison" – I watched both of them wince at the ugly implications of the *we* – "the President will never bless General Schmiesser as head of the Chiefs of Staff. All this as a result of us botching the PR over the Cuban crisis."

I was rubbing sand into lacerations, which must have already cut deep into Reich's hide, in the arguments with his colleagues over the President's broadcast. Nothing else could explain this unseemly, last-minute capitulation.

Reich must realise now that had the Disciples publicised my coup when it happened, the President would have looked unsafe and untrustworthy. Surprise missile threat. America unready, and only saved by the quick thinking of an agent on the ground. Me. As it turned out, the President had finally taken the news initiative by default, scored with the general public, and probably won four years of relative freedom from the plots of the Disciples.

"You don't have to explain the political situation to me!" Reich roared. "Your undertaking, Roger?"

"You have it, but may I have a similar one from you?"

"I don't know what you mean."

"The three CIA thugs at the party."

"I – we – don't know anything about them. You're suggesting they are there to… "

"Kill me."

"Not on our instructions. No way," Reich said.

"If there are dogs out there, they can be called off."

"There are none! I've told you!"

I didn't believe him. "Well, put it this way. I have your orders, clear and simple. I'll carry them out. If anything unfortunate happens, you can be absolutely sure it's not my initiative."

"Good. Thank you," Reich said, deflated, his eyes red and clouded.

"And I want to be officially replaced as head of security for the show. I look after Madison, and him alone."

"I don't see why…"

"You want me to stop the train I've started. OK, but I insist. I'll deliver Madison, but I won't be responsible for the rest."

"Agree, Otto," Rachel said. "Colonel Clark can take overall responsibility."

Reich gave a jaundiced movement of the jaw to make the concession.

Rachel Fernandez had said very little, almost distanced herself from Reich, her glance cast downward in her papier mache face. I fancied there would be more arguments to come, and perhaps some repositioning in the Disciples' camp. It was all very clever for dons to mastermind the broad and confusing currents in a vast sea of intelligence, but when it came down to action on the ground, to actual killing, the toll in stress was profound, and Reich had found that out. He looked as though his blood pressure would explode.

I was asked to wait for an orderly who would escort me to the plane while Reich and Rachel Fernandez departed. In a few minutes, the orderly arrived, and I followed him. Instead of striking out toward the jet, which I could see on the apron of the runway, the corporal led me to another hut. It was empty except for Rachel Fernandez, standing imperiously in her loose black suit, like a priest. She spoke when the orderly had retreated and closed the door.

"Roger, I want to tell you something privately and confidentially. You must do as Otto has asked, but you yourself are in danger. I don't know the details, but it is intended that you should not return from Fort Gaines. Personally, I have always been opposed to this... and that is why I'm telling you. I value your service very much."

It was helpful to have confirmed what I had already anticipated, and it was useful to have this special connection with a person of Fernandez' rank. Since our talk about Dolores Martinez there seemed to be a warm thread between us. Her attitude suggested the possible fall of Reich. I received the information imperturbably.

"Thank you. It's kind of you to tell me. I'll bear it in mind."

"You're a very cool character, Roger. You obviously knew already."

"Naturally. It's my job. But I'm grateful to you for thinking of me."

"I think of you as a kind of link with Dolores," she said sadly.

Although I had made my stance appear brave and gravely dramatic, I flew back to Fort Gaines with a relatively light heart. I did not have to go through the convoluted activity of showing that I was carrying out the Disciples' orders, while at the same time nullifying them. What had been tortuous and confused was now simple. I had to look after myself and Madison.

33

By the time the Learjet landed at Fort Gaines, the official orders from the Pentagon, under which the base was working, had been amended to place Colonel Gerald Clark in overall charge of security, with me remaining responsible for General Madison's person. Scott Maxell ribbed me about it when we met in the officers' mess. "Demoted, huh?"

"One general is enough for me to look after."

Maxell, I was sure, wouldn't have known what had happened. If he was the one with orders to kill me, he still had them. He regarded me for a long moment with his totem pole face, suspicious. "Why?"

I heaved my shoulders. "Obviously, it's easier. I do what I'm told without asking why. I'm like you, Scott, and all other agents – a mushroom."

"You're damn right! We're in the dark. What we get to know is a piece of information about the size of a rat's turd."

We could exchange these truisms about the service philosophically.

"The other thing is, Gerry Clark is my boss. Maybe being the security supremo on this picnic looks good to him."

Maxell was confused about this, because he probably knew there was going to be trouble, but he was a foot soldier, and knew better than to question higher authority.

Yarham's reaction was pleasurable when he heard my account of events at Andrews Air Force Base. "This means that the Conway reputation should be *virgo intacta*, Captain, assuming you come out of the tunnel with Madison. I should think Gerry Clark's a worried man. All sorts of nasties could happen."

The morning of the launch was clear, with a chill in the wind off the mountains. The jets were coming in from Washington, modified 727s with plenty of space for the Pentagon brass, contractors, scientists and engineers; and there were some smaller jets from other locations. The total complement expected was just short of a hundred and twenty persons. While Gerry Clark, who pointedly ignored me, was fussing about, I made sure the arrangements I had put in place were working, particularly the perimeter security, and the methodical checking of identities.

The programme had been timed to the minute: coffee on arrival in the mess hall, speeches and presentations on the tarmac, inspection of the deadly monster and the launch; and afterwards a relaxed lunch before departure.

I was at the foot of the gangway when General Madison's plane disembarked. He greeted me warmly. "I put myself in your hands, Roger." He introduced me to his aides: uniformed high officers themselves, greying and doing their fighting now with their waistlines in the gymnasium. They looked at me sceptically, a slim young man in well-tailored light grey flannel suit, and so obviously *an Englishman*. They would have heard a version of my exploits, but could not quite understand why the life of the second most important person in the US should have been committed to the hands of such a person.

I leaned toward them confidentially. "I hope it won't be necessary, but there could be circumstances in which I have to take the General with me, on his own, without you, for his safety."

"You're in charge on this, Roger," General Madison said, blocking any disagreement.

The aides nodded reluctant agreement, and were not too concerned that anything untoward could happen to their chief in this small, isolated gathering in the cool New Mexico sunshine.

The officer in charge of the ID verification drew me aside, and said that one of the perimeter guards was sick and would not be replaced, and there was an addition to the complement; an elderly scientist who had been omitted by mistake from the guest list.

Sally Greengloss had arrived with Gerry Clark. I assumed she was here to assist Clark. One had to be suspicious of everybody, and I remained uneasy about her. It was also interesting that she was discarding her cover as a publisher's assistant, and was coming out as an agent, certainly as far as I was concerned. I later gave her a cheery *hello*, but showed no sign of surprise at her presence.

The party finished their coffee and chatter after twenty-five minutes, and moved to the grandstand outside. Generals Madison and Schmiesser ascended the dais in front of the stand. General Madison made the first address. He described the R40 as the most deadly accurate long distance missile ever invented. Like the Gomez missile (although he did not refer to the Cuban missile or the Cuban affair), it travelled close to the ground at supersonic speed, and could be set on a varied course. It was believed to be unstoppable by any known defences. Versions of the R40, which was only ten feet long and eighteen inches in diameter, equipped with nuclear warheads, could be stationed on, and operated from, satellites. "This is indeed a formidable weapon," General Madison said, "a triumph of science, and yet it is a sad commentary on our times that we need it. Pray God we never have to use it."

General Schmiesser, free of any regret, outlined excitedly the kind of war he envisioned, with the US zapping its foes like a kid with a video game. "America is the big guy on the block and must never surrender that position to any other nation," he said. He presented personal letters of thanks, signed by the President, to a group of scientists and researchers who had led the project, designing more effective silos, more accurate firing controls, and vastly more powerful fuel and burners.

I watched and listened from the fringes, trying, impossibly, to see the poison lurking in a scene which looked as innocent as a crowd of parents gathered at a college baseball pitch to present prizes. Sally Greengloss, absorbed in the proceedings, looked quite attractive in her grey trouser suit. Clark moved restively at her side, picking his fingernails.

The speeches closed as planned according to time, and Gerry Clark stepped to the podium: "All those guests not cleared to visit the control centre, please proceed to the mess hall. You will find a video link set up there, which will give you a full view of events. All those visiting the control centre, please follow Colonel Stanley…"

The control centre was too small to accommodate more than a handful of people, and this choice group included the two generals, their chief aides, Scott Maxell, Clark, and myself. I moved into line behind Colonel Stanley, with General Madison, and a rising heartbeat.

We walked a short distance across the tarmac to the head of the bunker, entered an elevator, and travelled a hundred and fifty feet underground in silence. We exited into a long passage, circular in shape, leading to a number of control centres for different silos. Despite the air-conditioning, my skin was prickling and damp. Some conversation spurted in the gathering, but we were more like strangers in a weird art gallery, looking cautiously for the next exhibit.

I kept glancing about me for anything out of place, or any sign of agitation in my companions, but I could see none.

"You're sweating, son," General Madison said to me in a quiet and friendly undertone.

I didn't reply, but he knew fear, and he had detected mine. It was probably no bad thing. He began to look more serious. It wasn't merely an outing to look at the new toys.

When we reached the control room, I deliberately positioned Madison near the door. He was watching me now, understanding I knew more than he did. It wasn't such a good viewing point for Madison, because there was an array of computer screens, partly blocked out by those in front. A young woman lieutenant stood before the screens, and began explaining their importance. Two or three people motioned Madison to take a central place beside Schmeisser. He looked at me. I moved my head slightly to signal a negative. "I'm fine here," Madison said modestly. "I can see perfectly."

The lieutenant showed us a computerised map, literally the target range, which could be adjusted to cover any part of the surface of the earth within range with street-map precision. She showed how the target, if static, could be selected in detail down to a particular house in a particular street, or a parked vehicle, simply by moving a cursor on the screen to that point. She showed how a moving target, such as a motor vehicle, could be tracked.

"You don't need that much accuracy with a nuclear warhead," Schmeisser grinned.

"That's correct, sir. There are a variety of warheads. It depends what effect you want," she said, as though she was talking about painting and decorating a house.

The lieutenant took us through an imaginary arming and fuelling sequence, explaining that the missile we were going to fire was already fuelled, and did not have an explosive warhead.

"Pity about that. We could have tried one on Baghdad," Schmiesser chuckled.

I watched the group carefully, agonising whether I should get Madison out of there. Maxell was eyeing me. He was the only one, apart from me, not paying attention to the lieutenant. He seemed easy. Perhaps I was completely wrong in my assessment that the danger was underground. Then I realized that Clark had disappeared, slipped back to the lift unnoticed, and my worst fears came flooding back. But Schmiesser was present, and he was a safety indicator.

The lieutenant finished her piece, and a major at the control panel began a countdown. "We can fire instantly, but this is slow motion to illustrate the stages. By the way, this missile is going straight up into the atmosphere, and will destruct after four seconds," he said.

The earth trembled, and we had the vision, on a screen, of the missile leaping out of the ground and flaring upwards, its course obscured by smoke.

I grabbed General Madison's arm. "Time to leave," I whispered.

He looked at me, close and directly in the eyes, saw that I looked troubled, but perhaps doubted whether he should make a sly exit, when in the normal course he would have said a few words of thanks on behalf of the audience. There was a small round of applause, and no apparent danger. In his hesitation the years of discipline, and the understanding of why the event was organised in this way, came through. He moved his lips almost imperceptibly. "OK."

We slipped out of the control room while nobody was looking, and I made him jog along the corridor for twenty yards.

"Look, are you sure we need to do this, Roger? I mean… I feel like a fugitive… "

As we came past one of the bulkheads with steel doors, a circular side panel swung open. Yarham's face appeared. "In here, sir."

I bundled Madison through, and followed. Yarham took Madison away at a run. As I turned to close the hatch, Schmiesser came running toward us. "Where are you going? What's going on? Where is General Madison?" he shouted.

"Sorry, sir. No time to explain." He gobbled like a goldfish in a bowl as I slammed the thick steel plate shut in his face. I locked the hatch, and closed the wingnuts over the surrounding bolts.

Madison and Yarham had moved along the sodium-lit sub-passage for a hundred yards before I caught up.

"Who was that out there?" Madison asked.

"General Schmiesser."

"Why didn't you let him through?"

"He didn't want to come through. This is an exit route prepared exclusively for you. I'm responsible for you, and I'm not taking any chances. This is a set-up to kill you. I'm just hoping they don't blow the control room."

"Oh, surely…"

"No guards, sir," Yarham said, looking at me, alarmed.

I had placed part of the team of perimeter guards in the underground complex. "Maybe Clark withdrew them. We better go carefully."

I slipped the 9 mm Beretta out of my shoulder holster.

"It's that serious?" General Madison said, seeing the gun, and still feeling that he was the victim of security overkill.

"It's that serious. I'm taking a special route which should bring us safely above ground, but it should have been guarded. I'm concerned that there are no guards now."

Just then, from behind, there was a shock-wave which seemed to momentarily crush me, compress my head, and make my ears pop. And behind it a muffled roar. The ground shook.

"That wasn't another missile… " the General said.

"No, I don't think so. It was an explosion in the control room or the passage."

"All those people!"

"There are other escape routes, and they had a little time," I said.

"The TIFU factor, sir," Yarham said.

"What do you mean?" Madison asked.

"He means it's a fuck-up, General. An assassination attempt gone wrong, running out of control, and it's not over yet."

The lights went out, and we all broke our stride and stopped.

"My God!" the General said. "This is like war."

"We're ready for this." I spoke as calmly as I could.

Both Yarham and I had pencil torches, and I could work out our route in the tunnel complex in the dark. It was a simple matter of counting intersections, and knowing which way to turn. "Stay dark for the moment, and no talking."

I listened. There was unmistakable noise coming from the branch of the tunnel along which we should have gone, voices, movement sounds. The orders of the day were that apart from the guards, no person military or civilian was allowed in this part of the complex. I pushed Yarham and the General into another branch tunnel.

"We'll circumnavigate," I whispered.

A searchlight pierced the tunnel from the direction of the sounds.

A loudspeaker announced, "OK, Conway. We know you're there. Give up, man, and come out, or we'll come and get you!" said a voice I didn't recognise.

A pistol shot cracked and whined strangely down the tunnel.

"Bowl them one," I said to Yarham.

Yarham removed a grenade from the pocket of his flak jacket, and pulled the pin. "I'll get it as far down the tunnel as I can, right?"

"Don't show yourself too much."

Yarham exposed only his arm for a fraction of a second as he sent the grenade bouncing down the plastic floor of the tubular concrete tunnel. The grenade must have reached nearly to the searchlight before it exploded on its four-second fuse. Darkness. We huddled in the side tunnel, with our fingers in our ears, as a wave of smoke and gas and small pieces of debris blasted past us. Then silence in the dark.

"Effective, I think. Let's move on." I pushed the other two along the side tunnel, bringing the map of the complex back to my mind for our more complicated journey. We felt our way along, stopping every few moments to listen. The explosions had damaged the pipework in the ceiling. The floor was running with water, and a mix of other chemicals, judging by the acrid smell.

After half an hour of blackness, and scarcely a word between us, my navigation brought us close to the airshaft, stairs and elevator that I had been aiming for, an area bathed in red emergency lighting. I halted before we stepped into the wider main shaft.

"General, I want you to remain here with Mr Yarham, hidden. I don't know what I'll find up there. I plan to go up, see if the coast is clear, and then come back and get you. Once above ground we're relatively safe."

The General was appalled and confused. "Hell, this isn't like a war, it *is* war!"

"Almost a revolution, General, but not quite. You'll agree to my request?"

"You've managed up to now, OK," he said miserably.

I checked the slide on the Beretta, and stepped out into the red glow, keeping my gun hand slightly behind my back. I had hardly taken two steps before a voice rang out.

"Roger! You're OK?"

I saw Gerry Clark in the shadows, on the first landing of the escape stairway. I stopped. He was about twenty-five yards away. "I'm fine, Gerry. Having a nice time."

"Great," he said tensely. "Where's that clever-dick partner of yours?"

"Yarham's dead." I made it sound doleful.

"And General Madison?"

"Killed in a blast in the tunnel. I've been wandering round in the dark." I gave it a hysterical note.

Gerry Clark's voice lightened. "Well, there's got to be something good in a bad scene. Come on up. Don't stand there."

"I'm just about out of steam, Gerry," I said weakly.

"You sure are," he said, and looked up quickly.

There was another dark figure on the next landing. I had that sense of menace, and threw myself to the ground as a shot crackled past me. I had seen the flash of fire from that dark figure, and I squeezed three or four shots from the semi-automatic Beretta, roughly in the direction of the shooter.

I knew I had probably missed, but Yarham, hidden from Gerry Clark's view, had opened up too, with accuracy. The gunman had flopped on the stairs, and rolled to a landing.

"Nice shooting, Roger. Somebody didn't want you around," Clark said, under the impression that I was the marksman. "Come on up, and we'll take a look."

I holstered my gun, approached the stairs, and went up towards Clark. He had preceded me to the next landing, and was turning over the gunman with his foot.

"It's Greengloss," he said, and he didn't sound surprised. He sat down on the step above her head. "Come, take a look at the lady."

I went up the next flight of stairs and stood at Sally's feet. One of Yarham's shots had caught her in the eye, and her cheek, reddened with blood on its whiteness, was a grotesque carnival mask. Her hands, empty of the Ruger 22 she had been using, were like alabaster models.

"You knew her, I believe," Clark said.

"Not as a C3 agent. Which is what she is. Why should she try to kill me? I'm a loyal C3 man."

"Because you're also a dangerous, know-all cunt-sucker, Conway."

I could see now that Clark's crouch on the stairway, in his bulky uniform, hid a cradled semi-automatic. The light glinted on the circular opening of the barrel. I hadn't the slightest chance of reaching for my weapon.

"Greengloss didn't manage to send you to bye-byes, but I will," he grinned, his eyes disappearing into the blandness of his puffy face.

"Is this because I've been screwing your wife?" I said, wanting to check Clark for a second, and estimating that if I rushed him, I would take at least one bullet. If I moved fast enough, and swung sideways before the rush, the wound would be in the upper arm or shoulder.

A big vein that forked on Clark's forhead swelled noticeably as the impact of my words inflamed him. "You've been doing that, have you? Well, I didn't know, but this will make my work even more of a pleasure."

"And your cook. Surely you know about that? Oh yes,

Marie is something." I went on with the charade to distract Clark, and it certainly had that effect. I gathered my nerve for the rush.

"You're a lying son-of-a-bitch…"

There were three rapid shots from above, and Clark crumpled over Sally Greengloss's body, momentarily bloodless wounds in his shoulders and neck. As I glanced up, Barney Coultas, a gun in his hand, was coming down the stairs. I leaned over and put my fingers against Clark's throat. He was dead.

"Thanks," I said. "Is it all clear out there?"

"Yeah," Coultas said. "I think so."

"You mean there could be somebody roaming around out there with a killing agenda?"

"Could be."

I went back down the stairs, and rounded up General Madison and Yarham. "We have to get you on your plane straight away, and out of here, General."

Coultas waited on the stairs for us. General Madison cast a horrified and incredulous glance as we passed by the bodies of Clark and Greengloss.

"What happened in the control room?" I asked Coultas.

"Two dead in the elevator serving the R40 silo. It was mined. Believed to be General Schmiesser, and Scott. What a screw-up!"

"On the planning table a week ago, it was intended to be me and General Madison in that elevator!" I said.

General Madison's face was paper white. He turned and put his hand on my shoulder. "Thanks," he said in a faint, dry voice.

34

Laurie and I took Yarham and his wife, Iris, out to dinner at Rico's, to show my gratitude for his support in our latest exploit. Not a word of business was spoken at the table, but there was an added piquancy to the delicious food and wine, to share it in this peaceful American setting, with a comrade in battle.

Some weeks had passed since the tragedy at Fort Gaines. General Schmiesser had been buried with much fanfare at Arlington National Cemetery. The news media reported that a misfire had occurred during a missile firing demonstration, with the resulting loss of life. The shield of national security had been raised, and hid the fact that two people died of gunshot wounds. The military court of enquiry found no fault in the technical apparatus of the R40, and ascribed the explosion to unknown causes, a verdict never publicised.

The official, but of course top secret, view within the CIA and the NSA, uncovered and pieced together by Yarham in his persistent OPB operations, was that dissident liberals had clumsily assassinated General Schmiesser, killing themselves in the act.

Professor Otto Reich, a leading Harvard right-wing political theorist and consultant to the NSA, had been found drowned in the Potomac, as a result of a boating accident. This event was not connected with the assassination attempt at Fort Gaines.

The Disciples had cleverly finessed the assassination story

within the government agencies, so there was no suggestion that one need look further for traitors in the intelligence services. I knew, from Amory, that within the Disciples, Reich was blamed for failing to publicise the President's near-disaster in Cuba – "A failure which you acutely pointed out, my boy," Amory said – and Reich was held responsible for the debacle at Fort Gaines, of which he was principal architect. None of this information was available to the public.

My own management of the affair received the warmest congratulations from the Disciples, confused as they had become about the political utility of General Madison. And I should mention that quite apart from Madison's effusive thanks – which included dinner at his home with his family – I had a private audience with the President. As I was leaving the Oval Office, the President said, "Roger, I know there is someone there whom I can turn to in times of trouble, with absolute confidence."

When I talked to Yarham about the events at Fort Gaines, he turned his bright blue eyes up to the ceiling and said, "A pure case of the TIFU. I'll stick to that. The Disciples want to get rid of Madison. They appoint you to do it. Simple and straightforward. Then they concoct a scheme to get rid of you too. The political wind changes. At the eleventh hour they decide not to go ahead with Madison. But they decide to kill you, because you are an embarrassment, although there's dissension about that. On the day, you fool the people they've marshalled, Clark and Greengloss, by dodging out of the silo with Madison. They want to get you, and they nearly do, but…"

I thought Yarham had it about right.

I have been appointed, at General Madison's insistence, to head C3 for a year, while a permanent successor to Clark is found. With access to many more codes, I have used the opportunity to beef up Yarham's facility to carry out OPB ops. I expect, ultimately, to have the best overall picture of Anglo-American intelligence of any person alive.

Clark's bereaved wife has ceased to bother me, and formed an attachment with the older, but admittedly suave, widower, Carl Bolding. Bolding is a visiting professor at Georgetown, and the couple have acquired a twee little townhouse here – where I have been a guest. But alas the meal was not cooked by Marie. She has joined the Washington Philharmonic as a violinist, and is on tour with them.

I continue to be Chalmers Amory's golden boy, careful to dance just out of his reach, and he has promised me a high post when I return to London in a year – it would almost have to be his own job, to match the power I now wield.

The Disciples have regrouped around Amory, Bolding, Fernandez, Professor Kauffer whom I met at the time of my appointment to C3 in London, and a new young US general supposedly of great brilliance. But this is only a cell of the organisation, the one which happens to run me, and I am beginning to pick up evidence of other cells.

I have decided that if I want to continue to be a super-spy, I have no alternative but to exist within a cell of the Disciples, whether their influence is beneficial or malign. It would be blue-sky thinking to believe that I might one day produce a masterstroke which would expose and destroy them. But I might.

My work as director of C3, which includes being on the advisory committee of Fernandez' Special Collection Service, is mainly talking to politicians and members of the military, and planning. I do it exceedingly well, with Yarham to suggest some ideas and hoover up the details, but I find it boring. I'd like to get out into the field again, although I must say I'm enjoying the dinner parties, the charming Washington hostesses, and my awesome covert reputation as *The man who singlehandedly solved Cuban Missile Crisis II*.

Laurie stays with me when she's in town, and I still have the cat. Occasionally, I spare a thought for Roger Barmby, the second-hand car dealer from Oxford, England, with three A-levels and an accent that a half-colonel from Sandhurst didn't mind.